Praise for

T.M. LOGAN

'Smart, intense and with a humdinger of a mid-point twist. I loved it'

GILLIAN MCALLISTER

'Taut, tense and compelling. Thriller writing at its finest'

SIMON LELIC

'T.M. Logan's best yet. Unsettling and so, so entertaining.
The perfect thriller'

CAZ FREAR

'A tense and gripping thriller'

B.A. PARIS

'Assured, compelling, and hypnotically readable – with a twist at
the end I guarantee you won't see coming'

LEE CHILD

'A compelling, twisty page-turner, and that's the truth'

JAMES SWALLOW

'Outstanding and very well-written . . . so gripping
I genuinely found it hard to put down'

K.L. SLATER

'A terrific page-turner, didn't see that twist!
A thoroughly enjoyable thriller'

MEL SHERRATT

'Another blistering page-turner from psych-thriller god
T.M. Logan'

CHRIS WHITAKER

'Even the cleverest second-guesser is unlikely to arrive at
the truth until it's much, much too late'

THE TIMES

THE CURFEW

T.M. Logan's thrillers have sold over a million copies in the UK and are published in 22 countries around the world. His novel *The Holiday* was a Richard and Judy Book Club pick and became a *Sunday Times* bestseller in paperback. *Trust Me* was also a *Sunday Times* bestseller in hardback. Formerly a national newspaper journalist, he now writes full time and lives in Nottinghamshire with his wife and two children.

Also by T.M. Logan:

Lies

29 Seconds

The Holiday

The Catch

Trust Me

THE CURFEW

T.M. LOGAN

ZAFFRE

First published in the UK in 2022 by
ZAFFRE
An imprint of Bonnier Books UK
4th Floor, Victoria House, Bloomsbury Square, London, WC1B 4DA
Owned by Bonnier Books
Sveavägen 56, Stockholm, Sweden

A CIP catalogue record for this book is
available from the British Library.

Hardback ISBN: 978-1-83877-602-2
Trade paperback: 978-1-83877-674-9

Also available as an ebook and an audiobook

1 3 5 7 9 10 8 6 4 2

Typeset by IDSUK (Data Connection) Ltd
Printed and bound in Great Britain by Clays Ltd, Elcograf S.p.A.

Zaffre is an imprint of Bonnier Books UK
www.bonnierbooks.co.uk

For my brilliant wife, Sally,
from the luckiest guy in the world.
Happy 25th anniversary x

It is a wise father that knows his own child.
— William Shakespeare, *The Merchant of Venice*

Letting go is hard.

Maybe the hardest thing there is.

More than that; sometimes it's impossible.

Because sometimes, letting go threatens everything you love, everything you are.

But to do anything else, you have to lose a part of yourself. Forever.

I don't know the answer.

I guess that's why we ended up here.

SUNDAY
12TH JUNE

1

I should have known something was wrong.

I should have sensed it. Felt it in the air, like the build-up of pressure before a thunderstorm, that heavy, loaded calm.

I was his father, after all. His first line of defence. And his last.

But at this moment, at a few minutes past three o'clock in the morning, all I know is that I'm awake.

Perhaps it was a noise outside that pulled me from sleep, the call of a fox, or maybe a cat. Something else. But all is silent now in the warm inky blackness of the bedroom, both windows open, half the thin summer duvet thrown off. My phone is on silent on the bedside table, the screen's glow dazzling me for a moment as I look for a message from my son. The first of our three golden rules: *one – send a message to let us know where you are.* Closely followed by *two – stick to your curfew* and thirdly, *stay with your friends.* We don't tell Connor not to drink, because telling your teenager that seems like an exercise in futility. It's going to happen whatever we say, so we might as well just learn to live with it in a way that keeps him safe.

There is no message from my son.

But to be fair, he's more likely to text my wife.

She sleeps soundly beside me, her soft breathing a slow, comforting rhythm in the dark. I lay the phone back down and close my eyes again. Of the two of us, I've always been the heavy sleeper; Laura would have heard Connor when he came in. His curfew was midnight. Earlier than some, later than others. A normal Saturday night would be 11 p.m. but the first post-exams weekend of his summer holidays allowed for a little more flexibility.

He will have been back for hours by now, I think.

And then that's it – I can't get back to sleep. My mind is starting up, gears turning, thoughts pulling me up and away. After-images from the phone's screen still bright in my eyes. And for some reason I need the bathroom. *Ah*, the joys of middle age. I swing my legs out of bed and pad across the landing to the bathroom, softly pushing the door shut behind me.

On my way back, I realise there's more light than there should be, up here on the landing. A single bulb throwing a wash of pale shadows in the hall downstairs.

The porch light is still on.

Connor was supposed to turn it off when he came in. That was what we always said to him: *The porch light switched off means we know you're home, OK?* The light being left on means . . . probably nothing. He just forgot, that's all. Sixteen-year-olds forget things like that.

I move downstairs into the hall, the tiles cool beneath my bare feet, and hit the light switch. The hall is plunged back into full darkness. I stand for a second, blinking as my eyes slowly adjust, groping for the familiar wooden banister at the foot of the stairs.

Back on the landing, I go to the bottom of the small curving staircase that leads up to Connor's bedroom on the second floor, listening.

The house is silent around me.

He just left the porch light on, that's all. He leaves lights on all the time, and doors unlocked, plates unwashed, toilet rolls bare and wet towels on his bedroom floor. That's just what teenagers do.

But . . . I'm awake. Might as well double-check that he's home.

I climb the top staircase slowly as it curves right and then right again, missing the third step from the top – the creaky one – and move carefully onto the landing. Two doors. Spare room to the side, and Connor's room at the end, occupying two-thirds of the top floor beneath the sloping eaves of the roof.

His door is ajar and I push it open cautiously, taking a step inside, greeted by the familiar smells of summer sweat and trainers and deodorant lingering somewhere beneath. The earthy smell of unwashed clothes and a half-eaten sandwich lurking on a plate beneath the bed. The debris of scattered items on the floor – jeans, shoes, dishes and cups – softened into indistinct shapes by the darkness.

I squint into the shadows of his room. I wish I hadn't left my glasses on the bedside table, but I can still make out his familiar shape: long limbs sprawled beneath the duvet, dark hair against the pillow. No longer a boy, but not yet a man either. My whole body relaxes with relief. Connor is in bed. *Home. Safe.* Of course he is.

I'm struck by a pang of nostalgia for the years when I'd read him bedtime stories every night, when he had been my little shadow. We had been inseparable, father-and-son football in the garden, video games, *Mr Bean* and *Star Wars* and every single Roald Dahl story until we both knew them all by heart. Now he prefers to spend time with his cousin, his mates and he mostly confides in his mum. Probably because she's less judgemental. She sees his side and doesn't condemn. She doesn't necessarily condone, either, but she listens without jumping in as I'm prone to do. Now I feel I'm always on his back and increasingly we're like ships passing in the night, sometimes going days at a time without exchanging more than a few words. He's either in his bedroom, locked in the bathroom, or monosyllabic at the dinner table. Or just *out*.

But at 3.09 on a Sunday morning, none of that matters – because my boy is home. He's in his room, in his bed, where he is supposed to be. Everything is OK. I linger in the doorway, squinting into the shadows at my son's sleeping form.

Unaware, in that moment, of how badly mistaken I am.

Because I should have known then that something was wrong. I should have sensed it.

But I didn't.

Not until it was already too late.

2

I sleep fitfully and wake from a dream in which I'm convinced the front door is standing open. When I go to push it closed, the dream hallway gets longer and the door gets further away, the handle just out of my grasp.

By the time I'm showered and dressed, Laura is already back from her run, cheeks glowing red, phone strapped to her arm, long auburn hair tied back in a ponytail. In the kitchen, she hands me a cup of freshly brewed coffee from the Nespresso machine, sipping at her own.

'Double shot,' she says. 'Looks like you need it.'

'Thanks.' The coffee is strong and dark, the smell of it widening my eyes before the caffeine even hits my bloodstream. 'Do I look that bad?'

'Just kidding, you look as fresh as a daisy.'

'Doubtful,' I grunt. 'Did you hear Connor come in last night?'

She sits at the kitchen table and begins unlacing her trainers.

'He messaged me. You were asleep. Why?'

'He must be getting better at creeping around in the dark,' I say. 'Didn't hear a thing when he came in.'

'That's because you were snoring again.'

'Was *not* snoring.'

'I was going to give you a little kick, then you turned over.'

She gives me a smile. We've been together more than twenty years but I still can't always tell when she's winding me up. Especially first thing in the morning. I take another sip of my coffee, cradling the cup in both hands as I lean against the breakfast bar. Laura has already opened the double French doors out onto the patio, the smells of cut grass and blossom coming in on a warm breeze that promises another perfect midsummer day. The sky is a pure, cloudless blue.

'Anyway,' I say, 'Connor made his curfew, did he?'

'Like I said, he messaged me at twelve to let me know he was back.'

'But you didn't actually *hear* him come in either?'

She gives me a quizzical look. 'He's never broken his curfew before, has he? He said he was in at twelve, he did what we asked him to do. I trust him.' She shakes her head. 'You know, there comes a point when we *both* just have to trust him, Andy.'

She finishes unlacing her trainers and begins her warm-down stretches, resting one tanned leg on the windowsill and reaching over to touch her toes.

Toffee, our Cavapoo, pads into the kitchen with his lead in his mouth, dropping it at my feet like a sacrificial offering. He sits, tongue lolling, looking up at me with his big chocolate-brown eyes as his tail swishes a slow sweep of the kitchen floor.

I stroke the curly straw-coloured hair behind his ears.

'I know,' I say. 'I know that. I do trust him. He left the porch light on, that's all.'

'Well if that's all we've got to worry about, I think we're doing OK.'

I couldn't really argue with that. And I didn't want to admit that I'd checked on our son at 3 a.m., because that would make me sound even more paranoid. 'So where do you suppose they went last night?'

'Beacon Hill Woods, I assume.'

While we've been talking, Toffee has disappeared. He returns now with a well-chewed tennis ball, dropping it at my feet next to his lead, and looking up at me again.

'In a bit, boy.' I scratch under his chin. I know Beacon Hill well enough – it's one of Toffee's favourite places – but I've only ever been there during the day. 'What do they even *do* up there at night?'

It's a rhetorical question; we both have a pretty good idea of the answer. Connor and his cousin Zac are at that in-between age where they're still too young to get served in pubs but getting too old and restless to sit around at home on a Saturday night. A few of their mates have fake IDs saying they're eighteen, typically from an older friend who has sold, loaned or gifted their provisional driving licence with a picture that is generic enough to get them served in a bar. But they were the exception, not the rule. For everyone else, there were house parties, birthday parties, spur-of-the-moment gatherings when parents were absent – or Beacon Hill Woods.

Toffee is now watching my every move, his ears twitching at any gesture towards the front door. Finally, I pick up his lead and he gives a single happy bark of approval. In the lounge, I find my daughter, Harriet, cross-legged on the sofa in her *Team Gryffindor* pyjamas, eating a bowl of Coco Pops. Noise-cancelling headphones clamped to her head as always, laptop open beside her. Our cat, Pablo, is sprawled across her little lap, paws in the air.

'Harry? I'm taking Toffee for a walk, do you want to come?'

She gives no indication she's even aware of me standing there, headphones blocking out the world. She'll be a teenager soon but she's still so small and slight, already being left behind by the tall girls in her class and not remotely interested in clothes or makeup or TikTok or any of the things I assumed girls started getting into at her age. Maybe that was all around the corner. But for now, she was into coding club and *Minecraft* and her pets, still preferred jeans and T-shirts, had flatly refused to wear a skirt since she was tiny and never changed her mind since. Insisted on keeping her red hair boyishly short to stop it getting too curly. She seemed happy in her own skin and that was enough for me. She's an enigma, our Harry, is how my wife puts it. A little eccentric, my mum said.

'Harry?' I say again, a little louder.

She lifts one headphone off her ear, looking up at me. 'Did you say something?'

'Going for a dog walk, do you want to come?'

'I don't want to disturb Pablo,' she says, rubbing his tummy with her small hand. If it had been anyone else in the family, the cat would have taken their arm off at the elbow; but with Harriet he simply purrs softly and arches his back, asking for more.

I indicate the laptop on the sofa next to her.

'What are you watching?'

'Stuff. YouTube.'

'*Stuff*, eh? Sounds interesting.'

'If you must know, it's a video by a world-famous hacker explaining how he penetrated a top-secret Russian database.'

'Oh.' I stop at the door. 'Really?'

'No, Dad,' she says with a sigh. 'Just some TED talks.'

She puts her headphones back on and hits *play* on the screen.

Laura is making toast in the kitchen, the radio a low burble beneath the crunch of her knife cutting the crusty bread in half.

'Breakfast,' she says, handing me a thick slice smothered with blackberry jam. 'I'm going to grab a shower.'

'Thanks.' I take a bite of the toast, jam meltingly sweet on my tongue, and loop Toffee's lead over my shoulders with my free hand. 'See you in an hour.'

I walk up the block-paved drive to my neighbour's house, past his front lawn thick with summer growth and bursting with dandelions. I make a mental note to come back with the mower at some point in the next few days. There is a short wait after I press the bell, a familiar pause as the house seems to hold its breath, before a thin voice reaches back from somewhere deeper in the house.

'Who is it?'

I lean closer to the blue and red-coloured glass of the front door. 'It's just me, Arthur.'

'With you in a jiffy.'

The vague outline of a figure emerges at the end of the hall and begins to approach, making slow progress, until finally the door creaks open. There was a time when Arthur and I were the same height, but the years have curved his spine and stooped his shoulders so that now he looks up at me, both hands pressed over the top of his walking stick. He's been retired from teaching undergraduate law for more than two decades now, but his pale blue eyes are as sharp as ever.

'Good morning to you, young man.' Despite the early heat of the day he's wearing slacks with a long-sleeved shirt and a navy jumper.

'Morning, Arthur,' I say, Toffee sitting obediently at my feet. 'I'm taking the hound to the park, thought Chester might like to join us?'

Officially, Arthur is one of my patients, but he has an old man's reluctance to bother his GP so I like being able to keep an eye on how he's doing. His wife Marjorie had been able to cajole him into making an appointment when he needed to, but since he lost her he's become more stubborn about asking for help with the ailments common to his eighty-eight years. *Insomnia is God's way of telling you to make the most of the time you have left*, he liked to tell me. Our normal routine was for me or Connor to take both dogs out in the early evenings after work and school, although lately I've been doing it more and more.

'Are you OK for milk and bread, tea bags?' I ask, gesturing towards his kitchen. 'I can pick some up on the way back if you need anything.'

'No, I think I'm fine for everything, thank you, Andrew.'

'And how are you doing for whisky?' I give him a grin.

'Enough to last me until the apocalypse.' He winks. 'Or until Southend United win the Premier League, whichever comes first.'

He turns stiffly, whistles, and immediately I hear the soft click of paws on the parquet floor. A moment later a black and white Collie trots down the hallway, tail wagging. Chester is bigger and older than Toffee, the two dogs as delighted as ever to see each other.

'All right, Chester.' The dog sits obediently as his owner clips the lead to his collar with liver-spotted hands. 'Be a good boy now and don't give Dr Boyd any trouble.'

'It's Toffee who's the troublemaker.' I take Chester's lead from him. 'It's a good thing he's too slow to catch anything.'

Arthur squints up at the sky, one hand at the small of his back.

'Going to be another hot one again today.'

'Got to break soon, hasn't it?'

'Always does,' he says. 'But it'll get hotter before then I should imagine.'

'See you in a bit, then.' Both dogs are now sitting and looking up at me expectantly. 'Come on, you pair.'

I'm about to turn away when Arthur's papery voice reaches me again.

'How's that boy of yours?'

'Connor? Very well, thanks. Glad school's over.'

'Bet he'll be having a lie-in today, won't he?' He says it casually, as if he's still just making small talk. 'After such a late night, I mean?'

There's no malice in it, no snark, but something in his tone makes me stop. As if he knows something that I don't.

Relax. You're being ridiculous.

'Start of his summer holidays, Arthur,' I say, summoning another smile. 'Exams are over and every day is a lie-in.'

He stands framed in the doorway as I open the boot of my car for the dogs, raising a hand to wave as we pull away from his house.

I'm halfway to the park when my phone rings, my brother's number showing on the car's hands-free display.

'Hey Rob, how's it going?'

He doesn't waste time with pleasantries. 'Is Zac there?'

'Zac? No. Has he not—'

'He didn't sleep over at yours?'

'No. What's up?'

Our sons have always been close, have grown up going to the same schools and playing for the same football teams. Connor the dependable right back, solid and serious and unafraid of putting in the big tackles; his cousin Zac the mercurial striker up front, fast and skilful, a poacher's instinct for goal. As different as they could be on the pitch, but they had always clicked together like two halves of the same person. As close as siblings – they even looked like brothers – without the fighting.

'Have you seen him at all this morning?' my brother says. 'He didn't come round?'

'He and Connor were out together last night but I've not seen Zac today, no.'

'Shit,' he says quietly.

A pulse of unease touches the base of my spine. 'What's going on?'

I hear the intake of breath at the other end of the line, the shaky exhalation that follows.

'He didn't come home last night.'

3

It takes me a moment to digest what my brother is saying. There are less than two years between us and I've always looked up to him, always been able to rely on him, Rob, my calm older sibling, steady as a rock whenever I've needed him. But now his voice is flat and toneless, the words coming so fast they're almost falling over each other.

'You've tried his mobile?'

'Of course,' he snaps, tension crackling down the phone line. 'I had a message last night to say he might be going to Beacon Hill but now his phone just rings out. I got up this morning and his trainers weren't in the hall. Then checked his room and his bed was empty, hadn't been slept in. What time did Connor get back?'

I think back to what my wife said.

'Twelve.' I clear my throat. 'His curfew.'

'Did he mention Zac?'

'Not seen him yet this morning.' I try to think of anything I may have missed from last night, this morning, any clues as to my nephew's whereabouts. 'I'll get Laura to wake Connor up, ask him. I'm sure he'll turn up, Rob, he's probably just crashed at someone's house and forgot to tell you.'

'I've tried a couple of his friends' parents, but no one's seen him. Have you got numbers for Isaac's dad? Will's mum?'

I indicate and pull over into a bus stop, checking behind me for a gap in traffic.

'Laura will probably have them,' I say. 'I'll get her to text them to you.'

'I'm heading up to Beacon Hill now to have a look around.'

'I'll meet you there, I'm just—'

But he's already rung off.

I call my wife's mobile and listen as it rings six times, then goes to voicemail. I hang up and try again.

'Pick up!' I say to the ringtone. As it clicks into voicemail again, I belatedly remember what she'd said about going for a shower. I leave a message, asking her to call around to any parents who might know anything and send over the numbers Rob asked for.

'I'm going up to Beacon Hill to meet him, give him a hand. Call me when you get this. And wake Connor up,' I say. 'He might know something.'

I hang up and swing the car across the full width of the road in a quick U-turn.

Five minutes later, I'm pulling off the main road and up the potholed track beside the cemetery, climbing higher all the way. I park up in the little turnaround near the top, next to my brother's mud-spattered Mazda, and let the dogs out of the boot. I keep them on a long lead on the sunken path and after a couple of hundred metres we leave the tarmac and turn left, up the bank and out into the open of a farmer's field, a well-trodden path through waist-high wheat swaying in the gentle morning breeze. At the other end of the field is the entrance to Beacon Hill Woods, a few hundred acres of mature oaks, ash and beech trees, standing tall and full-green against the azure summer sky.

At the entrance to the woods there are two paths, one leading straight on and the other angling around to the left. I head straight, the dogs scampering ahead of me from tree to tree. It's cool and quiet up here, the only sound the echoing chatter of a thrush somewhere in the canopy of branches high above. The path is a strip of trodden earth through the trees, reddish-brown clay baked hard by the summer sun; twenty paces in and it's almost like being in a completely different environment, a world away from the city, from roads and houses, from normality. I assume that's why teenagers like it so much.

I'm already deep into the woods before I find my brother.

He's crouching down just off the path. Picking at the still-smoking ashes of a fire, a thick tree branch dumped in the middle that has not burned down to the end. As I approach, a twig cracks beneath my shoe and he stands abruptly, his head snapping around.

'Hey, Rob,' I say. 'Have you heard from Zac yet?'

He shakes his head. 'Not yet. Did you talk to Connor?'

'He was dead to the world when I left but Laura's waking him up and calling around some other parents. Have you tried the Cruickshanks or some of the other lads from football?'

'I've tried everyone I can think of.'

He looks away from me, his jaw tight, and I can tell that he's trying to put a brave face on it. Lines of worry on his brow, his eyes hidden behind sunglasses, dark stubble thick across his jaw. We've never been big huggers in our family but I put a hand on his shoulder, give it a squeeze.

'It's going to be all right, Rob,' I say. 'Before you know it he'll be back home with you, devouring everything in the fridge.

And you've got to promise not to give him too much of a bollock-ing, OK?'

'OK,' he says, his voice thick. I try to give him a reassuring pat, the muscles of his shoulder taut with tension. 'He's probably sleeping it off at a friend's house and his phone's out of charge. Maybe with a girl?'

'Has Connor mentioned anything about Zac having a girl-friend?'

'I'd be the last person he'd talk to on that subject.'

'Same here, just shuts me down whenever I ask about any-thing like that.' He squints into the trees. 'He ever mention Emily Ruskin?'

I turn to follow his gaze. 'The name sounds vaguely familiar. Why do you ask?'

'I'm sure he's mentioned her recently but I can't remember the context. Have you got a number for her parents?'

I take out my phone and send a message to my wife, asking the question. She's much better connected than me where school net-works are concerned. I unclip both dogs' leads and Toffee bounds off into the undergrowth, sniffing busily, tail wagging furiously. Chester stays close to me, the way he always does, padding more slowly from tree to tree, following scents, alert for squirrels. My brother and I rejoin the path and walk in single file further into the woods, looking for any signs of teenagers having been here, discarded bot-tles or cans or anything else left behind from an end-of-exams party.

'Do you really think,' I say, 'that Zac might have stayed out here all night?'

Rob shrugs. 'It's warm, the nights are short and school's finished for the summer.'

'All the same, wouldn't he at least tell you where he was going to be?'

My brother takes his sunglasses off, rubbing distractedly at a lens with the hem of his shirt, and I notice for the first time how tired he looks. Dark half-circles under bloodshot eyes, his skin a pasty shade of white in the summer sunshine. He looks as if he's barely slept at all; as if he's been up most of the night.

He puts the sunglasses back on, looks away into the trees.

'He came up here before,' he says. 'In April.' He seems about to say more but trails off. He doesn't need to finish the sentence; I know what he means.

In April. After the funeral.

'Overnight?' I say quietly.

My brother nods, grim-faced.

'Made himself a little hideout of branches, like a den. Brought his knife and his sleeping bag and some food. Came back at four in the morning, soaked and half frozen. I gave him hell for it, and we just ended up shouting at each other. He said he'd wanted to be on his own, where no one could find him. I thought maybe . . .' He swallows hard, fists by his sides. 'He's not the same boy anymore, Andy. Since he lost his mum. He's changed, he doesn't talk to me, just pretends nothing can touch him now, like he's built this hard shell around himself that nothing can penetrate. I don't know what to do, how to reach him.'

'That place he went before, where he built the den, have you checked there?'

My brother nods slowly. 'Nothing.'

'We'll find him. I promise you.'

'What if he doesn't want to be found?' His voice drops lower, as if he's afraid of even saying the words out loud. 'He could be anywhere.'

'Have you tried Find My iPhone? You can track the location of a device; I've used it once or twice on Connor.' *Once or twice*. Only a small lie.

'He disabled it. Said it was freaky and weird that I could see where he was. Like I was some sort of stalker.'

I want to give him more reassurance, to provide some small scrap of comfort, but I know he's not really interested in that. He just wants his son back; I'd be exactly the same, in his position.

We walk on, both of us calling Zac's name.

'This place must be pitch-black at night,' I say. 'How do they even see anything?'

'I think that's kind of the point.' He gestures to another blackened log near the path, a circle of stones laid as a makeshift fire pit. 'But they've had a few fires. And lights on their phones, I guess.'

Toffee trots out of the undergrowth dragging a tree branch in his mouth that is twice as long as him, a mass of leaves and twigs trailing in its wake. He drops it at my brother's feet and sits, panting hard. Rob snaps off a smaller stick and throws it, watching as Toffee bounds off to fetch it.

'I'm worried, Andy. What if he's done something stupid?'

I take my phone out of my pocket.

'We could . . . get the police involved?'

'No,' he says quickly. 'Not that. Not yet.'

'Let's cover some more of the woods first,' I say. 'Since we're here. Then we'll figure out what to do next, OK?' I point into the trees, the ground sloping gently away from us before rising again.

'You head up to the next crest then loop around to the right. If I follow the path up here and across to the left, we'll meet on the high ground there.'

'Sounds like a plan.'

He sets off striding down the hill, but he's only gone a few paces when he begins shouting his son's name again.

'ZAC!'

His deep voice echoes and bounces, until it fades to nothing among the trees.

It's not long afterwards that I find the keys.

4

The path splits and widens into a clearing, a pair of logs facing each other on the ground, empty cans and bottles between them. Chester trots over to have a good sniff at the remains of another fire, white ashes heaped inside a circle of stones, blackened fragments of dark fabric scattered around the edges. It was an unofficial tradition at the Comp, a rite of passage, that some Year 11 kids finishing their GCSEs would come up here on the last day of school and burn their blazers. Sit and watch as the navy polyester and viscose were consumed by flames.

It was a miracle they hadn't set the woods on fire years ago.

Off in the distance I can hear my brother still shouting for his son, his voice an incongruous echo amid the trees. I leave the clearing and cut into the woods, heading for the sound of Rob's voice. Echoing his calls.

Toffee bursts through a tangle of bushes to my left, tail wagging, panting, and drops a stick at my feet. He looks up at me, down at the stick and then back again.

'Where's the ball?' I say. 'What have you done with the ball?'

He pants up at me, tongue lolling from his mouth.

Picking up the stick, my eye is caught by something red lying at the base of a tree, partially obscured by a tangle of nettles and thick purple wildflowers. A key ring in the shape of a football shirt, the crest of Manchester United on one side and a name and number on the other. *Rashford 10.* Four keys attached, two normal sized and two smaller, like keys to a padlock or a desk drawer.

I pick up the keys, study the ground around them in case there is anything else discarded here. Throw the stick for Toffee and resume walking towards the sound of my brother's voice, turning the keys over in my hand. *Connor has a Man Utd key ring. He's always losing his keys. But how can they be out here? How the hell did he get in last night?*

My brother is on the far side of the hill, in another small clearing circled by mature oaks. He's squatting on the ground, his back to me. At the sound of my approach he stands up quickly.

'Anything?' His voice weighted with hope. 'Any sign of him?'

I hold out the keys in the palm of my hand. 'These were on the ground back there, just off the path.'

Rob's breath catches as he takes them from me.

'I think they're Connor's,' I say, 'but I can't work out how he'd have got in last—'

His voice is flat, toneless. 'They're Zac's keys.'

'You sure?'

He nods, turning the Man Utd key ring over with its player name and shirt number on the back. 'Connor has Bruno Fernandes. Zac has Rashford, remember? They're always arguing about which one is best.'

Every so often I'm reminded of the weird family parallels between me and my brother; between Connor and Zac. My older brother always more naturally gifted at sport, more confident and outgoing, more popular with girls than me when we were growing up. Our perennial argument about whether Bryan Robson was better than Mark Hughes. It was the same with Zac and Connor; the age gap between them only a month rather than two years but so much that was familiar in their relationship. The same dynamic, somehow passed down to our sons.

Rob wipes a smear of dirt off the key ring, his thumb moving reflexively up and down the red plastic. Up and down.

'How can he get home if he doesn't have his keys?' he says quietly.

'Has your neighbour got a key?'

He nods, his jaw tight. 'I already texted him to keep an eye out. No reply yet.'

'Connor's always losing his keys,' I say. 'On the bus, at school, in the wash.'

Then I notice something in his other hand, something soft and white, fabric of some kind. I gesture towards it.

'What have you found?'

Almost reluctantly, he opens his fist and holds it up by the shoulders: a thin white cotton top, a kind of cropped cardigan. Insubstantial and impractical, something a teenage girl might wear. Once it was white but now it's grubby and creased, dried reddish-brown smears on the sleeve, another on the back.

'Found it just over there.'

He indicates a thick log laid on the ground, bark worn smooth by time, on the edge of the clearing.

'Could have been here weeks, Rob,' I say. 'Months, even.'

'Smell it,' he says quietly.

'What?'

'Go on.'

Hesitating for a moment, I lower my face to the fabric and inhale, my nose instantly filled with an intense burst of fresh scent like berries and vanilla and white musk. Both brand new and somehow familiar.

'Recent, right?' he says. 'Must be from last night. Maybe you were right about Zac going off with a girl.'

I give him a reassuring smile. It feels to me that he's grasping at straws but now doesn't seem to be the time to point it out.

'Wherever he is, I'm sure we'll find him soon.'

He stares away into the trees again as if expecting his son to emerge at any moment. Shoves the cotton top into a pocket of his cargo shorts and checks his phone again.

'You need to be at home,' I say finally. 'For all we know, Zac could already be waiting for you there.'

'One other place I want to check first.'

We hike back to our cars and I follow him as he drives into town, doing a slow pass of the little high street, each of us scanning the pavements for any sign of Zac. At one point Rob slams his brakes on and I almost drive into the back of him as he stares at a group of teenagers outside the Co-op. But they are too young. He drives on another quarter-mile until we get to McDonald's, parking up and going inside without a word. I follow him in and we both stand inside the entrance, scanning the customers like a couple of store detectives trying to pinpoint a shoplifter. It's busy – it always seems to be busy – most of the tables filled with young families, couples, groups of girls and a few guys on their own.

'I really thought he might be here,' Rob mutters, his voice flat. 'Seems to spend half his life in here.'

'Let's head back to yours and—'

He stalks over to a corner table where four teenage girls are laughing loudly, phones in their hands and Diet Cokes in front of them. He holds up his own mobile. Their expressions shift from amusement to suspicion to shock as he shows the image on the screen to each of them in turn. Each shaking their head, *no*. I try to imagine Connor's reaction if I did this, a middle-aged man approaching a group of teenage girls to ask them *Have you seen my lad?* Imagining how fast that particular piece of gossip will travel around the school. But my brother is past caring about that, it seems.

'They're in Year Eleven as well,' he says as he pulls the heavy glass door open to leave. 'Said they hadn't seen him.'

We drive to his house and he almost runs up the drive in his haste to get inside. I follow him in through the front door and he's already calling out towards the kitchen, his voice raised in hope.

'Zac?' He goes to the bottom of the stairs, calling his son's name once more.

There is no answer.

As I stand in the hall, he moves quickly around the rooms downstairs, even the little toilet, heavy footsteps creaking loud in his silent house. He runs upstairs as I stand by the front door, listening as he criss-crosses the landing above me, knowing in the stillness of the house that there is no one here. It *feels* empty – and frankly has for a while now, too big for the two of them, like an oversized coat hanging from narrow shoulders. Rob hasn't said anything directly, but I know he's already dreading the day when Zac heads to university. When he'll be left alone here. A shoe rack at my feet holds a couple of pairs of my brother's size nine work shoes and Zac's trainers, two sizes bigger. But the left side of the rack is empty, unused, a blank. My sister-in-law's shoes gone, an absence that cannot be filled.

My eyes are drawn to a picture on the windowsill, a framed photograph of Rob, Vanessa and Zac smiling into the camera. Father and son on each side, mother between them. The three of them, all leaning in for a selfie. It was taken at a meal out for Vanessa's forty-fifth birthday last year, the table busy with glasses and tasting plates and a bottle of fizz in the centre. Before she got sick. Before the treatment. Before the assault of chemo and radiotherapy and surgery and the unstoppable march of an illness that consumed her from the inside out.

Rob reappears at the top of the staircase, catches me looking at the photograph.

'Anything?' I say.

He shakes his head and makes his way down the stairs, a deep frown of frustration on his face. He checks his watch again, his phone, the window onto the drive – his eyes always careful, I notice, to avoid the framed photograph on the windowsill.

I gesture towards the kitchen.

'Listen, why don't we—'

'I can't do this,' he says suddenly. 'Can't handle it, not now, not after everything.'

I put a hand on his arm, give it a gentle squeeze. 'We're going to find him.'

'He's all I've got, Andy,' he says suddenly, his face ashen. 'I can't lose him too.'

5

He's staring into space, blinking fast. He won't look at me, seems almost as surprised as I am at what he's just said. As if it's breached some wall in his mind, his worst fear articulated.

'Hey, listen to me.' I pull him into an awkward hug, his arms limp by his sides. 'You're not going to lose him. *We're* not going to lose him, I promise you. Let's sit down a minute, make a plan.'

In the kitchen, I pour a glass of cold water from the tap and hand it to him. He holds the tumbler against his chest as if he's not sure what to do with it.

'Drink,' I say to him. 'And you need to eat something too.'

I make him a couple of thick slices of buttered toast with Marmite – *the original comfort food*, our mum used to tell us – as he runs through everything he knows about last night. I find a pen and paper and tell him to make a list of all the people he's contacted already, so we can figure out who else to try. Leaning up against the kitchen worktop, I scroll through my phone's address book and call out names as he writes them down. Then we make a list of places Zac might be, where he likes to hang out with friends, the various parks and playing fields and pitches he normally spends time at in the summer.

All the time there is a faint echo in my head from last night, something that I can't quite hear, an itch I can't quite reach. Connor leaving the porch light on, after his silent return home? Arthur's remark when he asked about my son? *Bet he'll be having a lie-in today, after such a late night.* Was midnight a late night? Maybe it was if you were eighty-eight.

'What I don't get,' I say, blinking the thoughts away, 'is why Connor's not with him. They do everything together.'

My brother shakes his head, chewing on a piece of toast without much enthusiasm. 'Maybe they had a row, a falling-out.'

'Those two? No way.'

But even as I'm saying it, I know it's not beyond the realms of possibility. There had been one single spectacular bust-up earlier in the year, a wrestling match with a few punches thrown, Rob and me pulling the boys apart, both of them red-faced and refusing to apologise, saying the other started it. A week-long cooling-off period followed by a sudden truce and then – just like that – they were back to normal again, walking to school together, long *FIFA* sessions on the Xbox again, bike rides and football in the park as if nothing had ever happened. It was only later that Laura managed to coax out of our son the reason for the falling-out: a girl one of them liked. A crush, a disagreement over some perceived slight.

I know Rob is remembering this too. 'I wonder if it was a girl again,' he says. He picks distractedly around his thumbnail, fresh blood bright as he pulls off a thin strand of skin. I notice that the skin around most of his fingernails is scabbed and angry. *Idlejacks*, our mother would call them. 'You sure Connor never mentioned that Emily Ruskin?'

'He wouldn't talk to me about that stuff, but I'll ask Laura.'

I take out my phone and message her, three replies coming back almost immediately, one after the other.

Sorry was in shower and phone was charging, just got your message. Any news? How's Rob?
Am making calls now
He's not mentioned Emily R to me before

I send a reply back: *You need to wake Connor*

She replies instantly with a thumbs-up emoji. I'm about to put the phone away but the three dots appear again, indicating she's typing another response.

Do you mean Cathy Ruskin's daughter?

I don't know the answer to that, so I reply *Not sure* and put the phone back in my pocket.

My brother is now stabbing the screen of an iPad in a red Manchester United case. *Enter passcode.* He shakes his head and enters another six-digit number, frowning as the device's keypad shakes and a new message is displayed. *Incorrect passcode. iPad locked for five minutes.*

Abruptly, he stands up. He's barely touched his toast. He goes to a cupboard by the sink and I can hear the clink of glass as he moves bottles around.

'Shit.' He puts the bottles back and closes the cupboard door slowly.

'What is it?'

'There was a bottle of vodka in here, two-thirds full. It's gone.' He slams his palm down on the worktop. 'I've always told him

I'd rather he was open with me, told me stuff, than do it behind my back.'

'At least you know what he's drinking, I suppose. Better than drugs, right?'

I remember the two of us sneaking downstairs when we were teenagers, while our parents had dinner party guests in the other room, reaching to the back of the drinks cupboard for the bottles that wouldn't be missed. Optimistic holiday purchases that had been forgotten over the years – ouzo and Cretan raki, cherry brandy and Austrian schnapps, their lids gummed shut with neglect – smuggling a bottle back upstairs and daring each other to knock back throat-burning shots in our bedroom, me trying to keep up with my big brother, trying not to cough up a lung, trying not to be sick. Mum and Dad had never had any idea. Then, or now. *Like father, like son.*

Rob sucks at the blood from the torn skin on his thumb. 'Maybe there was a party,' he says, a spark of hope in his eyes. 'A house party, you know, end-of-term thing? Maybe it wasn't even local, one of those parties they put on Facebook, and loads of people turn up and it's a free-for-all. And maybe it was out in the sticks, and he's still trying to blag a lift home from someone.'

'Maybe.' I'm pretty sure that most kids our sons' age wouldn't be seen dead on Facebook, but I don't have the heart to tell him. 'But one of his mates would have mentioned it by now, wouldn't they?'

The glimmer of hope fades from his face.

'Something about this is really wrong, Andy. I can't get my head around it.'

I sit down on the stool opposite him, take a tissue from the box and hand it to him, indicating his bleeding thumb. There is a framed picture of Zac on the kitchen wall opposite me, his last school portrait taken at the end of Year 11, navy blazer, white shirt, tie askew below his undone top button. An awkward half-smile, his dark brown hair curly over his forehead and shaved high and tight at the sides. There is an almost identical picture of Connor on a bookcase in our lounge.

'Rob, I'm just going to ask you this because you're my brother, my family, and so is Zac.'

'Ask me what?'

'Zac's never talked about running away, has he? I mean, apart from that night he went to Beacon Hill on his own, a few months ago?' When he shakes his head, I add quietly: 'And he's never talked about . . . hurting himself?'

'No.' His head snaps up. 'Of course not. Nothing like that. He wouldn't do that.'

A voice in the back of my head says: *And you didn't think he'd stay out all night, either.*

'I just had to ask.'

'He would never do that,' he says emphatically. 'Not after everything else, not after we lost his mum.'

I watch as he wipes absently at his thumb with the tissue. If Vanessa – my late sister-in-law – had been here, she would have mobilised the whole neighbourhood by now, a blizzard of messages reaching out to friends, colleagues, neighbours, fellow choir singers and school-gate mums, lighting up a dozen WhatsApp groups and gathering information, urging everyone to nudge teenage children awake, to check spare bedrooms and bathrooms, gardens, sheds and garages until Zac was located and sent home without delay.

I guess my brother knows that too, but he's always preferred to sort things out himself rather than ask others for help. Has always preferred to be lost for twenty miles, grappling with a road map, instead of admitting defeat and simply asking a passer-by for directions. Rather keep it in the family than ask for strangers' help in locating an errant child.

Whatever progress Laura may have made at home, my phone remains resolutely silent. No messages. No word from Connor either.

'Listen,' I say carefully. 'We've contacted everyone we can think of, we've checked up at Beacon Hill and Zac's still not answering his phone. Maybe it's time to get the police involved?'

He exhales, covering his face with both hands. If it was Connor, I would have been on the phone to them already. But now, as before in the woods, my brother seems strangely reluctant to elevate it to this next level of concern. As if escalation is a bad omen, acknowledgement of the worst fear that neither of us wants to entertain, not even for a second.

'Don't people have to be missing for twenty-four hours, or something?'

'We should probably let them be the judge of that. Look, I can call them, if you like?'

He sits slumped in the chair for a long moment, fingers rubbing his red eyes that I'm sure are already aching from lack of sleep.

'No,' he says, his voice barely above a whisper. 'I'll do it. I'll call them.'

6

He punches three digits on his phone and puts it to his ear as I pull up another stool alongside him. The phone is loud enough for me to hear the other side of the conversation, his call answered after one ring by a flat male voice.

'Emergency. Which service?'

My brother clears his throat. 'Police. Please.'

'Hold the line.'

There is a click and a different woman's voice comes on, older, fifties maybe, clear and precise.

'Police. What's your emergency?'

He gives the call handler his details and takes her through what he knows – that he last saw his son around 8 p.m., has not heard from him since a text at 11.30 p.m., he's not been back home overnight – and she follows up with a string of questions that she's likely asked many times before.

Have you heard back from all his friends at this stage?

Not yet, no.

Has your son ever done this before?

Once.

Is there a reason to believe your son is in immediate physical danger?

No.

That he's a risk to himself or anyone else?

No.

Does your son have any pressing medical needs or conditions that require immediate attention?

No.

There's another pause, the faint clattering of her keyboard again.

'Hello, are you still there?' my brother says.

'I'm transferring you to our 101 service, sir, where one of our operators can assist you further.'

As Rob opens his mouth to protest, there is another click and a new voice comes on the line, younger, deliberate and unhurried. I can tell my brother is trying to keep the frustration out of his tone as he runs through all the same information for a second time. He paces as he talks, up and down the kitchen, gesticulating with his free hand. Finally, he hands me the phone and I put it to my ear, feeling the heat of it against my head. The call handler asks my name, address and mobile number, the tap-tap-tap of her typing a constant in the background.

'Mr Boyd tells me that your son and Zachary were together last night?'

'That's right.'

'And when did your son come home, sir?'

I hesitate.

'Midnight.'

The third time I've said this. To myself, my brother, and now to the police. Three times I've told what I believe to be the truth, what I *think* is the truth, each time convincing myself a little more, each time the words becoming a little more solid, a little more set in place. But still there is a twinge of unease in my stomach as I hear the call handler tapping on her keyboard at the other end of the line, typing my words onto her screen, into a report, a summary to be saved onto a hard drive somewhere. Probably – I tell myself – never to be seen again, deleted as a matter of course after the requisite period. Or maybe to be shared and read and circulated at some later date, my statement a part of the formal record.

Three times a denial. Just like ... Judas? And look what happened to him. I shake the thought away. I'm telling the truth.

The call handler is saying something, repeating herself.

'I'm sorry,' I say. 'What were you saying?'

'Have you spoken to your son yet, sir?'

'Not yet, he's still asleep but my wife was going to wake him.'

I hand the phone back to my brother. He finishes the call by writing down an incident number, the identifier by which this will all be logged on the police system.

'I've got to get back, talk to Connor. Let me know as soon as you hear anything.'

My brother nods. 'Tell me what he says?'

'Of course.' I put a hand on his shoulder. 'We're going to get this sorted, OK?'

He says nothing in reply.

* * *

Once Chester is safely back home next door, I lead Toffee around to our side gate, straight through into the back garden. Laura is on the bench by the back door in a pale pastel tank top and shorts, a wide-brimmed straw hat shading her eyes from the sun. She has her phone pressed to her ear, asking someone to call her if they hear anything.

She thanks them and rings off as Toffee trots over and collapses in a patch of shade under her seat. 'Any news?'

'Couldn't find him in the woods and he's not come home yet. Rob made a police report.'

'How's he doing?'

'Not great.' I peer through the kitchen window. 'What did Connor say?'

'I've been on the phone for the last half-hour. Shouted for him to come down but he's still dead to the world, I'll give him another try now.'

'I'll go,' I say.

I walk through the conservatory into the kitchen, kicking off my deck shoes.

The stairs creak and through the half-open kitchen door I catch a glimpse of Connor on the bottom step, wearing a hoodie that is going to be much too warm for June weather. *Finally*. His back is to me as he heads for the front door.

'Ah, you're up at last,' I say. 'Need to talk to you.'

He doesn't turn around, just keeps heading towards the front door, moving quickly as if he can't wait to get out.

'Connor, have you heard from Zac?' He doesn't seem to register what I've said. 'Are you all right?'

Laura appears beside me, her hand on my arm. 'Give him a minute, Andy.' She shoots me a familiar look.

Our son reaches for the front door handle, turning the key in the lock.

I walk out into the hall and put my fingertips lightly on his shoulder to get his attention, to make him look at me.

'Connor? Hey, this is important, your uncle is really worried about Zac. He didn't come home last night, when did you last hear from him?'

He turns to face me and for a moment my brain can't process what my eyes are seeing. There is a moment of disconnect, of *does-not-compute*, before the fog lifts.

But it still doesn't make sense.

Because the boy in the hallway is not my son.

7

I blink, trying to get my bearings. I'm disoriented, as if I've opened a familiar door and found myself in the wrong room entirely. A wash of emotions, swirling and mixing together: confusion, realisation, relief. Behind everything else a faint pulse of alarm.

'Zac?'

My nephew stares back at me, dark eyes squinting beneath the hoodie as if he's still adjusting to the brightness of the day. His face is pale, almost completely washed out, a smear of something dark – *mud?* – along the line of his jaw.

'I've got to go,' he mumbles.

'Zac, what are you doing here?'

'I really need to go,' he says again, reaching for the door.

I put a hand on his arm and feel him flinch, shrinking away from me as if I'm a threat, a stranger.

'Hang on a second.' I loosen my grip but don't want to let him go, don't want him to disappear again. 'Your dad's looking for you, he's worried out of his mind, we just spent the last two hours trying to find you. We've been up to Beacon Hill, driving around. You need to call him right now, tell him you're OK. You gave us a fright.'

He flinches again.

'OK. Sure.'

'We rang the police, Zac. Your dad made a report.'

That freezes him in his tracks. He turns to face me, the remaining colour draining from his face.

'What?' he says. 'Why'd you do that?'

'We had no idea where you—'

'What did you say to them?' His voice is rising now, an edge of panic creeping in. 'What did you tell them?'

'The truth.' I release his arm. 'That you hadn't come home. I mean, I realise now that wasn't completely true, was it?'

He looks at the floor, seeming to deflate a little.

'My phone was out of charge,' he says in a small voice. 'Connor said you wouldn't mind, he said it would be OK. I'm sorry.'

'We don't mind at all, it's not that.' I hold up my hands, palms out. 'Listen, it's fine for you to stay over whenever you like but you need to tell your dad where you are, OK? No exceptions.'

'OK.'

'You took the spare bed, did you? Is Connor up yet?'

Zac makes a non-committal shrug and moves towards the front door again.

'Are you all right?' I ask him. 'Is everything . . . all right?'

He makes a noise I can't decipher, pulls the front door open and steps into the porch.

With his back to me, I notice the design on his sweatshirt for the first time. A school hoodie to mark the end of GCSEs, end of Year 11, each one personalised to the individual pupil. *Class of '22*. A prickle of unease stirs in my stomach as I see my son's name below the school crest. They *did* sometimes borrow each other's clothes, it was true, but after the weird morning I've had it almost seems a deliberate choice, another attempt to confuse the adults.

'Why are you wearing Connor's hoodie?'

He doesn't reply.

'Zac?' I follow him out onto the drive, squinting into the dazzling midday brightness, the paving slabs warm beneath my bare feet. 'At least let me give you a lift home?'

'I'm sorry,' he says, hunching back into the hoodie, head down against the glare. 'For everything.'

Laura's voice comes from behind me in the hallway.

'Just leave him, Andy.' Her tone is emollient. 'Let him go.'

My nephew hurries away from me down the pavement and I watch him go all the way to the end of the street. He turns and disappears from view. It's the right way back to his house, but for a moment I think of grabbing my car keys and following him, to make sure he gets there. There is something *off* about the whole situation – normally Zac would talk us to death whenever we saw him. But today he can't get away fast enough.

I feel a soft hand on my arm.

'At least we know he's safe,' Laura says. 'What a day, eh? And it's not even lunchtime yet. Are you coming back inside?'

'He was almost shaking,' I say. 'It was as though he was frightened.'

My wife shrugs.

'He was trying to sneak out without anyone seeing, and we caught him.'

'It wasn't just that. It was more than that.' But there is something in her voice, something slightly defensive. 'Hang on a minute, did you know Zac was here?'

'What? Of course not.'

'You hesitated.'

'You need your hat, Andy.' She raises an eyebrow. 'The sun's getting to your head already. And you need to ring your brother, let him know.'

I dig the phone out of the pocket of my shorts and dial Rob's number, trying to think how best to phrase it. *Sorry, mate, I know we spent the last hour searching for your son but he was asleep in my house the whole time . . .* Because *that* wouldn't sound weird at all. His number is engaged, so I leave a quick message to say I've seen Zac, he's safe and on his way home now.

Laura is leaning on the banister, peering up the stairs as if expecting our son to appear at any moment.

'Can't wait to hear what Connor's got to say about this little stunt,' she says.

I take the stairs two at a time, breathing hard by the time I get to the second landing at the top of the house, and knock once on his closed bedroom door.

'Connor?'

Not waiting for an answer, I turn the handle and push the door open into his pitch-dark bedroom.

The blackout blind is pulled down and a heavy curtain pulled across it, only a tiny chink of daylight penetrating the gloom: a razor-thin strip of sunshine down one side. He's had a blackout curtain since he was small, when he was always an early riser with the dawn. I remembered holiday houses with paper-thin curtains which we quickly learned to hang with beach towels in an effort to get an extra half-hour of sleep.

As a teenager his sleeping pattern seemed to have flipped 180 degrees, sleeping through half the weekend until he emerged slow and grouchy like a bear from a cave, hunched and blinking into the light.

As my eyes start to adjust, I make out the shelf of books over his desk, another above it lined with trophies from his football. The dark shapes of posters on the walls, the dim outlines of football players, album covers, bands. The Weeknd, The 1975, Blossoms. I take a few steps into the room and stumble over a bowl that's been left on the floor, whispering a quiet curse as my foot pushes into something soft. I stand on one foot, trying to see what I've stepped in. The remnants of a bowl of cereal? I stoop to pick up the bowl off the floor as the smell of two-day-old milk rises to meet me.

'Connor?' I say softly. He doesn't stir, the bedclothes pulled up high on the double bed he'd insisted on last year when he said he was too big, too tall, for a single.

I take another step closer to the bed, eyes straining to make out more detail in the semi-darkness. Say his name again, a little louder this time, but still he doesn't flinch or make even the slight-est movement beneath the duvet. He really is dead to the world. I move a little closer, treading carefully around other half-visible objects littering his bedroom floor, my eyes still adjusting from the dazzling brightness of the day.

The bed is a mess, the duvet pulled up and humped in the mid-dle over my son's sleeping form. I reach over to give him a gentle pat on the shoulder and my hand sinks into something soft, my hand pushing into the duvet with almost no resistance.

Louder now, I say: 'Connor?'

With a flutter of unease in my chest, I pull back the duvet.

There is no one in the bed.

Instead, cushions and clothes have been laid along the length of it to give the impression it is occupied. A hastily gathered collection of items from the floor, by the looks of it. Zac, wanting to sneak out of the house without being spotted, left these here to make it look as if Connor was still asleep in bed. But we caught him.

The fluttering in my chest gathers momentum, a painful drum-beat against my ribs.

Not right. This is not right.

I go to the big dormer window, rip the curtains aside and grope for the white plastic blind cord. Pull it so hard I can feel it straining under my hand, the *tick-tick-tick* of the roller mechanism as the bedroom is bathed in light. Dust motes hang in the air, dancing in the sunlight and for a moment it's dazzling, all the corners of the room exposed to the blazing brightness of the midday sun. I pull the duvet all the way back – not even quite sure what I'm doing – before going back out onto the landing and pushing open the door to the spare room.

The spare bed has not been slept in.

There is a plunging, free-falling sensation in my stomach, steal-ing the strength from my limbs as the realisation hits me. A new reality shifting into focus, sharpening, like light refracted through a lens: we had combed the woods, called our friends, driven the streets of our neighbourhood, talked to the police.

But all that time we had been looking for the wrong boy.

8

When I come back downstairs, Laura is in the kitchen putting out plates for lunch.

'What did he say?'

'He's not here,' I say, trying to keep my voice even. 'He's not at home.'

'*What?*' She stares at me, the last plate clattering onto the table. 'You sure he's not in the bathroom? The en suite?'

I shake my head. We look at each other for a moment, then I take my phone from my pocket and dial Connor's number. Willing him to answer, willing him to pick up and be gruff and grumpy and monosyllabic and all the things that a sixteen-year-old boy *should* be on a Sunday. Just willing him to be *there*. To pick up. *Just pick up, son.* I listen to it ring six times before the tone cuts off.

'*Your call cannot be answered at this time. Please leave a message.*'

I leave a message, trying to keep my voice breezy and upbeat, as if everything is OK and I'm just checking in. Tamping down the acidic tension rolling in the pit of my stomach, telling myself that everything *is* OK. Of course it is.

I hang up, dial him straight back. Six rings and voicemail again.

Laura is staring at her own phone, checking for any messages that she might have missed.

I ring my brother's number and he picks up after one ring. 'Rob, it's me,' I say. 'Did you speak to Zac? He's fine and he's on his way back to you, should be home any minute.'

'You saw him?' His voice is instantly louder. 'Where? When?'

'It's the weirdest thing, but it looks like he was at ours all night. He slept here, we just saw him on his way out a few minutes ago.'

I describe what had happened, bumping into Zac as he tried to sneak out of the house, our one-sided conversation as he made his escape. It occurs to me that if I had got back a couple of minutes later I probably wouldn't have seen him at all. And then what? Would he have admitted to spending the night at our house? Would we have even found out, or would he have spun us a different line?

'Listen,' I say, my voice tight. 'This is going to sound weird, but we don't know where Connor is.'

'I thought you said he was at home?'

'Yeah, we thought he was but it turns out . . . he's not here, and we just want to make sure he's OK. If you're able to get any info out of Zac that would be really helpful.'

He doesn't answer straightaway and I think for a moment we've been cut off.

'Rob?' I say. 'You still there?'

'He's here! Zac's here, he's walking up the drive now, oh thank God! *Thank God.*' The relief in my brother's voice is palpable. 'Andy, can I call you back?'

'Sure.' I picture the reunion on his doorstep, father and son reunited. 'Let me know what he says about Connor, yeah?'

He hangs up without replying, the phone suddenly a blank silence against my ear.

'This is nuts,' I say, turning to Laura. 'What's going on? First Zac goes AWOL and now Connor. What are they up to?'

'Let's find him first,' Laura says. 'Worry about everything else later. What do we know for sure at this point?'

My legs feel weak suddenly, as if I've run a half-marathon, and I lean back against the kitchen counter. 'He was in by midnight, right? You said you saw him when he came back.'

'No,' she says slowly. 'I said he messaged me.'

'So you *didn't* see him?'

'I fell asleep, OK?' She shakes her head. 'I was tired, it's been a long week. Woke up just after midnight and messaged him, asked if he was home. He messaged straight back to say yes.'

'Did you *check*?'

'Of course I didn't *check*. I trust our son. And why am *I* always the one who has to stay awake?'

I put a hand up in apology. 'I was awake at three, went to check on him. He was there, in bed. At least . . . I thought it was him.' I think back to last night, only a matter of hours ago but it already feels distant, as if it belongs to a different week, a different time. 'I could have sworn it was Connor.'

'Did you have your glasses on?' Laura says. 'Did you actually see his face?'

I shake my head. 'I was in the doorway, saw someone in the bed and I just thought . . . it never crossed my mind that it wasn't him.'

'And the spare bed's not been slept in?'

I shake my head. 'Maybe he did come back last night and then went out early this morning.' It doesn't sound plausible, even to my own ears. 'Maybe he sneaked out before you went for your run.'

'To go where, exactly?'

'I have no idea.'

'But you said the spare bed's not been slept in, and we've only seen Zac this morning, which suggests . . .'

'. . . That Connor didn't come back at all.' A thrum of unease flutters low down in my stomach. 'But why would he lie, tell us he was home when he wasn't?'

'Why do teenagers ever lie?' She glances towards the front door again as if expecting our son to appear at any moment. 'So their parents don't worry about them. Did you ever stay out all night without telling your parents?'

'Rob went to a rave once, got in at 7 a.m. Mum stayed up all night and went absolutely *ballistic* when he got in.' I remembered that morning, being on the periphery of it, but I don't remember being worried about my brother. Not at all. It simply never entered my fifteen-year-old head that anything bad might have happened to him; I was just glad not to be at the epicentre of our mother's cold fury. 'He never did it again after that.'

'Maybe it's a one-off for Connor, like it was for your brother.'

We both fall silent for a moment, trying to put the pieces of last night together in a way that make sense. A new realisation hits me like a kick to the stomach: it was now almost midday and our last contact with him had been his text just after midnight. Which meant he was almost twelve hours gone, silent and out of contact.

Twelve *hours*.

Out there, somewhere. Maybe in trouble, desperate for our help.

'Why was Zac even sleeping in Connor's bed?' Laura says. 'Was he covering for him, or something? To convince us that Connor was home when he was still out? Why would he do that?'

Harriet appears in the doorway in cut-off jeans and a Hogwarts T-shirt, ever-present headphones loose around her neck.

'Why would Zac do *what*?' Harriet says.

'Nothing, Harry,' I say with a strained smile. 'It's all fine.'

'Mum?' Harriet says, pushing her glasses up her nose. 'What's going on? Is Connor in trouble?'

'No, sweetheart. We just need to speak to him.'

'He's not in his room?'

'Harry, why don't you go into the lounge, choose a film to watch and we'll be—'

'So my big brother broke his curfew, he's not in his room and you don't know where he is?' Her tone is flat – not sarcastic, just matter-of-fact. 'Mum? Is that what's happened?'

My wife gives her a tight smile. 'Kind of.'

'So where is he?' Harriet looks from her mum to me and back again. 'Is he safe?'

'I'm sure he's fine, H.'

'But you don't *know*.'

She puts the fingers of her left hand to her mouth, an unconscious habit she's had since she was a baby. Not biting her nails, just letting the fingertips rest there. An *anxiety response*, a paediatrician friend had called it.

'Hang on,' Laura says, frowning. 'Let's just rewind a minute. How do *you* know your brother broke his curfew?'

Our daughter blinks up at her wordlessly.

'Harry?'

'I don't want to get him in trouble.'

'He's not in trouble, Harry.' Laura puts a hand on her arm. 'We just need to know what you heard. That's all.'

'Will you be cross with him?'

'No.'

Harriet shrugs her small shoulders. 'I heard him when he came in. He woke me up.'

I turn fully towards my daughter as she stands framed in the kitchen doorway. Neither of us corrects her – she doesn't need to know yet that it was more likely her cousin that she heard. That her brother may not have come home at all.

'Do you remember what time it was? Was it around midnight?'

She fixes me with her intense, twelve-year-old stare. Her *Paddington stare*, she calls it.

'Not then, no.' A single, emphatic shake of her head. 'When he actually came home. At nineteen minutes past two.'

9

'Harriet,' my wife says carefully. 'Why don't you tell us what you heard? Your dad and I were thinking that your brother got home just after midnight because he sent—'

'No.' Our daughter shakes her head again. 'It wasn't then. I heard someone at 2.19. I looked over at my LED clock and remember thinking he was going to be in so much trouble with you for being so late.'

I exchange glances with Laura, my confusion mirrored in her eyes. Almost two thirty in the morning: how did *that* fit into the events of last night?

'You're sure?' I say to Harriet. 'Only, your ears can play tricks in the night, especially when you've been asleep and dreaming.' I give the parquet flooring a soft rap with my knuckles. 'This is an old house, lots of wood, so in the summer it gets really warm during the day and the wood expands a little bit, then at night all the heat slowly escapes and it makes the wood creak, you see?'

'I know about thermal expansion and contraction of wood, Dad.' She somehow manages to be both young for her age and mature beyond her years. Wonderfully naive one minute, a wise head on young shoulders the next. 'I know what I heard.'

'OK, OK,' I say with a nod. 'The thing is, Harry, we're not sure if that was Connor, or Zac. Maybe both of them, maybe not.'

'Zac was here? So you think Connor might not have come back at all?'

'That's what we're trying to establish.'

She frowns for a second then looks up, a new energy in her face. 'I can find out if you like.'

'Can you?'

She shrugs. 'Of course.'

I'm about to ask her how but she's already turned and hurried out, the tap-tap-tap of her light steps ascending the stairs following a moment later.

Laura and I return to our phones. I scroll to the Find My iPhone app and the screen switches to a map of our neighbourhood, all the surrounding streets laid out in green and blue and white. I pull up the list of phones that have allowed me access to their location, select Connor's. I expect the location to shift and zoom into something new but the map doesn't move, just shows a pulsing blue icon. I pinch the screen to zoom in, finding our house in the centre of the screen.

That can't be right.

According to the app, Connor is here at home.

At least his *phone* is here. I shake my head. Close the app and go back into it, repeat the process. Once again the map shows his phone is here. Maybe some kind of glitch. Or has he left it here, hidden it? I go up to his bedroom and spend ten minutes hunting through the clothes, towels, trainers and other assorted stuff on the bed and the floor, ringing his number three times and standing in silence in case it's on vibrate mode and I'm able to make out the sound of the handset buzzing. But there's nothing.

I stand by his desk, piled high on each side with notepads and textbooks, shifting things around in case his phone is hidden beneath the paperwork. Pens, pencils, highlighters, Post-its, loose notes, Blu Tack.

At the back of my mind, I realise this is a long shot. He has his iPhone with him all the time. Admittedly he does have a track record of losing it – leaving it on the bus, at McDonald's, even on a roller coaster at Disneyland Paris – but he hasn't done that for a while.

My hand goes to the top drawer of his desk and I stop. This is an invasion of my son's privacy, an intrusion into his personal stuff.

Am I looking for his phone now, or something else?

I know the line is there. But I'm going to cross it anyway. *He could be in danger.*

I pull the top drawer open halfway, just enough to reveal the jumble within: half-finished packets of sweets, a squashed Mars Bar, a ball of string, an old wristwatch, a small spiral-bound notebook with a Union Jack cover, a dog-eared pack of cards, a brown leather wallet containing a solitary £20 note. The next is more of the same, the bottom drawer thick with stacks of exercise books from his previous years at school. My eyes are drawn to the drawer in the bedside table. But it feels like a violation too far. And it occurs to me that finding his phone here would be a step back rather than a step forward – it would make it *harder* to reach him, not easier. Harder for him to reach us.

The Find My iPhone app must be glitchy, that's all.

I come back down to the lounge, check beneath the sofas and behind the cushions before finding myself back at our dark oak kitchen table, clicking on the app again in case I missed something, an update or some new permission box that needs to be ticked.

As I'm scrolling quickly through my messages, Laura calls to me from the lounge, her voice taut with urgency. 'Andy? You need to see this.'

I stand up and hurry down the hall.

'Have you heard from Connor?'

She holds her phone up but it's too far away for me to see the screen.

'One of the WhatsApp groups I'm in, the school PTA committee that organised the summer fair. One of the other mums has posted about last night.'

'About Connor?'

'No.' She won't look at me. 'Not exactly.'

'What then?'

'About her daughter. She's not come home either.'

10
EMILY

Sunday 12th June, 1.03 a.m.
Eighteen minutes before she disappears
Beacon Hill Woods

The woods were silent.

Silent and so dark that where she stood there were only shadows upon shadows, pools of inky black so deep that Emily's eyes couldn't adjust.

So dark that she could barely see her own hands, her own limbs, almost as if she too was melting away, becoming part of the night. She hadn't realised how impossible it would be here on a moonless night, how hard it would be to do what she had to do. She'd been here in the daytime, evenings too, but that had always been with other people, with a fire, with phone torches, voices, laughter.

At night, on her own in the true pitch black, it was like a hostile land she'd never visited before. She was already regretting the vodka, the weed. Because everything was different in the dark. Everything was harder, everything was against her. The heavy, unyielding trees a malevolent presence all around. The smells of hard earth, of rotting wood, stinging plants and the slow decay beneath it all. The only sound, the shallow rasp of her own breathing.

Emily trudged on, every step an effort. She thought of her dad, wondered whether he would be proud of her, or at least understand why she had to do this. Her mum always said she was just like him, just like this man she had never met. Would she even be here now, defenceless and alone in the dark, if her dad had been in her life?

No.

She stumbled through brambles, invisible barbs snagging on her jeans, scratching at her hands as she pushed through. The phone switched off because it had to be, a flat, useless slab of plastic in her pocket. No phone meant no torch. Her foot caught on something and she landed hard on one knee, stifling a cry against the flare of pain. She pulled herself to her feet. She was tired. So tired.

Nearly there. Keep going.

The woods were silent again.

Almost *silent*.

She was about to move off again when she heard it. There. A distant sound. Maybe an animal hunting, a fox biting down on small bones. An owl tearing the life from its prey.

No. Bigger.

Not an animal. A person.

Someone picking their way through the trees, slowly, stealthily, trying to approach without being heard.

Emily froze, the breath trapped in her throat.

She turned her head towards the sound, desperately searching the blackness –

There.

The sound came again, the muted rustle of a single step.

Behind her. Getting closer.

Hide. *She flattened herself behind a tree. Crouched down.*

Don't move, don't breathe. *She pressed herself close to the tree, the bark rough and rutted against the skin of her cheek. The sound of another footstep in the dark, closer again, and Emily knew for sure now they were following her. Here in this place of a million shadows, a million shades of black. She should have stayed by the fire, with the others.*

She put her palms against the tree to steady herself against a sick sweep of dizziness.

Silence returned but it was a loaded, deliberate silence. The silence of someone who knew they were close.

A soft footfall to the left—

Or was it on the right?

Fear. Bitter and sharp, like bile at the back of her throat.

Emily wanted to run now but her feet were rooted to the spot, her whole body frozen in place. She felt a sudden, overwhelming yearning so powerful it brought tears to her eyes: a wish to be somewhere, anywhere else.

Anywhere but here.

11

Laura holds her phone out to me and I scroll down a long thread of WhatsApp messages that started about half an hour ago. The first one in the thread is from someone identified in the chat as Cathy R.

Hi guys sorry to jump in with non-school stuff but am trying to track down Emily, she was supposed to be at a sleepover last night but have just found out she didn't stay there. Have any of your kids seen/heard from her? Really worried and I know I'm probably being silly but just want my baby back home. Thx all xx

A string of responses from other parents:

Sorry not heard Cathy, sure she'll be back home safe soon xx

Have asked my two and they've not heard, sorry hope ur OK

Ur not being silly at all hun have you tried the find iPhone thing? x

Sorry Millie was at Adam K's party says she can't remember seeing Emily xxx

A dozen more messages along the same lines, with lots of new members added to the group by the various admins. Then another message from Cathy R:

Thx guys please do pass it on and ask around just want to make sure she's safe xx

Emily. The second time her name has come up this morning, first tramping through the woods with my brother, and now this. I can't even remember why she was mentioned. Zac must have spoken to his dad about her at some point.

I point at the screen.

'Does Connor know this Emily girl?'

'She's in his half of the year group, not sure how many lessons they have together.' Her thumb scrolls further down the message thread. 'What, you're thinking they could be together?'

'Either that or it's just a big old coincidence that both of them stayed out all night.'

'We don't know for sure that Connor stayed out *all* night.'

'Don't we?'

She studies her phone again, new messages dropping in every few seconds. 'Shall I ask them about him too?'

Under normal circumstances, our son would be utterly mortified if we announced him as a missing person on a school WhatsApp group, among parents of people that he knows, his friends and classmates. To be the subject of discussion, of speculation about what he got up to last night and how *desperate* his parents must be to track him down. The school gossip grapevine will go into meltdown. But every minute that ticks by is a minute we slide further away from normal. And we need to get the word out.

'OK,' I say. 'Let's see if anyone knows anything.'

I watch as she types a message, thumbs flying over the screen.

Sorry Cathy we've not heard anything about Emily. This is going to sound weird but we're struggling to get hold of Connor too. Think he may have slept at a friend's house. If anyone's heard anything can you let me know pls? Thanks all x

She posts the message and then immediately adds me as a member of the group. We both sit for a moment, staring at her phone, waiting for the first replies. For a minute there is nothing, then the first responses start to drop in, more slowly and noticeably fewer in number than those to Cathy's message, each echoing *ping* pushing the last message further up the screen.

Oh no so sorry not heard anything about Connor xx

Dylan's at football with his dad have messaged him will let you know

Did he go to that 16th birthday party? x

Laura quickly adds another message of her own.

You can reach me on this number or my husband on his mobile. Thank you.

She types in my number in another message, adds it to the thread.

More messages drop in, each one saying the same thing in a different way, until someone called Emma S-L types:

Charlie was at Adam K's party but says he heard a few of them went on somewhere else after? xx

Laura types a reply. *Yes that's right did he say where?*

No but a bit of trouble at the party apparently, some people left. Not sure who, sorry xx

Before I've even finished reading the message, another one lands. This one is on a private thread, just Emma S-L and Laura, so none of the other commenters will see it.

STRICTLY between you and me there were LOADS of gate-crashers, Charlie says. Parents were out and not back until 1 a.m., drugs and kids passed out + being sick and stuff smashed up, neighbours threatened to call the police! Xx

The message ends with an emoji of a scared face, teeth bared. Laura frowns and types a rapid reply.

Sounds awful but thanks for the info, Emma x

Let me know when your boy is back safe and sound xx

Laura sends her a thumbs-up and switches back to the main message thread. Nothing new.

'Who is this Adam K. lad?'

'Adam King. One of the populars.' Seeing my frown, she adds: 'It's what Connor calls the popular kids, the in-crowd.'

My understanding of the social pecking order at the Comp had always been hazy at best. Connor and Zac hung out a lot together, and there were other friends in their orbit too, but I had only the loosest sense of the hierarchy. Connor had occasionally referred to *the populars* and *the plastics,* to *goths* and *indies, football lads, gamers* and *druggies,* some of the groups overlapping here and there. There were also *nerds* and *smart kids* – although I wasn't sure what the difference was – both terms that he used interchangeably for his little sister, in an affectionate way. She seemed almost pleased, wearing the names like a badge of honour.

'Connor and Zac weren't invited to Adam King's party?'

'He never mentioned it. I'll see if I can get a number for one of the parents.'

She sets to work sending more messages and a moment later puts the phone to her ear and walks out into the garden, her voice fading away.

'Hi, is that Mr King? Sorry to bother you . . .'

I dial my brother's number and he picks up after one ring. He sounds like a different man, a lightness to his tone that is far, far away from how he was this morning. He relates what little Zac has told him, which is that they went to a party on The Avenue, then left there and just hung out for a bit, chatting.

'Said he crashed at yours because he lost his keys,' my brother adds. 'Connor told him it wouldn't be a problem.'

'It's always fine for him to sleep over. We just want to know where Connor went, where he spent the night.'

'I'm sorry, Andy.' His tone shifts, as if he's finally picked up the concern in my voice. 'Zac didn't really say much more than that, he

was just the way he always is after a late night. Vague and monosyllabic. I mean . . . I got the impression he thought Connor was heading
back to yours last night. That he would be there when Zac woke up.'

'This is not like Connor at all,' I say. 'We're starting to get worried.'

'Of course.' There is a pause on the line, the sound of a tap running, a kettle being filled. 'You know . . . there was one other thing
he said.'

I feel a pulse of anticipation, a sudden wish that we were having
this conversation face to face.

'What?'

'He said there were five of them who left the party together,
some other lad and a couple of girls.'

'Which girls? Was one of them Emily Ruskin?'

'He didn't mention any names.'

'And did Connor go off with one of them after that? One of the
girls?'

'Zac didn't say.' There is a shrug in his voice. 'Just that they hung
out for a bit after the party.'

I try to come up with a tactful way of asking the question, but then
just jump in with it instead. 'Do you think he's telling us everything?'

'Are you saying he's lying?'

'I'm just saying it's all frustratingly vague.'

'Teenagers out on a Saturday night, right? Never going to give
us chapter and verse, are they?'

I ask if I can speak to Zac, but he tells me his son had wolfed
down a Pot Noodle, raided the fridge for some other food and gone
straight back out again. He didn't say where.

My ear is suddenly hot. My cheeks, my face too. I transfer the
phone to the other side, glancing over at the doorway, checking
that Harriet isn't eavesdropping.

'He knows his cousin's missing, doesn't he?' I try to keep the exasperation out of my voice. 'And Zac might have been the last person to speak to him?'

'I'm sorry, mate, if I'd known Connor was AWOL I would have sat Zac down, got all the info out of him. Do you want me to come over?'

'Right now I just want to speak to Zac.'

'Let me call him now and I'll come straight back to you.'

I wait for a minute then try Zac's mobile myself. I dial it twice but the line is engaged and goes to voicemail each time. I'm firing off a quick text to him as Laura comes back in from the garden to share what she's gathered from Jeremy King, who it seems regrets hosting his son's sixteenth birthday party last night. Around a hundred teenagers had turned up, he'd said, more than twice the number invited, although any mention of drugs or noise complaints were noticeably absent from his account. A group of Adam's friends had slept over in their summer house and he had been to grill them this morning after seeing the messages about Emily.

'They live in one of those big houses on The Avenue,' Laura says. 'Set in its own acre backing onto the fields that run up towards Beacon Hill Woods, you know that land where there always seem to be plans to build more houses, but it never happens? A couple of the sleepover kids said Emily was definitely at the party, at least earlier in the night. Apparently she'd been drinking, she was upset about something and then she left, with a few others in tow. They think they headed up to the woods.'

'And Connor?'

She nods, her face pale.

'Including Connor.'

12

My phone rings with an unrecognised number, and it takes me a moment to realise it's a WhatsApp video call. I hit accept and a woman's face fills the screen, mid-forties, long brown hair falling around her shoulders, worried eyes behind dark-framed glasses. I'm pretty sure I've never met her before but she still looks familiar.

'Hello?'

'Hi, is that Dr Boyd?' She's holding the phone out in front of her, walking through a high-ceilinged hallway as she talks. Her voice echoes, an undercurrent of anxiety beneath the words. 'It's Cathy Ruskin, Emily's mum. I know your wife but I don't think we've met.'

'Hi, sure, do you want to speak to Laura?'

'Her number was engaged. You're Connor's dad, right?' She runs a hand through her hair. 'I was hoping we might be able to help each other.'

Propping my phone against the fruit bowl, I sit at the kitchen table as we do a quick exchange of information about our missing children. I tell her that Connor seems to have been at a party with his cousin and may have gone on to Beacon Hill with a small group that included Emily. I skirt around the issue of his cousin sleeping in his bed and sneaking out of the house half an hour ago.

She tells me that Emily was supposed to be sleeping over at her friend Olivia's house after the party, but the two of them had got separated at some point and Olivia returned home alone. The confusion had only come to light when Cathy turned up to collect her an hour ago. As Cathy speaks, it becomes obvious that she's working hard to maintain her composure. That she's perhaps someone who is used to being in control, to persuading, to leading – and suddenly finds herself in an unfamiliar game in which she doesn't know the rules. There is an instant connection between us, an understanding that comes from our shared situation, and I have a powerful sense that we can help each other. I've *definitely* seen her face before, but I can't place her. Could she be one of my patients?

She tells me that her next call will be to the police and I wonder, with a lurch of panic, whether it's time for me to do the same.

'It's not—' Her voice catches and she takes a deep breath, then another. 'It's not like Emily. Not at all.'

'Is there a boyfriend in the picture?'

'No,' she says quickly. 'Nothing serious ... no. How about Connor? Does he have anyone?'

'Not that he's talked to me about.'

On the screen, Cathy looks over her shoulder, pushes a door shut behind her. It looks like she's in an artfully decorated study now, or some kind of snug with a large TV on the wall. More quietly, she says: 'He never mentioned Emily?'

'I don't think so.' I try to summon the correct teenage terminology. 'Were they ... together? I mean, like exclusive, or dating or whatever they call it now?'

'No.' She shakes her head, firmly, once. 'No, I don't think you'd call it that.'

Her change of tone throws me for a second. 'How do you mean? What would you—'

'I'm really sorry, Andy, I've got another call coming in.' She reaches towards the screen. 'Please *please* let me know if you hear anything about Emily. I really appreciate it.'

'Will do, and likewise if you hear about Connor.'

But she's already gone, leaving me pondering her closing words. *No, I don't think you'd call it that.* What did that even mean?

A message from my brother has dropped in while I was on the call.

Z not answering his phone, have left message. Going to check if he's at park. Let me know re: Connor

I come out of messages and scroll to the Find My iPhone app again, selecting Connor's number. The indicator is in exactly the same spot as before: according to this, his phone is here, in the house. I try it again then, getting the sense I'm being watched, look up to find Harriet studying me from the doorway.

'What are you doing, Dad?'

I angle the phone screen slightly away from her. 'Just a . . . thing with the phone.'

'Do you want me to help you?'

'I'm fine thanks, H.'

'Find My iPhone, right?' She takes a step into the kitchen. 'Is it working?'

Despite everything, I smile. Sometimes I think my daughter might be smarter than all the rest of us put together.

'Not yet.' I show her the screen with a sigh. 'It says he's *here*, his phone's at home. But that can't be right, it doesn't make sense.'

She glances at the map, gives a shrug of her little shoulders. 'Could be in his bedroom somewhere?'

'I've had a look but I couldn't find it up there. And anyway that phone goes with him everywhere, it never leaves his hand.'

'Maybe he removed your access to his location.'

'But . . . then his phone wouldn't show in the menu, would it?'

She pulls a face, wrinkling her nose in the way she does when I'm being particularly dense about technology.

'What is it, Harriet?'

'That app,' she says in a small voice. 'I think I might know why it doesn't work.'

'OK,' I say.

'I mean, there are ways to spoof it.'

I put my phone down. 'Do *what* to it?'

She pushes a two-pound coin in slow circles on the kitchen table with her index finger. Round and round. 'The thing is, Find My iPhone can't get *direct* access to the GPS chip, what actually happens is the phone's operating system monitors the location provided by GPS, then just passes that data on. But you can interrupt the process to substitute the real data with whatever you like.'

As is increasingly the case with my daughter, I find myself able to follow maybe half of what she's saying. Perhaps less than that. She might have got her dark brown eyes from me, but the IT side of things she'd definitely inherited from her mother. 'Harry,' I say, 'can you give me that again, but in English?'

She sighs. 'There are loads of GPS spoofing apps that let you change the system's location data, which is then reported to the tracking app like it's where you really are. You can make it so it looks like your phone is at our house, or at school, or at Asda or wherever you want.' She continues pushing the coin around the table. 'So it's sort of my fault that you can't find Connor.'

'Why is it your fault?' I'm still not really any the wiser about what she's saying, or what it means. 'How on earth do you even know this stuff, H.?'

She shrugs. 'Watched some tutorials on YouTube. Showed Connor how to do it to his phone.'

'Why?'

'He asked me to, and I wanted to help him, because he helped me at school. He's been nice.' She looks sheepishly up at me. 'I'm sorry.'

'He helped you?' I can't imagine a scenario in which Harriet would ask Connor for help, my effortlessly bright daughter who'd been sailing through every test and exam since she could hold a pencil. 'With your schoolwork?'

'No,' she says quietly. 'With the mean boys. In his year.'

13

I sit down next to my daughter, putting an arm around her little shoulders. She feels tiny, bird-like, and it makes me want to pick her up and carry her, shield her, protect her. She has always been small, too small when she was born to even fill the newborn sleepsuits we bought her.

'Harriet, what's been going on?' An ache spreads through my chest. 'Are you being bullied again?'

She nods, her eyes fixed on the coin beneath her finger, spinning in slow circles on the tabletop. 'I was. For a bit.'

'Tell me.'

'They've been picking on me after orchestra practice, the detention room's next door and they hang around calling me names and things, taking my bag and throwing mud and stuff.' I don't need to ask my daughter what they'd been calling her. *Freakshow. Weirdo. Greta Thunberg. Asperger's.* Names that seemed to follow her from primary school to secondary, passed on by some insidious teenage bush telegraph.

'You poor thing, why didn't you tell me or your mum? We could have talked to your head of year. Mum's worked with Tracey forever, they're good friends.'

Harriet gives me a look as if I can't *possibly* understand how embarrassing it is to have your own mother teaching at your school, of seeing her in the corridor, in assembly, having her as your teacher for IT, let alone asking for her to intervene on your behalf.

'Connor said he would sort it out for me.' She goes back to pushing the coin. 'He went to talk to them, told them to stop. They didn't like it.'

'Hang on, do you mean the thing that happened the other week with Connor and those three lads? Kieran Smith and Drew whats-his-name and that Fitzgerald kid?' I had only a vague idea of what they looked like, but I knew they were all four years older and a foot taller than my daughter.

Harriet nods.

According to the assistant head teacher, the cause of the 'incident' had been unclear, as Connor had said they'd simply got carried away playing MurderBall after school, a testosterone-fuelled game on a hard court that had got a little out of hand. But it appeared now this was a gloss to cover up what had really happened: a fight with teenage bullies who had taken on Connor three against one, and lost. Or at least, they hadn't won – which was just as embarrassing for them, given the odds. Connor had told us their names but said nothing more about the marks across his knuckles, the yellowing bruise under his eye. Only that it wouldn't happen again. He hadn't mentioned his sister was involved at all.

'He didn't want to get me involved,' she says. 'I promised I wouldn't say why he did it. Don't tell him I told you, *please*, Dad.'

As a parent, I knew what I should say to Connor in situations like these. *Don't sink to their level. Don't confront, don't fight. Tell a teacher. The school has a bullying policy, let them deal with it in the proper way.* Etcetera, etcetera. I know what we are supposed to say to our kids, what we've been conditioned to say since they were in infant school, that fighting back was wrong and bad and counter-productive. That they should turn the other cheek, walk away and let the grown-ups handle it.

I know all that, and confirmation that he was in a fight is a new worry to add to a list growing by the minute. And yet there is a fierce bloom of pride in my chest too, a part of me that's glad he stepped up, glad that – even though the two of them have almost nothing in common beyond their sibling connection – he went into bat for his little sister.

A part of me that's glad three bullies had got a taste of their own medicine.

'I won't say anything, Harry.'

'Drew told Connor afterwards that he was going to pay him back ten times over. Said he knew where he lived and how to find him.'

'And Connor thought that meant he might try to track him?'

'He wouldn't say, not exactly.' She sniffs. 'But he didn't want to get jumped by Drew and those others, so I showed him how to spoof the location on his phone. And now he's in trouble and it's my fault.'

I give her another hug. 'It's not your fault, H., it just would have been nice to know where he was, that's all. And it's not your fault you're being bullied, either. Listen, I'll email your head of year tomorrow and get a meeting set up—'

'They've stopped,' she says quickly. 'Drew and those other boys. They don't even look at me anymore, they don't bother me. You don't need to email Miss Nichols.'

'Good.' My throat thickens again at the thought of Connor standing up for his little sister. 'I'm glad they've stopped.'

'There's something else I need to show you too.' She slips off her chair and scampers out of the kitchen before I can ask her anything else.

Laura reappears in the doorway, empty-handed.

'No joy on Connor's iPhone,' she says. 'I've checked everywhere I can think of. Bedroom, bathroom, spare room, lounge.'

'I think we might have solved that mystery,' I say. 'He's probably got it with him. I'll explain later.'

Harriet returns to the kitchen, her laptop open in both hands, headphones around her neck.

'Mum, Dad, can I show you something?'

Laura turns to her, her face lifting with expectation. 'Have you found your brother's phone?'

'Not that, something else.'

She's setting her laptop down on the kitchen table when my mobile starts to ring with an unrecognised number, the opening bars of R.E.M.'s *Losing My Religion* piercing the silence. The voice on the other end is female, precise and clean-edged, the slightest trace of a local accent, and for a moment I think it's one of those recorded messages trying to sell me something.

'Hello?' I can hear the impatience in my voice but I don't have time for junk calls.

'My name's Detective Sergeant Priya Shah, Nottinghamshire Police.' There's background noise at her end, a crosstalk of other voices. 'Am I speaking to Andrew Boyd?'

I press the phone closer to my ear. 'Yes, that's me.'

'And you are the parent or legal guardian of Connor Boyd?'

And then the world is falling away beneath my feet, my stomach dropping with it.

Laura is looking at me in alarm, mouthing words. *What is it? What's wrong?*

I try to answer the detective's question but my tongue is thick with fear, the words colliding in my mouth, all clamouring to escape at once. I take a deep breath and try again. 'He's my son,' I manage finally. 'What's happened? Has something happened to him, is he OK?'

There is a pause on the other end of the line that feels like it stretches out for hours, for days. I want to reach through the phone line and grab this woman, this detective, grab her by the lapels and shake her, make her tell me.

'He's fine, Dr Boyd.'

The relief is instant, like the most powerful opiate mainlined straight into a vein. Laura is still frowning at me, mouthing another silent question. *Is he OK?*

I give her a shaky smile and a thumbs-up. 'Thank God, you found him. Thank God, we've been so worried. You're sure he's all right?'

'He's fit and well.'

I close my eyes, relief still washing warm through me.

'Thank you, thank you, that's such a relief. We've been so worried about him.'

'I'm calling to ask if you can come down here, Dr Boyd?' She gives me the address.

'Of course, I'll come to pick him up right away. I'll leave now—' I check my watch '—should be with you in ten minutes.'

'Great,' she says. 'Ask for me at the front desk and I'll take you down to the custody suite.'

'Thanks again for letting us know, it's such a ...' The word finally lands, like an anvil. 'Did you say *custody*?'

'That's correct, Dr Boyd.'

'What do you mean?' This is all happening too fast. 'He's being ... you mean he's been arrested? For what?'

'I can explain when you get here.'

14

The detective sergeant rings off and I relay our brief conversation to my wife and daughter, Laura already lacing up her trainers as she fires questions for which I don't have answers. *What's happened? Where has Connor been? Why has he been arrested?* The conversation seems ridiculously out of place, almost surreal, for the three of us standing in our kitchen on a beautiful sunlit Sunday afternoon.

Harriet gestures at her laptop. 'Dad? I really need to show you something.'

'There's no time for that now, Harry, we have to go.'

'Go where?'

'To pick Connor up from the police station in town.'

'Will the police want to ask us all questions?'

'No.' Laura shakes her head, an upbeat tone in her voice. 'Of course not. They'll talk to me and your dad, then we'll all talk to Connor for a bit and everything will be sorted out. We'll be back home before you know it.'

'You could drop me off at Unc's house instead?' Unc is her shorthand for my brother, her uncle Rob, the only family we have living nearby.

'No need,' Laura says. 'We won't be long.'

'But what if they do want to talk to me?'

'They won't.'

The three of us are in the car a few minutes later, reversing out of the drive, when Harriet picks up the thread of the conversation again. I can see her face in the rear-view mirror, her features pinched in concentration.

'What if they *do* though?' she says. 'What if the police ask me about Connor's curfew and Zac sleeping over and questions like that?'

Laura pauses and I can sense her weighing up the best approach. Harriet is like a dog with a bone when she gets like this and can sniff out adult flimflam from a mile away; at the age of five, she had set an alarm on Christmas night to discover the truth about Santa Claus. She didn't like to let things go until she knew the answer.

'Just say you don't remember, Harry.'

'You want me to lie?'

'Say you were asleep.'

'Even though I wasn't asleep?'

'That doesn't matter too much.'

'But it would be a lie.' She looks up, her eyes finding mine again in the mirror. 'What if they ask me about spoofing the location on his phone?'

I hadn't thought of that. *I guess we'll cross that bridge when we come to it.*

'They're not going to ask, Harry. They're not even going to want to talk to you.'

'But how do you *know*?'

She shakes her head and clamps her headphones over her ears again, blocking out the world.

Sunday traffic is light as we drive into the middle of Nottingham, windows up and the air conditioning on full blast. The satnav guides us to an anonymous 1960s building, three storeys of blocky grey concrete a couple of streets over from the main shopping centre. I pull into the visitors' section of the car park next to a white Range Rover with tinted windows. After a few minutes' wait a young guy in a dark blue suit, no tie, comes to meet us at the front desk and introduces himself as Detective Constable Harmer. He's tall and rangy, skinny trousers tight against his legs, mid-twenties maybe. He swipes a card to get us through a security barrier and we follow him down a blank grey corridor lined on the right with grey doors, all shut. Harriet's little hand grips mine tightly as we follow the detective towards the back of the station.

'I thought your daughter might prefer to wait in here?' He opens a door to a large open-plan office and gestures to a smiling blonde-haired woman next to an unoccupied desk. 'Jude Loughlin is one of my colleagues, she can sit with her while we talk to your son?'

It's more of an instruction than a question. Harriet grips my hand even tighter but says nothing, surveying the office. It's mostly empty, presumably a light Sunday rota or else most of the remaining staff are out and about.

'The other rooms are pretty cramped to be honest,' Harmer continues, 'and there's not really a lot of room.'

'It's probably better if you wait in here, Harry,' Laura says to her. 'We'll be out in a minute and we'll all go home together, OK?'

Reluctantly, Harriet releases my hand and hops up into the swivel chair, her feet not touching the floor. She's dwarfed by the chair, the desk, a child in a grown-up world. I don't particularly want to leave her on her own but I guess there can't be many safer places than the inside of a police station.

'OK, Harry?' I say to her.

She nods, once.

Jude Loughlin tucks a strand of hair behind her ear and gives Harriet a friendly smile. 'What's your name?'

'Harriet,' she says in a small voice. 'Are you a detective?'

'I am. A detective constable.'

DC Harmer gestures down the corridor. 'We're just down here.'

At the end of the corridor, he knocks once on a door and shows us into a small, cramped room, the smell of sweat hanging in the still air, of too many people packed in too close. A rectangular table on one side has four plastic chairs clustered around it, three of them already occupied. Connor has his back to us and doesn't turn around. Seated beside him is a balding, bearded man who is introduced as the duty solicitor and acknowledges us with a nod. Facing them in the third chair is a woman in her mid-thirties wearing a dark trouser suit, collarless white blouse buttoned to the neck, her thick dark hair tied back in a ponytail. She stands up as we walk in.

'Dr and Mrs Boyd, my name's Detective Sergeant Priya Shah. Thanks for coming in.'

Harmer opens the door to the corridor again. 'I'll get a couple more chairs, boss.'

He disappears, the door slamming behind him.

As we come around the table to get a proper look at our son, I hear Laura catch her breath beside me, a hand going to her mouth.

Connor looks as if he hasn't slept. But there is much worse than that. There is bruising above his left eye, the skin purpling, and his lip is swollen. A line of blood tracing a crack in his lower lip, another bruise spreading to his jawline.

'Connor,' she says, reaching for his hand. She leans towards him and I can tell it's taking all her effort not to go and hug him. 'Your face, what happened? Who did this?'

'What the hell happened to him?' I switch my attention to Shah. 'What did you do?'

The detective's expression doesn't change.

'If you're referring to the facial injuries, sir, he had those when we picked him up.'

'On the phone you said he was unharmed! He needs medical treatment, a doctor to look at his face, other injuries he might have.' I turn to face him again. 'Connor?'

'I'm fine, Dad.' He bites off the words through gritted teeth. 'Just leave it.'

'You're clearly not fine, son, look at you.'

Laura says: 'Does it hurt, Connor?'

'They gave me some paracetamol.'

DS Shah holds a hand up. 'He's been assessed and treated, sir. You need to calm down.'

'I am calm!'

Shah lets that go, her eyebrow raised just a fraction.

I'm pierced with regret for last night, when I had gone up to his room to check he was home. If I hadn't stopped in the doorway, if I had taken a few more steps into the room to be sure it was Connor in bed – if I had done my job as a father – maybe he wouldn't have got hurt. Maybe we wouldn't be sitting here now.

But it had never even crossed my mind that his bed might be occupied by someone else. I feel helpless, as sure as I can be that

I've let him down. I've failed him in the most basic way a parent can fail their child. Failed to protect him from harm. Failed to stop him from ending up in a police station. To prevent whatever happened last night.

'Are you OK, son?'

He nods, mute. I study him as if he's a patient, this boy with his angular teenage features, his mother's high cheekbones and soulful deep blue eyes. Thick brown hair like mine, messed into tousled curls at the front. He seems focused and alert, calm and not in any obvious discomfort.

Harmer returns to the room with two more plastic chairs, arranging them at the curved end of the table so we can see both Connor and the two detectives.

'Let's start again, shall we?' DS Shah says. 'As Connor is under eighteen he's entitled to have a parent or guardian with him while he's interviewed. Ideally one of you, rather than both, considering how tight we are for space.'

Laura folds her arms. 'Well I'm not leaving.'

'Neither am I,' I say.

The detective sergeant considers us both for a moment. 'Fine.'

'Why is he here?' I say.

'Connor was arrested near the city centre this morning, he's been cautioned and advised of his legal rights. So I don't have to repeat myself, let's just start the interview and take you through it, shall we?'

She presses a button on the digital display and recites her name along with the date, time and place of the interview. She then lists the names of the other five of us squeezed into the small interview room and proceeds to lay out the slim collection of facts they have gathered so far.

Connor had been arrested this morning near an upscale address in The Park after a neighbour spotted him loitering – first at the front door and then at the side gate – and assumed he was a burglar. Apparently there had been issues with prowlers and opportunist thieves in that neighbourhood over the last few months, and this was enough to prompt the neighbour to dial 999. When police arrived Connor had tried to run, pushing past one officer before being tackled to the ground by the other. A window at the house had subsequently been found to be broken. I listen with mounting horror as DS Shah describes all of this in a soft Nottinghamshire accent, flipping pages in her notebook.

Suspicion of burglary.

Criminal damage.

Resisting arrest.

My head is spinning, too many thoughts all colliding with each other. *This is not happening. This is ridiculous.* Laura's hand finds mine under the table, clasps it tight.

DS Shah leans forward onto the table. 'Connor, I'd like to know what you were doing near Beaufort Terrace this morning. So why don't we start with that? Why did you try to break into the property, Connor?'

Without looking up, without looking at anyone, my son says two words, the last words I was expecting to come out of his mouth. A flat monotone that is so unfamiliar I wouldn't have believed it was him if we hadn't been sitting at the same table.

'No comment.'

15

'Why did you run from the officers,' Shah says, 'when they challenged you?'

'No comment,' Connor says again.

'Was it because you'd just tried to break into a property on Beaufort Terrace?'

'No comment.'

'Do you know who owns that property?'

'No comment.'

'So you saw something you wanted and you broke in through a downstairs window?'

His eyes flash at this. 'I didn't break in! I didn't damage anything. I didn't *do* anything. The window was like that when I got there.'

'So you *were* on the property?'

My son shakes his head, seeming to retreat into himself again.

'No comment.'

'Do you know where Lower Farm Lane is?'

The switch is abrupt and I wonder why she's changed direction. But if the intent is to get another reaction from Connor, it doesn't seem to work.

'No comment.'

'Have you been to Lower Farm Lane in the last twenty-four hours? Or anywhere on the southern edge of Beacon Hill Woods?'

Question after question, a pregnant pause after each one waiting to be filled. *The bruising on your face, how did that happen? Where were you between 11 o'clock last night and six o'clock this morning? Did you go to a party at number seventy-seven The Avenue? How did you get to the property at Beaufort Terrace?*

Connor's voice, quiet and repetitive, almost apologetic. The same answer each time until the words are forming a dull echo, going round and round inside my head.

No comment.

He won't look at DS Shah, he doesn't look across at me or his mum either. Just keeps his eyes fixed on the table in front of him.

For a second I don't recognise him. His performance reminds me of a true crime documentary we had watched together recently – I can't even remember who it was about – the suspect putting up a 'no comment' response to hours of police questioning. How we both agreed it just made the guy look guilty, even if it did make things much harder for the police. Now that I thought about it, Connor did seem to watch a *lot* of true crime on Netflix, on iPlayer, on Sky Documentaries. The stuff seemed to be everywhere you looked now. Grainy CCTV footage of murder suspects being interviewed, time-stamped video from a fixed camera high up in the corner of a boxy interview room.

I thought he was just interested because he wanted to study law. But was *that* where he'd got this from? This refusal to cooperate, to stonewall questions?

There's no air conditioning in here, just a small window cracked open a few inches, and with the six of us crowded into such a small space, it's unpleasantly warm. Sweat is already dampening the collar of my shirt and gathering under my arms.

'Detective, my son's not a burglar. I've no idea what's gone on here but I'm sure there's a reasonable explanation.'

DS Shah looks perfectly composed, her white blouse crisp and unruffled.

'We've got some concerns about other . . . events that may have taken place last night and this morning.' It seems possible, she goes on to say, that there may be a connection between Connor's arrest at Beaufort Terrace and another incident currently under investigation. She won't elaborate any further.

She returns her attention to Connor.

'What were you doing, trying to break into that property on Beaufort Terrace?'

'No comment.'

'Was there something there that you needed? Something in that property?'

My son shakes his head.

With an almost imperceptible frown, Shah says, 'Suspect gave a negative response.'

'Connor?' I say quietly. 'What are you doing? Why are you not saying anything? Just answer the questions.'

His eyes meet mine for a second before he blinks and looks away. 'You wouldn't understand.' He shifts uncomfortably in his seat.

'Then *tell us*,' I say. 'Why don't you just tell us what you were doing there? The quicker we can answer these questions, the quicker all of this can be cleared up.'

I can feel the frustration building, a hard pressure behind my eyes.

I take a breath and turn to the duty solicitor, whose name I've already forgotten. 'Can we have a break, or something? I don't know what you've advised Connor to do, but I don't think this is the best strategy.'

The solicitor gives me a disinterested glance, the look of a man who would rather be anywhere else on a Sunday afternoon than here in this hot little room.

'All I can do,' he says, 'is present your son with his options. I've outlined his legal situation but in terms of what he chooses to say, that's not up to me.' He pauses. 'Or you.'

Laura touches our son gently on the arm. 'Just tell the truth, Connor.'

I look at him across the table, our studious child, who has always been serious and thoughtful and above all *kind*, trying to remember the last time he was in any sort of trouble at school or anywhere else. The only thing I can think of was a primary school prank years ago, Connor and Zac soaking wads of toilet paper in a sink and throwing them, dozens stuck up on the toilet ceiling by the time they were caught by the caretaker, still giggling and egging each other on. Laura and I sitting straight-faced on those tiny classroom chairs as his teacher gave us a stern talking to. Laughing about it later over a glass of wine after the kids were in bed. The boys had just got carried away, that was all. I can't even remember a detention since he's been at secondary school. Predictions of a good crop of GCSEs. This was *our son*, after all, who was already looking toward his A levels, who wanted to study law at university, who had his heart set on Warwick or Newcastle or Bath, top-ranked institutions that would be asking for A grades if not A stars.

Our son, who wouldn't stay out all night. *But did he?*

Who wouldn't lie. *But was sitting in front of us, refusing to tell the truth.*

Who wouldn't get into fights. *But had sought out a violent confrontation with three boys bullying his sister.*

Who'd never been in trouble with the police. *But was now under arrest facing a string of charges.*

For a moment I wonder if he has thrown it all away, if one night of madness will be the point on which his whole life hinges. A fork in the road at which his education, his career, his future shifts onto a different path. A darker, more uncertain one. If Connor has been changing imperceptibly into this *other* person, for months or years, and I have been too preoccupied to notice. Too caught up in my own work, my own life.

Because I barely recognise this angry, frightened boy sitting across the table from me.

What have you done, Connor?

What have you done?

16

'Let's talk about the house party on The Avenue,' DS Shah says abruptly. 'Did you see anyone with drugs? Anyone taking drugs, or dealing?'

Connor stares at the table. 'No,' he mumbles.

'Can you speak up, please?'

'No,' he says again. 'Nothing like that.'

The duty solicitor says: 'Would you like to pause, Connor?' He looks at his watch. 'We can take a break if you like, I can take you through the—'

'Let's carry on,' Connor says. 'Get it over with.'

He reaches up to rub his eyes and for the first time I notice marks on the back of his hand. The skin red and angry around them. Scratches? He drops his hand back to his lap and I wonder if the detectives have noticed too.

DS Shah looks at her watch. 'You know what? Let's take a five-minute break. I need a brief chat with my colleague.' She hits a button on the recording equipment. 'Toilets are down the corridor on the right, Dr and Mrs Boyd, vending machine too.'

She walks out. DC Harmer takes out his phone and scrolls through emails while the solicitor opens a page of his file and begins scribbling notes. The silence is leaden, me looking at Connor while he stares mutely at the table.

'Connor?' I say quietly.

He turns slightly towards me but still won't meet my eye.

'Connor?' I put a hand on his arm. 'Are you OK, do you want a drink? Something to eat?'

He shrugs, a universal teenage response with various meanings. *Yes, no, maybe, obviously, whatever.*

The vending machine is down the corridor, next to a set of double security doors controlled with a pass. As I reach in my pocket for change, I recognise the young female officer pressing buttons on the console.

'Just getting your daughter a 7UP,' DC Loughlin says. 'She's not allergic or anything, is she?'

'No. That's kind of you, thanks.' I peer down the corridor. 'Is she OK?'

'She's fine, Dr Boyd.' She collects the can from the dispenser and then selects another for herself. 'Asks a lot of questions, doesn't she?'

'It's her first time in a police station.' *And mine too.*

'Bright as a button, that one.'

'Thanks for keeping an eye on her.'

Loughlin gives me a nod and walks back into her office. I feed pound coins into the machine and try to remember what Connor likes. We used to play that game, the Richard Osman thing, the World Cup of Chocolate Bars – Mars v. Snickers, Crunchie v. Twirl. He wouldn't entertain it now, though. *You're so cringe, Dad.*

I get two Diet Cokes and a Mars bar. As I'm cradling the drinks under my left arm, the cans ice-cold through my polo shirt, a door opens opposite me. The room beyond is bigger than the interview room, less stark, a large window and a small round table against the wall. More comfortable chairs, a man in a shirt and tie sitting down with his back to me. Opposite him is Cathy Ruskin, her hands clasped in front of her on the table, her smooth face a picture of worry.

Our WhatsApp conversation returns to me, an unwelcome echo from a few hours ago.

Were they together?

No. Firm. Definitive. *I don't think you'd call it that.*

The door clicks shut before she sees me.

Back in the interview room, I put the drink and chocolate bar on the table in front of Connor but he doesn't touch either of them, his hands stuck resolutely in the pockets of his jeans. I open mine and put it to my lips, icy bubbles bursting on my tongue. I hadn't realised how dry my mouth was. I offer the can to Laura and she takes a long drink.

DS Shah reappears, her face still unreadable, and sits down opposite us.

'Right then,' she says, turning the recorder on again. 'Let's continue, shall we? So . . . at the moment we're piecing together a number of different events from the last twenty-four hours that may help us to locate a missing person. What we're really interested in is completing a timeline for you, Connor. In particular, where you were between the hours of midnight and 6 a.m. From our initial enquiries, there seems to have been a small group that went on from the party, up to Beacon Hill Woods. Is that right, Connor? Emily Ruskin, Olivia de Luca, Drew Saxton plus your cousin, Zac. And you.'

Five teenagers, just as Zac had told my brother. I wonder how many are being questioned by police – and whether my son is the only one who's managed to get himself arrested.

'No comment.' Connor's voice is fading, getting quieter with each refusal.

'Were you in that group, Connor?'

This time he doesn't even reply.

'I don't know who you think you're protecting.' DS Shah taps the table with her palm. 'Unless it's your cousin? Was that the idea, that neither of you say anything that could get the other one in trouble?' She lets this sit for a moment, the silence leaking out between us. 'Are you covering for Zac? Is that what this is?'

'No. Comment.'

'Did he do something?'

'Can I go now?'

'Because we'll be talking to him this afternoon, plus Drew and Olivia. I've already had a chat with your uncle, Robert, on the phone.'

Connor's eyes flick from one detective to the other. 'What?'

'He was very cooperative, says you and your cousin weren't invited to the party on The Avenue.' She checks her notes. 'Is that correct?'

'Yeah.'

'Was that where you got hurt, Connor?' She indicates the marks on his face. 'Was it a fight?'

'No.'

'It looks like a fight. Did you win?'

He shakes his head. 'I fell down on the way home. It was nothing.'

'Doesn't look like nothing.' She waits for him to respond, but he clamps his lips shut again. 'Anyway, as I said, we understand that a small group of teenagers left the house party and went up to Beacon Hill, shortly after midnight. We believe you were one of them.'

I glance over at Connor. He looks wretched, his jaw clenched, swallowing hard and doing everything he can to keep his emotions hidden. He's a six-foot teenager on the verge of manhood but he's still only a few years away from that little boy who loved *Mr Bean*. I try to imagine what he's gone through alone in the last few hours, handcuffed and arrested, surrounded by strangers.

This is my *son*. I *know* him.

I may not have brought him into the world but I was the first person to really hold him, to cradle him in my arms as surgeons completed the Caesarean operation. Gowned up in green scrubs, I had been the first person to look into his eyes: a perfect, tiny, red-faced baby handed to me by the nurse in the delivery suite. I have known him since he took his first breath.

Just a few words would sort this out, surely. All I had to do was vouch for my son and we could take him home, put this behind us. The scuffle with the police this morning, the arrest, that was just a bit of teenage stupidity, a misunderstanding. I couldn't see that they were going to actually charge him with anything, not a sixteen-year-old with no criminal record. And whatever happened in the woods last night, with Emily Ruskin . . . Connor didn't need to be dragged into that.

I just had to give him an alibi, that was all. Just a few words and Connor could put this behind him. Wasn't that all it would be? Words? Not a lie, not exactly, more like an *explanation*. The sort of thing a parent does for their child every so often, to smooth their path, to clear an obstacle out of the way so they don't stumble. Could I actually do it? More to the point, could I lie to a police officer, lie to her face, and do it convincingly?

Before I can even answer my own question, Laura beats me to it.

She gives the detective a definitive shake of her head. 'No,' she says firmly, 'that's not right. He was at home with us. He was home just after midnight.'

Connor's head jerks up in surprise, eyes widening at his mother.

DS Shah says: 'You're absolutely sure of that, Mrs Boyd? You're certain?'

'Yes,' she says firmly, squeezing my hand under the table. 'I'm sure. He was home by his curfew.'

'Just after midnight,' I add. 'That's when he came in. So this group that went up to the woods . . . he wasn't involved in that.'

I feel my pulse race a little quicker in my chest, a glimmer of warmth rising up my neck. DS Shah's deep brown eyes on mine.

Laura says: 'How does this relate to Emily Ruskin, anyway?'

Shah keeps her unblinking gaze on me, holding it for a long, uncomfortable moment – *she knows you're lying, she knows you're just covering for him* – before her eyes slide back across to my wife.

'Because our initial enquiries suggest,' she says, 'that five teenagers went up to the woods last night. But only four came out.'

17

For a horrible moment I think Connor is going to be held here, in a cell, for the rest of the day or perhaps even overnight. That they will keep on asking him the same questions, over and over, until he starts talking. So when DS Shah eventually says that as a juvenile with no prior criminal record, he is being released pending the outcome of further enquiries, I feel a rush of relief. Harmer takes him through to the main desk to fill out some paperwork, with the duty solicitor in tow. That leaves the three of us – the detective sergeant, Laura and me – facing each other awkwardly across the small plastic table like some hideously inverted parents' evening at school.

'Thanks for coming in today, both of you,' she says.

'I'm sorry about all that, about . . . Connor,' I say. 'We'll talk to him, I'm sure we can get this all sorted out.'

'That would be a big help.'

'He's a very honest boy, very truthful,' Laura interjects. 'He's not a liar, he's never been like that. It's not who he is.'

DS Shah nods slowly. 'I need to advise you that a standard part of post-arrest procedure is to take a DNA swab.'

A frown darkens Laura's face.

'Hang on a second,' she says. 'Does he have to do that? I mean, is he legally obliged to give a sample?'

'It's standard on arrest when—'

'So you're saying you've already done it?'

The detective nods. 'A sample's been taken, yes. Hopefully it will help us to eliminate him more quickly from our enquiries.'

'He's still legally a *child*, you're aware of that?' Laura says, her voice hard.

'It's OK,' I say to Laura. 'He's got nothing to hide.'

Shah hands me a business card bearing the silver and black logo of Notts Police.

'If you remember anything else unusual about last night,' she says, 'anything at all, please get in touch. We're particularly interested in the six-hour window after midnight. But you can say categorically that Connor was at home, at your property, between midnight and 6 a.m.?'

'Yes,' my wife says without missing a beat. 'He was home by 12.15. With us.'

'You saw him, did you?'

'Yes.'

'Did you speak to him?'

There is a pause, just a fraction of a second, and I wonder whether Shah has picked up on it.

'He just put his head around the bedroom door,' Laura says.

'And you're sure he didn't go out again after that?'

'Positive.'

'This morning, he left the house again at what time?'

Laura shoots a quick glance at me, as if this conversation is perfectly normal, even casual. Her face is totally calm, not a hint of the nerves I can feel fluttering in my stomach. 'Around nine,' she says. 'Yeah. Nine-ish.'

'All right then.' She closes her notebook with a snap and I feel a tiny relaxation in my shoulders, an easing of muscles I hadn't realise had been tensed. 'How about drugs?' she says abruptly.

'What?' I say. 'What about them?'

'Has Connor ever dabbled?'

I shake my head firmly. 'No.'

'Not even a bit of weed? Occasional spliff with his mates?'

'Not even that,' my wife cuts in. 'He's never been interested in that sort of thing.'

The detective nods slowly. 'Right. Smart lad.'

She and her colleagues, she explains, will be making further enquiries today and will probably need to speak to Connor again. They will be talking to a number of other teenagers through the rest of the day as they try to locate Emily Ruskin. Their hope is that she will be found safe and well and returned to her family before the day is out. In the meantime, she strongly advises us to keep Connor at home, and do what we can to get him to open up – because a full and frank account of his movements *would be in everyone's best interests*. She walks us around to the office next door. Harriet says a hasty goodbye to DC Loughlin and hurries over to me, gripping my hand tightly. In her other hand, she clutches her familiar blue key ring, her little talisman, that looks like a lip balm but *isn't* actually a lip balm – it's a USB stick. I make a mental note to ask her about it later.

When she catches sight of Connor, she runs to him without a word and buries her face in his chest, her little arms reaching around to hold him tight. He hugs her back, gently patting her shoulders. From the look on his face, Connor is as surprised as we are with his sister's sudden embrace. When they were both much younger, he would carry her around or give her piggybacks, get down on his hands and knees to be a horsey for her to ride around the lounge. But recently the physical contact had lessened, the four-year gap between them more pronounced as they grew, to the point where they hardly seemed to touch at all any more.

When Harriet breaks away from the hug, her face is lined with worry.

'What happened?'

'I'm fine, Harry.'

'What did they do to you?'

'Just asked me some stuff, that's all.'

'Why were they asking *you*?' she says. 'Are you coming home now? With all of us? I thought they were going to lock you up in a cell.'

He cracks a smile for the first time, tousling her red hair.

'Little nerd.' But there is warmth in his voice, the first time today he's sounded like normal Connor again, *our* Connor. 'They can't lock you up if you haven't done anything.'

Harriet stares up at her brother's bruises, concern in her serious brown eyes.

'What happened to your face?'

'It doesn't matter.'

'Was it Drew Saxton again?'

'No, Harry.' He shakes his head. 'It was just—'

'I'm sorry you got hurt.' In a small voice, she adds: 'I don't like it.'

'I'm fine, really.'

She holds out a hand and, to my surprise, he takes it. In the back seat of the car, she continues to clasp his hand tightly in her own as if she's petrified of letting him go. They haven't held hands in years, not since she was a bossy five-year-old leading him around the house in one of her endless games of *teachers* or *shopping* or *Dora the Explorer.*

I want to talk to him, to sit down with him, to tell him it's OK and just to tell us the truth so we can get all of this sorted out and put it behind us.

But Connor sits in silence, staring out of the window the whole way home.

18

Connor kicks his Nikes off in the hallway and heads for the kitchen.

I fetch the medical bag that lives in the boot of my car. By the time I find him next to the fridge he already has a pint of squash in one hand and a thick stack of digestive biscuits in the other, methodically feeding them into his mouth one after the other. He sees me opening the medical bag and his shoulders slump.

'The paramedics already checked me over.' He bites into another biscuit. 'Said I was fine.'

'It's always worth double-checking with head injuries,' I say, indicating a kitchen chair and then sitting down opposite him. I pull out a pen torch. 'Now just follow the light with your eyes.'

He sighs theatrically but does what he's asked. Up close, he looks younger, softer, more vulnerable. Defenceless. More like the sweet, wide-eyed boy he'd been before the teenage years hit him like a hurricane. I give him a thorough examination, checking his eyes are contracting equally in response to the light from the little torch. Checking in his ears for any signs of cerebrospinal fluid, and behind the ears for the telltale signs of an undiagnosed injury to the base of the skull. Finally, I check the site of injury itself for any boggy swelling beneath the skin that might indicate a fracture. It was possible – although uncommon – for serious head injuries to be missed on a quick examination. I remembered a case study we'd been taught at medical school, a young man involved in a Friday-night brawl, a head injury cleaned and dressed quickly, dismissed as superficial. In reality, he was dying of a slow bleed on the brain that was not diagnosed until it was too late: the patient had gone to sleep and never woken up.

My son continues to eat biscuits.

He has bruising and some swelling, but everything else checks out OK. He's lucky – it looks like he took a hefty whack from something. If he was one of my patients, I'd be recommending paracetamol and observation and a good night's sleep. I'm about to give him a proper GP-to-patient talking-to when Laura lays her palm flat on my chest and leads me into the lounge. She puts a finger to her lips.

'Let's take our time, OK?' she whispers. 'Give me a minute to talk to him.'

'I can—'

'If you jump in with your size elevens, he'll just clam up. Make us both a cup of tea while I have a chat with him.'

An objection is on my lips, but I know she's right. From the kitchen, I hear cupboard doors open and closing again, Connor foraging for more food. He's constantly hungry and it occurs to me that he must be starving after so long without a proper meal. Laura shepherds him towards the lounge. 'Give me ten minutes.'

'I'll make some calls,' I say. 'About the legal stuff.'

I call my friend Greg from the practice, whose wife is a solicitor. She does family law rather than criminal, but she's well

connected in legal circles and I ask if she can recommend someone. A few calls later and I have an appointment to meet with
Kay Barber-Lomax, a criminal law specialist with a fearsome
reputation.

The WhatsApp icon on my phone shows nine new messages.
I open it and click through some routine updates from work colleagues, which I ignore. Six others are on the school parents' group
that Cathy Ruskin used earlier, all of them arriving in the last hour.
More moral support – although most of them look as if they're just
fishing for updates, rather than offering anything new. But the last
one catches my eye.

> *Friend of mine who works for the police said a year 11 lad got
> arrested? Will private message you xx*

With an unpleasant lurch of recognition, I realise the message is
referring to Connor. News obviously travels fast on the school
grapevine and I wonder how long it will be before his name is
out there, spread around the neighbourhood attached to all kinds
of wild theories. A throb of panic lodges in my throat and for a
moment I have the urge to reply on the chat and tell the sender
to keep this kind of blatant gossip-mongering to herself. But that
wouldn't achieve anything apart from drawing more attention
to my son.

There's a response from Cathy from a few minutes ago.

> *Thanks all for your messages. Sorry can't reply to you indi-
> vidually, today has been awful but it's good to know you're all
> with us xx*

When I return to the lounge, my wife and son are sitting side by side on the sofa, their heads so close they're almost touching. Talking in low voices.

At the sight of me, the conversation stops.

'I've got an appointment with a solicitor booked,' I say. 'At her office in town, so we can get some proper legal advice. OK, Connor?'

He gives a single, curt nod, but says nothing.

In my peripheral vision I can sense Laura willing me to *back off, give him space*, but it's the first chance I've had to talk to my son face to face, on home turf, the first chance to hear his side of the story. It seems like I deserve that, at the very least.

'So what happened, Connor? Last night?'

'Nothing,' he says. 'Nothing happened.'

'We just spent two hours in the police station, so something must have happened,' I say, handing Laura a mug of tea. 'Why did you run from the police? What about this missing girl, do you know her? Was she with you?'

He shakes his head, but says nothing.

'You don't know her, or she wasn't with you? Which one is—'

Laura frowns at me a little.

'It's all right, Andy. We don't need to interrogate the boy all over again. He's home now, he's safe, and that's the main thing.'

'I just want to know what's going on.' I turn to our son again. 'And I'm sure Emily Ruskin's family do too – think about what they're going through today. Why did you say "No comment" for that whole interview, Connor?'

'Because I didn't do anything.'

'Then why don't you just *say* that? Tell them the truth. What about this house on Beaufort Terrace? They think you tried to break in.'

'Why don't you *ever* believe me?' he says. 'Why is it always everyone else that you believe, and not me? It's like I'm back at that police station. I didn't break in, and the resisting arrest thing is a load of crap, I didn't even realise they were police. I panicked, I heard someone coming after me and thought it was lads from school. I was just trying to get away.'

'All right,' I say. 'I believe you. But I don't get why you didn't answer any of the questions they put to you? You're going to have to tell the solicitor I've just arranged, so you might as well tell us now.'

He stares at me, his eyes dark with frustration. Or maybe disappointment.

'You wouldn't understand, Dad.' He stands abruptly.

'What about Lower Farm Lane, why were they asking about that?' I say. 'You didn't end up way over there last night, did you?'

He turns and walks out, the sound of his heavy footsteps on the stairs reaching us a moment later.

Laura is shaking her head. 'You know that thing I said to you a few minutes ago, about not jumping in with your size elevens?'

'So what did he tell you?'

She relates what she's gleaned from our son but it's barely more than he revealed to the police.

'And what about the other two, Drew and Olivia? What's the deal with them?'

'Olivia is Emily's best friend, apparently. The two of them are inseparable, BFFs and all that. Drew is a bit of a Jack the Lad, by the sound of it. Tried it on with Emily a few times but she's always knocked him back.'

'And he's the one who was making Harriet miserable.'

'Yes,' she says. 'He sounds like an absolute—'

She falls silent as Harriet comes in, standing in the doorway. Our daughter begins firing questions about Connor: *What's going to happen tomorrow? Will the police want to talk to him again?* I try my best to reassure her, then I remember something.

'In the police station, Harry, when the police officer left you alone, you didn't plug in your USB stick, did you? Didn't leave any little access programmes behind on that computer?'

Her last school had taken a very dim view of similar antics. I imagined the police would be even less impressed.

Harriet gives a quick shake of her head.

'No. Course not.'

'Good. That's good.'

'Although they are running an operating system older than I am.'

'As long as you didn't go poking around inside their—'

'That detective, Jude, said they were trying to find out what happened up at Beacon Hill Woods after the party,' she says abruptly. 'Was it something bad?'

'Whatever it was, Connor wasn't involved. We told them he was home by midnight.'

'You told the police that?'

'Yes.'

Her frown deepens. 'Why?'

'Because . . . we don't want him to get into trouble, darling.'

She gives me a strange look.

'I need to show you something.' Her voice is quiet. 'Back in a sec.'

She hurries out and I can hear her footsteps on the stairs.

I reach for Laura's hand and give it a little squeeze. She squeezes back. It's the first time we've had alone since the phone call from DS Shah, just the two of us for a moment with no one else in earshot.

'We did the right thing with the police, didn't we?' I say quietly.

'Yes,' she says. 'Anyone else would have done the same.' She glances quickly at the door to the hall, checking neither of the children is there. 'Now we both need to *stick* to the story,' she says. 'If we both say he was home at midnight, they can't touch him, right? We say he definitely made his curfew.'

I nod, wishing I shared her certainty. Wondering if it had been the right lie to tell. Although telling it was never in doubt, not really. Not after I saw his face in the police station, the bruises, the fear, the sense that I had let him down. 'Home by midnight,' I repeat. 'Keep it simple.'

'We should ground him for a week anyway.'

'At the very least. And we need to—'

She shoots me a warning look as Harriet bustles back in with her laptop under her arm.

'Look at this.' Our daughter opens the laptop, angling the screen to face us. She has that look on her face she gets when she's fully in the zone, fully engaged, the look when she's beating me at chess or solving some incomprehensible maths problem. 'Tried to tell you earlier but you kept ignoring me.'

Laura releases my hand. 'Tell us what, Harry?'

'This.' She jabs a little index finger at the screen. 'If you want to know who was actually *here* last night. And who wasn't.'

19

All I can see are lines of computer code or programming commands on the screen, an arcane collection of words and numbers and symbols stacked on top of each other.

'What are we looking at?'

'I interrogated our wireless router activity.'

I exchange glances with Laura. 'OK. I didn't know . . . you could do that.'

'It's actually really easy. There are loads of tutorials on YouTube about it.'

She launches into a complicated explanation of logs and files and protocols that loses me within the first ten seconds. She takes us through the data on the screen, showing us what is denoted by the lines of information. Activity on our home wireless network over the last thirty-six hours and all the devices connected to it: three laptops, three iPads, Connor's Alexa and various other devices, Laura's smart watch plus a variety of phones that she takes us through one by one, showing each time they connected to the house's wireless router. A log made each time a device connects to it, or leaves it. To me, the lines of data are completely meaningless, but Harriet seems to be able to discern the meaning of each datapoint. Time and date. A unique identifier for each device.

'This one here,' she says, tapping the screen with her index finger, 'is Zac's mobile. Connects to our Wi-Fi just before 8 p.m. on Saturday, drops off it eleven minutes later, the same time as Connor's phone which you can see *here*.'

I cast my mind back to last night. Zac had come to call for Connor and they had gone up to his room briefly before they went out.

She scrolls down the page. 'They left at the same time, but they came back at different times.'

'I don't think that's right, Harry,' Laura says, glancing at me.

'According to the router, it is.'

'He messaged me when he got in, H. Just like he always does. I keep my phone by the bed and I hear the buzz, rather than me listening out for him for hours. He knows to be super quiet and then he just lets me know when he's back in his room, so he doesn't disturb us too much.'

She shakes her head emphatically. 'No.'

'No?'

'Zac's phone reconnected to the Wi-Fi at 2.19 a.m. Connor's phone didn't.'

I look at where she's pointing on the screen, a line with today's date and the numbers *0219* next to it.

'That's the time, there,' she says.

I stare at the screen. 'How is it you *know* about this stuff, Harry?'

My daughter shrugs and gives me a pitying look, as if it's obvious. 'How is it you *don't* know?' she says. 'You're on the internet every day.'

It's true enough. Switch things on and they just *work* – I've never given a lot of thought to *how* they work, or what else they do. Then again I don't have a detailed understanding of what's going on under the bonnet of my car, either.

'Maybe Connor had his phone switched off when they came home,' Laura says. 'Or he ran out of charge, or something.'

Harriet turns her sceptical look on her mother. 'Connor's phone drops off the home network at 8.09 p.m. Doesn't come back again until this afternoon when we got back from the police station.'

'Maybe he . . . switched it off when he went to sleep?'

She raises her eyebrows again. She knows – all three of us know – that Connor never turns his phone off.

'See? I *told* you I wasn't lying. I told you I heard someone coming in at 2.19.'

Laura and I exchange a look. Despite our trust, and the story we had given the police, it is becoming ever more apparent that our son not only missed his midnight curfew; he had not come home at all. He had been out all night.

'It's very clever to have found this out, Harriet. But why are you telling us?'

'I don't want Connor to get into trouble. If I can find it, the police can find it, and when they do they'll know you told them a lie and you'll be in trouble too. *And* they'll think Connor did what-ever they think he did.'

She looks at me for the first time, eyes wide in her pale, freckled face, and I see that she's not done any of this to win an argument. She's worried. Scared for her brother. She doesn't even know the details of what he's been questioned about, but she's already think-ing ahead and trying to help him.

Laura points at the screen.

'Does that information get sent back to a central server, or up to the cloud?'

Harriet shrugs her shoulders. 'Don't know about a cloud backup, Mum. I could probably find out. Also stored locally for sixty days, but you can change that setting.'

'So it could be shorter, couldn't it?'

'You want me to delete the logs, Mum?'

'Not delete, no. Let me . . . have a think about it. Maybe just find out if it's possible?'

She looks at me meaningfully, unspoken words passing between us: *Better to know we can cover his tracks, if we need to.*

Harriet thinks about this for a moment, chewing on her thumbnail. Finally, she nods. 'I'll see what I can do.'

20
ZAC

Sunday 12th June, 12.44 a.m.
Thirty-seven minutes before Emily disappears
Beacon Hill Woods

She was a fake.

Everything about her was fake: she was a plastic person, just like her mum. A superficial, spoiled brat who used people and discarded them as it suited her. Emily Ruskin was toxic.

She wasn't worth a minute of Connor's time, not even a second.

But his cousin couldn't see that.

He couldn't see beyond her blonde hair, her perfect cheekbones and perfect lips and big slow-blinking eyes, beyond his own idea of who she was, never mind the reality.

But Zac had seen what she was really like.

And not just her; everything else, too. Zac's eyes had been opened and he had seen the world for what it was. The dark truth that sometimes life went so badly wrong it could never be put right again.

A truth denied, shunned, by the fakers and the plastics. By people like Emily Ruskin, who had no idea how lucky she really was.

Zac knew it was pointless saying this to Connor though. And there was no sense in falling out again, not over her.

Instead, the two of them walked side by side in silence, shining their torch beams warily into the dark, the glow of the campfire behind them. They had ventured away from the circle of light in search of a noise in the woods, Connor volunteering – at Emily's insistence – to check there was no one out there spying on their little group in the dark.

'You hear anything?' Zac said softly.

'Nope,' Connor said. 'Just us.'

Zac played the thin beam of his torch into bushes and trees, his eyes still adjusting after the bright dancing flames of the fire. It was weird how different Beacon Hill looked at night, how strange, how unknown. Hostile, almost alien. The trees seemed taller, their branches darker, brambles twisted with thorns as sharp as needles. He'd been up here on his own for a night, a few months ago, when he was really down about his mum. Connor had offered to join him but Zac had wanted to be on his own.

The truth was, he found it impossible to talk about that stuff, even with Connor. It was like a naked flame; he couldn't allow himself to get too close. He could only skirt around it, like maybe talking about his dad drinking too much or being crap at something his mum used to do, not knowing obvious stuff that his mum would have known, like the names of his teachers, his favourite curry, his favourite lines from Hot Fuzz. But no more than that.

'Probably a fox,' he murmured. 'Or a rabbit. There are a million creepy noises out here at night.'

Connor turned to go. 'Shall we head back?'

Zac put a hand on his cousin's arm. 'You're not going to help her, are you, mate?' He kept his voice low. 'It's messed up.'

Connor shrugged uneasily.

'I said I'd stay, so that's what I'm going to do.'

'Doesn't mean we have to be a part of this . . . It's not right. She doesn't know what she's saying. You can see that, can't you?'

'I feel sorry for her, I want to help her. That's all. It can't be easy living up to those expectations, her sisters and all that.'

Zac released his grip.

'You don't understand, mate. You can't . . . play at this stuff.' His voice was suddenly thick with emotion. 'It's not a game, it's real. What about her mum? It'll kill her. You want to be part of that?'

Connor stopped scanning the trees and looked instead at his cousin, face deep in shadow. Something in his voice, in his tone, that Zac had never heard before.

'Her mum is the reason for all this.'

'But you know Emily's stringing you along, don't you? Just using you, the way she uses everyone else.' He cleared his throat awkwardly. 'You're my best mate and I hate seeing her take advantage of you.'

Connor glared at his cousin. 'You've never liked her, have you? Why is that?'

'You can't see yourself, Connor, it's like you're in a daze when she's around. Like no one else is there and nothing else matters.'

'I'm going back,' Connor said abruptly. 'Are you coming, or what?'

He turned and walked back the way they had come, back towards the others and the orange glow of the fire.

Zac hesitated for a moment then hurried after his cousin, following his torchlight as he picked his way through the trees. Stung by a sense that – yet again – he was letting Connor down somehow. As if he was watching the same crash happen over and over again, and never doing anything to intervene.

They walked back to the clearing in silence.

Olivia was on the far side of the fire, the joint smoking in her left hand, a small silver hip flask in the other. Five red plastic cups were set out on a tree stump, a half full bottle of Absolut vodka next to them. He and Olivia had been exclusive for a bit, last summer, an on–off thing that had fizzled out after Zac got tired of being stood up. Olivia dropping everything whenever Emily called her with a new crisis until Zac realised he couldn't compete with Olivia's BFF.

He looked around the fire. For a second he thought Emily had disappeared before realising that she was still there, half hidden beneath Drew. Kissing him. Drew was leaning right over her, his mouth on hers, one hand in her hair and the other reaching up under her sweatshirt. And she was kissing him back, a hand on his arm, fingertips squeezing tight against his triceps.

Oh, shit.

Zac turned, seeing the heat already rising in a sudden rush to Connor's face. His cousin looked crushed, broken, as if his heart had been ripped from his chest.

But Zac felt only a disgusted anger that squeezed out everything else. Anger at this girl, and this boy, this total arsehole she had chosen over Connor. This moron, this idiot who didn't love her, probably didn't even like her, just wanted to have her because he could. And because she let him, had chosen him despite everything. Giving herself to him like it was nothing, like Connor's devotion to her didn't matter. He couldn't bear to see it but he couldn't tear his eyes away, either.

Drew was holding a fistful of her blonde hair, pulling her head back, her mouth up to his, kissing her harder, her sweatshirt riding up under his hand revealing the tanned skin of her stomach, a tiny red stone glinting in her belly button piercing, the black lace underside of her bra.

Was she kissing him back? Or trying to twist away?

It didn't matter because Drew was too strong, too big, lifting one leg up and over her waist, straddling her, pinning her to the ground. But he lost his balance for a moment and she levered one leg free, trying to swing a knee up into his groin.

Before Zac could react, Connor leaped across the fire and grabbed two handfuls of Drew's shirt, hauling him backwards.

'Get off her!' he shouted. 'Get the hell off her!'

For a second there was a blur of arms and legs, elbows and fists, grabbing and pulling, hands like claws, nails raking blindly as they separated.

'Leave me alone!' Emily said finally with a gasp, scrambling backwards. 'Get the fuck off me!'

Drew got to his feet and squared up to Connor.

'What?' he said in challenge, his arms wide. He was taller than Connor and big with it, his shoulders rounded with muscle. 'What? You got something to say?'

Connor looked down at Emily. 'Are you OK? Did he—'

Drew threw a short, vicious punch that knocked Connor to the ground.

Emily staggered to her feet, pulling her sweatshirt down. 'What the fuck, Drew? Leave him alone!'

'You were up for it. Don't say you weren't.' He touched a finger to his lip. 'Jesus, you bit me.'

Connor got unsteadily to his feet, squaring up to the taller boy again.

Zac stepped between them, trying to hold each at arm's length.

'Let's all just calm down, shall we?' He looked from Drew to Connor, and back again. 'Have another drink.'

Drew jabbed a finger at Connor. 'He started it.'

'You should leave her alone,' Connor said, his face flushed. 'She doesn't want you.'

Drew snorted, his face twisting into a crooked smile. 'That's not what she said a minute ago.' He scooped up a bottle from the ground and took a long swig then sprawled on a log by the fire, legs spread wide.

Zac took his cousin by the elbow and led him to another of the four old logs that served as benches in the clearing. A line of blood traced its way down from Connor's eyebrow where Drew's punch had landed.

Olivia sat Emily down with a drink, an arm around her shoulders.

For a long moment they sat in loaded silence, the five of them facing each other on different sides of the fire.

Connor looked across at Emily. 'Are you OK?'

She nodded, but said nothing.

Zac stood up, pouring generous measures from the bottle of vodka into five of the plastic cups.

'Hey, how about we do one last round of shots?' he said. 'It's Saturday night, exams are over, we've got the whole summer to do what we like. And we need to finish this Absolut.'

Olivia clapped her hands. 'Finishing the vodka is always a good idea.'

'Just one last round,' Emily said quietly. 'Then I'm gone.'

'Count me in,' Drew said with a belch. 'And no short measures.'

'Me too,' Connor grunted.

Zac gave his cousin a smile, squeezed his shoulder. The painful truth was that Connor was in a fight he couldn't win. Not with Drew. Not where Emily Ruskin was concerned.

Not unless the playing field was levelled a little bit.

And maybe tonight was the night.

21

We're outside on the patio eating a dinner of pizza and garlic bread when the doorbell rings.

My brother is at the front door, hands in the pockets of his khaki cargo shorts with Zac half a pace behind him, looking at the ground. The full heat of the day is spent but it's still a pleasantly warm evening.

Rob raises a hand in greeting. 'Are you eating? Sorry, mate.'

'It's fine, don't worry about it,' I say, waving away his apology. 'Should be some spare pizza if you want some?'

'Thanks, but we can't stay.' He rubs at his stubble. 'Listen, Zac said he left something behind last night, we were just on the way past so I thought he could pick it up.'

'Sure, of course.' Zac and Connor were back and forth between each other's houses so often that it was a common occurrence for things to be swapped, mislaid, left behind. A mysterious pair of trainers had appeared in the shoe rack earlier in the summer and it was a week before I realised they didn't belong to Connor. Although I couldn't remember the last time my brother had come by on a Sunday night to pick something up.

Zac moves past me, studiously avoiding my gaze, and heads up the stairs.

'Do you want me to give Connor a shout?' I say to his back, but he's already reached the landing. His feet disappear from sight as he turns towards the little staircase leading up to Connor's attic room.

I turn back to my brother. 'What is it he left behind?'

'Wallet. He'll only be a minute.'

'Come in, have a drink while you wait.' I gesture to the hallway behind me. 'Have a sit down, you look done in. We didn't really get a good chance to talk earlier.'

'Sorry, bro, can't really stay.'

'One beer?'

He shakes his head. 'Today's been a nightmare, just want to get him home.'

'Have you heard from the police?' I lean against the door frame. 'About this missing girl?'

'We've just come from the station.'

'So have they found her yet?'

He shakes his head. 'What did Connor say in his interview?'

'Almost nothing.' I lower my voice, scan the street behind him. 'He kept on saying "No comment", like he was hiding something. Like he'd been coached to give the same response over and over. It was the weirdest thing.'

'Yeah.' He looks over my shoulder, towards the stairs behind me. 'Zac did the exact same.'

I study him for a moment. He looks even more tired than he did this morning, his skin almost grey in the slanting evening sunlight. A scattering of tiny broken blood vessels across the bridge of his nose.

'Really? The detective who interviewed Connor made out like you were answering all their questions, being cooperative.'

Rob shrugs. 'So? That's what they do, isn't it? Standard tactic to get suspects talking. They told *us* Connor was being very helpful.' He glances over my shoulder again. 'So did he tell them anything?'

I relate the interview as best I can remember, the questions from DS Shah and the reasons the police had got involved. Emily Ruskin, Beacon Hill Woods and the scant information I have about the circumstances surrounding Connor's arrest.

'Zac staying over last night,' I say carefully, 'it's absolutely fine, you know he's always welcome, but it was almost like ... I don't know, like he was covering for Connor or something? To make us believe he was home if we checked in his room? Has Zac talked to you about that?'

Before he can reply, there are footsteps on the stairs behind me and Zac brushes past without acknowledging either of us, doing his utmost to make sure he gives me the widest possible berth in our narrow hallway.

Rob says: 'Found it?'

'Yeah, all sorted.'

Zac doesn't break stride on his way out through the front door. I call after him: 'You OK, Zac?'

If he's heard my question, he doesn't acknowledge it, just keeps walking down the drive and out to his dad's Mazda.

Rob gestures to his son's retreating back. 'I need to get him home. Let's talk tomorrow, yeah?'

'Let me know if you hear anything in the meantime.'

'Of course. Cheers, Andy.' With that, he turns and walks quickly back to his car.

I watch him drive away, closing the door slowly and trying to tamp down a feeling that Rob is holding something back, that there are things that maybe neither of us want to mention.

Back in the kitchen, my son is sitting on a chair as he laces up his trainers.

I lean against the kitchen counter. 'What are you doing, Connor?'

'Going out.' He doesn't meet my eye.

'No, you're not. You're grounded.'

'*What?*'

'You know the rules. We trusted you, we gave you a curfew and you broke it. So you're grounded.'

He looks up at me, a heavy frown lining his forehead. 'Are you serious?'

'Yup.'

'That's ridiculous.' He spits the words. 'It's not even eight o'clock.'

'What's ridiculous is that you won't even tell us where you were last night, why you didn't come home.'

He sniffs, looks away.

'Stayed with a friend.'

'Who?'

'You don't know them.'

'Try me.'

'Why do you have to know *everything* I do, *every* minute of *every* day? Why can't you give me a bit of space, a bit of freedom?'

'You *know* why,' I say, my voice rising. 'Because we just spent two hours in a police station.'

'Or is it because you don't trust me?'

'You only have to tell me and your mum, Connor. Just us. It doesn't have to go any further than that.'

He stares at me for a long moment, breathing hard through his nose. Finally, he unlaces his trainers again and kicks them into the corner.

* * *

By the time I've finished the washing-up, Harriet is ensconced on the sofa with her laptop and headphones. Laura is catching up on some Sunday-night marking at the dining table. I'm on leave tomorrow – Harriet's school has an INSET day for staff training – but I have a full list on Tuesday with morning clinic starting promptly at 8.30. Summer holidays are always a busy time as some of the eight practice partners head off on holiday and everyone else has to take up the slack. I have work to do as well, but today has been too strange, too outlandish, to concentrate on anything as mundane as clinic admin and emails. My attention keeps drifting, pulled away by an undercurrent of thoughts about the police, about my son and my brother, about a teenage girl who didn't come home last night.

I sit in the study with my laptop, open up a new browser window and type *Emily Ruskin* into Google. A string of search results with an Instagram account at the top of it. I click on the image results and the screen fills with pictures of a strikingly attractive teenager, honey-blonde hair with a streak of purple across her fringe. I don't remember seeing her before.

I check her name against any latest news but nothing comes up from today. Presumably the search for Emily is not yet public knowledge, not yet announced by the police or anyone else.

A search for Cathy Ruskin yields hundreds of results. The top result is a Wikipedia page which relates the story of a local girl made good: Nottingham born and bred, an actor from her early teens who featured in a popular kids' TV show before hitting prime time with high-profile roles in two of the biggest British soaps, making her a household name. Marriage to her childhood sweetheart and a gilded life through her twenties before tragedy struck when her husband died of an undiagnosed heart defect. A widow at thirty-one with twins aged six and their sister Emily just three years old, she had withdrawn from work for a year before a failed comeback in a period drama, cancelled after the first series. Years in the wilderness followed as acting roles slowly dwindled, before a battle with breast cancer two years ago brought her back into the public eye and onto a popular jungle-based TV show peopled with minor celebrities – which she went on to win. According to the Wikipedia entry, she was now on the verge of a career renaissance, cast as the lead in a new police drama due to air later this year.

I click on the next search result, an Instagram account with more than fifty thousand followers. I scroll through Cathy's posts, scanning images and captions, which broadly fall into one of three categories. One is resilience and self-reliance, of recovering when you're knocked down, under the hashtag #GetBackUp. The second is the world of acting and her new series in particular. The other category is her extremely photogenic daughters. I select a recent picture of them sitting down to a picnic in the park, big smiles and wholesome food, complete with hamper and blanket. The twins are in their late teens now, and even with different haircuts and outfits it's clear they are identical. Two beautiful dark-haired twins plus Emily, on the edge of the shot, younger and smaller and looking more like a cousin or a friend than a sibling. She's striking too but in her own way, icy blue eyes and long blonde hair.

I have Instagram on my phone but I don't use it much; a handful of pictures taken on a holiday, a few of Toffee, a few out on Sunday walks. My account is set to private and I've not used my own name or anything recognisable in my username. I'd heard too many horror stories of doctors, nurses, teachers – people in public-facing professions – being pursued and hounded on social media by parents or patients after a disagreement, and I had no desire to be tracked down online.

With a sigh, I close the browser. It's gone 9 p.m. This time yesterday, Laura, Harriet and I were watching *Ant & Dec's Saturday Night Takeaway* quite happily, unaware of all the troubles and worries today would hold. My attention is drifting again, my mind catching on something Connor said earlier this evening, like a hangnail snagging on skin. Two words. Maybe the only two completely honest words he's said to us all day.

I panicked.

He'd been telling us why he ran from the police this morning – a moment of fear, the urge to flee from a confrontation, a blind scramble that sent him headlong into a uniformed officer – but I can't help wondering whether there is more to it. If there is some wider significance in his words, something else he was trying to say but couldn't find the courage. Some other moment, some incident that he can't bring himself to relate. Not yet.

I panicked.

In my head I hear his words again, and again. Over and over.

A slow, cold creep of dread as my thoughts spool out in an unwelcome direction. Could something have happened last night in the woods? Is this why he won't talk to the police? Why he's lying?

I panicked.

Is that why someone else's child is missing?

22
ROB

Sometimes, when Vanessa had a nightcap before bed, she would fall asleep before him. He would hear her as she drifted off, her soft breaths going in and out. It reminded him of Zac when he was a newborn, lying in a Moses basket next to their bed. Rob would lie next to his wife and listen, feeling his own eyes growing heavier until her breaths lulled him, too, into a deep sleep. Never for a moment imagining a time when he wouldn't hear that sound anymore.

Nights had been the hardest, since she'd died.

And nights like this were the worst. When he felt like he was failing at everything, failing their son, who had grown up too fast and too hard in these last few months. Failing his family, failing in the one task that had been left to him.

He reached over to the bedside drawer, pulling it open. Gently, he slipped the single sheet of A4 paper out of the plastic wallet that protected it. He held it carefully by the edges; he had to preserve it for as long as possible and knew he shouldn't handle it too much. He had made copies, of course. But sometimes he just liked to hold the original, to hold in his hands this letter she had once held in hers, to imagine her filling the page with her flowing handwriting, all loops and swirls and flourishing capitals. Written when they both knew there was nothing more the doctors could do to stop the cancer's spread.

He knew her instructions by heart, all fifty-one of them, but he liked to read them anyway.

He sat back on the bed they had shared, and scanned the list.

- *Remember to kiss Zac twice when I am gone, once for you and once for me*
- *Tell him you love him*
- *Don't let him smoke or ride motorbikes*
- *Teach him to respect women and be kind*
- *Take him rock-pooling on our favourite beach*
- *Always help him and be there for him if he asks*
- *Tell each other the truth, always*
- *Don't get angry with each other; life is too short*

Rob felt the familiar lump in his throat, tears filling his eyes as he read on, turning the page.

Only one instruction was repeated. It featured once at the beginning of the list, and once at the very end. Bookmarking everything else to show it was the most important job of all.

- *Protect our beautiful boy, whatever it takes.*

MONDAY

23

I park up on a rough grass verge at one end of Lower Farm Lane, as close as I dare to the drainage gully running alongside. To the right are fields thick with summer grass, warm air heavy with the smell of bailed hay and foxgloves growing wild in the hedgerow. A handful of horses stand listlessly under the shade of wide-spreading oak, ears twitching at flies in the heat. To my left – the southern boundary of Beacon Hill Woods – trees spread their branches over the road, beech and ash and more oak, crowding right up to a wooden three-bar fence. This spot is only a couple of miles from my street, from my front door, but it feels like it's in the middle of the countryside. The middle of nowhere.

Lower Farm Lane has no path and isn't great for pedestrians. Harriet gets out of the back seat, clipping on Toffee's lead and lifting him over a stile beside the verge, into the field on our right. We set off along the path, following a trail of long grass beaten flat, the lead unspooling as Toffee scampers ahead. There's a shortcut here, a straight path into the next field that meets the road again as it bends back around, half a mile further along.

It was a question in Connor's police interview that drew me here today. A question that seemed significant, to carry particular weight with the detectives. *Do you know where Lower Farm Lane is? Have you been there in the last twenty-four hours?* Connor is still refusing to tell us what happened, but I have half an idea that if I can see this place for myself, see the ground, the location, I might get a better sense of how it relates to Emily Ruskin's disappearance. I'm not even sure what I'm looking for – all I know is that he's holding something back and I need all the information I can gather. I need to *understand*. Maybe there will be something here that Harriet and I can find, that might help.

The day is fresh and bright, the sun already hot on the back of my neck as Toffee bounds ahead through the long grass. There's a helicopter somewhere off in the distance, the *wup-wup-wup* of its blades muffled by the trees. We cross the next field, occupied by a single large bull, statue-still at the far end, facing away from us. Through a metal gate on the far side and we're back out on the tarmac of Lower Farm Lane.

Directly opposite is a short break in the fence. A narrow track leading off into Beacon Hill Woods.

The road is narrow here, the hedgerow growing higher and seeming to squeeze the tarmac inwards until it's easy to lose a wing mirror to a passing car around one of the bends. Not ideal for dog-walking. Or walking full stop.

Especially in the middle of the night.

'Dad,' Harriet says. 'Are you coming?'

'Yes.' I give her a smile. 'Just thinking about something.'

We cross the road and join the track as it winds into the woods. Harriet has her phone out and is taking pictures in her usual way, of the trees, of brambles, close-ups of nettles and flowers at the side of the path. Beneath the canopy of branches, it's several degrees cooler and I'm grateful for the shade, the morning air punctuated by the chattering of birds, invisible in the branches of this ancient woodland. A living, breathing, familiar landscape, unchanged by the passing of time.

But in the dark, it would be a different place entirely. I try to imagine being here in the dead of night, tree cover blotting out almost all the light thrown by a thin sliver of waning moon. Dark silence filled with a thousand shadows. Even with a torch, it would be easy to get disorientated, to lose your way, your sense of direction. I wondered how long it would be before an official search party was put together, friends and neighbours and concerned members of the community turning out to sweep the woods and help the police in the search for clues.

After five minutes' walk, the path opens out as it reaches the river, clear burbling water running over rocks and eddying around chunks of grey stone. It's much diminished in summer, barely even waist deep, the water looking deliciously cool against the heat of the morning. The old footbridge is little more than a shallow arch with handrails either side. My walking boots thud softly across the wooden planks as Toffee trots ahead of Harriet on his lead.

Harriet is cautious over the water; she's never liked it. I've always worried more about her than about Connor, which is painfully ironic, considering the events of the last twenty-four hours. She doesn't have a wide circle of friends – she's always insisted she prefers animals to people – she is too direct, too honest, and most girls her age don't know how to take her. Sometimes I think she is almost too bright for her own good. A move up to the comprehensive school last year seems to have accentuated the situation, making her a smaller fish in a much bigger pond. A specialist had finally confirmed last year what we'd suspected for a while: that she is on the milder end of the autistic spectrum. The fact that other kids at school tease her makes me so angry, so frustrated, and I have already been in to see the head of year three times since she started. Her obvious intelligence, her glasses and her boyishly-short haircut makes her an easy target for bullies.

On the other side of the bridge, the land starts to rise gently, the trees thickening further. From the beaten earth it seems that most walkers turn right here and follow the line of the river east, walking beside the water and beneath a couple of road bridges until the next village. Very few, it seems, continue straight on into the woods and this is where navigation becomes trickier, the faintest suggestion of a path leading away into the rising ground. It forks, fades, narrows, forks again, narrowing for fifty more yards or so until it is swallowed up in a mass of brambles. I retrace my steps and take a different fork, then another, the electric sting of nettles brushing against my legs on both sides until each path peters out into nothing.

Apparently there *was* one path through, but I had never found it – not with all the summer growth. Although I'd never really tried, not before today.

Maybe if I searched for long enough I could find the route through. Maybe Emily Ruskin had tried to find her way out too somehow, in the pitch darkness. It would be so easy to get disoriented, to get lost. I could barely make out a path even in full daylight; it would be virtually impossible for anyone to find it at night.

Maybe she was still here. Somewhere in the woods.

24

'Dad?' Harriet's small voice interrupts my thoughts again. I'd almost forgotten she was there. 'How do we find the right way?'

'Not sure, H. I thought the path might be a bit more obvious.' I shrug. 'Come on, let's head back.'

My daughter stays where she is, a stick clutched tightly in her right hand.

'Where is she, Dad?' She fixes me with a stare, somewhere between anxious and curious. 'Where's Emily Ruskin?'

I haven't told her specifically why we've come to this part of the woods, why today, why now. But I should have known she'd figure it out for herself in five seconds flat.

'Well,' I say slowly, 'that's what everyone is trying to find out. It's what the police are trying to find out.'

'But it doesn't make sense.'

'I know, Harry, it's hard to—'

'How can a person just *disappear*?' There is a note of incredulity in her voice, as if she cannot conceive of such a thing happening. 'How can they be there one minute, and then gone the next? And why are people saying it's Connor, that the police think he did something to her and he's going to jail?'

I stop and turn back to her, stung again by my failure to protect Connor, my impotence in all of this.

'What? Who's saying that?'

'Kids in my year. On Snapchat and stuff.'

'They're talking rubbish, just ignore them. Come on.'

Still, she doesn't move. 'Do you think she's dead?'

'No, Harry.' I put as much certainty into my voice as I can muster. 'Of course not.'

I hold out my hand to her and finally she takes it, her little hand slipping into mine. We retrace our steps back down the slope, over the footbridge. Back at Lower Farm Lane, I stop, out of habit, trying to make Toffee sit beside me even though there is still no traffic in sight. Across and through the gate will take us back through the fields, the same way we came in. Or we could turn immediately right and just walk along the road to return to my car.

The old woodman's hut is off to my left, around the next bend. A cobweb-filled ruin of moss-covered stones which had attracted various spooky stories since I was a boy. Perhaps it was worth a look.

We go left.

Cutting back into the woods, we follow the line of the road along a vague footpath that winds through the trees. Harriet unclips Toffee's lead and he hares off, the soft crunch of old leaves and dry earth beneath our feet as we follow. He has a tendency to run when he's let off the lead; we've been trying to train him out of it. So far, without much success.

The helicopter is back, invisible through the trees but getting louder as it comes closer, until there is a flash of movement above and it is clattering almost right over our heads, so low I can feel the deep throb of the rotors in my chest. A single word in bright yellow – *Police* – on the side. Harriet stares up with both hands pressed over her ears, only taking them away again as the noise recedes into the distance.

'So *loud*,' she says, snapping pictures of the helicopter on her mobile.

I take out my own phone and bring up Google Maps, trying to imagine how this place fits into the narrative being pursued by the police. Further along, Lower Farm Lane eventually joins onto the A-road running north back into Nottingham.

I remember something else DS Shah had mentioned in the interview yesterday, and type 'Beaufort Terrace' into the app's search bar. The map zooms out, a blue line appearing to indicate the route: 5.6 miles into the middle of Nottingham. A long-ish walk or a quick journey by car. Connor had been arrested there. Could Emily have been there too?

A noise reaches me from further into the woods. A voice. Low, male.

Perhaps thirty metres away is a line of people, a dozen or so, all identically dressed in black clothing, black boots, gloves, caps. All with their backs to me, moving deeper into the trees, 'POLICE' emblazoned in white lettering across the backs of their overalls. I watch them for a moment as they move slowly, tentatively, towards the river, a half-step at a time, prodding at the ground with thin poles.

A shiver touches the top of my spine as I realise they are looking for Emily. For *traces* of Emily. Evidence.

Or a body?

I push the thought away. *No*. Not a body. A child. Someone's child. Police officers looking for clues to help find her, bring her home safe to her family.

The police line keeps moving, all eyes on the ground, heads swivelling slowly, methodically, from side to side. As we watch, they all stop, an officer in the centre holding up a hand before dropping to one knee to study something at her feet.

The others lean on their poles, taking a breather while they wait for their colleague. In the pause, one of them turns. Sees Harriet and I.

We're totally exposed. It's too far away for me to read his expression but I have a sudden urge to turn and walk away, to get away from them as fast as possible. Before anyone recognises me, asks me what has brought us to this exact part of Beacon Hill Woods on this day, of all days.

But walking away would look weird. Guilty. As if I had something to hide.

The officer who has seen me reaches up to his lapel and keys his radio, his lips moving silently. His head is bent towards it as he speaks, but he keeps his eyes on me the whole time.

I walk on as if I'm indifferent to the whole spectacle, leading Harriet away from the line of police officers, a little closer to the road. Whistling to Toffee, somewhere up ahead of us. The old woodman's hut is not far away now, the tumbledown piles of green stone and ivy-clad walls emerging slowly, well camouflaged amid the trees. I remember coming here years ago when the kids were small, both still in primary school, and six-year-old Harriet had been frightened of this ruined hut, had not wanted to go near it let alone follow her big brother inside. Had asked me later if it was a witch's house, like in 'Hansel and Gretel', a place where children were taken away and put into the witch's oven. The roof of the hut is long gone, rotten and collapsed decades ago, a few remaining supporting stones projecting like broken teeth. For some reason, the whole sorry structure is encircled by blue and white police tape.

Toffee seems to have disappeared.

As I get closer, three figures emerge from around the side of the ruined hut. One talking, pointing, the others listening. Two men and a woman, their heads all swivelling towards me as a twig cracks beneath my shoe. An unpleasant tightening in my stomach as I recognise DC Harmer's tall frame. Jacket off, shirtsleeves rolled to his elbows, eyes hidden behind wraparound shades. The other man is unfamiliar: late twenties or early thirties, solidly built, in a pastel polo shirt and khaki shorts.

The woman stands between them, sunglasses pushed up into her long dark hair, a white vest top and dark blue culottes. Even from a little distance away I can see the tension in her stance, in her shoulders, arms crossed tightly over her chest. Her face etched with worry, with a mother's worst fear.

Cathy Ruskin.

25

We shouldn't be here. Shouldn't have come.

I nod a greeting to them, briefly thankful that Cathy doesn't betray any hint of recognition. DC Harmer seems to be ignoring me and is saying something else now, indicating the search team further into the trees. Her eyes follow where he's pointing as I scramble to calculate what would be less weird at this moment: to say something, or just walk away before she realises who we are? We could cut straight back to the road from here and walk that way to my car. Let the police get on with their search.

A police van and a couple of other cars are just visible through the trees, parked on Lower Farm Lane. I'm about to head that way when Toffee comes galloping out of the undergrowth, bouncing with excitement. He ignores the two men and singles out Cathy, putting his front paws up on her knees in enthusiastic greeting.

'Toffee!' I say. 'Come here!'

Toffee ignores me, his little tail wagging furiously as Cathy unfolds her arms, bending down to stroke his head.

I call to my dog again, jogging over with the lead in my hand, apologising as I reach them.

'I'm so sorry,' I say. 'He's old enough to know better but some-times with new people he's a bit excitable.'

Cathy waves my apology away.

'Don't worry about it,' she says, leaning down to gently stroke the curly fur on Toffee's head. 'He's a sweet pup, isn't he? We used to have a Cavapoo.'

'Sorry,' I say again. 'Your trousers, his paws, they might be a bit muddy . . .'

'It's fine.' She gives my dog one last scratch under his chin, talking to him now. 'You're a good boy, aren't you?'

Toffee gives a delighted bark of approval but both men – DC Harmer and the other guy, who I assume is Cathy's partner – are staring at me with barely concealed impatience. Toffee is still oblivious to both, and to me, all his attention and adoration focused on Emily's mother.

Finally, he comes to heel and I clip the lead hastily to his collar.

She stands up straight again and seems to look at me properly for the first time. She's a few years younger than me, maybe early forties, with olive skin and a kind, friendly face that is generically familiar in a way that I can't quite place. She's an attractive woman but today her features are buried beneath a layer of exhaustion, her dark eyes red-rimmed from crying.

'Oh.' Her face clouds. 'Hi. Sorry, do we . . . have we met? You'll have to forgive me, my head's all over the place at the moment.'

'We talked briefly on the phone,' I say. 'On WhatsApp.'

'Sorry,' she says again, 'I've spoken to so many people since yes-terday morning, I'm starting to lose track.'

She keeps apologising, and every time I think it's *me* that should be saying sorry. Even if I'm not sure why.

'It was yesterday.' I throw a quick glance at Harmer, wondering how much he has told Cathy about the kids they've pulled in for questioning. He's staring at me, his face unreadable. 'I was trying to . . . track down my son.'

One look back at Cathy gives me the answer, her eyes widening slightly.

'Oh.' A pulse of recognition. 'You're Connor Boyd's dad.'

'Yes.' I nod, trying to think of something else to say. 'And this is my daughter, Harriet.'

Harriet raises a hand half-heartedly and there is a beat of awkward silence, the indistinct chatter of a police radio crackling somewhere off in the distance.

'How's he doing?' Cathy says finally. I listen for any hint of sarcasm or spite in her words but can't hear any. She seems genuinely concerned. 'Is he all right?'

'Erm, yeah, he's . . . OK. He's fine. I was really sorry to hear about everything that happened at the weekend. I hope you get Emily back home soon.'

She gives me a quick nod. 'Thank you, so do we.' She indicates the blond man next to her. 'This is my partner, Karl, by the way.'

Karl sticks out a meaty hand and we shake, the automatic male reflex kicking in. His grip is a few notches tighter than it needs to be, his hand holding on for a moment or two longer than necessary. He's solidly built, thick through the chest, maybe ten years younger than Cathy.

Karl and I exchange a nod and after another squeeze he releases my hand, his sweat warm on my palm.

'And this is Detective Constable Harmer,' Cathy says.

'Yes,' I say. 'We've met.'

'The detective was just showing us—' She stops herself, throwing a questioning look at DC Harmer. 'Oh, sorry, Paul, am I allowed to say this, to tell people?'

DC Harmer nods. 'That's fine, Ms Ruskin. It's being released to the public this morning anyway.'

'I just feel like I want to tell everyone. To spread the word about Emily to encourage anyone with information to come forward.'

Harmer gives her a tight smile. 'Of course.'

Cathy turns back to us. 'So, according to what the police have pieced together from her friends so far, Emily wasn't intending to come home to us at all on Saturday night. She planned to walk south all the way through the woods, cross the river at the old footbridge until she reached this place, right here.' She holds her hands out to indicate the woodman's hut, the blue and white police tape jarringly out of place among the lush greens and deep browns of the clearing. 'She'd locked her mountain bike inside the hut the day before, so it would be waiting for her.'

'And then what?' I say gently. 'She was going to ... run away?'

'We don't know.' Cathy's voice cracks a little. 'No one seems to know. The thing is, Emily's bike is still here. Still locked up.' She takes a long, shuddering breath. 'Which suggests she never left the woods at all.'

She raises a hand to her mouth to stifle a sob. Karl puts a protective arm around her shoulders.

'It's all right, Cathy,' he says, his voice a deep bass rumble. 'Come on now, we don't know that for sure.'

I raise a hand in apology. 'I just wish there was more I could—'

'Has your son mentioned any of that?' she says. 'Or anything different? Has he talked to you or your wife about what really happened up here on Saturday night?'

'No, nothing,' I say. 'I'm sorry. He's not really said much to us at all. I don't know what's going on with him, to be honest. But I'll talk to him again.' I hold my hands up, starting to back away. 'I'll ask him. And if there's anything at all I can do in the meantime, please give me—'

Karl cuts me off.

'Never mind *you* talking to him,' he says, his tone suddenly belligerent. 'How about you start by getting him to cooperate with the police. Tell *them* what he knows, what he *did*.'

Cathy puts a hand on his arm. 'Karl, don't—'

'*That's* what you can do.' He takes a step closer and stabs a finger at me. 'Get him to tell the truth. If he's protecting someone or, hiding something, he'd better know that sooner or later he's going to pay dearly for it.'

His face is red now, a thick blue vein standing out in the side of his neck. Harriet is cowering behind my leg, Toffee growling low in his throat.

'My son didn't do anything,' I say quietly. 'He wouldn't hurt anyone.'

Harmer is standing off to one side, observing both of us. Not intervening. But Karl seems to be just getting into his stride.

'Just a massive coincidence that you're here then, is it? Our Em disappears, your lad's implicated and the next day you just happen to be out walking your dog where it's all supposed to have happened?' He looks over my shoulder, scanning the trees. 'Is he here? Is he with you?'

'He's not here,' I say. 'And he's not implicated in anything.'

Cathy moves to stand in front of her partner, a hand on his chest. 'That's enough, Karl.'

She gives me a weak smile, an apology in her eyes. 'Sorry.'

He's still muttering as she leads him away, back towards a big white SUV parked up on Lower Farm Lane.

Harmer stares at me for a long, uncomfortable moment.

'We'll be in touch,' he says, and follows them back to the road.

26

Harriet is silent on our return to the car. She grips my hand tightly all the way, keeping Toffee close and looking over her shoulder as if Karl might be following us.

We take the quick way back, along Lower Farm Lane rather than through the field. It's one of those winding, narrow country lanes where you often can't see oncoming traffic until it's right on top of you. As we walk, I wonder if Emily had taken this same route, whether a driver might not have seen her until it was too late. She might have been hit, thrown off the road. In the small hours of Sunday morning there would be very little risk of being seen by passing traffic. Maybe someone panicked and dragged her off the road, into the undergrowth, just drove away instead of reporting it? Or maybe Emily had left her bike behind because she'd decided to walk after all, she'd lost the key for her bike lock, something like that.

Someone could have simply driven past, given her a lift. Taken her away.

We've just got back to the car when my phone pings, three times in quick succession. A little numeral denoting three new items in Messenger, each stacked above the last, all three of them from my wife.

You need to see this
Posted by Emily's mum this morning

The third message is a link to Cathy Ruskin's Instagram account. I click on it and a video starts playing of her sitting at a table, a carved wooden bookcase behind her full of framed photographs. Family pictures. I angle the screen so Harriet can see it too, and turn the sound up.

Cathy speaks straight into the camera. 'This is the hardest thing I've ever had to do.' She takes a pause. 'But as a parent, as a mother, I want to appeal to anyone who might be able to help. My youngest daughter Emily went out to a party on Saturday evening at around 7.45 and she is now missing. The last message we had from her was at 9 p.m. on Saturday so it's now thirty-six hours since we had any kind of contact with her at all, which is very out of character for Emily. We're working closely with the police and they've been absolutely brilliant. But we need your help too. This is what we think she's wearing.' The image changes to a still of Emily, smiling in black skinny jeans and a white hoodie, 'Hollister' in large letters across the front. 'My daughter is my baby, my youngest, she's a very friendly, bubbly girl, very bright and outgoing, and her siblings adore her.'

She swallows, looking away from the camera for a moment. She looks pale and drawn. Then seems to gather herself and brings her eyes back to the lens.

'Emily, if you're watching this, we love you, we miss you so much and we all just want you to come home or just get in touch to let us know you're OK. Me, your sisters, Karl, all of us. It doesn't matter what's happened, you're not in any trouble. We love you and we miss you. Just get in touch, please.'

A tear rolls down her cheek and she swipes it away.

'And for everyone else watching, if you have any information about where Emily might be – anything at all, no matter how minor you might think it is – please pass it on to the police. Please help bring my baby home. Thank you so much.'

The screen fades to black with a police phone number and email, plus the hashtag #FindEmily.

I scroll down beneath the post. It was posted at nine this morning, barely two hours ago, but it already has almost three thousand likes and hundreds of comments. Most of them are friendly, positive – if not particularly helpful – from fans and well-wishers.

Thinking of you @CathyR_TV and sending hugs and love xx

I'm sure your baby will be back soon. Teenagers do crazy things sometimes, I know I did when I was Emily's age xxx

From our family to yours, we are thinking of you and praying with all our hearts for Emily's safe return xx

Lots of heart emojis, scattered everywhere. Some of the comments don't have any words but are simply two or three lines of hearts stacked on top of each other, pulsing hearts, hugging hearts, multi-coloured hearts. Lots of positivity and wishes for the best.

A few comments later there is a barbed little reminder of the worst.

Not surprised was BOUND to happen sooner or later put your family out there on display 24/7 for £££ cant be surprised when some nutter takes advantage

I shake my head. A bit further down, others have weighed in.

I say good for her she's well shot of you I reckon

A string of positive comments, more emojis, a brief return to normality. Then a response from @Red_Pill_97 that seems to have generated a thread all of its own:

Amazing what some people will do for likes and a few extra followers. Cannot believe someone would stoop so low. Shame on you #PublicityStunt #BeccaNorris

The same hashtags appear several times as more Instagram users reply to @Red_Pill_97's comment, most of them agreeing and amplifying whatever it is they are implying. *#PublicityStunt* scattered here and there among the hundreds of comments from well-wishers, venomous thorns waiting among the emojis and soft platitudes. It's true that the negative comments are in the minority, but their bile, their anger, their sheer simmering nastiness seems to give them more weight than the rest. I hope Cathy has got someone else to read and filter out the comments for her.

Harriet is peering at them from beside me, sadness etched on her face. 'Who's Becca Norris, Dad? And why are people so horrible?'

'Only a few, Harry,' I say. 'Most people aren't like that.'

'Creepy Crosby is.'

I look across at my daughter in the passenger seat, thumb-typing rapidly on her own phone now. 'Who's that?'

'You just met him.' She points a finger back down the road. 'Karl. He's a PE teacher at school, that's how he met Emily's mum.

Mr Crosby. Except everyone calls him Creepy Crosby. Especially the girls.'

'Why do they call him that?'

She shrugs. 'Because he is. Toffee didn't like him either, did you notice?'

'Toffee likes everyone, Harry.'

'Not everyone. He did that thing with his ears when they go flat against his head, that means he doesn't like someone.'

She holds out her phone to me – a mass of Google search results for the name Becca Norris, among them a Wikipedia page, stories in every newspaper and media site, a Channel 5 documentary. *The Strange Case of Becca Norris.* A seven-year-old in Worcester who'd gone missing on her way home from school, the subject of a huge police investigation, her distraught mother appealing for Becca's safe return. More than two weeks afterwards it was discovered that the whole kidnapping was a charade, a hoax instigated by the mother and her stepsister in a bid to claim a £100,000 reward. The little girl found alive and unharmed.

I scroll through a few more comments below the Instagram story. More of the same. Commenters arguing with each other about Cathy's motives, about her daughter, her whereabouts. More conspiracy theories sprouting from nothing, from literally *nothing*, like mushrooms growing in the dark. What was *wrong* with people? I feel another pang of sympathy for Cathy, a strengthening of my resolve to help her by talking to Connor again as soon as we got home.

And this time I needed answers from my son. For everyone's sake.

27

I call Laura when I get back, catching her in a break between training sessions at school. I relate the meeting with Cathy Ruskin and her partner in the woods near Lower Farm Lane.

'Is there any news?' she says. 'How was she?'

'Looks like she hasn't slept at all. The police have got search teams up there going over the ground inch by inch. DC Harmer was there, showing Cathy and Karl what's going on, where Emily's bike was found.'

I remember the look on Cathy's face, the fear, the dread of receiving the very worst news a parent could hear. She looked as if she was bracing for a blow. Her whole body tensed against an attack that might come from any direction, at any moment, with enough force to shatter her life forever.

'Must be absolutely awful for her,' my wife says. 'How was she . . . with you?'

'She was actually really kind. Thoughtful.' I fill a glass with water from the tap, take a long drink. 'Her partner wasn't quite so friendly.'

At her end of the line, the echo of a corridor changes as she steps outside. Her voice is lower, conspiratorial.

'Can't say I'm surprised.'

'Do you have much to do with him?'

'My esteemed colleague Karl Crosby?' Her tone is heavy with sarcasm. 'Don't have much to do with him at work but he's ... yeah. You always hear him before you see him.'

'How do you mean?'

There's another pause and I imagine her looking over her shoulder, making sure she's not overheard. 'Likes to think he's the big alpha male,' she says. 'That's Karl.'

I had always thought there would be some kind of rule about teachers getting involved with the parents of pupils at the school. Apparently not. According to my wife, Karl and Cathy had met at a school sports day where she was a PTA helper, and had been together for a couple of years now. He had moved into the Ruskin family home last year – the subject of much staffroom gossip at the time.

'Isn't it a bit weird?' I say. 'I mean he can't be much more than ten years older than Cathy's twins. Kind of a weird stepdad dynamic, isn't it?'

'To be honest, I try to have as little to do with him as possible.' She clears her throat. 'But you know what the kids at school call him, don't you?'

'Harriet told me.'

I describe Karl's aggression, his accusations about Connor. The sudden explosion of anger, as if it was just looking for an outlet. But I can't quite identify what else bothers me about our short encounter in the woods.

'He just went off on one, started really ranting at me,' I say. 'Out of nowhere. I've never met the guy before. One minute we're shaking hands and Cathy's telling us about Emily, the next minute he's accusing Connor of all sorts, that he either did something terrible or he's covering for someone else. But, I don't know.' I frown. 'It almost felt like he was doing it to impress Cathy, to make a point about something, or . . .'

'Or what?'

'I can't put my finger on it. But there's something *off* about him, something a bit . . . not quite right.' I notice the lack of reaction on her part. 'You don't sound surprised at all.'

'Some teachers get nicknames for a reason,' she says quietly. 'There *were* a few stories that followed him when he came to the Comp. But it was around that time he hooked up with Cathy, so I thought it was just gossip, stuff people said about him because he strutted around school like he was the bee's knees.'

'What kind of stuff?'

She lowers her voice further. 'That he'd left his last job under a bit of a cloud. His last couple of jobs. And no, I don't know any more than that, but it can't have been proven or upheld or he would never have got a position at our place.'

She lets that hang in the silence for a moment.

'Could you find out?' I say. I know in normal times she would never dream of digging into the background of a fellow teacher, of breaching staffroom solidarity. But these are not normal times. And she's built up a lot of contacts in twenty years of teaching.

'Just because I teach IT, Andy, it doesn't mean I can hack the school's personnel database.'

'I know that, I mean . . . can you do something discreetly?'

She murmurs a reluctant positive. 'Maybe. I can make a few calls, at least. Got to go, let's talk about this later.'

She hangs up and I head down the garden in search of Connor. Past the brick-built barbecue to the deck at the far end, half hidden behind a pair of small apple trees. Beams across the top of the deck are wrapped around with flowering vines, thick enough to throw plenty of shade on hot summer days. Connor likes it out there – it's as far away from the house as you can get but still just about in range of the Wi-Fi.

As I walk up the two wooden steps, I see he's hunched in a deckchair, long legs crossed at the ankle, thumb-typing rapidly on his phone.

'Hey, Connor,' I say.

'Hey.' He doesn't look up.

'How are you doing?'

He responds with a grunt.

On any other day, that would have been normal. But today I feel a prickle of annoyance at his monosyllabic response.

I change tack. 'I saw Cathy Ruskin today.'

His head jerks up. 'What? Where?'

'On a dog walk with Harriet, the far side of Beacon Hill.'

He swallows and his face softens a little. 'How's she . . . How's she doing?'

'Worried sick, really struggling. Desperate for news about Emily.'

My son drops his eyes to the wooden decking at our feet. 'Must be horrible for her.'

'You know, Connor, anything you can remember, anything you can tell us about Saturday night, it might help. We don't have to say it came from you, I can bypass the police and go straight to Cathy. To help her find Emily.'

He says nothing, still refusing to look at me.

I feel my anger start to bubble, the heat of frustration that he seems determined not to help himself, not to help Cathy, not to help the police.

'So is there anything?' I say quietly, trying to keep the exasperation out of my voice. 'Anything that might help to bring Emily home?'

He takes a deep breath and I think he's about to say something, to release what he seems to be holding inside, but instead he just resumes typing on his phone.

I try a different tack.

'I met Emily's stepfather too.'

Connor shakes his head. 'He's not her stepfather. Just some weird bloke who got his hooks into her mum.'

'Weird how?'

He snorts. 'He's, like, fifteen years younger than Cathy, a PE teacher and supposedly this *sports entrepreneur* on the side.' He illustrates the words with two fingers raised in air quotes. 'But he never seems to actually do anything apart from try to impress the Year Eleven girls and sponge off Emily's mum.'

'Did Emily tell you something about him?'

'More like stuff she *didn't* say. Stuff you heard about him, around school.'

'Like what?'

'Like . . . inappropriate things he says, does. He just gives off this really creepy vibe, like he wants to be your mate. Trying to be cool as if he's not twice our age or whatever.'

'Did he get along with Emily?'

Connor's face flushes red and he stops typing on his phone, shoving it into a pocket of his shorts. 'I don't know, Dad, why don't you ask him yourself? Since you're best mates now, apparently?'

He stands abruptly as if he's going to walk away.

My voice comes out as shout, surprising both of us.

'This is bloody serious, Connor! This is not a game!' I hold my hands up to him as if I can keep him there by force of will alone. 'You need to tell us what happened on Saturday night!'

His eyes widen momentarily. I don't swear in front of my children, and it's rare for me to shout. But he recovers quickly.

'I don't have to tell you anything.'

'Please just let us *help* you, son.' My voice is rising again. 'You can't keep stonewalling us.'

Harriet emerges from the kitchen, a half-eaten banana in one hand.

'What's going on?' She frowns at us. 'What's all the shouting about?'

'Dad's losing it,' Connor says through gritted teeth. He turns and walks down the steps to the lawn, back towards the house.

'Wait!' I say. 'Karl also said he thought you might be protecting someone.'

Connor slows but doesn't stop. He doesn't turn to face me, doesn't respond.

'Connor?' I say to his back. 'Are you?'

'What?'

'Protecting someone else from getting in trouble?'

He continues stalking across the lawn without answering. I watch him go as he disappears through the open French doors and into the house.

I stand there for a moment as the midday sun beats down from a cloudless sky. A pair of fat bees buzz lazily around the vines above my head, moving from one purple blossom to the next. A little team of two doing what they need to do.

With a horrible lurch of certainty, Karl Crosby's words finally hit home. There *is* someone Connor would lie for. Someone he would protect. Of *course* there is.

It made sense.

In fact, it was the only thing that did.

28

HARRIET

Harriet was young when she realised that she had a superpower.

Five, maybe six years old. It wasn't a Marvel superpower, not super-strength like the Hulk, or speed like Quicksilver, or flying or whatever. It wasn't quite like any of those, but it was nearly as good.

She could see things that were invisible.

Well, *almost*. Invisible to everyone else, anyway.

She could see things that other people would never notice, even if they were looking right at them.

Harriet had practised it for years.

She quite liked trying to be invisible herself, too. It was easier that way. She had always been small and naturally quiet, and didn't really *get* loud places or people. She didn't like it when her dad shouted; he hardly ever did it, and when he did he sounded like a different person. At school, it seemed like everything was all about being louder or shoutier than everyone else, about always putting your hand up, and being picked first for the team.

She just let the other kids get on with it. She had her own way of doing things, at school and at home.

She was good at finding what no one else could see.

29

My brother has stopped replying to my messages.

I text him again to ask if we can meet up for a coffee, keeping it vague even though I'm sure he knows what I *really* want: to talk about the boys, about the police investigation, about the missing girl, about all of it. To glean whatever extra information I can. It's my best chance of figuring out if Connor is covering for his cousin, protecting him. If my brother knows it, too.

I watch as the two ticks appear to show my latest message has been delivered, then turn blue to show the message has been read. Waiting for his response to appear in the green box below, waiting for something positive, something reassuring from my solid, sensible big brother.

He doesn't reply.

I give him ten minutes then call, getting his voicemail and, as I leave a message, doing my best to keep the exasperation out of my voice. It's not like him to be so elusive. Not like him at all. This last year has brought us close, maybe closer than we've ever been, those grim twelve months that saw Vanessa's diagnosis and the agonising spiral of treatment until the final weeks, the last few days, when the oncologists said they had done all they could.

The tragedy had drawn us closer together: I was always the first person he called and that felt right to me, like it was exactly how things should be. And it made his sudden reticence all the more troubling.

I make us a lunch of cheese and crackers but I can only pick at it, more through habit than appetite. My mobile remains stubbornly dark and silent on the table beside my plate. My brother is not at work today. There was that strange flying visit last night, and the strung-out look on his face when we'd combed the woods on Sunday morning, as if he'd barely slept. So what *is* he doing now? The answer seems fairly obvious: he's avoiding me.

After lunch, Harriet returns to the sofa with her laptop and headphones. Connor emerges from his room long enough to collect his lunch from the kitchen and take it back upstairs, closing his bedroom door behind him. Toffee is sound asleep in his basket in the kitchen; Pablo curled in the centre of the big armchair.

I tell my daughter I'm nipping out for half an hour and grab my car keys. Rob's house isn't far but I'm restless, agitated with unanswered questions, and don't want to waste time walking. He can't avoid me if I'm on his doorstep. The road is quiet, the June heatwave keeping most people out of their cars and off the streets, drawing them to rivers and gardens and parks instead, green open spaces with enough room to lay out a blanket, bask in the sun with an ice cream and watch the world go by. With Connor broken up from school after the end of his GCSEs, it almost feels like the summer holidays already. But it had always seemed to me that the summer never started – not really, not properly – until the schools finished for the year. Even if June had the longest days and the shortest nights, even if it had a heatwave, it still wasn't *really* summer until that last week in July when all the children were cut loose from the classroom and granted six blissful weeks of freedom. When life changed gear, easing down slowly into August.

It was normally a time I cherished, a chance to spend more time with my own family, my own children. But today those summers past feel like decades ago, like someone else's life.

There is a rigid band of tension across my forehead as I turn onto my brother's street.

Rob lives near the end of a small cul-de-sac that backs onto the local cricket pitch, his house one of a neat row of Edwardian semis. He doesn't usually work Mondays, compressing his working week into four days so he can spend more time with his son, but I don't see his Mazda anywhere as I park up. The heat envelops me again as I step out of the air-conditioned cool of my own car. There are no signs of life in the front room as I walk up the short drive; the slatted wooden blinds in the upstairs windows still shut despite it being early afternoon. The bell is muffled through the front door but I can still hear its dull echo in the hallway. I push my sunglasses up onto my forehead and cup my hands to the frosted glass pane beside the front door, trying to make out any movement. Nothing. I had assumed that Zac would probably be grounded too, after the weekend. And my brother *should* be here too.

I ring the doorbell again and knock three times, my knuckles loud against the wooden frame. More silence. Maybe they're in the garden getting some sun. Around the side of the house, the gate is locked. I call my brother's name and step up onto a pile of old bricks next to his wheelie bin, peering over the gate into his back garden. Just a washing line standing bare, arms outstretched, in the middle of his overgrown lawn.

As I come back around to the front I sense a flicker of movement in one of the upstairs windows, the slightest shift of the blinds as if one wooden slat is falling back into place. But the clang of the doorbell echoes in the hallway again.

I check my phone to see if my brother has responded – nothing – then dial his number again, leaning a bit nearer to the front door. Maybe I'll be able to hear it ringing inside the house, proof that he's actually at home. But it rings out again and I end the call as soon as I hear the first words of his voicemail message.

I'm about to leave him another message when the front door slowly opens, just a few inches, my nephew's face appearing at the side of it.

'Hey, Zac.' I raise a hand in greeting. 'How's it going?'

He looks over my shoulder, eyes flicking towards the street as if there might be someone else with me.

'Fine.'

'Is your dad in?' I say. A fly buzzes around my face and I bat it away. I've only been out of the car for a couple of minutes but sweat is already gathering at the back of my neck, dampening the collar of my shirt. 'Need a word with him.'

'He's not here.'

'Do you know when he's coming back? Where is he, Zac?'

He's still not opened the door fully, peering through the gap instead. He shrugs.

'Dunno.'

A thought occurs to me. I lean around, trying to look over his shoulder down the hallway towards the kitchen.

'Is someone else here with you?'

'No,' he says quickly. 'I'm on my own. There's no one here.'

'Been grounded, have you?'

He shakes his head. Zac has slowly become harder to reach since he lost his mum, as if he has retreated into a rigid shell, armour that he's put on piece by piece over the last few months. The same lad we have always known, but different somehow.

He moves to push the front door closed – to shut it in my face – and I'm so surprised it takes me a second to react.

'Wait,' I say, putting my palm flat on the door. 'What's going on, Zac?'

'Dad told me to stay away from Connor, OK?'

'*What?*'

'He said I couldn't see him for a bit, at least until the police . . . until they do whatever they're going to do.'

For a moment I think I've misunderstood him, misheard him. As if I've come to the wrong street, the wrong house and am talking to the wrong boy.

'He told you to stay away from Connor?' His words sting like a slap. 'Why?'

'Why do you think?'

I take my palm off the door and he pushes it hurriedly shut, a metallic *clunk* as he locks it from the other side.

30

Zac's parting shot rings in my ears. *Why do you think?* What the hell did that mean? That he was being punished for staying out overnight without telling his dad where he was? That he was happy for Connor to take all the flak, to cover for his cousin?

Or ... maybe that wasn't it. Maybe my brother had already decided Connor *had* done something, and didn't want him to pull Zac down with him? The thought coils like a knot in my stomach, a pang of nausea snaking after it. These boys had been together since they were babies, inseparable, as close as brothers. Cousins who had become best friends and had stayed that way through nursery, primary school, secondary school. But now my brother wanted to put up a wall between them, to keep Connor at arm's length as if he was some kind of pariah.

The nausea settles in my stomach, curdling into frustration. Anger, maybe.

I ring the doorbell a couple more times, to no avail. Zac has retreated back into the house, upstairs, and is not going to reappear. With one last look at the upstairs windows I get back into my car, slam the door and wrench the air-conditioning switch up to maximum, gunning the engine back up to the junction with the main road.

A bead of sweat runs into my eye. Swiping it away, I hit the right turn indicator to head home. But I have that same restless energy, a sense of things happening just beyond my eyeline, wheels in motion that can't be stopped. I should go home, bury myself in work for a few hours, go for a run, but it seems frivolous, pointless, while my son is still under suspicion.

My son.

There had been a time when I had known everything about Connor. Every last thing. His favourite breakfast cereal, his favourite pyjamas, favourite football player, his shoe size, his funny little tactics for delaying a visit to the dentist and which present he'd spend the most time playing with on Christmas morning. A time when my knowledge of him had been complete and absolute. When the first gaps had started to appear – years ago – they were so tiny it took me a while to realise they were even there. But slowly those gaps had grown, widened, my knowledge gradually becoming outdated and then obsolete.

Now it felt like there were more gaps than anything else. There was so much I *didn't* know about my son. A vacuum, a blank, a hidden world that teenagers didn't share with their parents.

I had to fill the vacuum with *something*. I had to know more, to discover things for myself.

The traffic is clear for me to turn right. The road home.

Instead I turn left, heading in the opposite direction, skirting the little high street with its curious mix of bars and charity shops, fancy restaurants and organic food stores, heading up towards the most exclusive part of the neighbourhood. The south-eastern corner, a handful of wide streets with well-spaced houses, each one different and unique from its neighbour, making up the most expensive postcodes in the area. It occurs to me that I don't actually know which one is Cathy Ruskin's house, but it becomes obvious as soon as I turn into The Avenue.

Outside a large three-storey Edwardian detached, a tastefully extended home set back from the road, a large white van with a satellite dish on its roof is parked up on the kerb, another car right behind it. There are three cars next to the house, including the white Range Rover I had seen earlier on Lower Farm Lane.

I make a slow pass of the house, keeping my speed down. A well-groomed young guy in a jacket and tie, boom microphone held down low at his waist, talks into a tripod-mounted camera. He has his back to the driveway, the house behind him. A camera operator peers into the lens, headphones on over her ponytail, giving him a thumbs-up. A few paces away is an older guy in jeans and a loose white shirt, notepad tucked under his arm, pen between his teeth, taking photos of the house on his mobile. It obviously hadn't taken the local media long to latch onto the story after Cathy's social media post this morning appealing for Emily's safe return. Her TV fame seemed to have definite advantages in terms of focusing attention – even if her proactive approach had already brought the worst of the social media trolls out of their caves. But I would have done the same, in her shoes, appealing for help as widely as possible, as quickly as possible.

The first hours, the first days, were crucial with a missing persons investigation. Wasn't that what the police always said?

Keeping my speed low, I carry on down the street, leaving the journalists behind. A silver-haired guy raking his front lawn gives me a look as I drive past, his eyes hidden behind wrap-around shades. The road curves around to the left and here the houses become even grander, a mixture of the original vicarage-style Edwardians and newer builds here and there, a sprawling red-brick with columns at the front door and its own turret, next to a Spanish-style villa behind high walls and gates. Beyond the houses to my right, behind their large gardens, is farmland – soft ranks of yellow wheat swaying gently in the summer breeze. Row upon row in fields that rise gently up towards the boundary of Beacon Hill Woods.

DS Shah suggested that everything on Saturday night had started on The Avenue. One of these houses was the home of Adam King, the teenager whose party Connor and Zac had gone to. I cruise slowly along the street. This house? That one? How many of them had access to the fields behind and the footpaths up to Beacon Hill?

I pull over and text my wife.

What number house was the party at on Saturday night?

She replies a moment later.

77 The Avenue I think
What you doing?

I type a reply, delete it, type a shorter version instead.

Just checking a few things out

Number seventy-seven is two doors up from where I've stopped. I get out of my car, walk casually up to the front gates of a sprawling art deco style home set back behind a wide paved drive. The gates are shut, curtains at the front windows of the house drawn tightly closed. My phone pings again with more messages, but I ignore them and go to the intercom at the side of the gate. The panel lights up when I press it, a sing-song chime echoing back at me. The big house can't be more than a few hundred metres up from the Ruskins', and I wonder how long it will be before the media realise the connection with Emily's disappearance and begin knocking on this door too. I wonder whether Mr King has already anticipated this unwelcome interest.

There is no answer, the intercom remaining stubbornly silent.

I get back in my car, grateful for the air-conditioned cool, and read Laura's latest – slightly exasperated – replies.

???

I already spoke to Adam King's dad on phone yesterday

I pull the car slowly away from the kerb again. Up ahead, The Avenue ends in a small roundabout planted with a few perfectly manicured trees, three more huge houses crowded around it. It is a road to nowhere – a dead end, where through traffic didn't belong. I pull my Renault through a slow turn around the roundabout and head back the way I came, the silver-haired guy leaning on his rake now to give me another hard stare as I drive back past him. I smile, nod, but resist the urge to give him a wave.

Turning back to the road, the smile freezes on my face. There is a jolt of recognition, that moment of disorientation of seeing a familiar thing out of context, like bumping into a work colleague at the supermarket checkout or at the gym. A car I recognise is parked up against the kerb, looking more than a little out of place in this neighbourhood. I brake and pass it slowly, checking the number plate again to be sure. There's no one inside.

A drumbeat of unease beats a rhythm in my chest.

I pull over and park up on the other side of the street, take out my phone to check for any messages or missed calls. Nothing. The car is parked opposite a modern glass-fronted detached house on my left, one of the biggest on The Avenue, all northern European styling, dark timber, hard-slanting roof angles and floor-to-ceiling glass. A high boundary wall at the pavement, an open gate onto an immaculate driveway shaded by fir trees.

As I watch, the front door opens. Three figures emerge into the covered porch.

The first is a stocky man in a pastel polo shirt and cargo shorts: Karl Crosby, turning and raising a hand to someone inside as he leaves. Behind him is a petite blonde woman, mid-thirties, in a pale blue sundress with sunglasses perched on top of her head.

The other one is my brother.

31

Karl Crosby strides off down The Avenue without giving me a second glance, slotting his sunglasses into place. The petite woman hurries out to her car, a small red hatchback parked in front of me. As she unlocks it with the remote, she looks up and sees me, her eyes widening in recognition. She hesitates for a moment, as if she's going to come over and speak to me. I'm sure I know her from somewhere. A patient from the practice? The kids' school? But by the time I've hit the button to buzz my window down she's clearly thought better of the idea and is getting into her car instead, slamming the door and bumping down the pavement as she drives away.

My brother lingers in the porch for a few moments longer. His arms are crossed and he's nodding, mostly listening to a tall, slender man in a white linen shirt and chinos who fills the doorway. I'm too far away to hear what they're saying but it's clearly an animated conversation, the white linen shirt guy gesturing with his hands, pointing across the road and up towards Beacon Hill, while Rob nods in agreement.

Finally, the guy in the linen shirt sticks out his right hand and they shake, once. Then it's over and my brother is walking quickly down the drive towards the street, checking his phone, the front door shutting behind him. He looks slightly more together than he did last night, but not by much. He's still pale and very much rough around the edges, his hair uncombed, bags hanging heavy under his eyes. I get out of my car and step down onto the tarmac. It's only as he glances up to check the road is clear that his head snaps around to me, a double take of recognition as if I'm the last person he expected to see.

'Hey, Rob,' I say, raising a hand in greeting.

'Hi,' he says, his voice tight with surprise. 'What are you doing here?'

'I've been trying to get hold of you, left you some messages. We've not really had a proper chat yet, have we?'

'Yeah, was meaning to get back to you.' He shoves his phone into the pocket of his shorts, going to stand by his own car rather than closing the distance between us. 'Sorry.'

'I didn't know you knew Karl Crosby?'

He shrugs, his shoulders tight. 'Through school.'

I wait for him to elaborate, to expand on this Monday afternoon gathering of parents. There is an unpleasant tingling sensation at the back of my neck.

'What's going on, Rob?' I gesture towards the big European-style house from which he's just emerged. 'Whose house is this? Who was the guy you were just talking to?'

When we were kids, my brother once stole a half-pouch of our dad's rolling tobacco from the high cupboard in the kitchen. We smuggled it down to our camp at the bottom of the garden and made terrible amateurish roll-ups, competing to see who could draw the smoke in deepest, hold it in the longest, until we were both sick.

That night, he was caught red-handed trying to stash the remaining tobacco back in the cupboard, and I've always remembered the look on his face. Shock and fear, but a measure of defiance too.

He looks like that now, ready to brazen this out. He puts mirrored aviator sunglasses on, looks away down the street.

'One of the dads from football,' he says tonelessly. 'Sponsors the boys' league.'

'Who?'

'Don't think you know him, actually.'

'Try me.'

A muscle in his jaw twitches. 'Alexander,' he says. 'Saxton.'

It takes me a second to make the connection.

'Drew Saxton's father?' I frown. 'He lives here?'

Rob nods an affirmative, pulling a bunch of keys from his pocket. My mind is spinning, the rigid bands of a headache cinching a little tighter across my temples as I put the pieces together. Alexander Saxton, whose son had bullied Harriet and fought with Connor as a result. Whose son was now somehow mixed up in whatever happened on Saturday night.

'Hang on a second, you're meeting with Drew's family behind my back? What for? Why?'

'It's not a big deal, don't make it sound like some kind of conspiracy.'

'Well it sounds like it—'

'He thought it would be a good idea to meet up, all right?' His voice rises, and he throws a quick glance back at the house. More quietly, he adds: 'To see what we could do to help find this girl. Find Emily.'

The acid burn of betrayal begins a slow churn in my stomach.

'So you met up with Drew's dad,' I say slowly, 'and Emily's stepdad, without even telling me? I could have joined you, helped you.' I think I already know the answer to my next question, but have to ask it anyway. 'And who was the woman in the blue dress?'

He swallows and finally has the decency to look a little bit sheepish.

'Does it matter?'

'Just bloody tell me, Rob.'

'Sophie. She's Olivia de Luca's mum.'

The other teenager who had gone up to the woods on Saturday night along with Drew, Emily, Zac and Connor. Their parents meeting up, the four of them, in solidarity with a desperate family – and in secret.

Only one of the five left out. One boy excluded.

My son.

It feels like my lungs are compressing, squeezing all the air from my chest. I'm standing in full sun and I can feel an angry heat climbing up my throat, beads of sweat prickling in my hairline.

'I don't understand, Rob, why are you talking to them, and not me? I mean, what the hell?' I realise my voice is getting louder. 'What did you even talk about?'

'I told you. Alexander's a school governor and he's got all kinds of other connections, said he was going to do everything he could to get the local community organised, and that we should all be sort of coordinating our efforts, working together.'

'By "all" you mean everyone except your own brother? Your own nephew?'

'He invited us, asked us to come over.' He shrugs as if to say *What else was I supposed to do?* 'Look, Andy, to be honest when I turned up I thought you'd be here too, OK? He asked me for your number and I gave it to him, but it wasn't my place to be inviting other people to the guy's house.'

I shake my head. 'This is messed up, Rob. I'm not *other people*, I'm your family.'

He opens his car door. 'I've got to go.'

'Why are you doing this, being like this?' I say. 'We've always looked out for each other. Always.'

He takes a sharp breath. 'Right now I have to look out for my son,' he says, his eyes hidden behind the mirrored shades. 'Maybe you should start doing the same.'

His words are like a punch to the stomach.

'What do you mean? Of course I'm looking out for him.' I take a step towards him. 'What does that even *mean*?'

My brother has one foot in his car, his right hand gripping the top of the door. People have always said how similar we look – same dimple in our jaws, same hairline, same straight nose inherited from our father – and sometimes when I see him it's almost like I'm looking in a mirror, seeing another version of myself. But today I barely recognise him. Today he looks like a stranger, his eyes hidden behind reflecting glass, his jaw tight with anxiety.

He shakes his head. 'Why don't you ask Connor?'

My mouth forms another question but Rob has already climbed into the driver's seat and slammed the door. The engine roars into life and I step back against my own car as he pulls away, the wing mirror missing me by inches. I watch the dusty rear of his Mazda accelerating down The Avenue, following the broad curve of the road until it disappears from sight.

The early afternoon sun feels suddenly very hot on the crown of my head, the throb of my headache digging in hard. The neighbourhood is closing ranks, leaving us on the outside. It feels as if I'm already ten paces behind everyone else, as if they know something about my son that I don't. I have the sick, dizzy feeling that I'm the very last person to realise what's going on, like I've walked into a room and everyone has stopped talking, all eyes turning in my direction.

The meeting of parents to help find a missing girl – excluding me.

The echo of Zac's voice still fresh in my memory, as he shut the door on me. *Dad told me to stay away from Connor.*

The gut-punch of my brother going behind my back. Almost as if he knows the hammer is about to fall, and he wants to be sure his own son is far away when it happens.

Fear and anger bubble in my chest, rising painfully into my throat. I reach into my car for a half-empty bottle of Volvic, drinking it all in one long unpleasant pull of lukewarm plastic-tasting water. *Be calm.* As I finish drinking, my eye catches on the house across the street, all huge planes of glass, steeply angled roof and heavy wooden door frames. Alexander Saxton had left me out of his little gathering of concerned parents, as if the stain of guilt had already attached itself to my family. As if it's all of them versus us. I screw the cap back on the empty water bottle and throw it onto the passenger seat, my hands shaking with anger. Do they know something I don't?

Maybe I should ask Alexander myself.

I cross the street and walk up the immaculate driveway to his house.

32

There are three cars parked side by side on the wide paved driveway. A Range Rover, a Tesla saloon and a low-slung sports car, maybe a Ferrari or a Lamborghini, all three of them in gleaming black, polished to a high shine. A discreet pair of cameras covers the vehicles from both sides. Close up, the house itself is even more impressive, a modern angular design of smooth wood and dark steel, the front elevation made up almost entirely of glass tinted heavily against the bright sunlight.

I pause at the wide front door. The sting of my brother's duplicity is still sharp, a barb buried beneath my skin. But I need to be calm now, need to be civil to a man who has gone behind my back. Not to mention the fact that his son has been bullying my daughter – but I can't get into that now. That's a conversation for another day. *Three deep breaths, slowly in and slowly out.* I press the button beneath the tiny glass eye of a camera, embedded in the brushed steel surround of the front door.

Nothing happens. I wait, listening for approaching footsteps, feeling the eye of the camera on my face. Knowing that he can see me, that he knows I'm here. With my shirt sticking to the sweat blooming at the small of my back, I press the doorbell again.

Almost immediately the heavy wooden door swings open and a wash of air-conditioned cool floods out, a blessed relief from the shade-free heat of the drive. Alexander Saxton stands in the doorway in white linen shirt and beige chinos, leather flip-flops on his feet. He's fortyish, tall and slender, fine brown hair swept back in a way that somehow makes him look like an academic or an artist. The resemblance to Drew is obvious in the handsome planes of his face, the clean angle of his jaw, his height.

At Alexander's shoulder, supported by his tanned right arm, is a blonde toddler in a white cotton sundress, her cheek pressed against his chest.

'Sorry about that,' he says, pulling the door fully open. His voice is deep and unhurried. 'Can I help you?'

I give him a tight smile.

'Apologies for dropping in on you out of the blue,' I say. 'My brother was here a few minutes ago, I just bumped into him outside.'

'Your brother?'

'Rob.' I gesture back towards the road. 'I'm Connor Boyd's father. Rob was saying about you getting the community mobilised to help find—'

'Oh! Yes, yes, of course, Dr Boyd, sorry.' He takes a step back into the hallway. 'Hello, come in, come in.'

I had been expecting him to be at least a little bit embarrassed to find me at his door, so soon after his little gathering of parents had ended. For him to be a little defensive about the fact that he's excluded my family from the conversation. But instead he ushers me into the high-ceilinged entrance hall, a smile on his face as if he's genuinely pleased to see me. With his right arm holding the little girl, he extends his left to me for an awkward handshake.

'Freya,' he says softly to the little girl, 'how about you go and find Mummy and tell her I said you could have an ice lolly?'

'No.' The girl doesn't raise her head, her voice muffled against his chest. 'Dada carry.'

He throws me an apologetic smile, and says: 'Can I get you a drink?'

'I'm fine, thank you.'

He leads me past a doorway into a sun-filled kitchen where a young blonde woman – at least a decade younger than him – stands at an enormous black granite island slicing fruit. She doesn't look up as we pass. Another doorway leads into an airy lounge; French doors open onto the smooth green expanse of the garden. The house is furnished in neutral Scandinavian colours, blond wood and creamy marble tile, and there's an open wooden staircase up to a mezzanine first floor. The air is wonderfully cool. Alexander leads us into another lounge, smaller and more intimate than the first, with deep soft brown armchairs arranged around a circular glass coffee table on which a huge arrangement of purple flowers is set in a vase. Soft music seems to be playing in all the rooms on connected speakers, some nineties Britpop I can't identify.

He gestures to one of the armchairs and sits down opposite me. The little girl still clings to his shoulder but is now tapping the screen of her father's smart watch, little fingers chasing pulsing colours on the screen.

'I was about to call you, actually,' he says, retrieving his phone from the pocket of his chinos. 'I hope you don't mind, but I asked your brother for your number.'

'Of course, no problem.'

'I'll send you a text now anyway, so you've got my number too.' He taps the screen of his mobile before setting it down on the coffee table.

'Great, thanks,' I say. My own phone buzzes in my pocket as his message drops in. My anger, the heat of frustration I'd felt when I stood at this man's front door a few moments ago has all but disappeared. Cooled by his welcome, his openness, the complete absence of defensiveness in his tone. 'So . . . I was just talking to Rob outside.'

Alexander gives a nod of approval. 'He's a good guy, your brother.'

'He said you sat down with him and the other parents this morning to talk about getting the word out, helping to find Emily.'

'Yes, Cathy's absolutely in *bits*, bless her, waiting to hear from Em. Our families have been close for years so we just wanted to do absolutely everything we could to make sure we get her little girl home safe. Even if that includes pulling a few strings.' He speaks with the air of a man who is used to being listened to. 'I mean, God, all of us hope and pray that Em's just acting out, maybe she needed some time to herself after all the pressure of exams, but either way, someone needs to get organised to find her, right?'

'Definitely.' I nod. 'The sooner she's back safe and sound with her family, the better.'

'So, Michael Freeman's a good mate of mine as it happens, solid guy, known him for years, all the way back to his days on the county council.' Seeing the confusion on my face, he adds: 'The Police and Crime Commissioner. Civilian who oversees the local force.'

'He's getting involved, is he?'

'Can't hurt to put a little pressure on the local plods, can it?'

'About that,' I say, 'I'm sure I can help with that kind of thing too if—'

'And the main thing with a missing person is to do it *quickly*, right? Strike while the iron's hot, get the messaging out everywhere and make sure everyone is singing from the same hymn sheet. Better to do it face to face than have a million WhatsApp messages flying around.'

He runs me briefly through their immediate plans to help trace Emily: a Facebook page */FindEmilyRuskin* and corresponding Twitter account, printed flyers, use of Alexander's own office staff to help with media liaison, a community meeting, the potential of a five-figure cash reward to be announced later in the week if there's no news – a sum which I assume Alexander will put up himself. All discussed at the meeting which had finished just as I arrived.

'I noticed that Olivia's mother was here as well,' I say evenly. 'Was there a reason why you didn't invite me to join you?'

He gives me a rueful smile and for the first time looks a little bit sheepish.

'Listen, it really wasn't how I wanted this to play out, and I can only apologise for how it looks, Dr Boyd, I just—'

'Please call me Andy.'

He nods. 'So, Andy, I'm aware of the various events of the last twenty-four hours and I just didn't want to put you in an awkward position.'

'*Events?*'

He shrugs as if he's sorry to have to be saying it out loud.

'Your son being arrested in town.' He shifts uneasily in his seat. 'Being held and interviewed under caution.'

'He was released without charge.'

'All the same I thought it might be super awkward for you and make the other parents uncomfortable, OK? I was trying to put everyone at their ease, which is tricky enough considering the circumstances. That's why I thought it would be better if I spoke to you separately, keep unhelpful emotion out of it. I didn't think it would be very productive if everyone was here at the same time. Particularly with Karl, he can be quite an emotional guy.'

'He certainly is that,' I say, recalling our encounter in the woods this morning.

'You've met him?'

'Briefly.'

Abruptly, the little girl detaches herself from his shoulder.

'Juice,' she says in a soft, sleepy voice.

'Mummy's in the kitchen, Freya. She'll get you a nice apple juice from the big fridge.'

She pads out of the lounge in bare feet, Alexander's wistful gaze following her.

'Sorry about that,' he says when she's gone. 'Drew's little sister. Half-sister, actually. She's a bit of a Klingon at the moment.'

I sit forward in my seat, choosing my next words carefully.

'Alexander, you said the other parents would be uncomfortable – but the police have been talking to their kids too.'

'Yes, they've spoken to Drew.'

'So how is Connor any different?'

He holds out his hands, palms up. 'Connor was the only one who was arrested. Cautioned, fingerprinted and all the rest. Not to mention his . . . history with Emily.'

'What do you mean? What history?'

He looks pained, almost embarrassed. 'I mean, it's no secret that your boy was somewhat obsessed with her.'

Obsessed. He elongates the word, pulling and stretching it out of shape until it's something obscene. I remember Cathy's response when I'd asked whether her daughter and Connor were an item. *No, I don't think you'd call it that.* How could it be that Laura and I were completely unaware of this part of his life?

'What are you talking about?' I say. 'He's never—'

'Been following her around for months apparently, messaging her, stalking her on social media, hanging around outside her house and not taking no for an answer.'

'According to who?'

He shrugs.

'Does it matter? I'm just passing on what I've heard and it's common knowledge anyway, half the school knows it. All her friends know it. The police certainly know it, that's why he appears to be their prime suspect. And that's why I didn't want to put you in an awkward position with the other parents.'

His words are like a punch to my solar plexus, forcing the air from my lungs. The room suddenly seems very bright, impossibly bright, the frigid air-conditioned chill of the room raising goosebumps on my bare arms.

'What?' I manage. 'Who says he's the prime suspect?'

Alexander shrugs apologetically. 'The detectives investigating what happened on Saturday night. Probably why your son said "no comment" through the whole interview.'

How does he even know that? How does he know what Connor said, what he didn't say?

And then I know how: Karl Crosby, Emily's de facto stepfather.

'My son didn't do anything, he's a good kid.' I shake my head in disbelief. 'This whole thing is a nightmare.'

He leans forward. 'If I could give you one piece of advice?' His voice is deep, emollient. 'Keep your son close.'

'What do you mean?'

'What I said about Karl, the way he reacts to things? As I said, he can get emotional and he's grown very attached to Cathy's girls. Very protective. If he convinces himself that Connor has done something, if he's involved, you don't want your son to be anywhere near him. Do you understand what I'm saying?'

I feel a sudden urge to get home, to check Connor's OK.

'Thanks for the warning.' I stand up. 'I should probably go.'

We shake hands again at his front door, properly this time, before I hurry back out into the heat of the day.

33

DREW

Sunday 12th June, 12.32 a.m.
Forty-nine minutes before Emily disappears
Beacon Hill Woods

She was the only girl who'd ever said no.

The only one who'd ever turned him down.

But what made her so special? Why did Emily Ruskin think she was different, better than everyone else? In the end it wouldn't matter, because Drew knew that sooner or later she'd give in. Girls like her always did. In the meantime, she was being a tease, as usual, she liked the attention and she was certainly milking it tonight. She enjoyed being centre of attention from suckers like Connor.

And fangirls like Olivia, too.

Drew had slept with Olivia, of course. She wasn't the sort to say no. Even though he knew that she only did it because of Emily.

Drew didn't really care either way. Olivia's friendship with Emily had always been a bit weird, a bit one-sided. For months at a time, it was like she and Emily were closer than sisters, they'd spend every minute together, they'd share clothes, Olivia would even do her makeup and style her hair the same way; then there would be some massive blow-up and they would be mortal enemies, not speaking for days or weeks. Followed by a reconciliation and then back to the beginning again, repeating the cycle. What was that word, that messed-up relationship thing that girls did? Frenemies. Best of friends, best of enemies. He couldn't really get his head around it. But tonight, it seemed like they were closer than ever.

He took another drink of the lime-flavoured vodka, enjoying the burn as it hit his throat.

Emily was at the edge of the circle of light thrown by the little campfire, where the undergrowth thickened with bushes and brambles. Using a stick, she pushed up a tangle of thorns and lifted some snapped-off tree branches, still thick with leaves, dropping them to one side. She knelt, with the torch in one hand, scraping handfuls of sticks and earth and old leaves away. Something black lay beneath, hidden under the branches but now revealed, a matte black fabric of some kind. She didn't seem so drunk anymore, not like the way she'd been at the party. Maybe it had just been a bit of an act. He wouldn't put it past her.

She pushed the last of the cover away and, with a grunt, dragged it out of the bush. A backpack. She unzipped it and began laying clothes out on the log, black jeans, dark baseball cap and a plain black sweatshirt. At the bottom of the pack, a pair of thick-soled black DMs. Clothes she wouldn't normally wear in a million years.

Drew grinned. 'Need any help getting changed?'

She gave him a frown of exaggerated disgust. 'You wish.'

She gathered up the dark clothes and took them behind a tree.

Olivia lit a joint, the end flaring cherry red, before passing it to her left. Zac took it from her and had a drag before passing it on to Connor, who did likewise. When it was his turn, Drew put the roll-up to his lips and sucked deep, feeling the smoke fill his lungs and his head, his stomach suddenly light and his limbs loose. He dug a hand into the pocket of his jeans, remembering again that it was empty. Had he brought them or not? Had he left them back at the house? In his jacket? He honestly couldn't remember, with the vodka and the cider and the weed. Anyway, whatever. Fuck it. Didn't matter either way. He could get more. And in the meantime, he still had his hip flask.

By the time Emily re-emerged into the light a couple of minutes later, Drew barely recognised her. Blond hair tucked up under her baseball cap, hood up, head down. Nothing like the Emily he knew from school. A pair of black-framed glasses completed the look.

'What do you think?' she said, flashing them all a grin.

Connor sat up straighter, like the sucker he was, refusing the joint as it came around to him again. 'You look . . . like someone else.'

'Well, duh,' she laughed. 'That's the whole idea.'

She repacked most of her original clothes in the backpack, folding them quickly, and then zipped it shut.

'Olivia is going to clear up here and take care of my clothes.' She pointed at Connor. 'And I've got a job for you too.'

'I can go with you,' Connor said. 'So you're not on your own.'

'That's very sweet of you, but there's something else I need you to do for me.' She took her mobile from the rucksack and dropped it into a thick padded envelope. 'Come sit down next to me and I'll explain.'

Drew watched the two of them, his contempt rising as she patted the log next to her and Connor went over and sat down to listen to her murmured instructions. Their heads close together, Connor nodded every few moments and finally took the envelope from her.

When she was finished, he said: 'But where are you going to be? How are you going to get there?'

'Like I said, Connor, it's better if you don't know.'

'You need a phone though, don't you?'

Emily and Olivia held up identical little black burner phones. Emily reached into the backpack and produced another one, handing it to Connor.

She indicated the padded envelope in his other hand. 'Send a message to let me know it's done. We'll use Telegram only because it's totally secure. Nothing else. And you've got to remember to chuck these phones in the morning. OK? Just bin them, they're only cheap burners.'

'OK,' Connor said, powering on the phone.

'You look worried, Connor,' she said. 'Don't be worried, it's going to be fine. It's going to be amazing.'

'It's not too late to change your mind, you know. You don't have to do this.'

'I'm doing it.'

Connor held her gaze for a moment. 'OK,' he said again. 'But tell me if you need anything else. Anything at all.'

She nodded, gave him a kiss on the cheek.

'Good to go?' Olivia said.

Emily gave her a big smile. 'I think so.'

'I'll walk you out as far as the river.'

Drew regarded the conversation with a sharp flare of annoyance. The night was still young. There was still lots to drink, to smoke, to say.

Still lots to do.

With the others' attention focused on Emily, Drew got to his feet and went to the edge of the little circle of light for a piss. In his pocket was one of the stones from around the fire pit. It was smooth and heavy, the size of a large egg, a good heft to it. When he was sure no eyes were on him, he drew his right arm back and threw the stone as hard as he could, launching it in a high arc above them and into the trees.

Wait for it, wait for it . . . one second, two seconds, three . . .

The stone landed with a distant crack-thud *that echoed through the dark woods.*

Emily's head snapped around towards the sound, the smile dying on her lips.

'Shit! Did you hear that?'

Olivia followed her gaze. 'What was it?'

Behind them, Drew reached for another stone and launched it high into the canopy of trees above.

'Seriously,' Emily said, her voice taut. 'What the hell was—'

There was another crack-thud *as the second stone landed, off to the left and a little nearer to their campfire.*

'Who's there?' Emily shouted into the trees. 'Whoever you are, you can piss off right now.'

Silence.

Connor got to his feet.

'Maybe someone else from the party followed us up here,' he said. 'I'll go and have a look.'

After a moment, Zac stood up too. 'I'll come with you.'

Drew allowed himself a smile of satisfaction. Connor and his cousin were so predictable, it would be funny – if it wasn't so tragic.

The two of them moved off cautiously towards the noise, away from the clearing, flicking torches on and shining them into the night. Drew waited until the beams were all but swallowed up by *the dark, then stood up and moved over to where Emily and Olivia were sitting.*

He glared at Olivia until she took the hint, making space for him and moving away to the big tree stump where the remaining red plastic cups stood side by side.

He moved closer to Emily, handed her a drink and tapped his own against it.

'Cheers,' he said softly. 'To Emily Ruskin, the hottest girl in the year.'

Tonight was a gift, really. It was an opportunity.

And this time she wouldn't say no.

34

A police Volvo is parked on the street when I get home, white, blue and yellow livery standing out against the plain uniformity of the other cars. I had driven home in a daze, sweat chilling my skin as it dried in the brutal cold of the car's air conditioning. Alexander's words crowding out everything else. *He was obsessed. The police's prime suspect. Keep your son close.* Now I feel a lurch of panic that they've come back for Connor, that they're going to arrest him again, charge him, take him away from us for good. But they seem to be more interested in our neighbours.

A uniformed officer, a small woman in a bulky stab vest, is standing on the doorstep of Arthur's house. She's nodding and taking notes as my elderly neighbour talks animatedly, his brown woollen cardigan buttoned to the neck despite the heat, Chester sitting obediently at his feet.

I nod at Arthur as I pass and give him a wave, but he looks at me blankly, then keeps right on talking to the constable. I'm pressing the key fob to lock my car when I notice someone at the door of our other neighbours on the far side, a tall guy in grey suit trousers and a white shirt, a lanyard around his neck. Detective Constable Harmer, chatting amiably with my neighbour Joe, the wine connoisseur whose boozy barbecues normally required a full day of recovery afterwards.

DC Harmer is making notes too.

The lurch of panic has receded, replaced by a sick crawl of unease, as if I'm watching a car crash happening from a long way away. As if I know what's going to happen but I'm powerless to stop it. Opposite our house, there is another suit with another lanyard around his neck. Another detective, talking to Barbara and John, whose now-grown up kids used to babysit for us when Connor was little. *They're canvassing all of our neighbours.* Bracketing our house to gather more information about what they might have seen or heard in the last thirty-six hours. Anything that might point in Connor's direction.

Will they knock on our door next? I'm not going to wait to find out. I hurry inside. Laura and Harriet are in the dining room, *Game of Thrones* Monopoly laid out on the table between them.

My wife and daughter both look up when I walk in.

'We need to talk to Connor,' I say. 'Where is he?'

'At work,' Laura says. 'Afternoon shift at the shelter.'

'What? You let him go?'

'Yes.'

I blow out an exasperated breath. 'I thought we grounded him?'

'Not for volunteering, surely? He was on that waiting list for a year.'

'I just thought we needed to make it clear to him that what he did was . . .' I shake my head with a sigh. 'Doesn't matter. When's he back?'

'His shift finishes at five thirty. Why?'

I'm about to explain when I notice Harriet's inquisitive eyes on me. This is not a conversation to be held in front of our daughter. 'Harry, I'm just going to borrow your mum for a moment, OK?'

She gestures at the board. 'But it's her turn.'

'We'll just be a minute.'

Laura stands and follows me out through the French doors and into the garden. We walk across the lawn to the deck by the back fence. Laura sits down in one of the reclining chairs opposite me as I recap my conversation with Rob, his invitation to join with parents of the other three teenagers involved in Saturday night's visit to Beacon Hill. I relate Alexander's assertion that Connor was being treated as the police's prime suspect.

'It's starting to feel like this is . . . some kind of contest, but no one's told us the rules,' I say quietly. 'Like Connor's going to be the one left standing when the music stops. I've got a really bad feeling about it.'

She considers this for a moment.

'Have you met Alexander Saxton before?' When I shake my head, she adds: 'I have – school parents' evenings for the last five years. Smooth operator, used to getting what he wants. And what he'll want right now is to protect his lad, and at the same time find out what everyone else is saying about that night. By excluding one family from his little gathering he turns it into an *us-and-them* thing, paints Connor as a suspect and diverts attention away from the other teenagers, including his own.'

'That's pretty cold,' I say. 'Pretty calculating.'

She shrugs. 'Like I said, he's a man who's accustomed to getting what he wants.'

'Says he's got all kinds of connections with the police, too. Although to be honest I'm more worried about what Rob said. It's like everyone is just trying to protect their kids – even my own brother – and it doesn't matter what happens to anyone else.'

'Well of *course* they are, Andy,' she says, a note of exasperation creeping into her voice. 'We'd be naive to think otherwise.'

'How can you be so matter of fact about it?'

'What else did you think would happen? Every parent of every child involved in this is going to protect their own offspring first and foremost. That includes your brother.' She leans a little closer. 'It needs to include us, too.'

I open my mouth to reply; close it again. The truth is it had never occurred to me that Rob and I would fall out, over anything. Twenty-four hours ago it had been unthinkable.

'I'm just surprised how fast things have started to turn ugly, that's all.'

She frowns slightly, as if she is not surprised at all. 'What else are you thinking, Andy?'

I check over my shoulder to make sure Harriet hasn't emerged from the house.

'So . . . five of them went up there: Emily, Connor, Zac, Drew and Olivia. Only four came out, and one of them must know *something*. If we exclude Connor and Zac, that leaves Drew and Olivia.'

'But what's the motive?'

'That's what we need to find out.'

'Or what about a third party?' she says. 'Someone else in the woods with them, someone we don't know about yet?'

I shrug, unconvinced. 'The police aren't going to waste time chasing shadows. They've got their suspects, now they're just whittling the pool down to one.'

'When are you meeting that lawyer?'

'Tomorrow after work, at her office in town.'

'Let's hope Emily's back home safe before then,' she says. 'Then maybe the police interest will go away and we won't need a lawyer after all.'

'Better to be prepared, although it would be a damn sight easier if Connor opened up about what happened on Saturday night. We need to get the truth out of him.'

'He'll tell us, he just needs a little space, a little time.'

'We don't *have* time.'

I twist in my chair as a small voice interrupts us.

'Time for what?' Our daughter has somehow crept up on us and is leaning on the brick surround of the barbecue, an expression of intense curiosity on her face. 'What don't we have time for?'

Laura gives her a reassuring smile. 'It doesn't matter, Harry.'

'Are you talking about that girl, Emily Ruskin?' Harry says. 'Have they found her?'

'Not yet,' Laura says. 'But a lot of smart people are looking for her, I'm sure there'll be news soon. Come on, how about we finish this game and you let me win for once?'

Laura and Harriet go back to their Monopoly game and I go to the kitchen, grabbing a cold can of Coke from the fridge. I take it up to Connor's room, standing in the doorway and surveying the mess, without any real idea what I'm doing here.

The untidy state of his room has been a constant theme for years but today it's different somehow, as if the chaos is now intended to hide something, to deceive, to conceal the truth from me. From everyone. I stand a moment longer, hoping that I might be able to discern my son's hidden life simply by standing here among his things, surrounded by his clothes and his books and posters. As if

I will be granted a glimpse of the truth that he seems determined to keep from us.

But it remains out of my sight, like undiscovered land lying just beyond the curve of the horizon.

35

I have some work emails to catch up on but after ten minutes at my laptop in the study I find myself opening an internet browser and checking through the news websites, scrolling through stories about Emily's disappearance. Her mother's TV profile has already given the story traction with the *Mirror* online and a couple of the other tabloids, all of them are running the video appeal she posted this morning, light on new facts and heavy on background, with a liberal sprinkling of speculation mixed in and a selection of family pictures lifted from Cathy's Instagram account.

The headlines are mostly variations on a theme.

MYSTERY OF CELEB'S MISSING GIRL

MISSING TEEN'S SOAP STAR FAMILY

'COME HOME TO US, EMILY'

But one of them jumps out at me.

KIDNAP RIDDLE OF TV STAR

I scroll down, further into the story.

Some fear that Emily may have been the victim of a kidnapping plot to extort a ransom from her wealthy family. Police said they are looking at a number of lines of enquiry.

Where the hell had *that* come from? A few lines later it quotes a variety of tweets and online comments on the kidnapping angle, relating how Cathy had talked in the past about her concerns around protecting her family, keeping teenagers safe in a connected world. Re-posting a series of videos she'd put up last year, where she had related some of the unsavoury comments and threats – including thinly veiled suggestions that one of her children might be snatched – during a discussion about responsible twenty-first century parenting and striking a balance between allowing kids to explore and shielding them from potential harm.

The story includes screenshots from various social media trolls. *So how about: maybe don't post your kids pictures to 50,000 followers every week?* I think of the comments I'd seen on her Instagram post. There seems to be a body of opinion among the darkest recesses of the internet that Cathy has somehow brought this on herself.

One line in the *Sun's* story stops me cold. *Detectives are quizzing classmates thought to have attended a drink and drug-fuelled end-of-school party with missing teen Emily on Saturday night.* How long will it be until they start putting up pictures of Connor and his friends in the search for a fresh angle, or using their names? Were they allowed to do that with teenagers? And how did they even know drugs were involved, or was that just an assumption?

I google Drew Saxton and find a handful of reports about the under-sixteen football team he plays for, accounts on Snapchat and Instagram. The fifth story down is not really about Drew at all, just a mention of him as the only child of Alexander Saxton and his first wife Josephine. A slightly amended search reveals it's just one of dozens of stories about Alexander, page after page of news items, deal announcements, events and website entries. He's a property developer – clearly a very successful one – with a string of deals in recent years involving housing developments, office blocks and a new retirement village in Leicester. There are numerous pictures of him on construction sites; shaking hands with government ministers and county councillors; in high-vis jacket and hard hat on brownfield sites; suited and booted for a glowing profile piece in a trade magazine.

The top *News* search result on his name is barely an hour old. I click on it and the link takes me through to a YouTube channel, *LuxuryLiving*, a two-minute video shot in his house, the expansive living room behind him. Alexander is in the same crisp white shirt he'd been wearing when I visited a couple of hours ago; he must have made this video soon after I'd left. I guess this is the first stage of what he talked about, of mobilising support from as many people as possible.

'This is the most important video I've ever made,' he says, looking seriously into the camera. 'So thank you for watching. You may have seen in the news that sixteen-year-old Emily Ruskin is missing, and we need everyone's help to find her and bring her home to her mum. We're very close to Emily and her family and our hearts go out to them at this incredibly difficult time. But what we *really* need is your help, your information, anything you've seen or heard that could be relevant. Please spread the word about Emily and if you have any info, *anything* at all that might help us find her, please get in touch. You can do it anonymously if you prefer . . .'

He reels off the various contact options and I watch the video to the end as the image changes to a still of Emily with the police phone number, an incident number, his email address and the hashtag #FindEmily.

His channel has almost ten thousand subscribers and more than a hundred videos, but this latest entry is the only one about Emily. I watch it again, then click on a quick selection of the others. In some he walks from room to room around his house while he talks architecture and design; other videos take viewers on site tours of ongoing projects, computer-generated fly-throughs of new buildings and a long series on the construction of his own hi-tech house, *Grand Designs* style. They're slick and professional; he's obviously very comfortable with technology. Many have the same backdrop as today's video: the cavernous and luxuriously appointed interior of his home, the huge lounge-dining-living space with light-reactive windows and multiple doors leading off to other areas. He likes the camera, and the camera likes him.

I go back to the search. There is something else interesting. A series of articles on a local news website, the *West Bridgford Wire*, about plans to clear part of Beacon Hill Woods to make way for a new housing estate. Back-and-forth news stories over the last three years with plans submitted, opposed by locals, rejected by council planners, revised and submitted again, approved provisionally then rejected again following an appeal by a local wildlife campaign group. The most recent story featured on the website at the beginning of this year under the headline NEW SETBACK FOR ESTATE PLAN.

I find a pad and pen and make some notes. I can't imagine why his business interest in Beacon Hill might be significant, but it seems like a weird coincidence. Something is still bothering me about our conversation too, although I can't put my finger on it. Something beyond his obvious charm, his unexpected welcome. Maybe something he'd *said*? But the words were just beyond my grasp.

A Google search for Olivia de Luca brings up much slimmer pickings. An Instagram account set to private, some mentions of a play in a school newsletter that are a few years old. There are no pictures but the school link gives me an idea and I fetch Connor's end-of-school yearbook from his bedroom, a full-colour hardback the school started producing a few years ago – another American import along with Year 11 Prom and 'graduation' for school leavers. I flip through until I come to the page with Olivia's entry. Each Year 11 student is allocated a third of a page with a head-and-shoulders photograph in school uniform, alongside the standard set of questions each child fills out in the spring term of their GCSE year.

Olivia de Luca
  Nicknames: Liv, Livvy, Rosie, Rosalee, Ro-Ro
  Favourite memory: Paris trip '21 with my forever bestie Emmy R.
  Where do you see yourself in 10 years: Fighting climate change with my husband Zayn Malik :-)
  Quotes: 'Sister from another mister'; 'Sometimes you've got to step back and let karma take over'

Facing her, on the right-hand-page, is Emily Ruskin's entry. I do a quick double-take: at first glance the two of them are weirdly similar looking, the same honey-blonde hair cut the same way, same fringe, same sculpted eyebrows, same blue eyes. Maybe all sixteen-year-old girls have a tendency to go for the same look? My eyes travel between the two images, a missing girl and her best friend facing each other across the pages. Where Emily's beauty looks completely effortless, almost casual, Olivia's is more deliberate somehow, more constructed. More *intentional*. A good copy of the original – but still a copy.

I flip through each class until I find the entry for Drew Saxton. He looks confidently into the camera.

Nicknames: Saxton AF, Boss

Where do you see yourself in 10 years: Cashing cheques 'n' breaking necks – making my second million

Quotes: 'You can catch a lot of flies with honey, but you can catch more honeys being fly'

I take out my phone and snap a photo of Drew's picture, then flip back to Olivia's page and take one of her too.

On the next page is Zac: just a picture of him staring blankly into the camera. There is no funny caption, no nicknames or humorous anecdotes. Just a simple generic message from his form tutor in its place: 'Zac is an academically able and talented student. We wish him all the best in his future.' I realise this would have been around the time his mother was already months into her one-sided fight with cancer. A premature end to his childhood, an end to the kind of banter and boasts and teenage in-jokes that his classmates would look back on with cringing recognition in years to come.

I shut the yearbook and enter Sophie de Luca's full name carefully into the search bar, letter by letter, with exactly the same result: lots of wrong answers. Absolutely nothing that links back to Olivia's mum. No social media, no email addresses, no mention on a company website. Sophie doesn't seem to have any online footprint at all.

*   *   *

I'm still puzzling over her online anonymity as I climb the stairs back up to Connor's room, to return the yearbook – no need for him to think I've been poking around his stuff more than I already have. I don't suppose Sophie de Luca's absence from the internet has to mean *anything*, really. Twenty-odd years ago there would have been nothing remarkable about it. Maybe she was just one of those people who had held back against all of that, who wanted to keep her private life exactly that.

I push open the door to Connor's bedroom and find I'm not alone.

My wife is standing up, turning to face me, a startled cast to her eyes that I hardly ever see. She's by the bed, next to his bedside table.

'Oh,' she says, a little breathlessly. 'You startled me.'

'Been looking at his school yearbook, you know it's uncanny how much Emily Ruskin and Olivia de Luca look alike.' I put the book back on top of the chest of drawers. 'Did you find something?'

'No,' she says quickly. 'Find what?'

I shrug. 'Thought you were looking under Connor's bed.'

'Just gathering up some laundry.' She scoops up a pair of jeans and some shorts from the floor. 'His room's like a bombsite again.'

'Always is.'

I pick up a crumpled shirt and hand it to her. She reaches out with her left hand, already holding the jeans and the shorts, gripping them awkwardly with two fingers.

Her right hand stays by her side. As I watch, I can see a telltale red blush at the top of her chest, already creeping up her throat.

'What's in your other hand, Laura?'

'Nothing.'

'Really?'

'Yes.' She clears her throat. 'Why?'

I raise my eyebrows at her in silent challenge.

'Whatever it is, it can't be good, otherwise you'd show me.'

For a moment I think she's going to walk past me without answering. That she's going to leave the room, act as if this conversation never happened.

Then she sighs, drops the clothes and opens her right hand.

Lying in her palm is a small, Ziploc bag, filled with transparent plastic shapes. I lift my glasses up to my forehead to peer closer and see that they're little plastic fish, perhaps ten of them, each one around an inch long and with a little red screwcap for a nose. I pick the bag up, hold it to the light. The fish are the kind of thing you might get with a sushi box, filled with a single serving of soy sauce for your meal. Except these are not filled with dark brown soy; instead, each one is filled with a clear liquid.

'I found the bag under his bedside table,' my wife says tonelessly. 'Just the corner was poking out. I thought it was a bag of coins or something.'

'What the hell are they?' I say. 'From a takeaway?'

She shakes her head. I open the bag and take one of the little containers out to study it more closely. Its plastic surface is dimpled with tiny details in imitation of a fish: rows of scales, two eyes, a fin and a tail. I start unscrewing the tiny red cap at the other end.

Laura puts a hand on mine. 'I wouldn't do that.'

'Why not?'

She goes to check the landing is empty before pushing the bedroom door closed.

'There was a circular at school earlier this term, the police sent it around to all the head teachers in the area and it was cascaded to all staff, so if we found any of these on pupils we'd know what we were dealing with.'

Even as she's saying it, I feel a recent memory surface. I *had* seen something from the police, circulated via our local primary care network weeks or months ago, an email among thousands of others, the kind of thing I would have given a cursory glance before moving onto the next message, the next case, the next prescription, the next patient.

'Do you know what this stuff is?'

'Yes,' she says, her voice so low it's almost a whisper. 'Drugs.'

36

We sit in frozen silence for a long moment.

I can see on her face that she's thinking the same thing as me. *Supplying drugs? Our boy? Not Connor, he wouldn't do that.* Never, *ever*, would I have thought Connor was into drugs. I couldn't even remember smelling weed on him when he'd come home from parties. The subject had come up at the dinner table from time to time because of the nature of my job, but Laura and I had never felt the need for a sit-down chat about the dangers. It had just never seemed like it was necessary; Connor was too sensible.

It seems we were wrong.

'Are you sure?' I say finally.

'I remembered it as soon as I saw it, how weird it was, because we always expect drugs to be pills or powder, resin or leaves or whatever. It was featured in the media too,' Laura says. 'There was a big awareness push by the police.'

A quick Google search brings up a string of stories. Among the top results is a story from last month's *Nottingham Post*.

CLUB DRUG FLOODING OUR STREETS
By Chris Dineen, Crime Correspondent

CRIMINAL gangs are flooding the city with a potent party drug that can kill, police warned today.

Detectives said the so-called 'club drug' GHB has been linked to dozens of allegations of sexual assault, rape, robbery, assault and theft this year alone, as well as users hospitalised with overdoses.

Effects of the drug include confusion, memory loss, impaired speech and blackouts, but it can also lead to breathing difficulties, seizures, coma – and death.

A spokesman for the Midlands Major Crime Task Force said: 'This is an extremely dangerous drug. There's a very high risk of overdosing with GHB because there's so little difference between the amount that causes the "high" and the amount that causes an overdose. That's why it's so important we get these drugs off the streets.'

GHB is sold in liquid form and dealers supply the drug in small containers chosen because they are the right size for a single dose – but this also makes it very easy to spike a stranger's drink, experts say.

The accompanying image shows hundreds, perhaps thousands of the little fish-shaped containers among a display of drugs, weapons and cash seized in a police raid.

I slump down onto the bed.

'Jesus Christ,' I whisper. 'What the hell's this stuff doing in his bedroom?'

'Maybe he was . . . holding them for someone,' she says slowly. 'Looking after them, doing a favour for somebody. You know what he's like.'

'I *thought* I did but I'm not so sure anymore. And a favour for who?'

'No idea.' She takes the bag from my hand. 'All I know is that we need to get rid of them.'

The shock of her words – the speed with which she's decided what has to be done – sends a wave of dizziness washing through me. And as I watch her tuck the little Ziploc bag into the pocket of her shorts, another uncomfortable thought edges its way in.

'You weren't going to tell me, were you?' I say. 'If I hadn't walked in on you just now, when you found them?'

She hesitates.

'I hadn't decided yet,' she says. 'I didn't know what I was going to do.'

'You tried to hide them from me.'

'You surprised me. I wasn't sure what was for the best.' She heads purposefully towards the door. 'But now I am.'

'You can't get rid of them.'

'Why not?'

'They're evidence. The police might . . . I don't know, they might relate to Emily Ruskin or whatever happened to her.'

She turns to me, a determined set to her mouth. 'No, Andy. These need to disappear. Right now.'

'We need to tell *someone*.' I stand, various scenarios cycling through my mind. 'What if Emily Ruskin took one of these? Or two of them? She could have had a fit or a seizure, she could have overdosed, she could have—'

'Keep your voice down!' Laura hisses. 'Harry will hear you!'

'We can't just pretend we didn't find them. We should at least—'

She cuts me off. 'We should what?' There is ice in her tone now. 'Do what, Andy? Take this little bag to our local police station and hand it over? Tell DS Shah they were in Connor's bedroom? Oh and by the way, please charge our son with dealing, possession and whatever else she can think of?'

'No,' I say. 'Not that. But there must be another way of making the police aware.'

My wife stares at me, her eyes blazing. '*Not* in a way that drops our son in it.' She points an angry finger at my chest. 'And it's their job to find Emily Ruskin, not ours. You need to work out where your loyalties lie and you'd better swear to me you won't say anything.'

'OK, OK.' I hold my hands up. 'Let's at least hang onto them for a little bit. Hide them. And we need to ask Connor about them too.'

She takes a breath then nods. 'Agreed.'

She wrenches Connor's bedroom door open and stalks out onto the landing without another word.

* * *

I spend an uncomfortable hour online, researching the effects and side-effects of GHB.

'Gamma Hydroxybutyrate is a central nervous system depressant that is commonly referred to as a "club drug" or "date rape" drug. GHB is abused by teens and young adults at bars, parties, clubs and raves and is often placed in alcoholic beverages. It is colourless, odourless and tasteless.'

Of course there was no way to be certain of the contents of the eleven little fish-shaped vials inside the Ziploc bag. In theory it could be something else, it could be nothing more dangerous than tap water, a lucrative placebo packaged up for sale to gullible users who didn't know any better. It could be harmless – but instinct tells me otherwise. And in any case, I can't think of a way of getting it officially tested that doesn't invite serious trouble with the police.

We're finishing dinner in the conservatory when the front door slams shut. Harriet has already finished her meal and disappeared upstairs to her bedroom. Laura and I both stop eating for a moment, forks suspended, listening for the progress of Connor's footsteps from the hallway and into the kitchen.

My wife half turns. 'Your chilli is in the microwave, Connor.' She flashes me a warning look that says, *Let me handle this.*

Our son emerges into the conservatory in jeans and a crumpled black T-shirt, his summer tan looking a shade darker, as if he's spent all afternoon in the sun. But he also looks tired, *so* tired, wrung out in a way I've never seen him before. He doesn't speak or make eye contact with either of us as he slides his plate onto the placemat and sits down. He mixes the food together with his fork, scooping and pushing the rice into the centre the way he's always done, blending it with the chilli, and then begins shovelling it into his mouth as if he's not eaten for a week.

Laura goes into the kitchen to warm up a pitta bread, adding it to the side of his plate.

'There's a bit more chilli in the pan if you want it,' she says. 'I can heat it up for you.'

He shrugs, chewing and swallowing another mouthful.

'Good day?' she says, pouring him a glass of water from the jug in the centre of the table. 'How was your shift? How were the cats?'

He grunts in response, picking up the tumbler and draining half of it in one long pull. On his left hand, gripping the glass, there are dark rings of dirt caked beneath his fingernails.

We lapse back into an uneasy silence, the only sound the clink and scrape of his fork against the rapidly diminishing plate of chilli con carne. I exchange frustrated glances with my wife before she tries again.

'We need to talk to you about a couple of things, Connor.'

'Uh-huh,' he says between mouthfuls.

'Your dad saw Drew Saxton's dad today.'

Connor finally looks up.

'What?' he says. 'Why?'

'I was looking for your uncle,' I say. 'Anyway, me and Drew's dad ended up having a bit of a chat. He said some things . . . about Emily Ruskin.'

Connor reddens visibly, a blush creeping up his jaw and staining his cheeks crimson.

'Like what?' he says. 'What things?'

'That you were really keen on her. You liked her.'

He exhales heavily, fork stabbing angrily into his meal.

'So?'

'So, the police will probably want to ask about that, and we want to be able to help you the best we can. But to do that, we need to know the full story.'

Laura leans forward and puts a hand gently on his arm.

'Please just talk to us, Connor, so we can deal with this together. It doesn't have to go any further than this room. We want to help you, to protect you, but it's difficult to do that if we don't know what really happened.'

He stares first at his mother, then at me, his blue eyes burning with anger and frustration.

'You two are unbelievable, you know that?'

'Connor, we're on your side here, we—'

'You think I did something to her, don't you?' There is a tremor in his voice, as if he is struggling to keep it under control. 'You think that's the reason why she's not come back? You've been listening to people talking shit about me, people who don't know anything, who don't know me, or her, like it means something. But I would never hurt Emily. *Never.*'

Laura shakes her head, giving him a sympathetic smile.

'Neither of us think that,' she says. 'You're our son, we love you and we want to look after you. That's all.'

He slams his fork down so hard I feel the table vibrate.

'I can look after myself.' He pushes his half-finished plate away and stands up, his chair scraping loudly on the tiled floor. 'Don't need you looking over my shoulder every minute of the day.'

'Sit. Down.' With considerable effort, I manage to keep my voice level.

Slowly, he does as he's told, staring at me with a look I've never seen before.

'Connor,' Laura says. 'There's something else, too.'

'What?' He looks at his mum, then me. 'What else?'

'We found drugs,' I say. 'In your bedroom.'

He freezes, just for a second, before regaining his composure.

'What *drugs*?' he says. 'What do you mean?'

'Eleven doses, in a bag,' my wife says. 'I recognised them from a police drug advisory warning we had through school last month.'

We lock eyes and in that moment he looks like a stranger, like someone else's child. The same, but transformed somehow: a changeling who has arrived in our house wearing Connor's clothes. My own child lost and gone, replaced by this angry, frightened, troubled young man.

'I have literally *no* idea what you're talking about.'

He stands and walks out.

TUESDAY

37

The morning passes with grinding slowness. Outside it's another beautiful summer's day, the air warm and clear, the sky as blue as the ocean with not a cloud in sight. But my cramped little consulting room has an airless, claustrophobic feel that seems to grow worse as the morning drags on. Patients come and go, the worried mother of a toddler with a rash, an elderly man in for a routine medication review, a woman with a persistent cough that she can't shift. I have a couple of no-shows which makes things worse, nothing to distract me from churning thoughts of Connor and the police and Emily Ruskin, from the sense of impending catastrophe. I have to resist the urge to refresh my email between every patient to see if there is any news, any update on Emily's disappearance.

Harriet insisted on having the day off sick, saying she couldn't face all the whispers and gossip at school from the mean kids, all the horrid things they were saying about her brother. Instead she ensconces herself in her bedroom – as usual – with laptop and headphones. Laura has taken a day of compassionate leave and will stay with her today.

I had slept fitfully, intermittently, my thoughts circling back to Connor's angry words at dinner last night. To one thing he'd said that stood out to me straightaway, taking on more and more significance with each hour I spent staring up at the ceiling in the too-warm darkness of our bedroom.

I would never hurt her.

Neither of us had mentioned anything about Emily being hurt. The police had not talked in those terms; they had talked about her being missing, or the possibility of self-harm, but had never suggested that someone else had hurt her. Even Alexander Saxton hadn't mentioned it. Connor had introduced it himself, unprompted. Was he trying to convince us, or himself?

I would never hurt her.

There is a gap in my schedule just before noon and I check my mobile again in between answering a medication query from one of the nurses and filing lab results on a patient's blood sample. There have been four WhatsApp messages from Laura in the last ten minutes, each green rectangle stacked on top of the next.

Have a look at this ASAP
Just posted this morning
Will be on today's lunchtime news apparently

The next message is a link. I click on it and the screen goes through to the Twitter feed of Nottinghamshire Police, a video that starts playing straightaway. Four people sit behind a long table arrayed with various microphones: Cathy Ruskin beside a uniformed officer in the centre, flanked on the other side by her partner, Karl Crosby. DS Shah sits at the other end, next to the uniformed officer. Behind them is a blue background emblazoned with a large silver-and-black police crest.

The uniformed senior officer, a silver-haired Scotsman in his late forties, begins by thanking the media for coming and explaining the background to the press conference, where and when Emily was last seen, her age and description, what she's thought to be wearing now. Then he hands over to Cathy. She's wearing a pale blue cap-sleeved T-shirt, her dark hair pulled back in a ponytail. She looks exhausted, as if she's barely slept in the last forty-eight hours, only desperation keeping her going. The contrast with the wholesome images on her Instagram feed is startling.

'We'd just like to appeal to anyone who can help us find Emily,' she begins, 'who might have seen anything, who might have seen her or know where she is, to please get in contact with the police.' She pauses to look down at a sheet of paper in front of her, blinking hard as if she is fighting with all she has not to cry on camera. 'You don't have to leave your name, you can do it anonymously but please pass on any information you have, even if you think it's not important. It could be the one piece of information that helps us to find her.'

The screen switches to a still image of Emily, a shot of her smiling in a white Hollister hoodie, alongside contact numbers for the police incident room and a police reference number.

'It's very out of character for my daughter to do something like this,' Cathy continues, 'to be away from home for so long without being in contact with us, and we all just desperately want her home safe. Emily is my youngest, my baby, she's so bright and beautiful and kind.' At this, her voice finally cracks, and the room switches back to Cathy, her face strobed with camera flashes. She takes a deep breath and continues. 'She's just the sweetest girl and we want her back more than anything else in the world.'

The video cuts away from the image of Emily and back to the press conference, four faces lined up behind a long table. The uniformed cop remains as impassive as a stone carving. DS Shah's expression is one of concerned professionalism, hands clasped in front of her, a brief nod of encouragement when Cathy glances across. At the other end of the long table, Karl is also giving little away, his eyes fixed on a point straight in front of him, dark rings of sweat visible at the armpits of his lilac polo shirt.

Cathy soldiers on. 'If there's someone who's with Emily,' she says, 'who might be ... the reason why she can't come home, I would say to you please just let us know that she's OK. Send a message to me or to the police, that's all we ask. Emily is such a lovely girl and she'll be so frightened, so scared, we've never spent more than one night apart since she was born and she needs to be back with her mum, with her family.'

She is wiping away tears now, a tissue clutched in her shaking fist. She's no longer looking at the sheet of paper on the table, her gaze focused instead on the cameras in front of her.

'Emily, if you're watching this, we love you. It doesn't matter what's happened, or where you've been, please come back to us. Me, your sisters, Karl, all of us. We just want you to come home to us. We love you more than anything and we want you back.' She wipes her eyes again. 'Thank you.'

The uniformed officer wraps up the press conference by repeating the incident room number to call. 'Emily is being treated as a high-risk missing person,' he says, his clipped Scottish accent a sharp contrast to Cathy's soft tones. 'There is a possibility that she's being held against her will somewhere; there's also a possibility that she may have come to harm in some way. Obviously we need to find her as quickly as possible. Thank you again for your assistance.'

The video finishes, flipping back to Emily's photo. I exhale a held breath, a little in awe of the dignified way this woman has kept on going under the pressure of every parent's worst nightmare. Clicking play again, I watch the video for a second time, listening more closely to her words this time and noting that they seem to cover two distinct possibilities – that Emily might have disappeared of her own accord, or that she's been taken by someone else and is being held against her will.

Which presumably means the police still haven't narrowed down their options either.

I think back to the first time I spoke to Cathy on Sunday afternoon, the hurried video call as we both searched for our missing children, trying to imagine what it would be like if we still hadn't heard from Connor in the intervening forty-eight hours – if the police still didn't know for sure whether he was a runaway, a possible suicide or a kidnap victim. The terror of it, the agonising wait for news, is almost unimaginable. The idea of keeping it together, of going on camera and pleading with strangers for help, makes my chest ache with sympathy. Was it true what Laura said, that every parent defaulted to selfishness when their own child was threatened? That we all just looked after our own and damn everyone else? I didn't want to believe that.

There is something else, too.

Guilt.

Nagging, gnawing guilt that my son was somehow involved in Emily's disappearance, that he is playing a part in her mother's misery, that the drugs we found in his bedroom are a factor in all of it.

The drugs we can't tell anyone about.

According to Twitter, this video was posted more than half an hour ago, so the press conference should be finished by now. I go back to WhatsApp and pull up the thread from Sunday's video call, Cathy's mobile number displayed, and type a new message to her.

Hello Cathy, we met briefly at Beacon Hill Woods yesterday. I've just seen your police appeal. I'm so sorry for what's happened, let me know if there's anything I can do to help. Anything at all.

I sign off with my name and press 'send' before I can change my mind. The two ticks appear to show the message has been sent; then a few seconds later they turn blue.

She won't reply; of course she won't. She'll be inundated with messages from well-wishers and friends, neighbours, colleagues and everyone else who wants to show their support but can't actually offer anything tangible in the search for her daughter. Never mind the fact that my son might have been one of the last people to see her.

Of course she won't reply.

I've almost convinced myself when my phone starts to ring.

38

Cathy sounds different on the phone, her voice quieter and more hesitant than in the press conference. The soft rounded edges of her Nottinghamshire accent coming through a little more clearly as she thanks me for my message and my offer of help. There are several other female voices in the background, an indistinct hum of activity. She doesn't waste time on pleasantries.

'Listen, Andy, I'm really glad you got in touch.' She's walking as she talks, the echo of footsteps punctuating her words. 'I would never normally ask this sort of thing, never in a million years, but I do need your help.'

'Of course,' I say. 'Anything.'

'It's just been driving me mad, feeling as if I missed all the signs. The police are supposed to be finding out but I don't know what's happened with that, or if they're not telling me, I'm not sure.'

It feels like I've arrived in the middle of a conversation, maybe one she's been having with herself.

'I'm afraid Connor's been very reticent about everything, we've tried to get him to talk about Saturday night but he just shuts us down every time.'

'You're a doctor at the Orchard Healthcare Practice, aren't you? A GP?'

'Yes,' I say cautiously. 'That's right. Before that I was at a practice in the city centre.'

The click of a door closing reaches me down the phone line and the echoes disappear, the texture of the background quieter, more intimate.

For a moment I wonder if we've been cut off.

'Cathy?' I say into the silence. 'Are you still there?'

'Yes,' she says quietly. 'Yes, I'm still here. Sorry.'

'I can't imagine how hard these last few days have been for you.'

'The thing is, Andy, there's just so much we don't know, so much the police can't or won't tell us.' She exhales, a deep, shuddering breath. 'So much about Emily that we didn't know. About what she's been going through. And one of the things that's been doing my head in, is not knowing whether Emily's been . . . taking anything.' Her voice cracks. 'Without my knowledge.'

She stops there, the question out in the open now, and suddenly I understand why she was so quick to respond to my message.

'You mean drugs?'

'I mean whether she had been prescribed anything to help with her moods, her anxiety.' She hesitates again, another heavy sigh coming down the phone line. 'Anything like . . . Prozac or whatever. Antidepressants. You hear of so many kids being prescribed them now and I've always been glad that my three managed to avoid going down that road, but then I wondered whether or not Em might have hidden it from me? Kept it to herself?'

'Cathy, I—'

'We're both registered at the Orchard, at your practice, have been since Emily was a newborn. My twins say we should have gone private by now, but I've always loved the NHS, loved what it's done for me and I'll never turn my back on it. Only now it's killing me, not knowing if Emily's been reaching out to someone else to help, talking to a doctor instead of me. Not knowing if I missed the signs that she was struggling.' Her voice wobbles again, on the verge of tears. 'I just need to know.'

She leaves the question there, setting it down in the silence between us like an offering.

The right answer to this question is obvious. And yet I can feel my resolve wavering, bending like a sapling in a storm, though this is a line I have never crossed before. Perhaps I could make this one exception to put her mind at rest, to help with this one small thing? Emily has never been my patient but all practice records are held centrally – the computer right here on my desk was all I needed, with a few keystrokes I could access Emily's full medical record and answer her mother's question, maybe give her some small measure of peace. After all, I had offered my help, volunteered it, and were these not exceptional circumstances?

I look up and my eyes come to rest on the framed photograph on my desk, a family shot taken on the beach in Turkey last year. Laura and Harriet in the centre, Connor and me on either side, tanned and happy, sunlight glinting off the Mediterranean behind us. All with our arms around each other, in our best clothes, poshed up before dinner on the last night of the holiday.

'I'm really sorry, Cathy . . .' I say finally, feeling like a fraud for offering my help and then turning her down. 'I can't do that. I'm bound by patient confidentiality and I'm not allowed to pass on that kind of information, even within a family.'

A pause, an exhaled breath, before she replies. 'Of course.' Her voice is smaller, quieter, as if she knew this would be the response. 'I understand.'

'I'm sorry,' I say again. 'I wish I could help, I really do.'

'No, I do understand. You're right, I shouldn't have asked. It was wrong of me. It's me who should be apologising, don't know what I was thinking.'

'Let me talk to the other practice partners, see if the police have been in touch already. Maybe I can push things along a little bit.'

It seems hopelessly inadequate considering the desperation of her plight, and I feel as if I've let her down. She thanks me anyway, following up with another question.

'There is one other thing, actually,' she says quickly. 'I'd normally do it myself but everything is so crazy and we all want to be here for Emily, to be at home for when there's an update from the police.'

'Tell me,' I say. 'I want to help.' And I do. It is, after all, why I love my job and why I chose medicine in the first place. Why I decided when I was Harriet's age that what I wanted more than anything else was to be a doctor. To help people.

She tells me. I check my watch: almost an hour before the clinical team meeting. I have one home visit to fit in before then, but it's in the same direction.

'No problem,' I say. 'I can be at your house in forty minutes.'

39

Satellite trucks, white vans and various other cars are parked up and down The Avenue so I have to leave my Renault half a dozen houses away and walk up, the sealed paper bag in my hand. As I get closer and see how many people are gathered there, I almost turn on my heel, but it feels like a sudden one-eighty would be even more awkward with an audience like this. The scrum of media outside Cathy's house has tripled or quadrupled in size since yesterday: photographers, camera crews and reporters mill about on the pavement by the Ruskins' front gate, aiming lenses at the front windows, scrolling phones, making calls or talking among themselves. Waiting for something – the next development, the next new angle – to feed the ever-hungry mouth of twenty-four-hour rolling news. I'm a little taken aback by the size of the press pack, but then I hadn't really appreciated the magnitude of Cathy's fame until now.

Yesterday the gate across the drive was open. Today it is firmly shut, vertical steel bars reaching seven feet tall and ending in decorative spear points, barring my way onto the drive. I sense some of the journalists turning towards me, stirrings of interest as it becomes clear I'm not a rubber-necking neighbour.

'Over here, my friend,' one of them says and – on instinct – I turn and find myself looking straight down the lens of a camera as he fires off three quick shots, *click-click-click*, before I can turn away again.

I find a keypad and press the call button, feeling exposed, surrounded, curious eyes on me from all sides. Finally, the gate clicks open, and as soon as I step through, it starts to swing shut again. Shouted questions from behind follow me down the drive, words overlapping.

'How's the family holding up?'

'Does Cathy have a message for her fans?'

'Can you confirm whether a ransom demand has been received?'

There is a small CCTV camera on the edge of the house, and another directly over the front door. I'm reaching up to press the doorbell when the wide door swings open, Cathy beckoning me inside and shutting it quickly as I step through. She's still wearing the pale blue T-shirt she had on for the press conference, dark hair tied back from a face lined with worry and exhaustion.

'Thanks for coming.' Her voice is softened with fatigue. 'I appreciate it.'

She leads me towards the back of the house, a hallway that opens up into a large kitchen-cum-dining area on one side, high stools pulled up to a black granite island and a long glass-topped table in the far corner surrounded by a dozen chairs. On the other side, a sunken lounge area full of low sofas, cushions and a huge wall-mounted TV showing *Sky News* with the volume low. Blinds are pulled across the skylights and lowered against the windows, cutting the natural light from this high-ceilinged space and muting it into shadow, accentuating the air of tension and strain. Two young women sit barefoot and close together on one of the sofas, absorbed in their phones, dark hair long and loose, their faces eerily similar. Even though I've seen the pictures on Instagram and I know Cathy's two elder daughters are identical twins, it's still disconcerting to see them in real life.

'My other daughters, Megan and Georgia.' Cathy lowers her voice, her eyes red. 'They're … really struggling. We all are, to be honest. Just waiting, waiting to hear something. Waiting for a phone call or a knock on the door.'

I can't think of a single thing to say, other than a variation of what I've just heard called out on the driveway, *How are you holding up?* And I don't feel like I know her well enough to ask this; it just seems like the world's dumbest question. Instead, I put the paper bag on the kitchen counter, the routine prescriptions I've picked up for her family from our in-house pharmacy. The bag is sealed with an adhesive tab but even if it hadn't been, I wouldn't have looked inside.

'Thanks for this,' she says again. 'You're very kind.'

'It's nothing, really.' I shrug. 'The practice pharmacy is just down the hall from my office.'

From here, a little closer, I can see a couple of grey strands sprouting at her hairline, incongruous on her otherwise-perfect head of chestnut brown hair.

'Would have gone myself,' Cathy says, 'but the media pack seems to be growing by the hour and every time I leave the house now it's like running the gauntlet, having the most horrible questions shouted at me, all that aggression.' She glances over at her daughters, then back at me, before gesturing towards an archway off to the left. She leads me into a white-painted study and perches on the edge of a wide desk. 'I can cope with media when they're at arm's length like in the press conference, but not like this. We had one of the photographers standing right outside the lounge this morning, pointing his camera in the window. Megan totally freaked out, Karl ran outside and nearly decked him.'

'Understandable, in the circumstances.'

'I wanted to apologise, by the way.' She lowers her voice further. 'For Karl, the way he talked to you up at Beacon Hill yesterday. It wasn't right that he said those things but he's very protective of the girls and he can get a bit . . . carried away sometimes.'

'It's fine, really.'

'He bottles it all up, you know? It's not easy being a stepdad but he does a brilliant job with my girls. Especially Emily. The two of them have a really special bond.'

I think of the conversation with my wife last night, of our efforts to dig into Karl's past, an acid burn of shame twisting in my stomach. Maybe I should just tell her about it, here and now? Or think of another way to warn her about Karl's work history, and what it might have led him to?

I do neither.

'It's already forgotten,' I say instead, 'don't worry about it. You're both under an unbearable amount of stress. I can't imagine how hard these last few days have been.'

She gives me a sad smile and changes the subject. 'How's that sweet little dog of yours?'

'Toffee? Still mad as a brush. Loves the summer though, loves the woods.' I smile too, despite everything. 'Sorry about him jumping up at you. He doesn't often do that, it's normally just with people he knows. But he really took a shine to you.'

She waves my apology away and indicates an alcove in the wall by her desk, a black-and-chrome machine that looks like it belongs in a café.

'I've got some fresh coffee on, by the way, would you like one?'

A large numberless clock on the wall says it's nearly 1.45 p.m. I'm already cutting it fine.

'Maybe just a quick one,' I say. 'Black, please.'

She moves to the machine, pressing buttons and placing delicate white china cups as it whirs into action. The aroma of fresh-ground coffee rises around us.

'And about what I asked you earlier, on the phone ... It was wrong of me to put you in that position.' She looks genuinely contrite. 'I shouldn't have asked you. It's just there's so much about Emily that I don't know, that she doesn't tell me anymore.'

'I know exactly what you mean,' I say. 'I guess we always want to know more than our teenagers are willing to tell us.'

The machine clicks to a stop and she holds out a cup to me, the coffee exquisitely dark.

'Maybe it's because she's my youngest, the twins have always said I baby her too much. Give her special treatment, you know? Try too hard to protect her.' Her voice cracks again and she takes a tissue from the box on her desk. 'Obviously I didn't try hard enough.'

I look at her, this woman, this mother, pushed to breaking point by circumstances beyond her control, fighting with every ounce of strength to do whatever she can for her daughter. A wave of sympathy rising through me, sweeping away everything in its path.

I take a deep breath, make a quick decision.

'Actually . . .' *Am I really doing this?*

She cocks her head slightly. 'What?'

Why not? I've already crossed the line.

I take a sip from the china cup, the coffee smooth and strong on my tongue, spurring me forward.

'The question you asked earlier, about what Emily might have been prescribed.' I lower my voice; I can't look at her. 'I did a quick check, and the answer is no. She wasn't.'

And there it is. Almost twenty years as a family doctor and I had broken one of the fundamental rules of the job. It was *that* easy to breach patient confidentiality, just a handful of words and a brief hot flare of shame at the base of my throat. In fact, it's scary how easy it was.

She holds my gaze for a moment, digesting the information, then drops her eyes to her own coffee cup.

'OK,' she says quietly, a tiny trace of relief in her voice. 'Thank you. I just couldn't bear not knowing if she's been struggling. These past few days it seems like I've been finding out so much that Emily's been hiding from us, keeping from me. Things that maybe she would have told me about a couple of years ago.'

I nod, wondering if she'll elaborate, but she doesn't. 'I know what you mean.'

'Thank you,' she says again. 'I know you're not supposed to . . . divulge those things.'

'It's fine,' I say. 'As long as it stays between the two of us. I just wish there was more I could do.'

She takes a sip of coffee, considering me. 'For what it's worth, I don't agree with what Karl said to you. I don't think your son's . . .

involved. Wouldn't have asked you to come here today if I thought he was. I don't think he's that kind of lad.'

You're certainly in the minority there, I think. After hearing so many people accuse my son, it's strange to hear words of support from *anyone*, let alone Emily's mother.

'I don't think he is either,' I say.

'He's always seemed like a sweet boy to me, whenever he's come to the house.'

Her words bring me up short. 'He's been *here*?'

Cathy nods. 'He was helping Emily with her homework, projects and things, then he went through a phase of bringing her things, like he got tickets for her and Olivia when Rock City had that under-eighteens night a couple of months ago. It was sold out but somehow Connor still managed to get some.'

I search my memory for any mention of a night out at Rock City, but come up blank.

'What did you mean on Sunday, when I asked you if Emily and Connor were in a relationship?'

'What did I say? Sunday seems like years ago.' She considers for a moment. 'I think it was just that Emily has always had lots of friends, lots of . . . attention from boys. Connor gave her attention too but he was always a bit different from the rest, more serious about it.' She gives me a tight smile. 'He kept asking her out, it was obvious he wanted to spend more time with her, but Emily wasn't . . . she wasn't really on the same page. He was keener than her, put it that way.'

I'm about to ask her another question when her phone rings loudly on the desk. She jumps, almost spilling her coffee in her haste to reach it.

'Hello?' She grips the mobile in both hands. 'Yes, this is Cathy Ruskin. Yes, yes, I can talk.'

'I'll get off,' I say quietly, gesturing towards the door. 'Leave you to it.'

She nods briefly before turning her full attention to the call.

I let myself out.

40

Cameras click as I walk down the drive but I keep my head down until I'm almost at the gate. It's only then that I see the throng of assembled media are not actually pointing their cameras in my direction but are focused instead on a couple of teenage girls, journalists surrounding them on the pavement like celebrities on the red carpet. I recognise one of the girls from her yearbook photo: Olivia de Luca, holding a photograph of Emily that's been blown up to A3 size. The other girl holds a large sheet of paper with the address of the *Find Emily* Facebook page, the hashtag and the police number to call with information. The two of them are dwarfed by the press pack, at the barrage of cameras gathered for this impromptu photo shoot. I'm just glad the media are distracted as I slip out through the gate.

Cathy's comment is still fresh in my mind as I reach my car. *For what it's worth. I don't think your son's involved.* A few kind words from a woman under unbearable strain, at a time when accusations are flying left and right. She didn't have to say that; she didn't have to say anything. Most people in her situation would be too wrapped up in their own fears to think of anyone else. The kindness of it, the generosity of spirit, feels remarkable – a tiny chink of light in the darkness of the last few days.

A selfish part of me hopes she might have said as much to the police, too.

I check my watch. I'll need to hurry to make it for the clinical staff meeting, if it's delayed it will knock on into this afternoon's list. Long experience has taught me that once you get behind with your morning or afternoon clinic, it's almost impossible to catch up. I look at my phone. There's a message from my colleague Sohail reminding me of the imminent meeting chaired by our irascible boss, the practice's lead partner Dr Henry Fraser. I type a quick reply.

On my way. Back in ten mins

I'm unlocking my car when a voice calls from behind me.

'Dr Boyd?'

One of the press pack has peeled off from the rest and has followed me back to my car. A skinny guy in his late forties, receding brown hair buzz-cut short, eyes hidden behind Wayfarer sunglasses. Dark trousers and a short-sleeved white shirt, the strap of a scuffed leather messenger bag slung across his chest. He looks vaguely familiar; I think he was one of the first journalists here when I drove by yesterday.

'Sorry.' I hold a hand up to him. 'I'm in a real hurry.'

'Can I have a word? It won't take a minute.'

I shake my head. 'Now's not a good time, I really have to go.'

He pushes his sunglasses up onto the top of his head, squinting against the brightness of the day.

'My name's Chris Dineen, I'm with the *Nottingham Post*.' He sticks out a hand to shake across the bonnet of my car, but I don't take it. He drops the hand back to his side. 'Just wanted to have a quick chat about Emily Ruskin's disappearance.'

'Not sure that would be a very good idea,' I say.

I get into the driver's seat and pull the door shut, the trapped air inside hot and stuffy. The reporter's face appears at the passenger window, still talking though I can't hear what he's saying. Something occurs to me and I open the window halfway.

'How do you know my name, anyway?'

He shrugs. 'Saw you here yesterday, did a little bit of asking around. Your son's one of Emily's close friends, right?'

I start the car, the engine rumbling into life, air con blowing. 'I really have to go.'

'Listen, it can be on the record, off the record, just for background like I said – whatever you want.' He reaches into his messenger bag. 'Here's my number if you change your mind.'

His hand comes through the window and drops a business card onto the passenger seat. The blue and yellow logo of the *Nottingham Post* and his name below it. *Christian Dineen, Crime Correspondent.* An email address and mobile number, but no landline.

'Thanks.'

'Alexander Saxton is a pretty interesting guy, right? Saw you talking to him on his doorstep yesterday.'

I frown. 'Are you spying on me?' I put on my sunglasses. 'Or him?'

Dineen checks over his shoulder to make sure no one else is nearby, then leans a little closer to my open car window. 'Anything about him that struck you as a bit odd? Anything he said?'

My phone pings with another message from Sohail at the surgery.

Meeting about to start. Henry already looks pissed off

'Sorry,' I say to Dineen. 'Got to go, I'm late for a meeting.'

He's saying something else but it's lost as I buzz the window up the rest of the way.

I put the car in gear and pull away, leaving him standing on the pavement in the blazing afternoon sun.

41

HARRIET

There were a *lot* of pictures.

A lot of images, never mind all the videos, stories, reels, comments, highlights, links and shares to investigate as well.

But Harriet didn't mind. She was patient. She imagined she was Hermione in *Harry Potter and the Chamber of Secrets*, when there was a monster roaming around Hogwarts at night and Hermione had to find out what it was. To discover its secrets.

That's what she was doing: trying to identify the monster.

And to find the monster, she had to find the pattern, to see where it was broken.

It had taken her a long while, a lot of trawling, but she was smart enough to know you never solved puzzles like this head-on. It was like writing lines of code; it was never obvious, never right in front of you. If it was obvious, everyone would be able to do it. *No.* You always had to go around the side, through the back door, find that one thing they'd overlooked. The one thing they'd forgotten.

She read a lot. She knew. They didn't get that big Chicago gangster on murder, after all. They got him for not paying his taxes.

She scrolled back to the start and watched the video again, all the way through. Checked back to the others, to make doubly sure she wasn't mistaken.

This meant *something*. She was sure of it.

Now she just needed to take the next step.

She'd already downloaded what she needed and had the email ready with its sneaky link. She was pleased with the subject line of the email too – it was pretty irresistible. 'CCTV footage of Emily Ruskin'.

She checked the wording one last time, and pressed *send*.

42

I hurry into the clinical team meeting ten minutes late, met with a glare of unconcealed annoyance from Henry as I take the last seat at the big conference table. I open up the agenda on my tablet and try to pick up the thread of what's being discussed as he drones on about protocols and new NHS guidelines coming into effect later this month. But it's only a few minutes before I'm distracted, my thoughts pulled towards Cathy Ruskin, her daughter, my son and the events of the last forty-eight hours. Wondering again if I'd missed any warning signs, any clues in Connor's behaviour over the last few weeks. Trying to work out if there was a way – a discreet way – of testing the vials of liquid we found in his room. Maybe Laura was mistaken; maybe they weren't drugs at all but just dummies, sugar water or something packaged up to look like something more valuable, more potent. But short of turning them in anonymously to the police, or taking one myself, I couldn't think of a way to do it.

I'm glad to finally escape the meeting and get back to my afternoon list. My last patient of the day is a no-show. Jason Corker, twenty-two, his record sparsely populated apart from asthma and a handful of minor childhood ailments, a recent history of making appointments that he did not show up for. I log another FTA to add to the rest on his file – *failed to attend* – and close it down. In theory we operated a three-strikes policy, three missed appointments in a row earned you a stern letter warning of further consequences, but in reality we had to be flexible and I hated to see patients getting kicked off our list, serial no-show or not.

There are some more notes I have to write up before finishing for the day, further observations of a couple of patients in particular and some emails from hospital consultants to whom I had referred patients. Reaching into my briefcase, my hand finds the sharp-edged business card I had been handed a few hours ago by Christian Dineen of the *Post*. Instead of finishing up my notes I find myself mulling over our brief conversation, his interest in Alexander Saxton. The reporter's parting shot, just before I'd pulled away.

Anything about him that struck you as a bit odd? Anything he said?

I had called Laura about it earlier, after the team meeting finally wound up.

'Do you remember yesterday,' I said. 'I talked to Drew Saxton's dad, at his house?'

'What about him?'

'There was something odd about what he said. Something's just reminded me of it. He said: "*It's no secret your boy was somewhat obsessed with her.*" Those were his exact words. I didn't quite register it at the time, but I'm sure that's how he said it.'

'So?' Laura said. 'We know Connor was keen on her.'

'He used past tense. *Was* obsessed.'

She had paused before replying. 'Maybe he just meant . . . in the sense that it was a school thing, like a temporary crush.'

'Maybe.' But I'm not sure I believe that.

I switch my computer off and start to clear my desk. During clinic, I normally kept my phone on do-not-disturb mode, all its functions disabled apart from phone calls and texts so I could focus on my patients. I switch it back to normal function now, all the greyed-out icons shifting back to full colour as messages and personal emails drop in. An email from Kay Barber-Lomax, the lawyer I'd engaged, confirming my appointment with her at 5.30 p.m. A text from Laura reminding me she's gone with Harriet to the Showcase Cinema and will be back about 6 p.m.

Connor had been asleep when I left for work this morning so I'd messaged him at lunchtime, asking him if he was OK and what he was doing today. Reminding him that I would pick him up from home for the appointment with Kay Barber-Lomax. He hadn't let me have another look at the injuries on his face, to check they were healing OK.

It tears me up that he wants to keep me at arm's length.

I want to keep an eye on him but don't want him thinking I am breathing down his neck. His reply to my lunchtime message had been short and to the point.

Taking Toffee and Chester for walk

He was still officially grounded, but walking the dogs was our one concession for the day. On my way out to the car park, I dial his mobile. A shuffling, echoing noise comes down the line when he finally picks up.

'Hello?'

'Connor, it's Dad. How are you doing, are you OK?'

'Yeah.'

'How's your head?'

'All right.'

'We've got that meeting with the lawyer at five thirty, remember? I'm just leaving work now but it's a quick turnaround so you need to be ready to go when I get home, all right?'

'I *know*, Dad.'

'What have you been doing today?'

'Not much.'

'Where are you?'

'At home.' There is a hint of teenage exasperation in his voice. 'Obviously.'

'Have you heard from any of your friends?'

From his end of the line comes the two-tone ding-dong of our doorbell, muted by distance but still instantly familiar.

'Hang on a sec,' he says. More of the shuffling, echoing noise as he goes to answer the front door, the line still open on his mobile.

I hear the click and squeak of the door as it's opened. I press my own phone closer and stick a finger in my other ear to mask the noise of the street at my end. A disembodied conversation reaches me, as if I'm listening to my son talking to a woman at the other end of a long tunnel.

Are your parents at home?

No.

Are you on your own?

Yes.

Detective Sergeant Shah is at my house.

In my mind's eye I imagine her flanked by DC Harmer in suit and tie, solid and unsmiling.

My first thought is that they've found Emily Ruskin, that she's OK and that's what they've come to tell us. *Would they come to the house to do that?* Then a flicker of fear pulses through me as I realise Connor is at home on his own with the police at the front door. I'm a fifteen-minute drive away, Laura and Harriet are at the cinema with their phones likely switched to silent. My son is alone. Unprotected.

Another thought hits me like a blast of icy water.

The drugs.

What if they search the house? What if they have a warrant to go through everything? Where did Laura hide them? She didn't actually tell me, although I have a pretty good idea where they'll be. *Shit.* I should have moved them, should have taken them myself.

Should have got rid of them.

'Connor?' I say. He doesn't respond.

DS Shah's voice returns and I strain to hear what she's saying to my son on the doorstep.

'Connor,' she says. 'Remember me, from Sunday? DS Shah from Notts Police. New evidence has come to light with regard to Emily Ruskin and we'd like to talk to you about it at the station. Why don't you get your shoes and we can take you down there now, get this sorted out?'

My son's reply is a deep mumble, indistinct words not picked up by his phone.

'Connor!' I'm almost shouting now. 'Connor! Let me talk to her.'

His voice finally returns to my ear, soft and hesitant. 'Dad?'

'Let me talk to her, mate,' I say. 'Give her your phone.'

A rustle as the mobile is handed over.

'Hello?' DS Shah's voice is loud and clipped. 'Who am I speaking to?'

'Connor's dad,' I say, feeling a powerful lurch of helplessness. 'What's going on? He's a minor, a child. Are you arresting him?'

'We have a warrant to search your property, Dr Boyd, and we're going to drive your son to Central Police Station for further questioning. Are you able to meet us there?'

43

I ring Kay Barber-Lomax on the hands-free while I'm en route, asking her to meet us at the police station instead of her office. By the time I fight my way through early rush hour traffic, she's already there, talking on the phone in the car park beside a coral-blue Audi TT, all business in a dark grey skirt suit, immaculate chestnut-brown hair falling stylishly to her shoulders. Her heels give her an extra three inches but she still can't be much over five feet tall.

We've only met once before at a barbecue held by a mutual friend, but she seems to recognise me, waving me over to her car as she hangs up the phone.

After introductions, I gesture towards the heavy double doors of the police station. 'Should we go in? They're waiting for us.'

'They can wait a little bit longer,' she says, hitting the car remote to unlock the doors of the sports car. 'And besides, walls have ears in my experience. Let's have a quick chat first.'

She listens as I give a brief recap of the situation, asks me how Connor has been, then takes me through his legal options for today. She doesn't seem fazed when I relate how few questions he was willing to answer on Sunday, how often he blanked the detectives with *No comment*.

'Much less likely to dig himself a hole that way,' she says matter-of-factly, 'than if he gives them chapter and verse.'

'But he's not *done* anything. He's got nothing to hide.'

'Of course not, Dr Boyd,' she says, reaching for a slim black leather briefcase on the back seat.

'Shall we go in now?'

Ten minutes later we're being buzzed through a security door by the duty sergeant and led into the bowels of the station by DC Harmer. The solicitor is slightly ahead of me, her heels clicking confidently on the tiled floor, and it feels better to be here with her. She clearly knows her way around, knows some of the officers here, nodding a greeting to a couple of the detectives as we pass. The station is busier today, a weekday shift, phones ringing and doors open, a background hum of conversation and activity.

It's the second time in three days I've been here, the second time in my life. I'd like nothing better than for it to be the last.

DC Harmer leaves the three of us alone in an interview room and Barber-Lomax introduces herself to my son, giving him broadly the same spiel she'd given to me in her car, advising him that there is nothing wrong – *nothing wrong at all* – with a 'no comment' response. That it was better to be safe than sorry, if he was in any doubt whatsoever about a line of questioning. Seeing him here again, pale and subdued as he waits for whatever is coming, makes me want to fold him into a hug and tell him it will all be OK. But I won't, I can't. Not here anyway, not now. When Barber-Lomax asks if he has any questions, he gives a sullen shake of his head.

'Just want to get it over with,' he says.

The two detectives return and we sit at the small table bolted to one wall, five plastic chairs crowded too close to each other. The atmosphere is cooler, more formal, than it had been on Sunday.

Today they are all business.

DS Shah turns on the recorder and cautions Connor, but she doesn't start with a question. Instead she takes a series of colour 10 by 8 inch photographs from a plastic wallet and lays them on the table one by one. She wears wedding and engagement rings, I notice absently, a plain platinum band and a small diamond.

'Can't show you the actual exhibits because they've all been sent to the lab for testing,' Shah says. 'But do you recognise any of these, Connor?'

Connor and I lean a little closer to get a better look. The first two shots appear to have been taken outside on the ground, photographed where they've been found. They have numbered yellow evidence markers alongside them.

The first image shows a provisional driving licence with reddish-brown smears down one side. The second one looks like a long fingernail, patterned with silver stars against a pink background.

A third image shows a piece of white cotton clothing, a top or a thin cardigan, inside a plastic evidence bag. It looks very similar – if not identical – to the one my brother found in the woods when we were looking for Zac.

'All of these items have been recovered from Beacon Hill Woods since Sunday morning,' Shah says. 'And all of them give us grave cause for concern.'

I lean a little closer to read the credit-card sized driver's licence. *Joshua Rice*, a name I don't recognise, a local address, a date of birth that would make him eighteen years old. The head and shoulders shot might bear a passing resemblance to Connor, if you didn't look too closely. The reddish-brown smears look like dried blood.

I frown, confused as to what this has to do with Connor.

Shah taps the first photograph with her index finger. 'We've spoken to Mr Rice. According to him, you purchased this from him for twenty-five pounds a couple of months ago. I'm assuming to use as a fake ID for buying alcohol?' Connor gives an almost imperceptible nod. 'A forensic search team found it up at Beacon Hill yesterday. Did you know you'd mislaid it?'

'No,' Connor says quietly.

'The blood,' Shah says, 'is a match to Emily Ruskin.'

She lets that sink in for a moment.

'Your ID,' she says again. 'Her blood. Can you explain that?'

Connor looks as if he might be sick.

'No,' he breathes.

'Speak up, please. For the tape.'

'No,' he says a little louder. 'I can't.'

Shah points to the third photo, on the right. The white top inside the evidence bag.

'This was actually handed in by your uncle, Robert Boyd. He handled it and removed it from the scene on Sunday morning, which is less than ideal in terms of chain of evidence and avoiding cross-contamination. But preliminary analysis has identified Emily's blood on the fabric and we believe there may be DNA from another individual as well. Initial results were not conclusive but we're getting it re-tested as a priority.'

Shah taps the second photograph, which sits in the middle of the three, in the middle of the table. 'Now we believe this—'

Barber-Lomax cuts her off. 'What you *believe*, Officer, is between you and your god. We are here to talk about the facts.'

DS Shah throws a withering look at the solicitor, who returns a small smile. These two seem to know each other professionally, as if they've sparred like this before, and it's clear there's no love lost between them.

'The *evidence* suggests that this—' the detective taps the photo of the star-painted nail again '—is an acrylic nail extension from a set that Emily Ruskin had applied to her own nails, the day before she went missing. We've recovered two sets of DNA from under it.'

No one speaks. No one moves.

'The first DNA sample is a match to Emily,' Shah continues, her tone neutral. 'The second is a match to you.'

'Me?' Connor blurts, blinking fast.

'How did your DNA get under her acrylic nail, Connor?'

He frowns but says nothing, eyes fixed on the colour photograph on the table in front of him.

Shah looks at him. 'One of her nails broke off when she was defending herself against you, didn't it?'

'I don't know,' he says in a small voice.

'She fought back, didn't she?'

Shah points to the three short red lines running in parallel across the back of Connor's left hand.

'Is that how you got the scratches?'

'She was—'

'Connor,' the solicitor interrupts sharply. 'Remember our discussion pre-interview?'

Shah waits for a moment, looking expectantly at Connor. When he doesn't say any more, she adds: 'We've done an initial proof-of-life enquiry on Emily Ruskin over the past twenty-four hours, and everything has come back negative so far. She hasn't used her phone, social media, bank cards, email account, she hasn't messaged anyone or been seen by anyone as far as we can tell. We've found nothing. Her phone drops off the grid at the same time as yours, pinging the same mast near Beacon Hill. Actually at the *exact* same time as phones belonging to you and your cousin, Zac, and a couple of other pupils from your year.'

'Olivia and Drew,' Connor says in a monotone.

'That's right. Those five phones all drop off the grid within a minute of each other. They stay off for a while and then all connect to the network at different points over the next few hours – all except Emily's. Her phone is only powered back on once, yesterday, in circumstances which add to our concerns. As far as *your* movements go, Connor, data from your own mobile contradicts what your parents told us.' She looks pointedly at me, and I feel myself reddening. 'It contradicts the statement given by your parents that you were home just after midnight. According to the network masts your phone was pinging, you switched it off near Beacon Hill Woods shortly after midnight and switched it back on again at 2.17 a.m., still in the woods. Data suggests you powered it off again less than ten minutes later. It was then switched on at 6.59 a.m. after which you visited a number of locations over the next several hours until ultimately you went to Beaufort Terrace in The Park, where you were challenged by patrol officers after acting suspiciously, tried to flee the scene and were arrested.'

He doesn't look at her, doesn't lift his eyes from the table.

'When we met on Sunday,' she continues, 'you weren't especially helpful in finding your friend, a lot of "no comment" answers.' She throws a pointed look at Kay Barber-Lomax. 'So I want to know before we get started – and in light of what I've just shown you, told you – are you going to do that to us again now?'

The solicitor puts a manicured hand on my son's forearm.

'Connor, remember, you don't have to answer.'

My son ignores her. Mumbles something inaudible.

Shah leans forward. 'What's that, Connor?'

'Not anymore.' His voice is not much more than a whisper. 'Not today. It's enough, now.'

'How do you mean, *enough*? Because today it's all starting to sink in? Because you've had time to think about what you've done, to think about Emily and her parents and her family?'

'It was only supposed to be, like, a couple of days.'

'What do you mean?'

Connor licks his dry lips, swallows hard. For a moment no one speaks, the only sounds a muffled conversation from further down the corridor, the distant click of footsteps. My son won't look at me. He won't look at anyone.

'Monday lunchtime,' he says. 'Yesterday. That was when she was supposed to come back.'

44

CONNOR

Sunday 12th June, 12.19 a.m.
Sixty-two minutes before Emily disappears
Beacon Hill Woods

She was the prettiest girl he'd ever seen.

Not just pretty, but properly stunning, like sometimes he could barely even talk when she was there, when they were in a lesson together or in the dining hall. No one else at school even came close to Emily Ruskin. And not just school – she was more beautiful than any actress, any celebrity, anyone on TV or Instagram or anywhere.

She got attention because of who her mum was, but Connor didn't care about any of that. He liked her because of who she was. The way he felt about her . . . he'd never felt like that about anyone before. He'd written songs about her, filled pages of his notebooks, verse after verse of heartfelt stuff he'd not showed to anyone, not even Zac. He didn't even sing the lyrics out loud when he played his guitar, just heard them in his head.

The way she looked at him, sometimes, that slow blink and the little smile that felt like it was just for him. He spent entire lessons thinking about her, couldn't focus on anything else. For the last two years, Connor had sat behind her in geography and IT and these were the high points of his week; sometimes he'd spend most of the hour staring at the faint outline of a lacy bra strap looping over her shoulder beneath the white school shirt.

But now it felt like all of that was about to change. Exams were finished, school was done and nothing would ever be the same. No more shared lessons; probably not even the same sixth-form college. Their paths would diverge, they would drift apart and he would lose her forever.

Even the thought of it made him feel sick.

Connor gazed at her now across the fire, the way her hair fell half across her face, the buttery colour of her skin in the flickering light of the flames, the perfect curve of her neck. The way her eyes shone in the darkness. For a moment it was just the two of them, just him and Emily and no one else, and he wanted so much for that to be true it was like a physical ache in his chest. For the other three to just disappear, to vanish, so he could be alone with her. To be able to tell her how he really felt about her. His heart bumped harder against his ribs at the thought of it.

Drew's obnoxious voice shook him back to reality, an unwelcome reminder of his presence.

'So,' he said. 'What's this big surprise you've got planned, Emily?'

Connor glanced over at the taller boy, his white shirt open a couple of buttons too many, his dark hair clippered almost to the scalp at the sides and back, elegantly messy at the front. It was typical of Drew, he thought, always trying to make out like he was in charge, the big alpha male asserting his dominance. He was the captain of another team in their under-sixteens league, a gobby midfielder who wouldn't think twice about an off-the-ball foul if the ref was looking the other way. Who would fly studs-up into an ankle-snapping tackle one minute, then drop to the ground clutching his head if you came within three feet of him. But he had something, some swagger like he didn't give a shit about getting a red card, or abuse from the other players or their dads, or anything. The only thing he hated was losing.

Whatever it was he had, girls seemed to like it. Emily seemed to like it, Connor thought, as he watched the smile light up her face.

She sat forward, tucking her hair behind both ears.

'OK,' she said. 'What's the best prank you've ever pulled?'

Silence.

'All right, forget that,' she said, waving a hand. She looked around the circle of faces lit by the flickering log fire 'What I mean is, aren't you sick of it? All of you?'

More silence, the only sound a crackle of logs as they snapped on the fire. A bright orange burst of sparks rose up, eddying and circling into the black night air.

'School, you mean?' Connor said.

'Parents. Families. Feeling like you're on show, twenty-four-seven. You've always got to look the right way, to be perfect all the time, to perform, to get top grades in your GCSEs, to live up to what your parents think you should be doing. To never have an off day, never have a time when you can just kick back and not bother about anything. I'm not even supposed to be out tonight. Knowing that everything you do, even if you fuck up this much—' she held her thumb and forefinger a half-centimetre apart '—your parents will find out about it. Everyone always being compared to everyone else. It's like a fucking disease.'

'I can still help you,' Connor said. 'With homework and stuff. Essays. If you want.'

He had picked up bits of this in the last few months, from what Emily had said – as well as the things she hadn't. From the fact that it always seemed to be her sisters front and centre on her mum's Instagram account with Emily mostly in the background. So much of the content was devoted to her sisters – the twins, first year students at Oxford and Cambridge respectively – rather than Emily. The national papers had loved that, these tall, super-brainy identical daughters with their semi-famous mother, who had pulled in six A-star grades between them to secure places studying medicine and English literature at the top two universities in the country.

Everyone made a fuss about how drop-dead gorgeous they were, like two mini-me versions of their mum. But Connor could only see Emily.

'I'm not going to get the grades for sixth-form college,' she said, shaking her head. 'And I'm sick of trying to keep up. Don't you wish you could tell everybody to just do one?'

'I'll drink to that,' Drew said, taking a pull on the bottle. 'Cheers. I tell you what though, this lime vodka is a game-changer.'

Connor had never seen Emily like this. So serious.

'I thought you were doing OK,' he said. 'With your marks and stuff.'

She snorted, her face lit a ghostly orange by the fire. He'd noticed she had eased off on the drinking and had barely touched the joint that was going around the circle, holding up an imperious hand whenever Drew held it out to her. Olivia put the spliff to her lips now, pulling the smoke deep before handing it to Connor. Connor took a drag, felt it bloom in his lungs, the fluttering lightness in his stomach, his chest, inside his skull, willing himself not to cough as he exhaled a blue-grey cloud into the night sky. Drew's dark eyes glittered as he reached for the joint again. Every time he leaned forward to take it, he sat back down on the log a little closer to Emily until now he was right next to her, their legs touching.

Seeing them so close together made it feel like someone was reaching into Connor's chest, a fist slowly closing around his heart.

Emily was getting into her stride now. 'Don't you ever want to be in control, for once? To be the one calling the shots?'

Drew rested a hand on her knee. 'What are you talking about?'

'I'm talking about parents. *Take my mother, for example. She's built this whole TV persona around being the perfect mother with these perfect twin daughters who never got stoned on a school night and messed up an exam, never dropped a grade, never screwed up anything. And of course every interview with her makes it sound like she's some kind of parenting genius instead of the actual truth that she's a complete fucking control freak, and her fans lap it up.' She swipes a tear angrily away. 'At first I used to like it, being different to my sisters, looking different. Took me ages to realise that I've always been the extra, the fucking hanger-on, the one at the edge of the picture. The* mistake. *Getting in the way. Letting the side down.'*

'Emily,' Connor said quietly, 'you're not any of those—'

She cut him off.

'Took me a while to realise it was a game I couldn't win, I could never win. Not unless I changed the rules, made it about something she couldn't control. Showed her what life could be like, if she got her wish. And as an extra bonus, I get to show everyone my perfect mother isn't so fucking perfect after all.'

'Wait,' Drew said, holding a hand up. 'You're not going to blow the fucking school up, are you? Not saying I'd be against it, but it would be . . . major.'

'No, Drew, we're not blowing anything up,' Emily said. 'Stop thinking like such a lad. I'm talking about a giant wake-up call to our families and to the school and all the bullshit constant pressure about GCSEs and grades and uni and careers and the future.'

In the moment of silence that followed, a noise reached them through the trees. A soft rustling, almost imperceptible. In the day-time it would have merited no attention at all. But now, all five of them turned towards the sound, staring into the darkness.

'What the hell?' Connor said softly. His eyes still burned with after-images of the fire, the woods around them totally, impossibly black.

'It's just the wind.' Drew jabbed at the fire with a stick, sending more orange sparks spiralling up into the darkness. 'No need to shit your pants.'

'The wind's dropped,' Zac said, indicating the smoke rising straight up into the dark. 'Look.'

'Must be one of those escaped warthogs from the farm then.'

Olivia scanned the darkness. 'What are you talking about?'

'Like a pig but crazier,' Drew said, index fingers curved at his mouth. 'With big old tusks.'

'God, are you serious?' Olivia said. 'I hate pigs.'

Zac was shaking his head. 'He's messing with you. Ignore him, it's an urban myth.'

Drew turned towards the noise, made a clicking noise with his tongue. 'Here piggy piggy piggy! Come on!'

Emily slapped him on the shoulder. 'Shut up, Drew, you moron!'

He gave her a wounded look. 'What's the big deal?'

Silence settled on the woods again, as they all turned back to the fire.

'So,' Emily said finally, 'who can keep a secret? Who's in? Livvy is my partner in crime, my BFF, she's already done her bit by meeting us with all the stuff.' She indicated the rucksack, the bottle of vodka, the fire. 'So who else is staying? 'Cos if you're too scared you can run home to your mummies and daddies now and leave the fun to us.'

Connor caught Zac's eye and saw only contempt there. His cousin had never liked Emily, he thought she was superficial and fake. But that was only because he didn't really know her. He didn't know the real girl, underneath. He and Zac tended to avoid talking about her because it only ended in a disagreement.

Emily came around the fire and sat down next to Connor, tilting her head to rest on his shoulder.

'My lovely Connor, you'll help me, won't you? And keep my secrets?'

Connor could feel the heat from her leg beside his, smell her light musky perfume, berries and vanilla. If he turned his head, he could kiss her if he wanted to. His heart was doing the weird thudding thing and there was a lightness in his stomach that made it feel like he was lifting up, floating. Just to have her so close, to feel her touch, it was almost impossible to think straight.

'Yeah,' he said, clearing his throat. 'I'll stay, if you want.'

'Me too,' Drew said immediately.

Emily clapped her hands.

'Perfect!' she said. 'Zac? Not going to abandon your cousin, are you?'

Zac looked at Emily briefly before his eyes flicked back to Connor, a silent exchange between them. Both of them knowing what his answer would be, even before the words had formed in his mouth.

'OK.' He shrugged. 'I'm up for whatever. What exactly is it that you're going to do, though?'

She tucked a stray strand of blonde hair behind her ear, flashed them a nervous smile.

'I'm going to disappear.'

The silence that greeted her announcement was broken only by the crackle of the fire.

'So,' she prompted finally. 'What do you think?'

Connor frowned. 'What do you mean, "disappear"?'

'Exactly that: just vanish for a bit. Be mysterious. Go off the grid, offline for a couple of days.'

Connor studied her across the fire, this beautiful, amazing girl, seeing a brand-new side to her. A side he never even knew existed before tonight.

'What about your mum, though? Won't she go mental?'

'She'd go mental if I walked in on Sunday morning,' Emily said. 'By Monday lunchtime it'll be a whole different story, she might even be pleased to see me for once. She might be able to talk to me without giving me shit about exams and A levels and not working hard enough. When I walk back in to the house, maybe she'll appreciate me for once. Make her realise what she might have lost.'

Drew whistled under his breath.

'Jesus, Emily, that's . . . cold.' He smiled wolfishly at her. 'It's kind of cool, though. I like it. But . . . what? You're just going to climb a tree and wait until Monday? Hope no one finds you before then?'

'No, I'm not going to climb a tree, Drew.'

Her plan, she told them, was to hike through to the far side of the woods where she had hidden her bike the day before, then cycle into town to a rental property her family owned on Beaufort Terrace. There were no tenants at the moment, so it was empty – and her mother, she announced, would never think to look there.

Emily stood up.

'So, that's it!' She held her hands out, like an actor welcoming an ovation. 'The best prank, the best disappearing act ever. They're going to talk about this for years – and you guys all get to be a part of it.'

Olivia stood too and looked nervously at her friend, a bottle of peach schnapps in her hand. 'You're sure you want to go through with this?'

'I'm one hundred per cent sure, Livvy.' Emily pulled her into a hug. 'Hey, you're shivering,' she said, rubbing Olivia's back. 'What's the matter? There's nothing to worry about.'

'Just . . . nervous. Can't believe this is actually going to happen. That you're going to be . . .'

'It'll be fine.' Emily released her from the hug, holding her friend by the shoulders. 'And it's only till Monday. Then I'll be back from the dead!' She flashed a wide smile, her teeth white in the firelight.

Something passed across Olivia's face, an expression that Connor couldn't identify. Then it was gone.

'Yeah,' she said quietly. 'Then you'll be back.'

'We should have a toast!' Emily said, looking around for the bottle.

Connor handed her a drink as Emily talked excitedly about her plan and how she expected things to unfold tomorrow – and how they were all sworn to secrecy until the big reveal.

Connor listened in silence, accepting a drink passed to him, thoughts tumbling through his head. Thoughts of this amazing girl and how close they were right now, of how they might never be closer. Of how everything was going to change. How Emily was going to disappear tonight, just like she was going to disappear from his life, slowly but surely over the summer now that school was finished. The thought of losing her was unthinkable, impossible – that they might part ways before he could tell her how he really felt.

Maybe tonight would be his last chance.

45

Once Connor starts talking, it seems he can't stop. His relief visible in the relaxation of his shoulders, the sadness in his eyes.

Emily had planned it all out.

She was convinced her GCSEs had been a disaster. Her family had no idea how far behind she'd got, how much she'd struggled with a million distractions. She couldn't bring herself to admit it, not with the constant comparisons to her high-flying sisters, spoken or unspoken.

'She's not like the twins,' Connor says. 'It's just not as easy for her. Her sisters got grade nines in every single GCSE they took, and A stars in every single A level. How do you compete with that? So Emily couldn't tell her mum, or her sisters. Didn't want to admit how bad things had got. Thought if she disappeared for a bit, gave them a shock, they'd see past all of that. They'd see *her*, for once.'

'What about her mother's partner?' DC Harmer says. 'Could she not have talked to him as a neutral, someone a little bit outside the family unit?'

'Karl?' Connor gives him a strange look. 'No. *Definitely* not him.'

'What makes you say that?'

'Have you met him? He'd be the last person she'd confide in.'

'He didn't like her?'

'Sort of the opposite of that, if you know what I mean.' He crosses his arms over his chest. 'From what I heard, anyway.'

Harmer makes a note on his notebook, both detectives letting the silence gather until it fills every corner of the small interview room.

'What *did* you hear, Connor?' Shah says finally. 'Are you suggesting that Karl Crosby had inappropriate feelings for his step-daughter?'

Connor reddens. 'Nothing. Forget it.'

'No, go on. We're interested, and it could be relevant.'

Connor shakes his head.

Shah waits again, patient and still, until it becomes clear that nothing else is forthcoming. She turns to another page of her notebook.

'So why did Emily not just do this on her own?' she said. 'Take herself off somewhere? Why did she need you four?'

'Don't know.'

'I think you do. I think you know exactly what it was all about. You helped her with this plan, you helped her put it together and you helped her carry it out. Was it your idea in the first place, for her to go off into the woods on her own?'

'*No,*' he says, frowning. 'Of course not.'

The detective is shaking her head. 'I don't believe you, Connor.'

'She wouldn't have listened to me even if it had been my idea.'

'So how did you all come to be up there in—'

'She wanted an audience, OK?' His voice rises for a moment before he gets it back under control. 'She wanted to be *seen*, to have people there. To be listened to, for once in her life.'

I remember something Harriet had said to me recently, when I insisted that Toffee had once sat patiently when I let him off the lead, rather than bolting into the distance. Whenever I said any-thing of which she was a bit sceptical. *Pictures or it didn't hap-pen, Dad.* If it wasn't witnessed, photographed, shared, posted or commented on, then it might as well have not happened at all. Was that what this was? An audience to validate Emily's cry for help?

Shah says: 'So Emily wanted to be the centre of attention for once? Not her mum. Not her super-brainy sisters. A captive audi-ence of admirers.'

Connor gives a reluctant nod. 'I guess.'

'You're one of her admirers, aren't you? You've got a crush on her.'

He shrugs, not meeting anyone's eye. Finally, another reluctant nod.

'But it was more than that, wasn't it?' Her tone softens. 'How long have you been in love with her?'

Another shrug.

'She knew, didn't she?' Shah continues. 'She knew you'd keep her secret, she knew you'd do anything for her. Even if it meant getting arrested.'

'It was never supposed to come to that.'

'And yet here we are.' She gestures to the small interview room. 'She's vanished and left you to pick up the pieces. How does that make you feel?'

'No one was supposed to get arrested. But I guess we didn't realise how much pull her mum would have after that first appeal on Instagram.'

DS Shah shifts in her seat, her dark eyebrows drawing together slightly.

'We respond to the evidence, Connor. To risk analysis, the specifics of each case and the likelihood of harm coming to those involved.'

I don't say it, but I'm sure I'm not the only one to think it: *Being a mid-list celebrity probably doesn't hurt either.* I wonder, not for the first time, whether Cathy's profile has elevated Emily's disappearance. How things might have unfolded if her mother had been anyone else.

'If any of us *did* get interviewed by the police, we were supposed to just say "no comment" until Monday lunchtime, otherwise it would all be for nothing. We had to keep the story going.'

'You all agreed to lie for her?'

'It wasn't lying,' he says, a heart-breaking naivety in his voice. 'And it's not as if there was any actual crime involved, so we couldn't get in to trouble as long as no one said anything.'

DC Harmer flips to another page of his notebook. 'How about when you texted your mum?' he says. 'When you told her you were safely home in time for your curfew? That was a flat-out lie, wasn't it?'

'I didn't want them to worry,' he says quietly. 'And I wanted to be sure that Emily would be OK.'

'Prompting your parents to lie to the police on your behalf.'

Connor's eyes flick briefly across to mine.

'I didn't ask them to do that.'

'And what about your cousin?' Harmer says. 'Didn't he have a curfew?'

'He said his dad would be so drunk by that point that he wouldn't know if Zac was home or not.'

'I don't believe you.' Harmer's voice is as hard as tarmac. 'You're making it up as you go along.'

Abruptly, his phone buzzes on the table in front of him. He checks the display, shows it to his partner, then stands and heads for the door.

'Excuse me,' he says tightly.

As the door clicks shut behind him, Shah says: 'So, Connor, keeping secrets and telling lies, is that right?'

'But no one actually *did* anything,' Connor continues. 'We were just helping her. It wasn't supposed to be like this, she was supposed to be back by now and she'd sort it out with her mum and everything would be OK again.' His voice cracks on the last words. 'Won't it?'

'Connor, we've gathered evidence over the last forty-eight hours that gives us real cause for concern about what *actually* happened in the early hours of Sunday morning. The *truth* – rather than what you've told us.'

'What?' Connor says quietly. 'What are you talking about?'

'You all went up there with her. You enabled her to carry this plan out. You were all part of it.'

He swallows hard. 'I just wanted to help. We all did.'

'Emily was going to make it look like she'd taken herself off somewhere, run away and maybe harmed herself, right? Maybe even killed herself. A cry for help, a shock to get her mum's attention; an elaborate prank to make her think she'd lost Emily forever. Make her parents appreciate her. But here's the thing, Connor.' She leans forward, elbows on the table. 'It's starting to look as if she *did* come to harm.'

46

Connor looks stricken, like a small boy lost in a crowd.

'What are you talking about?' He stares at DS Shah. 'What do you mean?'

'The events you all took part in on Saturday night, the staging of her disappearance, the evidence we've found since. All of it gives me real concern that Emily may have come to grievous harm.'

'No,' he says, his eyes filling with tears. 'That can't be right.'

'Did you hurt her, Connor?'

'No! I would never do that. The last time I saw her she was walking away into the woods, doing what she planned to do. Everyone went their separate ways.' He begins to talk fast again now, the words tumbling out. 'She had it all planned. She was going to get her bike, cycle into town and hide out at the house on Beaufort Terrace. There was, like, renovation work or something going on there, so it didn't have anyone living in it.'

The detective studies him for a moment, a cat studying a mouse.

'Except that's not what happened, is it, Connor? You got rid of your cousin by asking him to cover for you back at home, then looped back and followed her into the woods so you could finally be alone with her. Isn't that right?'

'That's not true, I—'

'I get it,' Shah says, nodding. 'I honestly do. You're a nice lad, but you'd started to realise that being nice doesn't get you very far. Not with girls like Emily Ruskin. They prefer the bad boys, don't they? Boys like Drew, who take the lead, who take control. Who see what they want, go out and take it. They've got that confidence, that charisma.' She pauses for a moment, her voice lowering. 'There was something about him that Emily couldn't resist, wasn't there? You wanted to show her you could be just like Drew, but it went a bit too far, didn't it? Got out of hand. And that's when she fought back, when she scratched you, trying to defend herself.' Shah pauses to let the words land properly. 'Defend herself from you.'

He shakes his head, tears spilling.

'Suspect indicated a negative response,' Shah says. Her voice is softer now, gentler. 'There's one thing I've learned in fifteen years of doing this job, Connor. One thing I can absolutely, one-hundred-per-cent guarantee. And there are not many things you can say that about in life, are there? But this one thing I can promise you.'

I'm expecting her to say *Sooner or later we will solve this*, or maybe something like *We're going to nail the person who did this*, and from the look on his face I can tell Connor's thinking the same thing. He looks desperate, panicked, like a drowning child caught in a riptide who can see the shoreline but knows he's being dragged further away with every stroke. I look to Barber-Lomax, hoping she might jump in, but her face retains the impassive look of someone who's heard this all before.

'What?' my son says in a half-sob.

'You will feel a thousand times better if you just tell us the truth, Connor. You don't have to carry this thing all on your own, it's not fair on you. You don't have to keep it locked up inside. It's not your burden to carry alone.' She pauses for a beat, her voice softening further. 'Just tell me, Connor, get it off your chest. You'll be able to sleep again, eat again, you won't feel like you're going crazy thinking about it twenty-four hours a day. I absolutely *promise* you. All you have to do is tell me what happened up in the woods. What *really* happened.'

She sits back in her chair. Silence. The room holds its breath, as if she's placed a hand grenade in the middle of the table and we're all waiting for it to go off. There's a stinging pain in my palm and I realise my fingernails are digging into the flesh, fists curled tight in my lap.

Connor shakes his head, a small desperate movement. He wipes away tears with the heel of his hand.

'She was—'

'Connor?' The solicitor does jump in now, putting a hand on his arm. 'Remember what I said? You don't have to answer. You're not obliged to say anything at all. OK?'

Shah's voice is still soft. 'Why did we find your DNA under Emily's acrylic nail, Connor? Did it happen when you were struggling with Emily?'

'What?' He looks up. 'No. I wasn't ... I didn't struggle with anyone. I was trying to get him off her.'

'She chose Drew, didn't she? She rejected you, didn't she, Connor? After all you've done to help her, all your feelings for her. But she rejected you when you were all up at Beacon Hill. And you snapped.'

Connor's lips barely move. 'No. After she'd headed off into the woods, all of us went our separate ways.' He tails off. 'Me and Zac had almost got back to my house but then . . . I don't know. There was just something that didn't feel right.'

'What?'

He looks at the table.

'I just had a bad feeling, like something was wrong.'

'A *bad feeling*?' Shah repeats.

'Yes.'

'Based on what?'

Connor swallows hard. 'Dunno, just like a gut instinct or—'

He flinches as the door bangs open and Harmer strides in, his face impassive. He sits back down at the table, shows his phone to DS Shah. There is an image on the screen but I'm too far around the table to make out what it is. The two detectives exchange a look and Harmer nods at DS Shah before sliding the phone into his jacket pocket.

'So,' Shah says, returning her attention to Connor. 'You *did* go back into the woods?'

Connor nods, once. 'But not to . . . do anything. I just wanted to find her, make sure she was OK.'

'Because of this *bad feeling*.' She illustrates the two words with air quotes.

'Yeah.'

'What, like Spiderman with his spider-sense?' Her words are heavy with sarcasm. 'Or maybe a disturbance in the Force?'

'I dunno. Maybe.' He won't look at any of us. 'There are some bits I can't quite remember. Like . . . blank spots in my memory.'

She shakes her head. 'Were you drunk?'

'We'd all had some drinks. But I wasn't, like, really drunk or anything.'

'When you headed back into the woods, why didn't your cousin go with you? Why not the two of you?'

Connor rubs at a faded grey scar on the tabletop, a years-old cigarette burn in the plastic.

'There was no point both of us getting in trouble,' he says quietly. 'And I asked him to cover for me. Go back to mine and pretend to be me until I got back. My dad . . .' He glances up at me, the first time he's looked at me properly since we sat down. 'My dad often comes in to check on us, just stands in the doorway like a weirdo to make sure we've not, like, died in our sleep or whatever. He's done it ever since I can remember. Since me and my sister were little.'

Shah turns to me. 'Is that right, Dr Boyd?'

Her question catches me off-guard. I'm still digesting Connor's rather elaborate answer, the details that Shah had not even really asked for.

'I suppose . . . I do that sometimes, yes.'

She returns her gaze to my son. 'And Zac agreed to cover for you?'

'Of course. He's my cousin, my best mate.' He says it quickly, almost too quickly. 'I'd do the same for him.'

'So it wasn't just because he'd lost his keys?'

Connor shakes his head. 'His dad always leaves a spare under the yellow pot by the back door.'

The detective changes tack. 'Where's Emily's phone, Connor?'

My son looks up, eyes wide. He glances across at the solicitor, then back at DS Shah.

'I don't know.'

'Are you sure?'

'She had a ... plan for it. She asked me to post it for her. She sealed it up in a padded envelope and gave it to me before she set off.'

'*Post* it?' Shah's voice drips with disbelief. 'To where?'

Connor shrugs. 'This place in Norfolk, she said friends of her family owned it but it was a holiday home and would be empty. Emily said she'd scheduled the phone to power on automatically at five on Sunday evening, at which point it would be on its way. And if her mum or anyone else tried to track her, it would send them off on a wild goose chase. Keep everyone guessing for a little bit longer.'

'Why didn't she just post it herself?'

'There's only this one postbox that does a midday Sunday collection but it's on London Road and there's loads of CCTV cameras down there. She didn't want to be spotted. And anyway it was in completely the wrong direction for her.'

'So posting it was a job she allocated to you, was it?'

'Yeah.'

'Except it never arrived in Norfolk, did it?'

Connor shakes his head. The interview room falls silent again. DC Harmer has his arms crossed, a slight frown on his wide fore-head. DS Shah finishes writing something in her notebook.

'When I went back into the woods to look for Emily,' Connor says, 'I was trying to find a way through to the other side where I thought her bike would be. Down by the river and the bridge and that road—'

'Lower Farm Lane?' Shah says.

'Yeah. I was in the middle of the woods walking around, trying to find my way, and it was *so* dark but I thought I saw something, some*one*, a person. Thought maybe it was Emily. I went towards her and that's when it happened.'

'What?'

'I was attacked, from behind,' Connor says.

Hearing him say it brings a painful lump to my throat.

'Someone whacked me on the side of the head,' Connor continues. 'Next thing I knew I was waking up face-down in the leaves, blood in my hair and a splitting headache. And Emily was gone.'

Shah's eyes narrow in suspicion.

'You didn't see or hear anyone else?'

'No.'

'So you're saying you were attacked, but didn't see the person who attacked you? You didn't hear them coming, which direction they came from, whether they were male or female, what they struck you with? They took you completely by surprise?'

'Yes.'

'Hmm.' Shah makes another note on her pad.

After a full minute of leaden silence, Harmer takes out his mobile and shows Connor a picture on the screen. The solicitor and I both lean in for a closer look at the image: an iPhone with a purple case, a slight crack in the screen in the top-right corner. It appears to be inside a clear plastic evidence bag. The screensaver is an image of Emily pouting at the camera, two fingers up in a peace sign, her hair in pigtails.

'Do you recognise this phone, Connor?'

'It's Emily's.'

'You never posted it, did you?' Shah says. 'You didn't do what she asked you to do. You kept it instead. Didn't you?'

'No.' He shakes his head emphatically. 'It was taken from me when I was attacked. I woke up and the padded envelope was gone.'

'And what about the burner phone that Emily had given you, to use on that night?'

'That was gone too.'

'*Really?* That *is* unfortunate. So we can't verify any of what you told us.'

Connor shrugs, a tiny movement of his shoulders.

'That's how it—'

'As you can see from the picture, Connor, we have now recovered Emily's phone. Any idea where we might have found it?'

'No.' His voice is almost inaudible.

'Speak up for the tape, please.'

'No. No idea.'

'Sure about that?'

'Yes.'

Shah lets the silence build, second by second, pushing all the air from the room until it becomes almost unbearable.

Finally, she says: 'So you can't think of a reason why officers just found Emily's phone at your home address?'

Connor's head snaps up.

'What? No.'

I hold up a hand. 'Hang on, what are you talking about?'

Harmer says: 'Emily's phone was recovered from a wheelie bin on your property during this evening's preliminary search.'

'But . . .' My heart starts to knock painfully against my ribcage. 'Anyone could have put it in there.'

Shah ignores my protest. 'I'll ask you again, Connor,' she says. 'Can you think of a reason why Emily's phone was there?'

'No.'

'Well, I'll tell you what, Connor: I can. I can think of a very good reason.' She crosses her slender arms. 'Do you know what an unreliable witness is, Connor?'

My son says nothing.

'A witness whose testimony can't be relied upon because it contradicts itself or other provable facts. You know what I think? I think you lied to your parents, you lied to your friends, you lied to your cousin.' She points an accusing finger at his chest. 'And now you're lying to me.'

47

Shah and Harmer suspend the interview while they go out to confer in the corridor. My phone rings, buzzing in my pocket. I take it out and see Laura's name on the display.

'Just came out of the film and saw your message, what's going on?' My wife's voice is a nervous staccato. 'Where are you? What's happening?'

I don't want to leave the room – don't want to let Connor out of my sight – so I give Laura a brief outline of what's happened in the last hour, telling her I don't know how much longer we will be at the police station.

'The police have a search warrant,' I say instead, hoping she understands why I'm telling her. 'They've already started looking through stuff.'

She pauses just for a beat, just long enough for me to know that she's got the message, the question that I'm asking without saying it out loud. *Are the drugs well hidden?*

'At the house?' she says calmly.

'Yes.'

'OK.'

'They've started with the outside but I guess they'll want to check inside too.' I'm aware of my son's eyes on me. 'Connor's room especially.'

'Right,' she says, her voice even. 'I'd better get back there.'

'I'll stay with Connor until I can bring him home, you stay with Harry and I'll fill you in later.'

But Connor isn't coming home. They're holding him overnight.

Shah returns to the interview room to inform us that my son will be held in custody at the station and re-interviewed in the morning.

'Dad?' Connor's voice is small, stripped bare, a boy looking to his father for reassurance. For protection. Suddenly he's ten years old again, limping off a football pitch and sobbing inconsolably into my shoulder. He's seven, knees bloodied and speckled with gravel, as I lift him from a fallen bike and carry him indoors. 'What's happening?'

All the teenage bravado is long gone.

I swallow down hard on the lump in my throat.

'One night,' I say, with all the confidence I can muster. 'Just one night, Connor, and then we're going to get you out of here, OK?'

Barber-Lomax leans forward, puts a hand on his arm. 'You don't say anything to anyone, do you understand? Not the duty sergeant, not the nice chap who brings you a cup of tea in the morning, or anyone who might pop their head around the cell door to check you're OK. No one. Unless I'm with you. I want to be very clear on that, do you understand me?'

Connor nods, wordlessly.

A sense of dread settles on my shoulders like a heavy blanket. It takes a moment for me to work out where the feeling is coming from – and then I realise. *She's talking to my son as if he's guilty.*

The duty sergeant leads him away down the corridor, Connor following, looking smaller and younger with every step he takes. As he's led through another set of heavy grey double doors, he turns and gives me one last look over his shoulder, his frightened eyes finding mine.

It feels like my heart is going to tear out of my chest. It occurs to me that I could just charge down the corridor and grab Connor before they can go any further, before they can lock him in a cell, just grab him by the shoulder and run him out of here. Bring this process to a halt *right now*, refuse to cooperate, stop playing by their rules and start doing whatever it takes to keep my firstborn child safe from harm, safe from—

The heavy double doors shut behind him.

And then he's gone.

Shah is about to follow them when I put a hand on her elbow. 'Actually,' I say, 'can I have a quick word?'

She gives me a quizzical look, then gestures to the empty interview room we've just vacated and follows me in, standing with her back to the open door. My solicitor stays out in the corridor, thumb-typing rapidly on her phone.

'Dr Boyd,' Shah says, 'I can understand that you're upset and you—'

'My son is being set up,' I say. 'He didn't do this.'

DS Shah's expression doesn't change.

'Didn't do *what*, exactly?'

'He didn't harm Emily Ruskin.'

'Officially, she's still a missing person, unless you have new information that she's been harmed?'

'No.' I shake my head. 'No, I don't. All I can tell you is my son would never hurt anyone.'

'Right.' A single word, stretched and weighed down with scepticism. 'Who do you think is setting him up?'

I take a deep breath and then I tell her about the gathering at Alexander Saxton's house yesterday morning, attended by my brother, Olivia's mother, and Emily's stepfather. The scant details I'd been able to glean from Rob afterwards, from Alexander himself; the fact that my family had been excluded.

Shah doesn't look particularly interested. 'I see,' she says. 'And you think there's some kind of collusion going on, do you? To put the blame on Connor?'

'Honestly? I don't know,' I say. 'But I *do* know my son, better than all of them, better than anyone – it's just not possible that he's done this. This latest thing with Emily's phone being found on our property? Anyone could have put it there. Our wheelie bins are just behind our garden gate, which is usually unlocked and not hard to climb over even when it is.'

She considers me for a moment but I can tell from her stony expression that she's not buying what I'm saying. She's not even surprised. I wonder how many other parents have spoken these exact same words in this cramped little interview room before me. Insisting that their offspring would never – *could* never – have done the terrible thing of which they were being accused.

'A couple of days ago,' she says, 'you assured me that your son was at home by midnight when you knew nothing of the sort. It wasn't true, was it, Dr Boyd?' She doesn't wait for me to reply.

'So forgive me if I take your latest assertion with a large pinch of salt.'

I feel myself colouring, warmth creeping up my neck. The reminder of an alibi I'd provided in the vain hope that it would put an end to police interest in my son. Instead, it had been just the beginning.

'But *this*—' I gesture at the file in her hand '—whatever this is. If someone has been hurt I can tell you that's just not in his nature, it never has been. Connor would never do something like that.'

She opens the folder, flips a few pages, finds what she's looking for. 'Although he did attack another pupil at his school two weeks ago, I understand? Left him with a black eye?' She reads further down the page. 'Split another boy's lip? An unprovoked attack, according to witnesses.'

My throat is tight with anger. There was only one place that information could have come from: Drew Saxton, getting his version of the story in first, no doubt encouraged by his father.

'*Not* unprovoked,' I say, trying to keep my voice under control. 'They'd been bullying his sister, my daughter. The three of them against him, and one of those boys was Drew who must be still holding a grudge, telling you all kinds of stories to make Connor look guilty.'

'Your son must have been pretty angry to pick a fight with three of his classmates. Does he tend to get angry a lot?'

'What? No.' I hold my hands up, trying to get back on track. 'Listen, somebody is making it look like he's involved. They're using him, trying to throw you off the scent. I've been thinking about this all day and it's the only explanation that makes sense.'

'I disagree.' Her tone is steely calm. 'As does my boss. There are a number of other scenarios that make much more sense, chief among them that your son was directly involved in Emily Ruskin's disappearance – since he's already forensically linked to the case and still seems to be withholding crucial information that could help us find her.'

This isn't going the way I'd planned. I'd wanted them to see the truth, to give them a glimpse of the *real* Connor, the boy I've known since the moment he took his first breath. Rather than just another anonymous, sleep-deprived suspect who had to be pushed and pushed until he told them what they wanted to hear. But I still had one more card to play.

'Cathy Ruskin doesn't think he was involved,' I say. 'She told me that herself.'

Shah snaps the folder shut. 'Yes, I heard about your visit to the Ruskin family.'

'That must carry some weight, surely? The fact that—'

'Let me be clear about one thing.' She holds her index finger up. 'Any attempt to coerce or intimidate a key witness in this case is in direct contravention of Section 51 of the Criminal Justice and Public Order Act, and could lead to serious legal trouble for you.'

I open my mouth, close it again. Try to recall anything from the few minutes I'd been at their house that might have prompted a complaint. 'I wasn't doing anything like that,' I say. 'I wasn't coercing anyone. Cathy invited me over there, asked me to drop some repeat prescriptions around to the house.'

'Yes, I've had a colleague contact your employer to look into that.'

'You spoke to the practice?' I swallow hard. 'To my boss?'

'That's right.'

I feel a sick roll of nausea in my stomach at the memory of Cathy's tearful request about her daughter – of accessing Emily's patient file and passing on confidential information. Of breaking my oath, crossing a professional boundary that should never be crossed.

I clear my throat. 'When I went to see Cathy Ruskin, it was totally amicable.'

'That's not the version I heard from Mr Crosby. He was extremely unhappy when he called, quite agitated by the whole thing.'

'He wasn't even there!' I say, my voice rising. 'I didn't say a word to him, didn't even see him. In fact, you might want to look at *his* involvement in this. *His* background. You heard what Connor said about his relationship with Emily. Why aren't you investigating *that*?'

'I'd advise you to take a step back from all this, Dr Boyd. You've already lied about your son's whereabouts on Saturday night – impeding our investigation – and right now I'm about *this* close—' she holds out her finger and thumb, a centimetre apart '—to charging you with perverting the course of justice. Do you understand?'

It's the first time she's raised her voice, her words ringing in the empty interview room.

'This is not right,' I say quietly. 'It's not right.'

She frowns, as if drawing on her last reserves of patience. 'Listen, Andy, I get that you're Connor's dad and no parent wants to believe their child is capable of something like this. I get it, OK?

I've got two little ones at home myself. But the fact is, the more evidence we gather, the more of it points towards your son. Staying in denial is not helping him. Or yourself.' She checks her watch. 'Now if you'll excuse me, I've got to give an update to the SIO. We'll be in touch. Soon.'

She turns and leaves me alone in the interview room, the sound of her flat shoes on the concrete floor receding into silence.

I stand for a moment in the oppressive quiet. My son is a stranger in this world of concrete floors and steel doors, of locks and wire-mesh safety glass, of bolted-down chairs and panic alarms and the ground-in smells of sweat and desperation.

Connor doesn't belong here.

I refuse to believe he has done this.

I refuse to believe in a world where such a thing could be possible.

Someone is trying to cover their tracks by shifting the blame onto my son: it is the only conclusion that makes any sense. And the police are a whisper away from charging him with a terrible crime.

But the police are wrong.

And I'm going to prove it.

48

Kay Barber-Lomax walks me back out to the car park. The air is still warm but while we've been sitting inside, packed into the windowless interview room, the darkness of evening has crept in.

I blow out a heavy breath. 'Did you have to talk to Connor like that? As if he's guilty?'

'It's sound advice in any situation. At this point, he's his own worst enemy.'

'He didn't do anything to that girl,' I say. 'He wouldn't. It's not in his nature to lie.'

The solicitor considers this, car keys in her hand. 'He seems like a nice young man.'

'What happens next? Tomorrow?'

'We just need to sit tight, Andy,' she says. 'The police have a lot of ground to cover yet. They can hold him until tomorrow, or charge him, or apply for a warrant of further detention – which a magistrate won't grant, because he's sixteen. The fact that Emily Ruskin's a photogenic sixteen-year-old blonde with a famous mother – it's going to keep the story in the public eye. More news coverage, more visibility, more pressure on the police to get a result. Pressure from above, from their bosses, and pressure from the media. Some pressure can be good, too much pressure not so good. Not for us, anyway. But we'll have a clearer picture in the morning. I'll speak to you then, OK?'

We shake hands and she heads off to her little blue Audi, its lights flaring in the dark as she hits the remote unlock.

When I open the front door of our house, Laura is waiting for me. We stand there in the hall for a minute, the door still open behind me, hugging each other. She has a dozen questions about Connor and I try to give her as much reassurance as I can.

She leads me upstairs and we stand in the doorway of Connor's empty bedroom. The bed sheets have been stripped off and taken, drawers cleared out, clothes piled on the floor where wardrobes have been dumped out by officers searching for evidence. Somehow it looks even worse than it does normally, as if it has been abandoned in haste by someone fleeing a natural disaster. Our son's absence hangs like a dark shroud over everything. He is everywhere in this room. And nowhere.

'They said it was just a preliminary search and they might be back,' Laura says as we continue to survey the damage.

'Did they find anything?'

'They wouldn't say. Took a lot of stuff away.'

'And what about the ... other thing?' I lower my voice. 'The Ziploc bag.'

'Still where I put it.'

'Good. Thank God you found it when you did.'

'Do you think Connor will be OK tonight?' she says, her voice breaking a little.

I hug her again, pulling her to me and holding her close.

'I think the sooner we can get him out of there, the better.'

Back downstairs, the ten o'clock news muted into silence on the TV, she pours us both a glass of wine as I give her a more detailed update, taking her through the events at the police station. Harriet, she says, has been very upset and has only just gone to bed.

We sit in frozen silence when the local BBC bulletin comes on at 10.30, Emily Ruskin's disappearance the top story for the second night in a row. Laura grabs the remote and turns up the volume.

They run the same press conference I watched earlier today, Cathy's appeal for information. There is a surreal feeling of seeing people we know, people we've *met*, reduced to two dimensions on a TV screen. The image on screen changes to a wide shot of Beacon Hill Woods, then to footage of Olivia de Luca outside the Ruskin house earlier today. Standing there with the big blown-up photograph of her best friend, I'm struck by how relaxed and confident Olivia looks, how she hasn't hesitated to put herself forward into the maelstrom of media coverage. Not fazed by it or flinching from it. If anything, quite the opposite, embracing the attention. The reporter wraps up his piece with a new line about police continuing to question one suspect who is being held overnight.

The presenter moves on to the next story but Laura hits a button on the remote to rewind.

'Don't think I can face watching that again,' I say. 'Shall we turn it off?'

'Hang on a second,' she says, hitting 'play' again as the press conference begins on the screen. 'Look.'

'What am I looking at?'

'There,' she says, pausing, rewinding, playing again. 'Did you see it that time?'

I hadn't even noticed it earlier, was too focused on what Cathy was saying. But now Laura has shown me, I see it, right at the edge of the shot. Cathy and Karl's hands are close together, but not clasped. Not even touching. He moves to grip her hand at one point and she shifts it away, clasping her hands together in front of her instead, the movement so subtle it's easy to miss.

'That's interesting.'

'Body language gives us away.' She rewinds again, pauses the clip just as Cathy moves her hand away. 'She can't bear to touch him. Can't bear him touching her.'

'Maybe she didn't want to be distracted?'

'Look how she moves her hand away,' she says. 'She thinks he's hiding something.'

She mutes the sound.

'It's interesting how she phrased it, too,' Laura continues. 'She used exactly the same wording in her appeal on Instagram, the same words. "*Me, your sisters, Karl, all of us.*"'

'Just means they're all in it together, right? They're a family.'

'But why would she feel the need to list them all? Surely it's obvious that "we" means all of them, the whole family?'

'Suppose so. What are you getting at?'

'Just think it's curious, that's all. A strange choice of words. Almost like . . . Emily's had some kind of falling out with one of them and that's why she's run away, so Cathy's making it clear that she can fix it, patch things up, make them apologise to Emily if only she'll come home.'

I think about this for a moment. My wife has always been a student of human nature but this seems a bit of a stretch.

'Sure you're not reading too much into it?'

'I'm telling you, there's something weird going on between the two of them.'

She heads upstairs to bed and I tell her I'll follow in a minute. I pour another glass of wine and sit at the kitchen table, scrolling quickly through my emails. Mostly work stuff, but one of them stands out. The subject line reads: 'Need to speak to you urgently'. The sender is Chris Dineen. The local reporter. There is no text in the body of the email, just his mobile number. I delete the message.

Laura is finishing up a phone call as I walk into our bedroom.

'Thank you again,' she says, 'Sure, yes, of course.' She pauses to listen, nodding. 'Yes absolutely, I understand. I really appreciate this, Trish.'

Still clutching her phone, she goes to shut the door behind me. Then sits back down on our bed.

'What is it?' I say, perching beside her. 'Who was that on the phone?'

My wife looks furtive, her eyes shining with secret knowledge.

'So,' she says quietly. 'I've just had an interesting conversation about Karl Crosby. *Strictly* off the record.'

'Tell me.'

Her voice lowered, she lays out the details of the conversation she's just had with a long-standing friend, a deputy head she has known for more than twenty years – who nevertheless had insisted on off-the-record anonymity.

By the time she's finished telling me, my wine glass is empty but I don't feel tired any more.

'As soon as she saw the news stories about Emily,' my wife says, 'it was the first thing she thought of. That it related to him in some way. To Crosby.'

'We can't prove any of it though, right? It's just inside knowledge, basically staffroom gossip?'

She shrugs. 'Guys like him, incidents like this . . . these are the stories that travel on the grapevine, that people talk about, the kind of things that are whispered about in the pub when you get a bunch of teachers together. The bad apples tend to get a reputation, whether the police get involved or not.'

'Maybe you were right about the strange body language in that press conference today.'

'I *told* you there was something weird.'

'I've got to call it in,' I say. 'DS Shah needs to know about this.'

'Hang on a second,' Laura says, holding up a hand. 'It will be obvious that it came from me. I'll get in all kinds of trouble.'

'Well, we can't just sit on this information, we can't do nothing. Crosby's right there, still in the heart of this family, Cathy could be at risk, her other daughters too.'

She considers this for a moment.

'You can't say where it came from, or who, or connect me to it in *any* way.'

'I know,' I say. 'Better for me to do it anonymously in any case – if they know it came from me, they might not take it seriously. They might assume I've got an agenda.'

She raises an eyebrow. 'We *have* got an agenda.'

'True.'

'Just make sure you keep my name completely out of it.'

An anonymous call seems like it could be fraught with hazards. Not least of which would a phone number being recognised, or traced, or my voice being recognised. Too risky. Would they be able to trace an email? I wasn't sure. The smart thing would be to go to an internet café – did they even exist anymore? – use a different device. But with my son behind bars, it seems like an unnecessary delay.

I grab my laptop from my bag and sit back down on the bed. I go to Google and create a new Gmail account with a generic name, using both my grandfathers' first names. Then dig out DS Shah's business card which has both her email and an address for her team. I wonder briefly how many crazy anonymous emails she gets; probably too many to count.

To: priya.shah@nottspolice.gov.uk
From: RobertArthur619@gmail.com
Cc: majorcrime@nottspolice.gov.uk
Re: Emily Ruskin - URGENT

Dear Detective,

Regarding the investigation into Emily Ruskin's disappearance. You should be aware that her mother's partner, Karl Crosby, has a history of concerning incidents relating to his teaching career, and specifically to incidents involving female pupils in his care. There are at least two incidents which have come to my attention and which may indicate a specific and worrying interest in teenage pupils of Emily's age.

Sir William Crane School, Portsmouth 2013–15. Crosby was employed as a newly qualified PE teacher at this private school. Left before the end of his second year after allegations were made about his conduct with a number of Year 11 pupils. No formal charges brought but complaints apparently made by the parents of two sixteen-year-old girls. Allowed to leave with references intact after signing a non-disclosure agreement.

Caxton International School, Dubai 2016–18. Crosby was again employed as a PE teacher at a school for international students in the UAE. I understand that his contract was terminated without notice after he was found to be in a relationship with a seventeen-year-old pupil. However, the girl's parents and the school wanted to cover up any potential public scandal and allowed him to leave without any formal proceedings taking place.

I hope you will find this information useful.

Yours sincerely,
A concerned citizen

I read it through with a twinge of shame, thinking about how fast I'm abandoning my principles in the attempt to divert police attention away from my son. An anonymous poison pen email with the potential to sink a stranger's career. But there was no smoke without fire, right? And Connor needed all the help he could get.

I ask Laura to check I've got the details right. She scans the text and gives me a nod.

I press 'send'.

WEDNESDAY

49

Connor looks as if he has not slept at all.

His skin is dull, dark hair sticking out in all directions, his eyes half-lidded with fatigue. We're back in the little interview room, as stuffy and under-ventilated as it was last night, Connor on the chair next to me and Kay Barber-Lomax on his other side, pristine in a cobalt blue tailored jacket, her perfume distractingly fresh. She's already explained to me that keeping him in a cell overnight is partly intended to sap his spirit, to grind him down to the point where he wants to cooperate fully.

It looks to me like it might have worked.

Connor seems smaller somehow, diminished by his overnight ordeal and I want more than anything else to fold him into a hug, to rub his back and tell him everything is going to be OK. But he's shied away from hugs for a few years now – even today, even here, he'd be mortified if I tried. I settle instead for a silent squeeze of his shoulder. He won't even make eye contact with me.

Barber-Lomax reiterates to Connor her advice from yesterday – a brief repeat of her *rules of engagement* – and a reminder that DS Shah is not his friend, not *anyone's* friend. That her main aim is to return him to a cell like the one he's just spent the night in, for the foreseeable future. She tells us that this morning we'll likely hear more of the same questions, unless they have new evidence or test results back from the lab, in which case she will ask for a break so she can discuss them with him first.

Connor nods, eyes on the table, but says nothing.

DS Shah comes in, on her own this time, laying a green cardboard folder on the table between us. The folder seems thicker, bulkier, than last night.

I can't help wondering whether she's already read the anonymous email I sent, whether it has risen to the surface of all the other messages and calls and tips she and her team must be sifting through each day. Whether she is already looking into Crosby's past, putting the pieces together.

Whether she's already figured out who sent the email.

If she has, she gives no sign of it. She goes through the same routine as before, sets the recorder running and specifies the resumption of the previous interview along with who's in the room.

'So, Connor,' she says, 'you've had a little more time to think since we spoke yesterday. Is there anything else you'd like to say about what happened on Saturday night? Anything you've remembered? Something that will help us to find Emily, perhaps?'

His eyes flick up to Barber-Lomax, then back to the table. He shakes his head.

'It's been more than seventy-two hours now since she was last seen,' Shah continues. 'As you can imagine it's an incredibly hard time for her mother, for the whole family. I'm sure you don't want to prolong their suffering any further, do you?'

Another tiny shake of his head, the movement so small it's almost imperceptible. Shah lets the silence spool out for ten seconds. Twenty. Thirty.

'Where is she, Connor?' The words are soft and gentle. 'Where is Emily?'

'I don't know.'

Shah indicates the solicitor.

'I'm sure that Ms Barber-Lomax will have given you advice on what to say, or not say. But that's all it is: advice. It's not an order. She's not in charge here – *you're* in charge. It's *your* choice whether you follow her advice, or not. Your decision.'

He nods, wordlessly.

'And this is your chance to put across your side of the story, Connor.' She leans forward. 'Maybe your last chance.'

Those last four words land like a punch to the kidneys.

Connor shifts in his seat beside me, wrapped in obstinate silence once again.

The detective leans forward, putting both elbows on the table. 'We can do this all day, Connor, if you like. We can sit here all day and all night going over what—'

'Come on, Priya,' Barber-Lomax cuts across her, speaking for the first time since the interview started. 'At this point you can either charge my client or release him. And since you seem unwilling or unable to do the former, it seems the latter would be the logical path at this stage. For all of us. I'm guessing you're still waiting on lab results, your boffins have a backlog because of the summer holidays, yes?'

Shah frowns and I can tell that the solicitor's use of her first name has really pissed her off. 'If we choose to, we can hold your client—' she checks her watch '—for another eight hours.'

Barber-Lomax gives her a chilly smile. 'In which case I would remind you, *again*, that my client is a child with no criminal record, an academic high-achiever from a stable family background, and

I would just *love* to hear you argue in front of a judge why you decided it was essential to detain him further without good cause.'

Shah throws a disgusted look at the solicitor. Then returns her gaze to my son, tapping the end of her biro on the cover of her notebook. *Tap, tap, tap.* Giving him one last opportunity, to say what she clearly wants to hear.

Finally, she slides the pen back into her jacket pocket and closes the folder.

'Connor Boyd, you're going to be released under investigation until such time as you are summoned for a follow-up interview. Once further enquiries are completed and a decision has been made you will be notified and you will be required to attend further interviews here at the station, at which time you may be rearrested whether or not new evidence has come to light.'

Relief washes through me like a cold wave.

Shah tells Connor he is to stay at the family address and not to contact any of the Ruskin family, speak to other witnesses or go to Beacon Hill Woods.

'That's it?' he says tentatively.

The detective stands up. 'For now.'

Behind my sense of relief there is another, stronger instinct: to grab hold of Connor and get out of here as fast as possible in case she changes her mind. This doesn't feel like a victory. More like a temporary reprieve.

The snatched breath of a drowning man, before he goes under for good.

50

Connor is silent on the drive home, his body turned slightly away from me to look out of the passenger side window, hands listless in his lap. I try to get him talking a little but he won't engage, nodding wordlessly to a few of my questions before retreating further back into silence. The bruises on his face are yellowing, diminishing, no longer the angry purple and black of Sunday night. At least his physical injuries seem to be healing OK.

In the kitchen, Laura pulls him into a hug without either of them saying a word. This boy she carried and nurtured who now towers over her, whose chin rests awkwardly on her shoulder while she rubs his back in a gentle circular motion. Finally, she clasps his shoulders and leans back to study his face more closely.

'Right,' she says firmly. 'Food.'

She sits him down at the kitchen table, fetching drinks and cutlery, heating soup for an early brunch. Connor picks at thick buttered slices of melted cheese on toast and spoons half-heartedly from a bowl of tomato soup. It's the only soup he'll touch, his favourite since he was in primary school.

To me, she indicates a small envelope on the kitchen side, already opened.

'This came through the door while you were out.'

The envelope says simply 'FAO: ANDY AND LAURA BOYD' in hasty capitals. There is no note, just another *Nottingham Post* business card from Chris Dineen, the local crime reporter. On the back he has written: *Please give me a call ASAP – urgent. Thank you.*

'How did this reporter even find out our names?' she says. 'Where we live?'

'God knows.' I shrug, dropping the card and envelope into the recycling bin. 'Electoral roll?'

We sit with Connor while he lifts slow spoonfuls of soup to his mouth, mechanically, automatically, as if he can't taste anything at all. Laura gently tries to draw him out, to get him talking.

'I've put fresh sheets on your bed, so it's all ready for you,' she says softly. 'Were you able to get much sleep last night?'

He shakes his head, slack-faced with exhaustion.

'No,' he says. 'Not really.'

'You poor thing. Was it . . . really awful?'

Connor puts the spoon back in the bowl and pushes it away, still half-full. There is a tiny tremor in his hand. He looks up at his mother, then at me, then down at the table.

'It was the worst night of my life, Mum,' he says, his voice cracking. 'The stink, and the noise. There was just so much *noise*. All night. The guy in the cell next to me spent most of the night kicking his door, over and over and over again, then every few minutes he'd shout a load of swear words. Felt like I was going to be in that cell for the rest of my life.'

There is a burn of useless anger building deep in my chest; frustration, pity and remorse all swirling together in a toxic cocktail. But most of all I feel an overwhelming, paralysing sense of failure.

I've failed him. *We've* failed him. Failed to protect him from this accelerating nightmare.

I see all of this on Laura's face too.

Connor rubs a hand across his mouth.

'The whole time, I couldn't stop thinking about Emily being out there somewhere. And it's my fault. My fault that she didn't come home, my fault because of everything that happened and I'm never going to see her again. I realised that it was all *real*, that this is really happening, and it's . . .' He blinks fast, a single tear brimming before he cuffs it angrily away. 'It's all my fault.'

Laura covers her hand with his. Her voice, when she finally speaks, is as soft as a feather.

'Why is it your fault, Connor?'

He shakes his head, but says nothing.

'Connor,' I say quietly. 'I want to make sure you know something, OK?'

He glances up at me with red-rimmed eyes. 'What?'

'There's nothing you could ever do or say that would make us love you any less. Nothing. Whatever it is, whatever happens next. You do know that, don't you?'

And then, almost like a switch has been flipped, his eyes fill with tears and he begins to cry. Any remaining bravado dissolving before our eyes. Big shaking sobs wrack his shoulders, tears streaking his face and splashing in fat drops on the polished table between us.

Laura goes to sit by him, putting an arm around his shoulders. I fetch a box of tissues and hand some to him. He holds them against his face as if he's trying to cover up, to hide, to block everything out.

When he finally drops the sodden tissues onto the table, he looks utterly traumatised. Broken. Defeated.

Laura tries again, gently probing. *Why do you think it's your fault, Connor? What happened? Tell us how we can help you.* But he's closed down again. All he'll say is that he wants to go to bed.

But first, we have to ask him one more question, one last question to which there are no good answers.

Laura reaches into her pocket and lays something on the table between us: the small Ziploc bag, liquid GHB contained in the little plastic vials.

Our son looks at the bag, then at each of us, before his eyes return to the vials again.

'What's this?' he says.

'That's what we want you to tell us,' Laura says. 'We found it in your room.' She waits a beat before asking the question we've both been dreading. 'Is it yours?'

Connor frowns.

'I've never seen that bag before. Those things.' He's shaking his head. 'They're not mine, honestly. I *swear* to you.'

Before this last weekend I would have been happy to leave it at that, satisfied with his answer. Content to take my son at his word, to trust him. But now there is a splinter of doubt, jagged and sharp, that has forced its way into the space between us.

'Do you know what they are?'

'I can guess; I mean I've heard stuff. But they're not mine.' Our son swallows hard. 'You do believe me, don't you?'

'Yes,' Laura says without hesitation.

'Of course,' I add, my words trailing in her wake.

She presses on. 'So someone put them there?'

'I don't know, Mum.'

Laura gives voice to something that's been bothering me since we found the bag of drugs. Something we hadn't even discussed with each other yet: a creeping sense of hidden forces at play, of things happening just beyond our view. Maybe the drugs were a part of that: an effort to undermine Connor's credibility in the eyes of the police, to give him a hidden agenda, a motive for secrecy. It was only by sheer fluke that Laura had found them before last night's police search.

'Zac was in your room,' she says carefully. 'He slept here on Saturday night, then came back with his dad on Sunday evening.'

'No,' Connor says quickly, his tone adamant. 'Not Zac.'

'I know you're super loyal to your cousin, and that's great, but we need to—'

'It's not him,' Connor says again. He picks up the small bag and turns it over in his hand, studying the little fish-shaped vials. Abruptly, he looks up, as realisation dawns. 'Wait, so, this stuff . . . you didn't give it to the police. You didn't tell that detective you found them.'

My wife shakes her head. 'No, we didn't. We would *never* do that.'

He considers this for a moment, digesting the implications. Then his face crumples and he starts to cry again.

'I'm sorry, Mum, Dad,' he sobs. 'I just wanted to help Emily but everything's gone wrong, now she's gone and it's all messed up. I've let everyone down. I'm sorry.'

Laura pulls him in for another hug, his head on her shoulder as the tears flow. I've not seen him full-on cry like this in years.

When the tears finally subside, he rubs his face with the hem of his shirt, sitting up straight again.

'Maybe it's true, what everyone is saying,' he says, his voice dull with resignation. 'Maybe I did it.'

51

His words land like shattering glass. I stare at my son, his face wretched.

The shoulder of Laura's pale cream top is mottled dark with his tears. 'What are you talking about?' she says, her voice trembling a little.

'There are bits of Saturday night I can't remember.' Connor can barely look at us now. 'Gaps in my memory. The more I think about it, the more I think it must have been me that did something to her. We were out there in the woods when something happened and maybe I blocked it out of my memory. My subconscious blocked it out because it's too horrible to remember. It's a definite thing that can happen sometimes.'

Laura shakes her head. 'I don't know about that, Connor.'

'It is,' Connor says. 'I looked it up. When the brain makes memories at a time of extreme stress or trauma, they can get locked away in a place you can't normally reach. It's called dissociative amnesia. Maybe I did hurt Emily like everyone says I did. Maybe that's why I've got the blanks in my memory. That can happen, can't it, Dad, especially when you get knocked out?' He prods the Ziploc bag with his finger. 'Or maybe I was spiked with one of these.'

This is a long way from my day-to-day expertise as a GP but I try to reach back to my medical school training, to the examination I'd given Connor when we brought him home on Sunday afternoon.

'It would be very rare, Connor, it might only happen in cases with—'

'But you can't be sure! Everyone's saying it was me, maybe they're right.' His hands are shaking. 'Where's Emily, Dad? Why wasn't she at the house where she said she'd be? Why has she not gone home? And why was her blood on my fake ID?'

'Why don't you start by telling us everything you *can* remember, absolutely everything, and maybe that will help us piece it all together?'

Our son blows out a shuddering breath, shoulders slumping. In a low voice, he begins to relate the events of Saturday night, who was there at the party, who he recognised from school, about Zac, Drew and Olivia; what Emily had said and how she'd seemed. Rumours that had been going around school about girls being spiked at parties, having their drinks adulterated – with drugs just like the ones we'd found in Connor's room.

'That's why I went with them up to Beacon Hill,' he says. 'In case the same thing happened to Emily.'

The implication of what he's saying takes a second to sink in, as I think about the five of them: two girls who were best friends, two boys who were cousins.

Plus one more boy. The odd one out, if you looked at it that way.

'You think *Drew* might have been spiking these girls?'

Connor traces a pattern on the table with his index finger, back and forth across the polished pine. He shrugs, but won't look at me. 'He's just . . . I don't know. Maybe. He pretty much gets whatever he wants, you know?'

'Do you have any proof?'

Connor shakes his head.

The three of us sit in our own silence for a moment, digesting the potential of his words, the awful possibilities they suggest. According to Connor's account, there had been a couple of spiking incidents at parties and gatherings, he tells us, one at an under-eighteens event at Rock City, a nightclub in town; another at a sixteenth birthday party in the upstairs function room of a pub.

I try to swallow down my shock. These terrible things had been going on for *months*, and we had no idea about any of it. Perhaps if our eldest had been a girl, the subject might have come up. But Connor had either thought it wasn't relevant, or – more likely – didn't want us to overreact, which was why we were only finding out now. He had withheld the information from us. And now we were doing the same – withholding information from the police about the drugs we'd found, to shield our son. And so it went on, a circle of lies and evasion and half-truths, a missing girl at its centre.

'What about the police?' I ask. 'Did they get involved either of those times?'

He shakes his head.

'What if Emily knew something about it?' Laura says quietly. 'Or she found out something Drew didn't want her to know. It might be a motive for him to confront her, to intimidate her.' She pauses. 'To keep her from saying anything.'

Connor is about to answer when there is the squeak of a floorboard from the hallway. All three of us look towards the kitchen door, which is slightly ajar.

I walk to the door and pull it open.

Harriet is standing in the hallway, Toffee cradled in her arms like a baby. She looks up at me, wide-eyed, in a way that makes it impossible for me to be angry at her for eavesdropping.

I sigh. 'How long have you been listening, Harry?'

'Toffee wanted to come in.'

'How much have you heard?'

She shrugs. 'Everything.'

She puts the dog down and slips through the door to her brother. She gives him an awkward hug, chin on his shoulder, her small hand patting his back. Toffee follows her into the room, pads around the table and sits down next to Connor's chair, gazing up at him with big brown eyes and letting out a small whine.

Harriet reaches down and strokes the dog's head. 'Connor, do you remember when Toffee ate a whole bar of rum and raisin chocolate and he had to have his stomach pumped? And then when he came back from the vet he absolutely *stank*?' She scratches under his chin. 'Didn't you, Toff?'

Connor snorts and a smile cracks his face for the first time in days. 'Worst thing I've ever smelled in my life,' he says.

Toffee gives a single happy bark of approval, his tail swishing a slow back and forth on the laminate floor.

'I'm going to help you,' Harriet says. 'Help prove that you didn't do what those people are saying you did.'

The smile fades from Connor's face, the moment of lightness vanishing like smoke.

'Mum, Dad,' Harriet says, turning to us. 'I want to help. Tell me what I can do.'

'That's very sweet of you,' I say. 'But this is really for the grown-ups to sort out and—'

'I'm not a *baby*, Dad, I'm twelve.' She crosses her thin arms tightly across her chest. 'I can *do* things. I can find things out.'

I grasp for something my daughter can do that will keep her busy and assuage her feeling of being left out.

'Social media,' I say. 'You could help by keeping us up to date on that Facebook page that's been set up to help find Emily, let us know what everyone is saying. You can use my iPad.'

'Seriously?' She looks at me as if this is the lamest idea she's ever heard. 'Facebook is for pensioners and conspiracy people.'

'You can also help us by keeping all of this secret,' Laura adds, '*top* secret, all the things you've just heard, standing behind that door. And by looking after Toffee. Why don't you take him into the garden for a bit now, make that agility course that he likes with the jumps?'

Harriet gives a disgusted sigh and marches out of the room, Toffee trotting after her.

I push the door closed again, waiting for the *click* as it shuts properly before Laura picks up the thread of the conversation, asking Connor how else the drugs might relate to Emily's disappearance. 'I need you to think, Connor,' she says. 'Has this ever happened to Emily?'

He shakes his head. 'Don't think so. Not that she told me, anyway. There were rumours it happened to a friend of hers, at a party in the Easter holidays. Stories were flying around school when we went back for the new term. The girl it supposedly happened to, apparently she was off sick the first day of the new term with a *flu bug*.' He illustrates the two words with air quotes. 'It was never, like, confirmed or anything.'

'Who was the girl?'

'I don't know for sure.' He swallows hard, sharp Adam's apple bobbing in his throat. 'But the story going around was that it might have been Olivia.'

Laura leans forward. 'Was she assaulted?'

'I told you, I don't *know*,' he says quickly. 'I have no idea. I wasn't even invited to the party. It was all, like, top secret and no one was supposed to talk about it. Which meant literally everyone at school *did*, even though no one really knew the actual facts.'

Laura thinks for a moment. 'Wasn't she the girl Zac was going out with?' she says. 'I remember him saying something about her.'

Connor looks up at his mother, gives a reluctant nod. 'For a while, yeah. They split up around the same time.'

Laura shoots me a quick glance, eyebrows raised.

Our son yawns hugely for the second time in as many minutes, eyes drooping shut, and I'm reminded again of how little rest he got last night.

'You need to sleep,' Laura says to him. 'Go on upstairs now.'

He nods wordlessly and we both watch his exhausted rise from the table, then listen to his slow footsteps retreat up the stairs to his bedroom.

I push the dining room door shut again and sit back down opposite my wife, neither of us saying a word. I reach out and squeeze her hand on the table. There is no question of telling DS Shah about the drugs we'd found in Connor's room. No question of pressing this angle, telling them *why* they should be looking more closely at the girls being spiked as a possible motive for whatever had happened to Emily.

But maybe there was a way around that.

52

I open my laptop, click into a new browser window and navigate to the staff login page at the surgery. The actions are so familiar, so ingrained, that they are completely automatic – movements I have made a thousand times before. On the laptop screen, a cursor blinks at me in the first of two rectangular boxes.

Please enter your login and password.

In theory every time a staff member accessed the system – either at the surgery or remotely – it was logged on the central drive. And every time a patient record was accessed or updated, this was also recorded against your login ID. But it was an old, creaking system and it had flaws – the main one being a vulnerability to human nature, to the human tendency to look for shortcuts and workarounds, the quick fix rather than the boring security proto-col. When we had temporary locum doctors to fill in for sickness and absence, for example, they were *supposed* to use a new guest login to access the system so they could update the records of the patients they saw.

The guest logins were *supposed* to be randomly generated and changed on a weekly basis. But they weren't. Not since a chaotic Monday morning a few years ago when three locums couldn't get onto the system simultaneously and couldn't see patients for hours on end, dozens of appointments piling up in the waiting room as tempers flared. Since that day, locum doctors had always been given one of the same handful of guest logins, with the same passwords.

One of them is written on a Post-it note in the back of my day planner.

My fingers hover over the keyboard. Laura is outside in the garden with Harriet and Connor is up in bed, lost to a deep sleep, blinds pulled down against the midday sun. I'm alone in the kitchen.

What I'm about to do is unethical, improper, maybe even illegal. Enough to get me in seriously hot water with the GMC, at any rate. But I've already broken the rules once, when I accessed Emily's patient file to answer her mother's question. And the police had already contacted the practice after my visit to the Ruskin family yesterday, although I've yet to learn what consequences I would face from my boss.

Nevertheless, I feel a pinch of unease at how fast my scruples are fading into the background. Though the stakes have got higher since yesterday.

I type in the details on the Post-it note and press 'enter'. If anyone checks, for any reason, they should see a guest ID rather than mine. There would be an audit trail somewhere with an external IP address, but only if someone looked. And only if they knew exactly what they were looking *for*.

I navigate quickly through the system to Olivia's patient record, scanning quickly through the last six months. Nothing much of note; antibiotics for an ear infection, a prescription for migraine tablets.

There. April 9th, a Monday just over three months ago. Olivia had come in for what was described on the record as a 'Follow-up check/blood test/general assessment'. I scan the notes made by the GP who had seen her. The blood test had come back negative for GHB and had also been tested for any traces of ketamine or Rohypnol, also negative. I pull up another browser window to check how long traces of these drugs might remain in the system and read that they are normally metabolised and purged from the body within twenty-four hours, which was one of the reasons the crime was so hard to prove and prosecute. The evidence literally vanished. I assume the party had been on a Friday or Saturday night, and Olivia had not been tested until Monday. Testing for a broad spectrum of drugs might be routine or it might just mean they weren't sure what they were looking for. Maybe they were just hoping to find *something*. Her test had come back positive for cannabis, but that can hang around in your system for weeks. Did that mean anything? I wasn't sure. It seemed as popular now as when I had been a teenager; maybe even more so.

Other than that, her notes showed she was maybe borderline underweight for her height and age but otherwise in good general health.

I make a note of the home address and log out of the system.

* * *

The street is right on the far edge of the school catchment area, a featureless cul-de-sac backing onto a light industrial park of warehouses and workshops. The house is a small sixties semi-detached with dandelions sprouting through cracks in the short concrete driveway. I have to ring the bell three times before the front door finally opens a few inches and Sophie de Luca looks out at me through the gap. Messy shoulder length blonde hair, dark roots, a deep tan. She is dressed in a pink vest top, shorts and flip-flops. A furtive set to her shoulders, as if she's been caught out.

'Oh,' she says, squinting up into the afternoon sun. 'Hey.'

'Hello,' I say brightly and introduce myself. 'I was wondering if we could have a quick chat?'

She studies me for a moment, blinking fast as if she's still struggling to place me. Her eyes are bloodshot and the GP part of my brain is automatically thinking *Afternoon drinker?* I've had alcoholics in the surgery before – some who've come in steaming drunk first thing in the morning – but there's no telltale smell of alcohol here. She's younger than I'd expected, perhaps mid-thirties, and must have been a teenager herself when she had Olivia.

'A chat?' she repeats nervously, her fingers gripping the frame of the door, pink nail varnish chipped and dull.

'Just five minutes, that's all.'

She seems to finally remember who I am, recognition dawning on her face. 'Listen, if it's about the other day, sorry I drove off but I was rattled by Alex Saxton, all the shit he was spouting.' She looks past me, out into the street. 'How's your boy doing, anyway?'

The question surprises me but I wonder how much she already knows, how far the news of his rearrest and second police interview has already travelled on the bush telegraph of school parents. 'He's OK.' The lie comes out smoothly. 'He's doing all right.'

'He's a good lad, your Connor, he's walked Olivia home more than a few times. He told you where we live, did he?'

I nod, give her another smile. 'About Connor and the others . . . do you mind if I come in for a few minutes?'

She opens the door wide and ushers me into a small front room, overfilled with two tired armchairs, a sofa and a wide TV muted into silence. On the screen, two expensively dressed women are having a row, manicured fingers pointing, somewhere sunny and shiny and exclusive, the sea glinting blue behind them. All the windows are open but the air is still thick with a sweet, spicy, familiar smell. She gestures me towards the sofa and slumps down in an armchair, the fabric of both arms worn bare.

Olivia, she says, is out doing another photo shoot with the press, another story about Emily's disappearance, an appeal for the safe return of her best friend.

'It's been non-stop these last few days, the media can't get enough of my girl,' she says with a snort. 'If only they knew.'

'Knew what?'

'About Emily Ruskin.' Her voice is ripe with disdain. 'What she's *really* like.'

53

OLIVIA

Saturday 11th June, 11.58 p.m.
Eighty-three minutes before Emily's disappearance
Footpath behind 77 The Avenue

She was the best friend Olivia had ever had.

And the worst.

Emily was like the sun, warm and bright and beautiful, the blazing centre of their little universe with all others in a pale and grateful orbit. You could bask in that warm reflected glow if she let you come close.

She could burn you, too. Olivia knew that better than anyone.

But still, she wanted more than anything to protect Emily, to possess her too, to have her all to herself. To have all of her time and all of her attention, fully and completely. To be a sister to her – the best she would ever have, better than her stuck-up older sisters. She and Emily would be best friends forever, she knew that for a fact.

It was more intense than anything she'd ever felt for a boy. Olivia couldn't explain it to her mum; she couldn't explain it to anyone. But she couldn't get enough of Emily, she was like the richest cake or the most expensive champagne, Olivia just had to have more and more even if she knew she was gorging herself, even if she knew deep down that it wasn't good for her. She told herself that didn't matter because their relationship was pure, not in a romantic way, it was deeper than that. Not that she would ever say that to Emily, not in so many words.

She had told Emily they could do this – they could carry out her plan – without anyone else. Just the two of them together, like Sansa and Arya Stark on Game of Thrones. But that wasn't Emily's way. She had to have an audience, had to have eyes on her – even if she ignored them – had to have boys falling at her feet. Even when they only wanted one thing. She absorbed attention, like a sponge soaking up water, more and more and more, even if everyone else around her was dying of thirst.

It was as if Olivia on her own wasn't enough. Would never be enough.

Sometimes it made Olivia so . . . angry? No, not angry exactly, but . . . yes. Angry. Furious. And frustrated, heartsick, so black and low that the only thing that helped was to retrieve the little razor blade from its hiding place under her mattress and make a few cuts to release the pressure. The sharp purity of pain that seemed to help when nothing else would.

Olivia waited for her friend at the place they had agreed, the path above the party house at the richest end of The Avenue. The field where she stood rose gently up towards Beacon Hill Woods and gave her a good vantage point into the large garden below. It was almost midnight, but the party was still in full flow, all the outside lights blazing, music pumping from somewhere inside, shouts and laughter and splashes from the pool, teenage voices raised in celebration of a summer Saturday night. Olivia shifted the backpack to settle it more comfortably on her shoulders, and absentmindedly patted her back pocket again, feeling for the curve of the slim silver hip flask, a sixteenth birthday gift from her mum. She checked her phone. It was almost time.

As she watched, shadows shifted and coalesced at the bottom of the garden and a figure emerged through the back gate, turning to make its way up the path towards her. Olivia's eyes were still a little dazzled from looking at the lights around the swimming pool but she knew who it was just from her walk, her size, the way she flicked her hair. Emily was in the lead with short, purposeful strides, three taller figures following behind her. Three boys.

One of them was Drew Saxton, she could tell by his self-confident swagger as he moved to catch up with Emily. She was pretty sure the one behind him was Connor Boyd – he was never far away from Emily. As they moved closer, she recognised the third figure too, felt herself bristle with annoyance at the sight of Zac Boyd bringing up the rear. Her ex didn't like Emily; had never liked her. Not that Emily would care even if she knew.

Emily reached the meeting place and greeted her with a hug. 'You got everything, hon?'

'Yeah,' Olivia said. 'You ready?'

'All good,' Emily said. 'Let's go.'

With the two girls leading and the boys behind, the five of them made their way up through the field, the sound of the party slowly receding behind them. Shouting voices and the bass beat of the music fading as they picked up the path through waist-high wheat, golden stalks swaying and rustling in a gentle night-time breeze.

Beacon Hill Woods loomed ahead of them, a dark mass at the top of the hill. It was a cloudless night, the moon barely a sliver of light in the sky above. The street lights were spread out below them in dusky orange strings.

Olivia had been up here plenty of times before, but mostly during the day or the evening, when there was at least some light. When she was younger, she'd sometimes come sledging with Emily in the winter snow. On a clear day, she could find her own bedroom window down there among all the thousands of houses spread out below them in West Bridgford. Far away from Emily's house, in just about every way imaginable.

She heard Zac's voice behind her, low and soft.

'Don't look at your phone,' he was saying, presumably to his cousin. 'The light will ruin your night vision. Got to keep your eyes on the dark until they get used to it.'

'Just need to send this text.'

'You telling your parents you're back home already?'

'They won't know,' Connor said quietly. 'They won't check. As long as I text, it'll be OK.'

Zac's response was too quiet for her to hear. Drew appeared on Emily's other side as they made their way up the uneven path, his arm snaking across her back and around her waist, holding her, so they were walking hip to hip. She didn't move his hand, or push him away, matching his footsteps stride for stride. Then Drew whispered something in Emily's ear and they both snorted with laughter, the two of them half turning to look at Connor, almost as if to check he was watching this little intimacy taking place.

Olivia felt her cheeks burn with anger, that feeling of being discarded, suddenly unwanted, that she always got when the boys started buzzing around her best friend. Drew was too full of himself to realise that Emily was just doing it for the attention, basking in it before *she held him away at arm's length again. The same way she'd done before. But he literally didn't know how to take no for an answer.*

'What's in that big backpack, Olivia?' Drew said. 'Looks heavy.'

Olivia gripped the strap a little tighter against her shoulder. 'Surprise,' she said coolly.

'Mysterious,' Drew said with extra emphasis. 'I like it.'

The five of them walked on in silence along the well-worn path to the boundary of the woods, a three-bar wooden fence with a staggered gateway. The woods themselves covered several hundred acres, extending along the ridge and down the far side of the hill before rising to another ridge, but most of the people from school just stayed on the south side nearest to town where the paths were. The far side, the backwoods sloping down into the valley, was thicker and less inviting. She'd ventured over that way with Emily yesterday, in preparation for this, but what few paths there were narrowed and dwindled into nothing, thickets of brambles and nettles and fallen trees blocking your way until you had no idea which direction you were heading. And that was in the daytime.

Darkness enveloped them now as they walked in: among the trees, it was total. In the daytime you could find your way around pretty well, at least in the part that was nearest the entrance. But now, what little light there was from the thin sliver of a crescent moon was blotted out by the thick canopy of leaves above them.

Emily turned and stopped them in their tracks.

'Tonight's going to be cool,' she said. 'I've got a surprise planned. But first, you all have to do something for me.'

'What?' Zac said.

'You have to promise me you'll do it first.' At the party, Emily had seemed drunk. But Olivia knew that was part of the act, part of

the performance that would be relayed back to her family tomorrow to add to the effect her friend wanted to create: a drunk, emotional teenager who might have done something terrible. Now, Emily's words were clear again. 'Then we can properly get started,' she said.

Drew snorted. 'I'm not promising anything, Ems, until—'

'OK, Emily,' Connor said. 'What do you want us to do?'

She studied the four of them in turn, her gaze sweeping from one face to the next.

'You have to switch your phones off,' she said finally. 'All of you.'

'Why?' Zac asked. 'And how are we going to see anything?'

'Switch it off and you'll find out.'

Four phones were dutifully powered down while Emily watched, arms crossed. Olivia handed out small black torches to each of them from the backpack she was carrying.

Emily turned on her torch. 'OK then,' she said, her voice lifting with excitement. 'Let's go.'

Drew draped an arm around her shoulders and the two of them led off into the dark, thin beams of light from their torches dancing off trees and bushes, Emily's perfume lingering in their wake. She was whispering and giggling with Drew again.

Ignoring her best friend, again.

Olivia zipped up the backpack and swung it over her shoulder, hurrying to fall into step behind them. Convinced now – absolutely certain, in fact – that this would have been so much better if it had just been the two of them. Partners in crime. On a mission, two best friends who would do anything for each other. Instead of bringing in these stupid boys to make more of a performance out of the whole thing.

Drew, who just wanted to have sex with her.

Zac, who seemed to hate her.

And Connor, who'd put her on a pedestal higher than he could reach.

Emily and Olivia didn't need any of them. They just needed each other. The thoughts churned inside her head as they walked, Emily and Drew up front, Connor and Zac still bringing up the rear in silence. Olivia in the middle, alone and glad of the dark.

A ten-minute hike through the woods brought them to a little clearing, with fallen trees laid on three sides around a fire pit ringed with blackened rocks. Olivia went into the backpack again and handed a lighter to Emily, who held it low down to a pile of wood. The flame bloomed in her hand and immediately it began to catch, orange and blue flames licking around the base. Olivia had been up here earlier today to prepare the fire pit ahead of time, stacking it with twigs and paper for kindling, bigger logs propped over the top.

For a moment they all stood and watched the orange flames catch and grow, twigs crackling as the fire took hold, smoke curling up into the black. Beyond the light of the fire, the circle of darkness around them was pure black, a shroud that had fallen over everything. Nothing existed beyond the circle. It was as if they were the only five people in the world; maybe the last five left.

Olivia looked up at Emily's flawless face, tanned skin glowing in the firelight. The best friend she'd ever had, the only one she needed. Sometimes she loved her so much she almost couldn't stand it.

Maybe tonight, this one night, was Olivia's chance to really show her how much their friendship meant.

How she was the only one Emily could rely on.

54

I try to sit up straighter on the spongy sofa, feeling tired springs give beneath me. This was not what I'd been expecting.

'I've never actually met Emily,' I say. 'But the police seem extremely concerned, I guess it's a long time for a sixteen-year-old to be missing.'

'*Missing.*' She smothers the word in sarcasm. 'Right. Of course.'

In four days where Emily Ruskin has loomed large in our lives, where her name has become a national headline, this is the first time I've heard anyone suggest something negative about her. A lot of mud has been thrown since Sunday, trolls on social media have accused Cathy of being a terrible mother, police and parents – my own brother – have basically accused my son of a terrible crime, but Emily herself is golden, untouchable, unimpeachable, a missing child made perfect by her absence.

'You don't think . . . she's missing at all?' I assume Olivia has told her mother about Emily's plan. 'So where is she, what do you think is going on?'

Sophie snorts again.

'Emily will be doing what's best for Emily,' she says, her voice a nervous staccato. 'That's what she always does. She's a bloody expert at it. Believe me, she's probably off with a boy somewhere, she's certainly not short of admirers. Loves to be the centre of attention.' She's hitting her stride now, as if she's been burning to say this for days but had no audience with whom to share it. 'All the sympathy, the media going on and on and on, all this *crap* about what a lovely girl she is. It's a joke.'

There is a fizz of adrenaline in my blood. *Emily will be doing what's best for Emily.* Instinctively, I want it to be true, despite the venom of her words. Because maybe those words offer a chink of light for Connor, for Cathy, for all of us.

'So you don't like Emily?'

'*Like* her?' Her face creases as if she's recoiling from a bad smell. 'No. I don't like her. There were girls at my school who were just the same as her. Let me tell you about my daughter's so-called best friend. About what kind of girl she really is.'

She snaps open the lid of a small Fisherman's Friend tin on the low table in front of her. Takes out Rizlas and tobacco, then expertly rolls a cigarette and sprinkles in dark resin that she unwraps from a small piece of cling film and crumbles between her small fingers. She rolls it shut and puts it to her lips, tongue flicking out to seal the paper. The whole procedure takes maybe thirty seconds from start to finish.

After lighting it with a pink Bic, she pulls in a deep drag and then holds the joint out to me. 'Want some?'

I shake my head. It feels a little surreal, coming here to talk about drugs as she smokes weed in front of me – never mind the fact that she's a patient at the practice where I work. Then again, so much of the last four days has felt so surreal that this latest moment barely registers. I guess it might be the reason why Olivia's tox report showed a positive result for cannabis.

She sees my expression.

'Need it for my nerves,' she says. 'Anxiety. Don't worry,' she adds, her voice tight with smoke. 'I never roll up when Olivia is here. And I don't normally in the day, but I'm sort of in between jobs at the moment, and her dad is as useless at paying mainte-nance on time as he was at everything else.'

She blows out a stream of smoke, taps ash into a coffee mug, and settles back into the armchair. Starts to tell me about a sixteenth birthday party at the Grosvenor, a pub in the city, a few months ago. It was after a girl at another school had been spiked, and all the talk had been about how no one should leave their drink unat-tended when they went to the toilet or the dance floor, or accept drinks from lads they didn't know, how they should all buddy up and look after each other.

'The rule was that they should always stay together, a pair of them at least, the more the better,' Sophie says. 'That was the only rule I gave her. I made her promise. So that if anyone did get spiked they'd have, like, a wingman, wingwoman or whatever, to make sure they didn't get taken advantage of. Make sure nothing hap-pened to them.'

I nod, encouraging her on. 'Connor mentioned something hap-pening at a party at the Grosvenor.'

'Yeah, your boy was there.' I try to ignore the fact that this contra-dicts what Connor told us barely an hour ago. Sophie takes another drag, another deep lungful of smoke. 'Anyway, so Emily and Olivia were buddied up and they were so excited about the party. They were going to look out for each other, take care of each other. That was the deal, the arrangement, that was why I let Livvy go.'

'So, what happened?'

She pauses to take another deep drag, lips puckering around the roll-up.

'I got a call at half ten from someone I hardly knew, the mum of the girl having the party, to say that Olivia had been found slumped in the ladies' toilets, practically comatose, and someone's said she *thinks* my girl might have been doing vodka shots but she's not sure, or *maybe* she took something, or *maybe* something else has gone on. No one really knows what the hell's happened.'

'Where was Emily?'

Sophie's face contorts with anger.

'Off with some boy. Outside in the beer garden, just the two of them in the corner. Barely spent ten minutes with Olivia after they got there, just hooked up with this lad and went off with him. Left Olivia to fend for herself – and that's when she got spiked.' She gestures at me with the smoking joint clasped between her fingers. '*That's* what kind of girl Emily Ruskin is. A fake, just like her mother.'

'Christ,' I say, 'I'm sorry that happened to her.'

'I drove down there to pick her up. I was so fucking angry and freaked out that all I could think about was getting her home, safe. She's my only child, just the two of us since her dad buggered off.' She taps more ash into the coffee mug. 'And right in the middle of it, while I'm getting Olivia on her feet, trying to get her downstairs to the car, Cathy storms in at eleven on the dot like some fucking prima donna and demands Emily comes home. Virtually drags her out of there, oblivious to everything else, not a word about Olivia or the state she was in, banging on about Emily having an eleven o'clock curfew and that *trust had to be earned,* all that kind of crap. The two of them had a shouting match in the car park, neither of them even thought to *ask* how my girl was doing.'

'But . . . the girls are best friends again now, aren't they?'

'Yeah.' She snorts, puffs of blue-grey smoke curling from her nostrils. 'Although God knows why. They had this big falling-out afterwards, screaming phone calls, crying, sobbing and drama, Olivia refusing to come out of her room, the lot. The whole thing was a completely shit experience for her to go through, but I thought one positive might come out of it – that she'd see what Emily Ruskin was like and be shot of her for good. Except I was wrong about that as well. A couple of weeks later it was business as usual, back to how they'd always been, best buddies again. She's like a drug that my daughter just can't quit.'

She looks at the joint in her hand, raises an eyebrow as if appreciating the irony of her last sentence.

I wait a beat before asking the question I came here for.

'The party at the Grosvenor – did you get the police involved?'

'I wish I had, but Olivia begged me not to.' The joint is down to almost nothing now and she takes one last drag, the bright-burning tip almost touching her fingers. 'Took her for a check-up, blood tests and stuff Monday morning but they never showed anything. Apparently these drugs are out of your system pretty quick.'

I nod slowly as if this is new information. 'And did Olivia mention a lad called Drew Saxton being there?'

'Drew? Yeah. He gets invited to everything, as far as I hear.' She frowns at me, fine-lined eyebrows drawing together. 'Why?

You think he's the one who did it? He's the little bastard spiking these girls?'

'I don't know, but his name keeps coming up.' Seeing the look on her face, I'm already regretting dropping Drew's name into this conversation. 'Although it's probably better if you keep that under your hat for now.'

She stubs the butt out, grinding it into the bottom of the cup. 'Sure.'

Back in my car, I sit for a moment with all the windows down, getting some fresh air into my lungs. I haven't had a joint since I was at uni, and even being in the same room with all that smoke has left me a bit light-headed. There's a lukewarm bottle of water in the glove compartment and I take sips of it, trying to get my thoughts into order.

If what Sophie said was true, Emily had abandoned her best friend when Olivia needed her most. Left her vulnerable, defence-less, against a serial offender who had never been caught. And yet Olivia had forgiven her, it seemed. She'd wanted to be friends again. Best friends.

Even if it meant slipping back into Emily's shadow, not quite as pretty, not quite as self-assured, not quite as popular with either boys or other girls. These two best friends from opposite ends of the neighbourhood, with this strange connection they had.

She's like a drug that my daughter just can't quit.

Olivia had forgiven her. Forgive and forget.

Except . . . what if she hadn't?

What if she had slipped over that perilously thin dividing line between love and hate? She was the only other person with prior knowledge of Emily's plan. Who knew, in advance, *how* Emily was planning to disappear. And what if Olivia had been playing a different game? Biding her time, waiting for her chance to get revenge? To give Emily a taste of what it felt like to be alone, helpless, at someone else's mercy?

And what if it had gone too far?

55

I fill a glass with water from the kitchen tap and drink half of it in one long pull, looking out into the back garden. Harriet's sitting with her laptop in the shade, cross-legged on our wooden bench, the one that's close enough to the house for Wi-Fi. She has her headphones on and is busy typing, the little line appearing between her eyebrows that she gets when she's fully engrossed.

When I turn around Laura is there behind me, iPad in hand. Her face is flushed, her jaw set tight.

'Hey,' I say. 'Just had a really interesting chat with Sophie—'

'I take it you've not seen this yet?' She hands me the iPad, crosses her arms tightly. 'What the hell were you doing? What were you *thinking*?'

I frown at the tablet's screen, most of which is taken up by a news story, the red and white masthead of the *Mirror* at the top of the page. The main picture is a collage of three images: me next to a gate, then a shot of Cathy standing in her doorway as I walk in, and then another shot of me walking back down the driveway on my way out a few minutes later. There's a sudden plunge in my stomach, as if I'm falling but still on my feet. In both images where I'm shot from the front, my face is blurred out. But it's little consolation when I read the headline: SUSPECT'S DAD IN DRUG DASH TO TV STAR.

I skim the first few paragraphs, my stomach sinking lower with every word.

A MYSTERY visitor to TV star Cathy Ruskin was the dad of a suspect in her daughter's disappearance, we can reveal.

Friends and family have been rallying around Cathy, 44, since her 16-year-old daughter Emily vanished after a booze-fuelled party.

But onlookers were shocked when the suspect's dad made a delivery to the front door yesterday. One witness said: 'It looked like a bag full of prescription drugs. Boxes and boxes of them.'

Presumably my face is blurred out because they've made the connection between me and Connor, and he will have anonymity as a juvenile. But people around here – everyone who knows what I look like – will still be able to figure out pretty easily that it's me. How did this reporter find out? How did they know my name, link me to the investigation? Although if the local guy, Dineen, could find out then presumably others could too.

'Christ.' I swallow painfully, scrolling further down the story. 'What the hell?'

'What were you *doing*? How do they even know Connor's a suspect?' Her nose wrinkles as she takes a step closer. 'God, have you been smoking *weed*?'

'Olivia's mum, Sophie,' I say with a shrug. 'She rolled up while I was talking to her. Couldn't exactly just walk out, could I?'

'Stinks,' she says, stepping back.

'So does this story,' I say, gesturing to the iPad. It was hard to explain that the article was right but wrong at the same time, the inference of the words, the spin of the headline, the way the whole thing was made out to be some illicit drug drop. 'It's crap.'

'But you did go there? To her house?'

'Yes, but the bit further down about me—'

Her voice, incredulous, rises above mine. 'Are you out of your mind? It doesn't *matter*!'

'Look, it was yesterday afternoon, I didn't know Connor was going to be questioned again, that they'd be zeroing in on him with all this new stuff. I didn't know, OK? I thought Emily would have come home by now, she would be safe. I was trying to help, just didn't realise how many media were going to be there.'

She shakes her head. 'Help who?'

'Cathy Ruskin. Her family.'

'How about you try to help your *son*? Instead of drawing more attention to us, to Connor? Instead of waltzing around with a bag of drugs like some kind of neighbourhood dealer?'

'They were repeat prescriptions for her family, her other children. Stuff they needed.'

'You're not listening to me – that doesn't matter either!' She takes a deep breath, an effort at calm. 'All that matters is the way it looks.'

I scroll further down. Midway through the story is another image, a shot of Connor and I from maybe a year ago, shoulder to shoulder. He's in his football kit, knees muddied, holding a small Man of the Match trophy; both our faces digitally obscured with an oval blur.

I gesture at the picture. 'Where'd they get that one from?'

'Facebook,' she says, almost sheepishly. Her anger seems to have spent itself. 'I posted it last year. Tightened up my profile today, only friends can see my posts now.'

It obviously didn't take long for the journalist to connect me to Connor, and both of us to Laura, and it occurs to me that restricting her profile now is probably too late. If they've copied one photo, they've probably copied them all for potential future use. *Jesus.* I wonder what else they might have found out about us, what else we've put out there as a family. The business card from Dineen, the *Nottingham Post* reporter, sits like a guilty secret in my wallet. He hadn't written this story but he was from the same camp, the same side of the fence, as the journalist who had.

Laura sighs, closing the iPad and laying it face down on the kitchen table. 'Tell me what you found out from Sophie.'

* * *

I'm still talking her through the exchange, and Olivia's toxic friendship with Emily, when a text drops in from Kay Barber-Lomax. It's a link to the *Mirror* online story accompanied by a characteristically blunt two-word text.

Not ideal

My phone rings before I can start typing a reply, the solicitor's number displaying on the screen.

She doesn't bother with a hello. 'I take it you've seen the *Mirror* story already?'

'Yes,' I say, leaden with the certainty that I've let my son down. 'What do you think, is it bad?'

'Well it's not good, put it that way.'

She quizzes me on what I was doing there, what was said, and tells me in no uncertain terms that I'm not to visit the Ruskins' house again, under *any* circumstances. Putting myself in the media spotlight was *not* going to help Connor's situation, and anything relating to the Emily Ruskin case would be leaped upon by the media looking for a fresh angle. Our faces had been blurred out, she confirms, because the suspect is under eighteen and identifying me would naturally identify Connor too. Even so, they were sailing pretty close to the wind in legal terms. She concedes finally that I had *perhaps* been a little unlucky that we were heading into the summer because there wasn't much competition in terms of other news.

Once the dressing-down has finished, I tell her about my conversation with Sophie de Luca, the potential link to several other girls in the same year group who have been drugged at parties in the last few months. I choose my words slowly, carefully, sensing myself walking a tightrope between being either too specific or not specific enough. We may have found drugs in Connor's room but I still don't believe he is responsible for what happened to those girls.

'Is there any way you can flag that with DS Shah or one of her colleagues? If Emily found out who's been spiking these girls, that could have put her in danger.'

'And you think Drew Saxton is the culprit, do you?'

'His name keeps cropping up. And he was one of the five in the woods on Saturday night.'

She considers this for a moment. 'Is there any other reason why you're interested in these drugs?' Barber-Lomax says carefully. 'Anything else you want to tell me?'

I swallow, thinking of the small Ziploc bag currently tucked under a pile of old bank statements in a box on top of my bedroom wardrobe, wondering if she can read my mind. Laura had wanted to get rid of them, to empty the vials and burn them, bury the ashes, pretend they never existed. But I had argued to keep them, just for a few more days, just in case. *Just in case what?* she'd replied, exasperated. And I didn't really have a good answer. But they were evidence of criminality, maybe the start of something that had ended up with a missing girl and a police hunt and a picture of Connor's face blurred out in a national newspaper.

I don't tell Barber-Lomax about the drugs. 'It just seems like there might be a link.'

'I can have a word in a few ears,' she says, 'see if that's being followed up. But in the absence of any drugs being found at the scene, or since, I'm not sure how much of a priority it'll be.' She hangs up.

Laura is staring at me across the table, her face grim.

'These drugs,' she says, her voice barely above a whisper, 'how much do you know about them? I mean, through work?'

'I've been reading up a bit.'

'Can you overdose?'

I nod. 'Yes, quite easily, particularly if you add alcohol into the mix, and the fact that with illicit drugs the dosage can be all over the place – they can be far more potent than you think. Anything that depresses your central nervous system is inherently dangerous. And GHB is basically a sedative that slows the heart and breathing, so . . . too much would be a very bad idea.'

'Potentially fatal?' I nod, and she adds: 'So maybe Emily was spiked before she set off by herself on Saturday night? And the drugs didn't kick in until she was out there, in the dark, on her own.'

I think back to Connor's account of Saturday night, five teenagers in the woods, smoking and drinking around the flickering light of a campfire. How hard would it have been for one of the others to spike her drink?

'Could be,' I say. 'But then where is she now?'

Harriet bustles in, laptop open in her hands, and we both fall silent.

I go back to the iPad, scrolling through the story to the readers' section at the bottom. Three-quarters of the comments are negative, general trolling to the effect that Cathy Ruskin is getting what she deserves, that she is somehow an unfit mother whose other children should be rescued by social services. There is very little about me or my role in the story – all the bile and blame seems to be directed at Cathy. But I'm still kicking myself for getting into the situation in the first place, however inadvertently it had happened. I shake my head and close the browser window.

The *Find Emily* Facebook page is a different story. As requested, Harriet has been keeping an eye on it and she turns her laptop screen towards me now to give a rundown of who's been saying what, who's getting involved and links to other media articles about the case. The page seems to be run by Olivia and it looks like she's been *very* busy coordinating publicity, fielding interview requests and replying to the hundreds of messages that have flooded in. It strikes me again that Olivia seems to have really come into her own over these past few days. Quick to set up the Facebook page, to bask in the flood of attention afforded to her as the official best friend of the missing girl, to stake her claim in the media as the anguished voice of all Emily's classmates. The image of her holding up a photo of Emily has become one of the most widely shared across social media, in the press and on TV.

Olivia's face has become almost as famous as that of the missing girl herself.

No, I tell myself. *She's just trying to help.* And yet, I can't shake the suspicion I had left her house with only an hour ago, like a nagging itch that won't go away.

Harriet is still talking, telling me about something happening this evening – a candlelit vigil she wants to attend. It's due to be held tonight at seven, at the entrance to Beacon Hill Woods.

'I'll come with you,' I say.

Laura puts her hands on her hips. 'Is that a good idea, bearing in mind today's *Daily Mirror*?'

'I'll be inconspicuous this time,' I say. 'And I want to see who else turns up.'

She doesn't look convinced.

'Just try to stay in the background, OK? And whatever you do, don't talk to any reporters.'

56

A large crowd has already gathered by the time we get there, candles glowing like fireflies against the approaching dusk.

Parents and children, teenagers, people pushing buggies and walking dogs have come together at the top of the field leading into Beacon Hill Woods, stalks of wheat beaten flat on either side of the path where the crowd has made its way up. By my quick count there are 150 people here at least, maybe more. All of them waiting in a loose semicircle, a low hubbub of voices as they light candles for the vigil and nod hellos to friends and neighbours, school gate acquaintances made solemn by the reason that has brought them all here on this warm summer evening. The sun is sinking, the trees throwing long slanting shadows across the field.

As we'd walked up from the house, I'd explained to Harriet the need for us to be inconspicuous, to stay away from cameras and media and not draw attention to ourselves if we could possibly help it. She simply said, *I know, Dad,* as if she is well used to flying under the radar. Nevertheless, she's wearing her favourite *Minecraft* cap, the brim pulled low, and I'm wearing a navy baseball cap and sunglasses. There had been no suggestion of Connor attending and Laura had not wanted to leave him alone in the house; in any case, he had still not emerged from his bedroom after this morning's tearful conversation.

The mood in the crowd is strange, an odd mix of enforced familiarity, but with an edge of tension in everything. Every look, every hello, every half-wave to a neighbour weighed down with a shared fear that none will openly acknowledge: that *this could happen to any of us.* Harriet grips my left hand tightly; she's nervous anywhere she feels boxed in by too many tall adults. We take a place on the edge of the crowd, away from the front but with enough of a gap so she can see through to where the Ruskin family are gathered in the centre of the semicircle.

Cathy is there, her right arm looped through Karl's beside her. On the other side are her two other daughters, one dabbing at her eyes with a tissue, the other impassive behind dark Jackie O. style sunglasses.

'Beautiful, aren't they?' It's not awe or envy in Harriet's voice, but more a statement of fact. Something undeniable.

'You know what?' I say quietly. 'I'm still not quite sure which one's which.'

'Next to her mum is Megan, and the one with the sunglasses is Georgia.'

I look down at her, impressed. She gives a little shrug, adding: 'And the horrible stepfather on the end is Creepy Crosby.'

'Harry,' I chide her quietly. 'You can't say things like that. Not here.'

'He *is* though,' she says seriously. 'He's creepy.'

Alexander Saxton stands with them, a smooth and assured wingman, his face a picture of concern. He's giving an interview to a TV reporter, hands clasped in front of him as if in prayer.

All four members of the family – plus Saxton and a dozen or so teenage girls moving among the crowd, with Olivia de Luca at the vanguard – are wearing *Find Emily* T-shirts, emblazoned with a picture of the teenager's smiling face and the police hotline number. All members of the same team. The friends are busily handing out candles from a box and lighting them for well-wishers; one of them hands one to Harriet, lighting it for her. Others are giving out *Have you seen Emily Ruskin?* flyers with more detailed information about where the sixteen-year-old was last seen, what she was wearing and all the contact information for the police. I notice DS Shah standing off to the side, a little away from the family, her grey trouser suit a contrast to the shorts and T-shirts of most of the people around her.

Arrayed in front of the Ruskins, like a firing squad waiting for the order, is a bank of photographers and camera operators. A thick rank of lenses focused on the family with a second row on mini-stepladders to get a better view.

Cathy raises a hand to acknowledge everyone, and the murmurs of the crowd fall silent.

'Thank you, everyone,' she begins, accompanied by a barrage of clicks and flashes from the cameras. 'Thank you so much for coming to be with us here tonight. To be here for Emily. It has meant so much to us to have your support as we've gone through these terrible last few days, to know that our friends and neighbours are spreading the word, staying vigilant and doing everything they can to help the police to bring Emily back to us . . .'

I scan the crowd, feeling myself starting to tune out. It's disconcerting how fast the words, the platitudes, start to wash over you when you've heard the same thing for three or four days in a row. The tragedy of it is that there's not much new to say because the main thing – the only thing – that matters is that Emily is still missing. She's three full days gone, four if you count Sunday, and the family don't seem any closer to being reunited. Perhaps there's only so much heartbreak we can all cope with, so we change the channel, turn the page, scroll on to something less painful.

A black thought slithers out from the darkest corner of my mind.

What if Connor is the reason we are all here this evening? The reason we're all gathered on a hillside, watching this spectacle of tortured hope? What if he's lying?

No. No, not Connor. Not my son.

I shiver as if someone has just walked over my grave, shaking the thought free. Harriet looks up at me, a question in her dark brown eyes, clutching my hand a little tighter. I give her a tight smile and return my gaze to the Ruskin family.

The twins are arm in arm half a pace behind their mother, both of them crying now. I try to picture Emily alongside them. But even if she was here, I'm not sure I would have put them all together as siblings; where Emily is blonde, petite and fair, the twins are dark, tall with their mother's olive complexion. I guess Emily got a different shake of the genetic dice.

Karl Crosby looks like he's coming apart at the seams. He's grey-faced and unshaven, his *Find Emily* T-shirt already creased and stained dark with sweat. By contrast, Cathy looks like the glue that's holding the whole family together. I tune back into what she's saying and I'm struck again by her strength, her stamina.

'. . . so I just want to thank everyone again for being with us here this evening,' she says finally, her lower lip trembling. 'For helping us to keep the faith and joining us in praying for Emily's safe return. I hope you'll continue to keep us in your thoughts and prayers until the day that she comes back to us.'

There is a polite smattering of applause from the crowd, people unsure of the correct response to her speech but still wanting to show their support. The assembled media move forward and Cathy is taken to one side by a high-heeled TV reporter, camera operator in tow. One of the daughters, Georgia, I think, steps forward into the glare of artificial light to field another interview request a few metres away.

The low hubbub of chatter starts again in the crowd, people looking around and a few taking pictures, no one wanting to be the first to leave. There's a shift in front of us, a ripple as the gathered journalists continue to disperse among the residents. Through the gap I see Olivia again, two reporters holding out their phones to record as they ask her questions that she must have answered dozens of times already this week. *Are you still hopeful Emily will be found safe and well? What's your message to Emily? What would you say to people who might have information?* She's immaculately made up, blonde hair straightened, not showing any sign of fatigue at the repetition of the questions being directed at her. In fact, she is almost glowing with the attention, like a flower turned up to the sun. She's saying something about another event she's planning for Friday night, then more people crowd the space in between us and her words are lost.

I'm scanning the crowd for my brother when a tall, thin figure appears at my shoulder.

'Tried to warn you,' a male voice says. 'About that story.' I turn and see Dineen, the local reporter, standing next to me. He's in a short-sleeved black shirt and jeans, leather messenger bag across his chest, his eyes hidden behind mirrored aviators. 'The guy from the *Mirror* was asking everyone in the pack who you were, what your connection was to the family. Did you not get the card I put through your letterbox?'

'Why were you trying to warn me?'

Dineen shrugs. 'Don't like to see a good bloke getting turned over. And those guys on the nationals will always turn you over if they have to, because they know they're probably never going to see you again.' He puts a hand to his chest. 'Whereas your *local* media have a stake in getting things right, because we know we'll probably see you around.'

The crowd is thinning, shifting, as a few parents with pushchairs start to head back down the hill. Other people mill about, serious faces lit by the late evening sun, still keen to do *more*, to do something that might make a difference beyond just showing solidarity with a desperate family.

'Wasn't even a story,' I say, more to myself than him. 'Not really.'

Dineen gestures to the scene around us. 'Day four of this case and there's no solid progress. Everybody's news desk is screaming for a new angle, something fresh. Anything.'

'It's a good turnout this evening, at least.'

He leans in, conspiratorial. 'We're into that weird time of the investigation though, aren't we? Big elephant in the room.'

'What are you talking about?'

'I mean, day *four*, right?' He lowers his voice. 'Day four is not really about finding her alive, anymore, is it? After the first twenty-four hours in this kind of case, the chances of that start to drop exponentially. It's about finding a body now. Everyone *knows* that's the reality, but no one's saying it out loud.'

'I don't believe that.' I shake my head. 'There's got to be hope, there must be a chance otherwise what the hell are we all doing here?'

'People are drawn to tragedy, they always have been, always will be. To see it up close, really close, and think, *There but for the grace of God go I.*'

'That's pretty cynical.'

He shrugs. 'It's human nature.'

Harriet is staring up at the reporter with a deep frown of dislike. Dineen gives her a small wave but she doesn't reciprocate.

'Me and Toffee are going to have a look around,' she says to me. 'See if we can find Florence.'

'Stay where I can see you,' I say. 'Don't go far.'

She trots off in search of her friend, Toffee straining at his lead.

Dineen holds his phone up high, snapping a couple of pictures of the crowd. 'You're right though, it is a good turnout.' When I don't reply, he lowers his voice and adds: 'But I find it's always more interesting at these things to see who's *not* here, rather than who is. Don't you think?'

'First one of these things I've ever been to,' I say. 'Hang on a minute, are you going to quote me on this?'

'Hey, don't worry.' He shoves the phone in his pocket and holds his hands up. 'No notes, no quotes. We're fully off the record here.'

I manage ten long seconds of silence. I don't really want to play his game but I can't resist.

'So who's not here?' I say, scanning the crowd. 'Looks to me like half of West Bridgford has turned up.'

He leans in, close enough for me to smell the coffee on his breath. 'Drew Saxton.'

My son is not here either; nor is my nephew. But I don't particularly want to get into that with a reporter.

'So?' I say instead. 'What does it mean that Drew didn't show?'

'I mean no one's even seen him for *days*, apparently. Parents have been keeping him at home under house arrest.'

I turn to him with a frown. 'Where'd you hear that?'

'I could tell you.' He winks. 'But then I'd have to kill you.' Realising what he's just said, he adds quickly: 'Sorry, probably not appropriate considering the circumstances. Let's just say I have it on very good authority that young Drew has been properly grounded since the weekend.'

Something in the way he says it reminds me of conspiracy theories, the way people talk to each other on social media with such ironclad confidence about 5G masts causing coronavirus and vaccine shots carrying secret microchips. *I have it on very good authority that the moon landings were faked.*

I'm starting to make my excuses and walk away to find Harriet when the reporter puts a hand on my arm.

'Something else interesting, about Mr Saxton senior.' He leans in a little closer. 'The whisper is that he's one bad deal away from going under.'

57

Dineen grins, pleased to have reeled me in again.

'That's right.' He nods. 'You wouldn't know it to look at the guy, but his whole business is on a knife-edge. Three of his flagship projects got mothballed during the pandemic and ever since then he's been in a hole he can't dig his way out of. He's one more blown deal away from losing everything.' He holds up a fist and opens the fingers, blows air through his lips. 'All of it, gone.'

I think about the size of Alexander's house, the posh Avenue address, the three flashy cars on the drive. The security cameras, the expensive wristwatch. He had seemed the very picture of affluence, a successful businessman who knew how to make money – and spend it. But maybe it was all hanging by a thread, all of it an expensive mirage to hide the precarious truth of his situation?

Or maybe that was just another conspiracy theory.

'According to who?' I say.

'I've been at the *Post* a lot of years, my friend, spent quite a few of them digging into Saxton's business affairs. Some murky stuff in there as well, let me tell you. It's been one of my little side projects, hasn't paid off yet but when it does . . . it's going to be a big story.

A real bombshell. When he goes down, a lot of people are going to go down with him.'

I check over my shoulder, to make sure we're not overheard. 'And the deal he's depending on . . . ?'

Dineen points a long index finger straight down at the ground on which we're standing.

'Houses,' he says, with a knowing nod. 'Right here. The Beacon Hill estate, the one he's been trying to get planning consent on for the last couple of years. It's his lifeline – he either gets it through or his company goes under.'

'So run the story then, if you've got it.'

He gives me a knowing smile. 'Not yet. Not until I can get the facts I need on the record. His lawyers will have me for breakfast otherwise.' He spots Olivia through a gap in the crowd. 'Better get some fresh quotes for tonight's piece, I suppose. It was nice to see you again, Dr Boyd.' He pulls a notepad and pen from his messenger bag and lopes off towards the bustle of people and cameras surrounding the Ruskin family.

For the first time since we arrived on the hill, I'm alone, at the far edge of the crowd. Feeling more cut off, more isolated than ever. Feeling like I shouldn't be here. I've not seen Sophie de Luca here either, although judging by our conversation this afternoon – and what she felt about her daughter's friendship with Emily – that's not a great surprise. There is a shift in the milling crowd and I spot my brother on the far side of the gathering, standing apart, with his hands in the pockets of his jeans. He seems to be on his own, no sign of Zac. Each of us alone then, each of us on the periphery of this vigil for a missing teenager. With more at stake than we can bear to lose.

I raise a hand to wave to him. For a moment our eyes meet, but his hands stay in his pockets.

He turns and walks off down the hill.

Harriet and Toffee reappear, accompanied by another small girl with another small dog.

'Dad?' my daughter says brightly. 'Can I walk home with Florence and Marmite and her parents? Her mum and dad are just over there and they'll be going past our house, they said they don't mind.' She points to a couple I know a little further down the path. It occurs to me that this isn't a safe neighbourhood anymore; it's the kind of place where sixteen-year-old girls go missing. Maybe the kind of place where you don't let your kids out of your sight.

I bite down on the instinct, telling myself that Harriet will be perfectly safe walking home with a friend and her parents.

'As long as you all stay together,' I say, 'and text me when you get home, OK?'

'Are you not coming?'

'Soon.'

The two girls head off, already chattering away to each other, half skipping as the two curly-haired dogs lead the way. I watch them for a moment as they join up with the parents, the dad raising a hand to me as the group turns to walk down the hill. Other people are already starting to drift away, the sun glowing orange now as it dips towards the horizon. But Cathy is still the centre of attention, people clustering around her to talk to her, put a hand on her arm, taking turns to embrace her. DS Shah stands nearby, talking with a small group of parents. Dineen's comment about Alexander Saxton is stuck on a loop inside my head. *He's one bad deal away from going under.* And if his son Drew was implicated in Emily's disappearance on this very spot, the negative press alone would likely sink any chance of the house-building project going ahead.

I'm still thinking about it when I spot a slim figure near the woods, separated from the crowd. Georgia Ruskin, a navy hoodie over her *Find Emily* T-shirt, the hood pulled up over her head. But the big sunglasses give her away. She's looking at her phone, typing fast. It's strange to see her out on her own, away from her family, but maybe the vigil had just got too much.

Then she does something interesting.

She slides the phone into her pocket and starts walking. But instead of heading back into the throng, back to her family, she turns and heads *up* the hill. She's alone, striding fast, angling across the field towards the entrance to the woods. A moment later, she's through the three-bar gate, ducking under a line of police tape and disappearing into the trees.

Where are you going, Georgia? What are you looking for?

I follow her.

58

At the entrance to the woods, on both sides of the gate, colour posters have been pinned to the wooden uprights. Emily's face is at eye level as I walk through, urgent capitals above the picture. *HAVE YOU SEEN EMILY RUSKIN?* The flyers tucked inside clear plastic wallets to protect them from the elements, between blue and white police tape nominally supposed to keep people out of the woods. Another one is pinned to the noticeboard just inside, alongside a curling flyer about the next meeting of the Friends of Beacon Hill.

Through the gate, the trees make the evening a few shades darker and I take off my sunglasses before catching sight of Georgia ahead of me, moving quickly along the path that leads deeper into the heart of the woods. She's picked up her pace; she seems to know where she is going. The woods are still busy with calling birds in the branches above us, one last song before the sun disappears for the evening. The path is compacted earth baked firm by the summer sun, my footsteps muffled almost into silence.

Georgia walks through the trees ahead of me and I quicken my pace to keep her navy hoodie in sight. As I watch, she takes her phone from her pocket again and raises it to her ear, but I'm too far away to hear any of the conversation. She moves left, off the track, deeper into the trees. Again, there is no hesitation, no pausing to check her bearings. She knows these woods. Far better than I do, at any rate.

She's well off the trail now and it seems to be getting darker by the minute, thick-limbed trees snuffing out the daylight even before the sun has fully disappeared. I follow her through a clearing, recognising the smooth fallen logs facing each other across the campfire's blackened remains; the navy blue fragments of a blazer burned on the last day of school last week. I know this place. My brother and I were here on Sunday morning, searching for Zac – unaware he was safe in Connor's bed. Unaware that Emily was the one who actually needed help.

Another hundred metres further in, Georgia slows next to a fallen tree, turning first left then right. She stops, stands still for a moment. I conceal myself behind a wide oak, leaning out slightly to see what she's doing. Georgia crouches down with one hand against the earth, her palm flat to the ground almost as if she's trying to feel a vibration through the soil. She stands and moves around the same spot, scuffing at a few patches of dirt with the end of her trainers. Her eyes are fixed on the ground the whole time, like she's looking for something she's left behind or lost. Or perhaps just revisiting the place where all of this started, hoping for a trace of her younger sister, a sense of her still lingering among the trees.

She sniffs, her shoulders shaking, and I realise she's crying.

Abruptly, I remember Dineen's words. *It's about finding a body now. Everyone knows that's the reality, but no one's saying it out loud.*

The thought is like a shock of cold water on the back of my neck. *No. Not that. Please don't let it be that.*

My phone beeps, the electronic sound loud and out of place in the stillness of the woods. Georgia looks up sharply as I duck back behind the oak and snatch the phone out of my pocket. A message from Harriet.

Home safe. Toffee chased a squirrel! Mum says when u back? xx

I switch it to silent and shove it back into the pocket of my shorts.

When I look back again, Georgia has disappeared. How can that be? She was here moments ago, and now she's slipped away. I peer further around the tree. Gone.

I wait a minute to see if she reappears from the undergrowth, but the woods are silent. I make my way carefully forward until I'm standing where she was standing, next to the fallen tree, its roots ripped from the earth and exposed like entrails torn clear by a giant hand.

Why here? Why was Georgia drawn to this particular spot? In the gathering gloom, I scan the ground to see if I can make out any signs of disturbed earth or anything out of place. A scattering of leaves and patches of grass, nettles and weeds sprouting in the shadow of the fallen tree. Nothing that looks immediately suspicious, no freshly turned earth piled up and bulging darkly from the ground.

A crack behind me snatches my attention. Heavy footsteps crunching through leaves, not making any attempt to be stealthy. For a moment I can't work out how Georgia has circled back so quickly, until I make out a stocky figure approaching through the trees, brushing branches aside as he strides towards me.

It's Karl Crosby.

As he comes closer, moving out of a shadow and into a slash of light from the setting sun, I can see his face is red with engorged blood, veins standing out in his neck like steel cords. He looks angry. More than that; he looks *enraged*. He looks quickly left and right, then back over his shoulder as if he's checking there's no one else around. A twig snaps off to my right and I turn my head instinctively towards the sound, but can't see anything beyond a screen of bushes.

Crosby throws the punch as I'm turning back.

For a big man, he's very fast. His right fist snaps forward like a piston and there is an explosion of pain in my jaw, a bomb going off inside my mouth. I must black out for a few seconds as the punch connects because there is no sensation of falling, of impact with the ground. One moment I'm standing in the woods as his fist arcs towards me, the next I'm flat on my back in the dirt. A throbbing, pounding pain radiating from my face and up the side of my skull.

The warm, coppery taste of blood is in my mouth. *Get. Up.* I raise my head, a sick wave of dizziness washing over me before I lie back down in the leaves. Through a fog of pain and fear, I think of the phone call Georgia had made as I followed her through the woods. I guess I had not been as stealthy as I thought.

Crosby stands over me, fists clenched at his sides, contempt radiating from him like a solar flare. Out here, deep in the woods, there is something animalistic about him, something savage and primal shining from his eyes as if he'd like to hit me again and again. Georgia appears, standing a little behind him, her face lined with fright. The pair loom, silhouetted against the swaying trees and the darkening sky above, the teenager and her de facto step-father separated in age by barely a dozen years.

Crosby leans down, meaty hands on his knees.

'Why were you following her?' he spits. 'What kind of weirdo follows a young girl into the woods?'

'I want to help find Emily, just like everyone else.'

'Of *course* you do.' His tone is heavy with sarcasm. 'But Georgia wanted to be on her own for a minute, get away from all the people. Bloody good thing I was here to protect her too.'

'I was just curious, wanted to see what she was—'

'You're a weirdo,' he says loudly. 'Just like your son.'

I swallow down my nausea. 'My son is innocent.'

'Your son's a fucking menace and you're just as bad for not turning him in.' He shakes his head. 'He needs to do the decent thing, tell the police what he did to Emily.'

'He would never hurt her.' Every word sends a fresh burst of pain through my jaw. 'He wouldn't hurt anyone.'

'By the way,' Crosby says, leaning closer so he's right in my face, 'if you've got a problem with me, be a man about it, come to *me*. Don't go skulking around behind my back, sending anonymous emails, spreading shit about things that never happened. The way I hear it, the police are about to drop the hammer on your boy so it doesn't make a difference you spinning your pathetic lies anyway.' His face twists with anger again. 'And yes, I know it was you who emailed the cops, so don't try to deny it. If I ever hear of you trying to drop me in it again, I will come down on you like the worst shitstorm you've ever seen. Do you understand?'

He leans in closer, flecks of spittle on his lips.

'And if you ever come near my girls again, I'll fucking kill you.'

THURSDAY

59

DS Shah is on the road when I call her, a background of traffic and engine noise.

'So you're saying Mr Crosby assaulted you?' She sounds bright and full of energy. 'Last night?'

I've had another night of broken sleep, a few hours snatched in between long periods lying awake, my racing thoughts taking me to ever-worsening places. A darkening bruise along my jawline where the punch landed, the pain settling into a low, steady throb. When I came home bruised and muddy from the woods Laura had insisted on fixing me up with a bag of ice cubes to lower the swelling, and a large whisky-and-water on the side. Since this morning, I'd just been dosing myself on paracetamol.

'Yes, but that's not why I'm calling,' I say, taking another sip of coffee. The ache in my jaw makes even this small movement painful. 'After the vigil I saw Georgia Ruskin going into the woods, to a very particular place—'

'Because Mr Crosby is saying a similar thing. Except he says *you* assaulted *him*.'

'What?'

'He called me last night. Said Georgia was upset and overwhelmed after the vigil and went into the woods to be alone. She got worried because she thought someone was following her, so she called Karl. You then confronted this *young woman*—' she emphasises the words '—and when Mr Crosby arrived you became abusive and physical and he had to defend himself.'

I'm reminded of Connor's account of what happened by the campfire on Saturday night, Drew trying to force himself on Emily. Connor dragging him off. Except Drew had said it was the other way around.

A twisted mirror image of the truth.

Accuse your enemies of the exact things you have done yourself, fill the air with confusion and counter-accusations until it's almost impossible to discern the truth. It seemed to be more and more common these days.

'I've got the bruises to prove that's not true.' As if on cue, my jaw starts to throb again. 'Do I strike you as the kind of person who starts fights? He threatened to kill me, he's a dangerous guy. In fact, if you look into his professional history you'll find some pretty concerning stuff relating to some of his previous teaching roles, jobs he left in a hurry.' She makes a noise that I can't quite decipher, and I wonder if she knows it was me that sent the anonymous email on Tuesday night. But at this point I'm past caring. 'Maybe you should get *him* into an interview room, ask him about Saturday night.'

'No need,' she says calmly. 'He's got an alibi for the period in question.'

'From whom?'

'That doesn't really concern you.'

'All the same, I'd like to know.'

She sighs. 'His alibi is solid, put it that way.'

'You mean Cathy?'

'I mean, it doesn't concern you.' She lets that hang in the air for a moment. 'Look, this thing between the two of you last night, it would be your word against his, I'm afraid.'

'Georgia Ruskin saw it too.'

'Georgia is too upset to speak to us, according to Mr Crosby. But if you want to go forward with a formal allegation I can get a colleague to take your statement at the station. Obviously we're stretched pretty thin at the moment so I can't promise it will be top of the priority list.'

I shake my head in exasperation and tell her I don't want to make a statement. I repeat instead how Georgia had seemed interested in one particular spot in Beacon Hill Woods, one specific place near to where the five teenagers had gathered on Saturday night. My suspicion that she might have been looking for something.

'I can lead you there,' I tell her. 'With the sniffer dogs, ground-penetrating radar or whatever kit you have. I remember the route, I can show you exactly where she was looking, right by this fallen tree. There must be evidence, maybe something that could help the investigation. Or something . . . buried.'

In truth, I was worried that even if the police went up there right away, it might already be too late. Last night Crosby had stood and watched me as I picked myself up off the ground and stumbled away, back to the path and out of the woods. With his feet planted wide, arms crossed, he'd made it quite clear he wasn't moving, wasn't going to relinquish the little piece of territory by the fallen tree until I was gone. For all I knew, he had spent what remained of the fast-fading light removing evidence, or other-wise obscuring anything else that might shed light on Emily's disappearance. Had Georgia gone up there because she suspected her stepfather knew where Emily was? Or was Georgia somehow involved too?

'No need,' Shah says crisply. 'We've already checked. Carried out a thorough sweep of that area earlier this week and we didn't turn up any potential disposal sites.'

For a moment I think I've misheard her.

'Well . . . how about you do it again?' I try to keep a lid on my frustration. 'Now that I have new information, I can take you to literally the exact spot.'

Shah sighs. 'Thanks, Dr Boyd. But how about you stick to doling out antibiotics and I'll stick to being a police officer?'

With that, she tells me she has to go to a briefing and rings off. With a muttered curse, I toss the phone down on my desk with a clatter. How can the police be so obtuse? Are they really so laser-focused on Connor that they won't entertain any other possibilities?

I have a four-hour clinic this morning but it's only a half-day cover for a colleague so I should be able to get away by 1 p.m. I can go back up to the woods myself this afternoon, while it's still full daylight.

Maybe I can find what Georgia had been looking for – now that I know exactly where to look.

* * *

For once, I keep pretty much to time and I'm only ten minutes late for my last patient. I've been distracted all morning, half my mind on Connor, hurrying patients along and sidestepping a few questions about the bruise along my jawline. Closing down a couple who want to just have a *quick word* about this *one other thing* that's been bothering them. Normally I would listen but today I don't have time, I just need to get through my list and get back out there. A quick check of my mobile in between every patient in case there are any updates on the case. As my last appointment finally leaves, I type up some cursory notes, ignore the unread messages stacking up in my email inbox and shut down my PC.

I retrieve my phone from the drawer, heart lurching in my chest as I see two missed calls and three texts from Connor in the last few minutes. After his night in the cells it didn't seem fair to confine him to the house for the rest of the day. He had begged us to be allowed outside, to get out of the house, anything so that he didn't feel four walls closing in on him.

My mind races with new possibilities: he's been arrested again? Or maybe this time it's Olivia's turn? Or perhaps the police are searching the woods again after all? As I switch the phone out of silent mode it rings in my hand, Connor's name on the display.

'Dad?' His voice is tight with panic. 'I need you, can you come and pick me up?'

'What's happened? Where are you?'

'Can you just come? Right now!'

I try to think where he might be: traffic noise in the background, a busy street, shops and people and the far-off wail of a siren.

'Yes of course, I'm going to my car and leaving work now, OK?' I grab for my keys, knocking the dregs of my coffee across the desk. 'Are you all right? Are you hurt? Are you in a public place?'

'I'm scared, Dad.' Every word is brittle, like glass that could shatter at any moment. 'There's someone following me.'

60

HARRIET

It wasn't snooping. Not really.

It was no different to walking down the street and looking into someone's front window. Seeing what they were watching on TV, or what kind of wallpaper they had. And Mum did that all the time, so it couldn't be *that* bad, could it? And besides, she'd heard her parents talking, she'd listened to what they were saying. She *agreed* with what they were saying. At the end of all of this, when they had figured it all out, they would probably claim it was their idea in the first place. That was what adults usually did.

And her brother? He couldn't see it, couldn't seem to see anything clearly at the moment. But then the pre-frontal cortex of a sixteen-year-old was still not fully developed; the rational part of his brain in a daily struggle with all those tendencies towards impulsive, emotional, risk-taking behaviour.

Her mum and dad were too busy worrying about Connor to listen to her. They thought she was too young to do anything useful.

Admittedly, what she'd done might not be strictly *legal*.

But soon that wouldn't matter. As soon as she *proved* what she'd found, she'd tell them.

She would show her mum and dad. She would show everyone.

Until then, it would be her secret.

Harriet checked her information for the third time, the digital breadcrumbs that had been inadvertently left behind. It was all there: pulse, step count, calorie burn. Elevated levels across all three, with particular spikes between 1.10 a.m. and 2.03 a.m. Elevated levels between those two times that showed intermittent exertion.

Someone had been busy in the early hours of Sunday morning.

61

There is an uncomfortable plunging sensation in my stomach.

'Who's following you, Connor?' I wedge the phone against my shoulder as I lock the door of my consulting room. 'Is it Karl Crosby?'

'What?' There is a rustling on the line and his voice comes back quieter, as if he's speaking very close to the mouthpiece. 'I just came into town to get out of the house for a bit, try to clear my head, and I noticed these people following me. I'm sure one of them was on the bus with me and there's a guy in a car and another one dressed like a bike courier and they're like, *stalking* me. They're police, I'm sure of it.'

'Tell me exactly where you are, I'm coming now to pick you up.'

I'm still talking to him as I hurry out of the surgery and down to my car, wanting to keep him on the line as long as I can. He sounds frightened, freaked out, as if he might be on the verge of doing something foolish. I keep the call going on the hands-free as I drive into town, not minding the silences between us as long as I can retain this one tenuous link with my son. Then he's on the move again, phone pressed to his ear as he walks the half-mile through busy shopping streets to the bottom of Mansfield Road.

He's still being followed, he says.

I finally hang up when I spot him on a bench near the Victoria Shopping Centre. He has his hoodie pulled up over his head, hands buried in his pockets, barely acknowledging me as I sit down on the other end of the bench.

'I tried to shake them off but they're still there,' he says, chin almost on his chest.

He nods up the street towards a silver Ford Mondeo parked against the kerb in a lay-by. A bald guy in his late thirties is behind the wheel, phone to his ear. Talking, half smiling, not looking at us.

'And don't look now,' Connor says, 'but the woman in the bus shelter over your right shoulder is one of them too. Three buses have been past and she's not got on any of them.'

I half turn on the bench, trying to be casual, and scan the handful of people at the bus stop. A couple of pensioners, a young guy in a suit, a mum holding a toddler's hand. A blonde woman in a denim jacket, partially obscured by a poster advertising the new iPhone.

'I said don't look!' Connor hisses.

'We don't know for sure they're police, they might just be—'

'They are!' he says, teeth gritted. 'There was a bike courier too and maybe others I haven't spotted yet. Why are they following me, Dad?'

I don't want to say it out loud. If he's right, there's only one obvious answer that springs to mind. *Because they think you might incriminate yourself further, son, might try to dispose of evidence. Might lead them to a kidnap victim, a body.* I wonder now whether this was why DS Shah released him from custody yesterday. Why she wasn't interested in following up the lead I gave her about

Georgia's walk in the woods. Whether it was part of her game plan all along, for Connor to lead them to Emily.

Or whether the strain my son has been under is tipping him into paranoia.

'The woman at the bus stop,' he says under his breath. 'I swear she's been watching me for the last ten minutes.'

I turn my head slowly, casually, to look over at the blonde woman again. She's early thirties, hair tied back, sunglasses on, one strap of a rucksack over her shoulder as she peers at the bus timetable.

There *is* something about her, something oddly familiar.

I can't quite put my finger on it. Am I imagining it? And then . . .

A tingle of recognition.

She turns her head slightly, her eyes falling on us just for a moment before they move away, and I know where I've seen her before.

Central Police Station, Sunday afternoon.

Detective Constable Jude Loughlin. She had sat with Harriet in the main office while Connor was interviewed for the first time. We'd only exchanged a few words, but I remembered her – everything about that grim day seemed to be imprinted on my brain and I couldn't forget it even if I tried.

I stare at her for a moment longer, until all the doubt is gone. It's definitely her.

It *could* be a coincidence, I guess.

But not today.

'I think they might be getting desperate,' I say to my son. 'Come on, the car's not far. Let's get you home.'

I keep one eye on the rear-view mirror as we head south, out of town, over the Trent and back into West Bridgford. The silver Mondeo stays a few cars back all the way until we get to our street, then it peels off and disappears. Connor spends the journey slouched down low in the passenger seat, the hoodie still pulled forward over his head.

When we get home, he goes into the lounge, peering nervously through the window at cars parked on our street before drawing the curtains and plunging the room into a warm semi-darkness.

'Make them go away, Dad. Tell them it wasn't—'

The landline rings beside him and he flinches away from the sudden noise. I answer it and listen to the first few words of a recorded message about a tax rebate before I hang up.

'Just junk,' I say to him. 'Listen, let's go into the kitchen, I'll make you something to eat.'

He shakes his head. 'I need to go to my room.' His footsteps thud loudly as he takes the stairs two at a time.

I go back out onto the pavement, looking up and down the street for the silver car or DC Loughlin. But there's nothing that looks out of place for a Thursday afternoon. No one sitting in a parked car or loitering on the corner, smoking a cigarette. Laura and Harriet are at the kitchen table, each with a laptop open in front of them plus a scattering of A4 notepads, torn-out sheets covered in Laura's looping handwriting, school yearbooks, photos, pens and newspapers. They both look up when I walk in, their quiet conversation stopping mid-flow.

'How is he?' Laura says, concern etched on her face.

'Tired,' I say, dropping my keys on the kitchen side. 'Anxious. Depressed. Looks like the police have put surveillance on him.'

'What?' she says. 'Really?

'There was one in town, shadowing us on foot, another one in a car.'

'Isn't that harassment, or something?'

'I imagine they'd claim they're just doing their job, but I don't know. They've both gone now, as far as I can tell. Connor's gone to his room for a bit.'

'And how's your face?' Laura says.

'Same,' I say. I gesture at the paperwork piled on the table. 'What are you two up to? You look as if you've been busy.'

They glance at each other, then back at me. 'We found a couple of things,' my wife says. 'And you're not going to like either of them.'

Harriet turns the screen of her laptop towards me: a story in the *Daily Mail* online with images of the Ruskin family taken at last night's vigil on the hillside. The headline in heavy black capitals is EMILY COPS ZERO IN ON SUSPECT. I scan the first few lines.

An arrest is imminent in the case of missing teenager Emily Ruskin, according to police.

The net is closing on a prime suspect, believed to be a school friend of 16-year-old Emily – who has been missing since Sunday.

A source close to the investigation said police had made significant strides and were 'very, very close to making a key arrest'.

As I read the words, my stomach knots. Is this a leak from DS Shah, to put more pressure on us? Perhaps someone higher up the food chain desperate to show that progress is being made in the case? Or another story spun up out of almost nothing by a reporter desperate for a fresh angle?

Maybe a little bit of all three. But it feels like time is running out.

Harriet says: 'They mean Connor, don't they? That they're going to arrest him? I didn't want to put it on the family WhatsApp in case he saw it.'

'He's probably seen it anyway, sweetheart.' I fetch a tall glass from the cupboard and fill it from the tap. 'Try not to worry about stories like that, they're out of our control.'

My daughter tucks her laptop under her arm and hops off her chair.

'Going back up to my room,' she says. 'Do some more.'

I give her a quizzical look. 'More what?'

'You know.' She shrugs. 'Detective stuff.'

I watch her scamper into the hall and head up the stairs before turning back to my wife. 'So what's the other thing you've found?'

Laura points at her own laptop. 'We've been checking social media, see who's saying what on Twitter and the rest, and *oh my goodness* there are a lot of hideous people on there, saying the most horrible things about Cathy and Emily.'

'I know. The trolls have been having a field day.'

'But it gave me an idea. Cathy Ruskin has most of her followers on Instagram, like fifty thousand, so I thought I'd concentrate on that. Spent quite a few hours going through her recent posts and seeing who commented, especially the unpleasant ones.'

'And?'

My wife gestures to a kitchen chair. 'You look done in, Andy. Why don't you have a seat?'

I stay standing. 'Just tell me.'

She sighs. 'OK. So, we've been trying to work out what's been going on, right? All of us. Trying to figure out who wants Connor as a scapegoat for whatever happened up in the woods. You've been digging up stuff on Drew and Alexander; wondering whether Olivia might have some sick love/hate thing going on with Emily that went too far. According to Olivia's mum, Emily's just gone off with some boy and is lapping up all the attention. And there are things I've found out about Karl Crosby's seedy past that I wish to God I'd never known.' She wrinkles her nose as if reacting to a bad smell. 'But we might've been overlooking something much closer to home. Something that's been right under our noses the whole time.'

62

My throat is suddenly parched and I take a sip of water. 'What are you talking about?'

'Sit down,' my wife says, 'and I'll show you.'

Reluctantly, I pull out a kitchen chair and sit at the table opposite her, clearing a small space amid the papers.

Laura half turns her laptop screen towards me and begins to give me a rundown of Cathy Ruskin's Instagram account – @CathyR_TV: 52k followers, 1139 posts, 325 following.

'Look at this.' She selects one of Cathy's recent posts, from a couple of weeks ago. The picture is of Cathy and Karl on sunloungers by a back-garden pool, looking relaxed and happy.

'What am I looking at?' I say.

'She has loads and loads of fans, right?' Laura says. 'Tens of thousands. But also some trolls who seem to follow her just so they can have a go at her and make nasty comments. Some of them are horrible. I mean, like, *really* horrible.' She clicks into the comments and points out a few in particular as she scrolls through, vitriol dripping from the words like battery acid.

Hope u get skin cancer #bitch #rotinhell
Me + my paedo boyfriend chillin by the pool

The second comment is accompanied by a string of emojis, a laughing/crying face, vomiting face, a baby with a dummy, dollar signs.

'These are actually quite tame,' Laura says, 'compared to some of the worst ones.'

'Why doesn't she just block these people?'

'Because blocking them is validating them, telling them they've got through to her. It's like a badge of honour to them – *I got blocked by @CathyR_TV*. Allowing them to have a little piece of her time. And because if you block them they'll just come back ten minutes later with a new account, new username. She said that in an interview on *Loose Women*. It's on YouTube.'

I remembered the hashtag *#BeccaNorris* that had been trending on social media right at the beginning of this, the casual suggestion that Cathy was somehow copying what had happened in Worcester, where a mother had falsely claimed her daughter had been kidnapped in order to collect reward money for her return.

'It's just so grim,' I say. 'The things people will put out there for the whole world to see. The way some people respond.'

'Exactly.' Laura points a finger at the laptop. 'So I started thinking, what if the person who's got Emily is one of *these* people? One of the haters? What if they've been doing all of this trolling online but they see it never makes any difference because Cathy is still this successful, resilient person with this amazing family. Then one of her online haters got so frustrated and angry that they wanted to do something to her in real life? More than just leaving nasty comments, they wanted to *really* hurt her, so they kidnapped Emily?'

'Seems like a big leap from one to the other,' I say, rubbing my chin. 'But I'd assume the police are already looking at that angle.'

'Doubt it,' she says sceptically. 'Those police station computers are running on an unpatched operating system that's nearly as old as Harry.'

'How do you know that?'

My wife shrugs her shoulders. 'She told me. After that first visit to the police station on Sunday.'

She switches screens on her laptop to bring up a spreadsheet of usernames, avatars, dates and links. 'Anyway, never mind that. I've gone through all of her posts from the last two months, making a list of the main offenders, all the worst trolls, the persistent ones. I divided them into three categories – just casual meanness, properly nasty and then actual physical threats.'

She points at the screen. The first group, colour-coded in yellow, contains dozens and dozens of usernames. A few pages' worth. The next group is coded orange, maybe fifty in all.

The red group is at the bottom of the spreadsheet.

'The worst of the worst,' Laura says. 'There are about fifteen who make regular appearances, usually saying things which are either clear or implied threats of physical harm to Cathy, Karl, some or all of the children.'

I scan the list of usernames and avatars in the red group. None of them use a recognisable name: they have online identities like @wolfkiller401K and @$tillOnTilt$. Outwardly, in real life, these people were probably unremarkable. Average. Normal. But online, they vented at the world, vented at life, vomited their bile into the digital void. I try to work out if any of the usernames look familiar in any way, but nothing jumps out.

'But they're anonymous, right?'

'Not necessarily.'

I stare at more of the usernames: *@battlebitchXX*, *@Eat_Me1111*, *@fu_fu0606*. 'They look like nonsense to me.'

'But each one is a real person on a real device.'

'I suppose . . .'

'So I bought this software called IP Finder. It's mostly sold to police and tech companies, people like that, but they have a home version as well. You know what an IP address is, right?' I nod before she continues. 'It's like a unique label that identifies a device connected to the internet. Well, this software, it's like a search tool for finding out what IP address someone is using. Even if you only know one thing about someone, you feed in that one thing—'

'Like someone's Instagram account?'

'Yes. Like that. It's kind of like giving one of those police sniffer dogs a piece of your clothing to smell, and then turning them loose to track you down. So you feed in what you have and it goes off and trawls the web for clues to who that person is, like similar usernames on other sites, online reviews where they've used the same avatar, social media profiles, email addresses, websites, public-facing databases, horrible comments they've left on other social media sites. Even anonymous trolls often use variations of the same name – there are patterns that can be found. The software looks for any kind of similarity, any matches, marries it up with location data, online habits, reused avatars and that sort of stuff, then collates all of that together and triangulates it to an IP address, and trawls again to associate it with a *physical* address.'

I'm just about keeping up with my wife's machine-gun delivery. 'Kind of like a reverse phone number search?'

She frowns. 'A bit old school, but kind of like that, yes.'

'So it's a way of taking the mask off anonymous trolls, right?'

'Exactly.' She points to the fifteen usernames on her red list. 'Took a day for the country results to come back on these. With three it was a complete blank, it couldn't find anything at all. Four others were in North America or Asia so I crossed them off, same with another in Poland and one in Cyprus. Six in the UK: in Cornwall, East Sussex, south London and Fife. They all seem like a long way away. But there are two accounts associated with a physical address within a twenty-mile radius. And I reckon the people who are physically closer are more likely to take things to the next level, because they might actually see Cathy Ruskin in real life, maybe in their town. Much worse than just seeing her on a screen.'

Despite the heat of the afternoon, there is a coldness growing at the back of my neck. 'You've got the two addresses?' I say.

She clicks on one of the red-coded usernames, pointing out some technical gobbledegook I can't understand, a long sequence of letters and numbers. Next to it, an actual physical address in the nearby town of Loughborough. *The Gables*. Maybe twenty minutes down the road; not far at all.

'This one,' she says, 'turns out to be an assisted living facility. Most residents are seventy-plus.'

'A retirement village?' I have a sudden image of someone's sweet old granddad, a blanket over his knees in the day room, posting lurid abuse on social media to pass the time. 'Doesn't seem very likely that a septuagenarian has gone from trolling to kidnapping though. Does it?'

'No,' she says. 'I didn't think so either.' She hesitates, her hand hovering over the laptop's touchpad. She looks up at me nervously. 'Which left this one.'

She clicks on the one remaining username on her list, revealing the street address.

I recognise it instantly.

An address I've known for years. A house I know almost as well as my own.

My brother's house.

63

EMILY

Saturday 11th June, 11.43 p.m.
Ninety-eight minutes before she disappears
77 The Avenue

The house pulsed with music, tall speakers vibrating with bass, the air heavy with the smells of spilled cider and sweet perfume, and the thick spicy smell of weed underlying it all.

It was on OK party, Emily supposed. All the usual suspects were here. There were the awkward sobers, all clustered in one corner of the dining room. The ravers dancing in the lounge; an emotional crying girl in the corner being comforted by a friend. A sleepy drunk already passed out on the sofa; rowdy football boys in the kitchen; two lads standing at either end of the dining table, shirtless, playing beer pong, the same two rugby lads who always seemed to take their shirts off. Out here in the garden, someone retching into a flowerbed; a couple on a bench nearby, kissing enthusiastically in the shadows. Another bench occupied by giggling smokers.

Usually, the day after a party like this there would be lots of gossip, lots of who-got-with-who, who got knocked back, who was sick and who was hilarious. But not tomorrow. Tomorrow there would only be one topic of conversation: Emily Ruskin. Where she'd gone and what might have happened to her. The thought gave her a little shiver of excitement, of anticipation, the delicious knowledge that right now only she and Olivia knew what was going to happen. Only they knew how the next couple of days were going to play out. It was good, almost too good – almost like playing God – and she wanted to prolong the feeling, but knew it was nearly time to set things in motion.

Next to her on the wooden bench, Drew was talking but she wasn't really paying attention. He was going on in his usual way, something about how his house was bigger and more expensive than this one, how it had a cinema room in the basement, a gym and a summer house and a tennis court.

Connor returned from his errand to the kitchen, making his way carefully across the patio towards them, three glasses clenched in his hands.

'Peach schnapps in the front one,' he said, 'vodka lemonade on the right and vodka and Coke on the—'

'You know what?' Emily said, plucking the right-hand glass from him and taking a gulp from it. 'I've changed my mind. You don't mind having the schnapps, do you, Connor?'

'No worries, I don't mind,' Connor said with a shrug. He took a seat beside her.

Drew grabbed the other vodka and knocked half of it back in one go.

'Cheers, mate.' A heavy, unfriendly emphasis on the second word. His hand gripped the glass so tight the knuckles stood out white against his skin.

'You know what, Connor?' Emily leaned over and gave him a breathy kiss on the cheek, the air around them filling with the strong

summer scent of her perfume, fresh and sharp and intoxicating. 'One day, you're going to make someone a wonderful wife.'

'Thanks,' Connor said with a half-smile. 'I think.'

She could tell he was unsure whether this was a compliment or a diss but didn't really care either way. She put her hand on his arm, giving his bicep a squeeze.

'When did you get so chunky?' She laughed. 'Used to be skinny but you're getting proper hench, aren't you?'

'Dunno,' he said, a flush of red spreading to his cheeks. 'Been to the gym a bit.'

She let her hand rest on his arm for a moment longer, smiling up at him as if she'd only just thought of something else.

'Hey, a few of us are going up to Beacon Hill soon if you want to come?'

'Sure.' Connor glanced back at her, at Drew with his arm draped casually over her shoulders. 'Yeah, why not.'

'You're not going to get in shit with your parents, are you? My mum is such a dick about curfews.'

'No,' Connor said, checking his watch. 'I'll send them a text. It's no big deal.'

'Perfect.' She handed Connor her glass and stood up. 'Bathroom before we go, I think. I can trust you to look after my drink, can't I?'

'Of course,' Connor said, taking it in his left hand, a smudge of bright red lipstick on the rim.

Emily left the two boys in awkward silence on the bench and headed inside, weaving through milling partygoers in the conservatory and the kitchen, into the long hallway, moving through a gaggle of lanky guys clustered at the bottom of the stairs who parted to let her pass. Muddy footprints had turned the thick cream stair carpet to a deep churned brown in places, mud from the garden trammelled into the shag pile as people tracked up and down to the toilet on the first floor. At the end of a long corridor off the landing, the bathroom door was open.

A girl lay on the floor, on her side in the recovery position, eyes closed, mouth open, a faint sheen of sweat on her pale face. A thin slick of saliva tracking down her cheek onto the bath towels stacked under her head. Zac Boyd knelt on one side of her, a girl in a pink crop top on the other, short skirt riding up high on her thighs.

'Oh my God,' Emily said, kneeling down by the stricken girl's feet. She recognised her from school, from the other half of their year group. She put a hand on her bare ankle, the skin warm and clammy to the touch. 'It's Rosie, isn't it? I know her.'

'Rosie McKinlay,' Zac said, without turning to acknowledge Emily. 'She's in my tutor group.'

'Poor thing, what happened to her? Has she been sick?'

'Just found her in here,' Zac said. 'On the floor. Someone spiked her. She's totally gone.'

Spiked. With a shiver, Emily remembered the only other time she'd seen this. A girl sprawled in a corner, hair hanging down around her face, zombiefied with whatever had been dropped into her drink when she was looking the other way. Unable to think, resist, remember. Unable to talk, barely able to walk.

And not just any girl: Olivia.

'Shit,' she said under her breath. 'Do you know who might have done it?'

'Not sure,' Zac said. There was a hard edge of hostility in his voice, but Emily couldn't tell whether it was directed at her or someone else. 'But I've got a few ideas.'

Emily's heart lurched in her chest at the idea that someone here at the party, someone she probably knew, had done this to Rosie.

'Who?'

Zac turned to look at her for the first time, not bothering to disguise his anger. 'Heard about this sort of shit happening in clubs but not here, not at someone's house.'

'It was lucky you found her in time,' the girl in the pink crop top said.

Zac stood up. 'You sure you don't want me to call an ambulance? Get her to A & E?'

The girl shook her head quickly.

'She's not supposed to be here. None of us are, we're supposed to be sleeping over at mine, our mums will freak if they hear about this.'

'You're going to stay with her?'

'I'll look after her, get her home.' She put a protective hand on Rosie's shoulder. 'Thanks, Zac.'

He gave her a curt nod and walked out of the bathroom without giving Emily another glance.

'Do you want me to . . . do anything?' Emily said. 'Get anyone else up here?'

The girl glanced down the empty corridor. 'You could send Ayisha up if you see her?'

'Sure.'

'There's an en suite in the guest bedroom.' She pointed back across the landing. 'If that's what you were looking for.'

Emily stood up, pulling the bathroom door shut behind her. She went back to the landing, finding the guest bedroom on the second attempt, with its huge TV screen on the far wall, a king-sized double bed piled with jackets and coats and rolled sleeping bags and—

Zac Boyd.

He was standing on the far side of the bed, straightening up, his hand withdrawing quickly from something amid the pile of possessions heaped there. A furtive, defensive set to his jaw.

Emily looked from him to the open door of the en suite, dark and empty. 'Waiting for the bathroom?'

'Nah,' Zac said, shoving a hand into the pocket of his jeans. 'Just getting something.'

He bustled past her and was gone.

64

I stare at the screen, my eyes fixed on the address. *Sixteen Robinson Road*. The semi-detached they'd moved to when Zac was in nursery, squeezing their budget to the absolute limit to get into the catchment area for a good primary school. The house we'd been to for drinks and meals and babysitting and birthdays, hundreds of times over the years. The house where my brother had nursed his wife through the final weeks of her illness.

'It must be a mistake,' I say tonelessly. 'Some sort of glitch in the software.'

Laura waits a beat before she answers; she knows I'm clutching at straws. 'So of all the millions of results it could have thrown up,' she says softly, 'it just *happened* to give the address of someone who knows her, who goes to school with her, who was in the woods with her on Saturday night?'

I grasp for a response, a rebuttal, but nothing comes.

'Why would he do this?' I say instead. 'Why would he post those messages?'

My wife shrugs. 'Does it matter?'

'Show me the Instagram account.'

Laura pulls up another tab on her laptop and I'm looking at an account with the username @*Chuckiee74__xx*. No posts, thirty-nine followers, following eighty-one people. Set up four months ago; something about the date rings a vague bell. The avatar is a picture from the movie *Hellboy*, a red-faced demon with his horns filed down to stumps.

'But it could be either of them,' I say quietly. 'Either Zac or my brother. And we don't know which one.'

'No,' Laura says. 'Just that it's a device at that address.'

It doesn't matter – I don't believe it. At least, I don't *want* to believe it. Maybe that's the same thing.

Not my family. Not my brother's kid, my nephew, my godson.

'It doesn't mean he actually did anything,' I say finally.

My wife pushes her laptop out of the way, leans forward onto the table between us. Puts her warm hand over mine. Waiting, weighing the moment, choosing her words carefully.

'I remember something you told me, something your brother said a few days ago. That Zac had been up to Beacon Hill Woods at night. Camping out on his own.'

I pull my hand away. 'So what?'

'*So* it means he probably knows those woods better than most. Knows the paths, the trails, knows his way around there at night.'

'And?' I try to keep the edge of anger out of my voice.

My wife and I face each other in awkward silence for a moment.

'I'm saying you need to look at the facts, Andy,' she says finally. 'Your brother's been avoiding you like you're contagious. Talking to Alexander Saxton behind your back. Zac wouldn't even let you in the house, the last time you went around there. He was clearly freaked out when he left here on Sunday morning. But he gave chapter and verse to the police about Connor's movements, which is one of the reasons they suspect him.' She points to her laptop, where the @Chuckiee74__xx account is still displayed. 'And now this, these messages, they're unbelievably vile. *Think* about it, Andy.'

I stare at my wife, trying to decide if this is the hard truth that I've spent all week deliberately not thinking about, ever since I met my brother in the woods on Sunday morning. Deliberately not asking myself why he'd been hollow-eyed from lack of sleep. Not questioning how he had 'found' a white top in the woods, which subsequently turned out to have Emily's blood on it.

Perhaps Rob hadn't found it at all. Perhaps he had put it there himself.

'But Zac was *with* him on Saturday night,' I say instead, 'they were together most of the—'

'No,' she says quickly. 'They split up, remember? According to what Connor told the police, the five of them all went their separate ways just before 1 a.m. At some point after that, Connor turned around and went back to look for Emily, to check she was OK. That was the last time he and Zac were actually together. But Zac didn't get to ours until 2.19 a.m., when his phone reconnected to our wireless network. That's a fifteen-minute walk back from the woods that took him almost an hour and a half – a lot of time unaccounted for.'

I've never been good at arguing with my wife. She's always so certain, so clear. So convincing.

But I shake my head anyway.

'I'm not going to sell my brother out,' I say. 'I'm not selling my nephew out.'

She slaps her palm down on the kitchen table with a loud *smack* that jolts me upright.

'We're a long way past that now!' she shouts. 'That train has already left the station. It is *gone*. The police are about to arrest our son again, our *child*, they're going to take him away and if he gets charged, and doesn't get bail, he could be locked up for the next nine months while we wait for a trial.'

'There has to be another way we—'

'*You're* the one who convinced *me* our son was being set up! And it was *your* brother who turned up here on Sunday evening with some story about Zac looking for his missing wallet so he could go up to Connor's bedroom. The following day we find the drugs. Is that some incredible coincidence? Because if you were right about our son being set up, we may well have found the culprit – and you have to wake up to that before it's too late.' Her face is colouring, her cheeks red with anger. 'At the very least we need to give the police a convincing alternative. It's time to choose, Andy. Right now. Your brother's family or your own.'

Looking at her, I finally realise something.

What's the most dangerous thing in the world?

A mother whose young are threatened.

Her only concern is to protect Connor, by whatever means necessary.

I put my head in my hands. 'This is a nightmare.'

There is another silence between us in that moment, a silence so deep and wide it seems to fill the room, the whole house, to freeze everything in place.

Her voice quieter again, Laura says: 'Why did we give Connor an alibi on Sunday, the first time we talked to the police? We weren't certain whether he made his curfew or not, but we said it anyway. Both of us.'

I spread my hands as if the answer is obvious. 'Because . . . because we didn't want him to get into trouble.'

'Exactly. This is no different.'

'Of course it's different, a girl is four days missing and the police think she's come to harm!'

She shakes her head. 'But *our* priority is no different. The same instinct that made us give him an alibi when the police first started asking questions.' She points again at the laptop. '*This* is a chink of light for Connor, a life raft. This might be the thing that turns the police around. Because the alternative for our son is his future *gone*, twenty years in jail and his life ruined. And you're going to just let that happen, are you? Because I'm not.'

'You're talking about stabbing family in the back.' Nausea is rolling in my stomach. 'My brother . . . it would kill him.'

'I'm talking about our son's *life*.'

'I know that,' I say quietly. 'I know.'

She looks away for a moment, and when her eyes return to mine they are as hard and cold as chips of ice.

'If you don't go to the police with this, I will.'

'No.' I stand up. 'Not yet. Let me talk to my brother first.'

65

My brother is not at home and not answering his phone. He's not at the office either, the engineering company where he works as a draughtsman. The receptionist tells me he's called in sick today but is hoping to be back in work tomorrow.

I eventually find him at the Three Tuns, the pub nearest to his house.

By the time I walk in, it's late afternoon and the place is mostly empty, too late for the lunch crowd and too early for post-work drinks. There are a couple of old guys at the bar nursing pints and a group of middle-aged women gathered around a small table filled with coffee cups and paperback books. Three lads who don't look much older than Connor play pool under the wall-mounted TVs silently showing horse racing and cricket. My brother is alone in the back room, in a corner booth on his own, absorbed in his phone. As I approach my own phone beeps with a message from Laura.

What did Rob say?

I shove it back in my pocket and take the seat opposite him.

'Been looking for you,' I say. 'You weren't answering your phone.'

He takes a swig of his half-finished pint of bitter. He's always liked a drink but I wonder when his enthusiasm tipped over into alcoholism. Something else I had missed, evidently.

'I've been busy.' His eyes have the glassy belligerence of the daytime drinker. 'But now you've found me, *bro*.'

'I need to talk to you about Zac,' I say, ignoring his sarcasm. 'About what happened on Saturday night. About all of it. You've been acting weird, keeping me and Connor at arm's length like we're not even family any more, and I want to know why.'

He turns his phone face down on the table. 'Same reason you've been going around stirring up shit about people, asking too many questions. To protect my kid.'

'And what about protecting other people from *him*?'

His face twists into an angry frown. 'What?'

I think back to Sunday, to how this had all started with Rob's phone call. Where this nightmare had begun. Maybe it was going to end with him too.

'When we met up in the woods on Sunday morning,' I say, 'you looked like absolute crap. Like you'd been up most of the night.'

'So?' he says. 'I had a hangover. It was the weekend. So what?'

'No, I've seen you with plenty of hangovers, it wasn't that. You looked as if you hadn't slept. *At all*.'

He stares at me across the wooden table and I see the toll this week has taken on him. The stubble, the dark shadows under his eyes, the grey pallor of his skin.

'Some nights I just don't sleep.' He takes another hefty swig of his pint. 'I *can't* sleep.'

'Were you out?' I say. 'Did Zac call you? Did you drive over to meet with him at Beacon Hill Woods? Did you help him?'

'Help him with *what*?'

I take a breath. 'With Emily.'

There. I've said it. Two words out in the air that can never be retrieved.

Rob blinks at me. 'What are you talking about?'

'I think you know *exactly* what I'm talking about.'

He shakes his head. 'You're seriously asking me that? Have you been dipping into the prescription drugs at the practice?'

I press on. 'And all that stuff on Sunday morning about how you couldn't find him, us tramping around the woods together, what was that really about? Was it just a smokescreen? A false trail to help cover your tracks?'

His eyes narrow, thoughts swimming through the fog of alcohol. 'You've lost the plot, Andy. It really is mad, what you're saying.'

'I'll tell you what's mad,' I say, leaning closer. 'The fact that one of you hates Cathy Ruskin with a passion, has been trolling her for months with incredibly vile stuff on social media, about her family, how she deserves to rot in hell, how she's a parasite and a phoney and a disgusting fake. Was it you, or Zac?'

'Why don't you tell me, Andy?' he says. 'You seem to have all the answers.'

Looking at my brother, I see myself reflected in his features: this man with whom I now had so much in common. Both of us becoming liars for our children. Willing to deny and deflect and defend our sons to the last.

The answer is suddenly obvious.

'It's Zac, isn't it?'

I expect him to react, for his body language to betray anger or shame. But there's nothing. He's not even surprised at the accusation, just sits back in his seat and meets my gaze. It takes a moment for my brain to catch up, for the evidence to filter through. Then it clicks, like a light switch being turned on.

'And you *knew*, didn't you?' I lean forward. 'You knew he was doing it, posting all those hideous messages, all that hate? Jesus! How long have you known?'

He drains the last of his pint and stands abruptly, grabbing his phone off the table and making for the side door out to the car park.

I hurry after him, catching the door as it swings back at me. 'Did Zac just decide to put his words into action?' I say to his back. 'Only he couldn't get to Cathy so he took it out on someone close to her instead?'

He's striding across the car park, ignoring me. I jog a few paces to catch up with him.

'Hey!' I put a hand on his arm. 'I'm talking to you, Rob! You knew Zac was doing this, threatening Cathy online?'

He shakes me off and keeps on walking across the potholed tarmac, towards the exit onto the main road.

I grab his shoulder, more firmly this time. 'I don't have time for you to walk away,' I shout. 'Connor doesn't have time for—'

He spins and punches me once, hard, a sharp jab with a lot of anger behind it. The shock of it knocks me to the ground, gravel stinging my palms, my head ringing from the blow.

My brother leans down to me, the face of a stranger. 'Of course I fucking knew.'

He turns to walk away again, to dismiss me, and I feel a surge of rage I haven't felt since we were kids. The particular rage of the younger brother, always shorter and lighter and slower and weaker, never able to measure up. Never able to get an even contest with my older sibling. I charge my brother and rugby-tackle him to the ground, and then we're grappling and grabbing, punching and kicking with no holds barred. We haven't had a fight for thirty years and even they were never really proper fights, just dead arms and Chinese burns and wrestling moves copied from WWE. But nothing really serious, not blood and bruises and loosened teeth.

Not like this.

Rob ends up on top of me, pinning my arms to the tarmac with his knees, his hands gripping the collar of my shirt. 'You want to know why he hates her?' He leans closer, his breath sour with beer. 'Because she's a fucking liar, a charlatan, the worst kind of fake. She took someone else's tragedy and turned it into a career opportunity.'

It's my turn to be confused. 'What?'

'You know about her, right? What happened to her last year?'

'I've read a bit, the last few days. She's an actor, done lots of TV—'

'Not for *years*,' he says. 'Her career was dead in the water, she was in a couple of things that got totally panned by everyone and roles started drying up for her. She wasn't getting offered anything. She was one of those sad has-beens who could barely get a mention in the local media, never mind the nationals. Her career was over.' He waits for a beat, catching his breath. 'And then she got the worst news: she had cancer.'

His grip slackens, the fight draining out of him. He lets out a choking sob and releases my shirt, rolling off me and sitting back on the tarmac.

I struggle up to a sitting position. 'I think I read that online. On her Wikipedia page.'

'She kept it secret for a while, only revealed it last year when she was in remission after some new miracle treatment in the US. Lost all her hair, loads of weight, but there she was, this miracle story, former household name fighting back and surviving against the odds, and suddenly the tabloids couldn't get enough of her. An inspirational story, right? All packaged up nicely on social media, her journey and her recovery. She does some chat shows and podcasts, and then off the back of *that*, she gets picked for that reality TV show full of C-list celebrities.'

'Right,' I say. 'I don't really watch that show.'

He stands up, brushing gravel from his jeans, and I do the same.

'Me neither,' he says. 'Anyway, she goes on to win the show and immediately donates all the prize money to breast cancer charities, and the media fucking *loved* that. Phoenix from the ashes kind of thing. And her star keeps on rising, before you know it she's been cast as the lead in a brand-new ten-part drama on Netflix due to air this autumn.'

'It's quite a comeback.'

'It is.' His eyes bore into mine, months of pent-up anger pouring out of him. 'There's only one problem with it.'

'What's that?'

'She's a fake. A lot of people think she made it up. Having cancer. A *lot* of people.'

I can't believe what I'm hearing. My sensible big brother, peddling what I assume is a conspiracy theory bandied around dark corners of the internet.

'Including you?' I say. 'And Zac?'

'Loads of other people online too. Google it, there's a ton of stuff out there, lots about her story that doesn't add up. Getting treated at a private clinic in the US, who does that? Having some secret new treatment rather than going on the NHS? Only revealing it when she's already in remission and back in the UK? And she never *looked* ill, not the way Vanessa looked, she never looked like she was fighting for her life, like her own body had turned against her, the way someone looks when they *really* have cancer. Trust me, I know what that's like.'

I remembered my sister-in-law as she had undergone chemotherapy, her skin increasingly drawn and grey, the onslaught of chemicals that had barely checked the fast-growing cancer. How she had seemed to shrink and diminish before our eyes as the disease consumed her pound by agonising pound.

'You think Cathy Ruskin made up her cancer to get back into the public eye? To get back on the TV?'

'Yes.'

'But if she ever got found out, she'd be absolutely crucified—'

'Her career was starting to take off again right when Vanessa was diagnosed. Do you have any idea how fucking sick it makes you feel, to know someone has used this disgusting, horrible disease like a PR tactic?' He leans closer, flecks of his spit landing on my cheeks. 'This thing that took Vanessa at the age of forty-five, the worst thing that could ever happen to your family, used like a tool to get a career back on track? And the sickest part is that Nessa loved Cathy's social media posts about *resilience and honesty* in the face of illness, and there was the extra novelty of living in the same neighbourhood, of seeing her at school fetes and sports days, of chatting to her. Particularly after Nessa was diagnosed.'

'I'm sorry,' I say. 'I didn't know any of this.'

His eyes are suddenly full of tears.

'Imagine you're a teenager, and you've lost your mum,' he says. 'Imagine how angry you'd be. How *furious*. So yes, of course Zac hates her. And yes, I knew what he'd been posting online. But it doesn't mean he did anything to her daughter.'

We stand like that for a moment, still breathing hard, blinking in disbelief. Two brothers, two people who had always been able to rely on each other, reduced to brawling in a pub car park.

'Sunday evening,' I say quietly. 'When you dropped by our house. You said Zac had left his wallet in Connor's room but that wasn't true, was it?'

He drags a sleeve across his eyes, angrily cuffing away tears. 'No,' he says. 'It wasn't true.'

'He was planting those drugs, wasn't he? The doses of GHB in that little bag.'

Rob swallows. 'No.'

'What then?' I hold my hands out, palms up. 'He was planting them to incriminate Connor. So that when the police—'

'No,' he says again. 'He wasn't planting the bag. He was trying to find it.'

His answer catches me off guard. 'What do you mean?'

'He had the stuff on him when he crashed at yours on Saturday night. When he slept in Connor's bed. He said they must have fallen out of his pocket at some point, but he didn't realise they were gone until Sunday afternoon. Then he started freaking out, saying we had to find them, get rid of them, so we came back round to yours. Zac went up to Connor's room but he couldn't find the bag.'

'I don't believe you.'

'Believe what you like, but that is God's honest truth.'

'Then you should have just told me on Sunday.'

'Yeah, right.' He shakes his head, the way he always used to when we were kids and I'd come out with something particularly naive. '*By the way, Andy, please can I have my son's class B drugs back if you happen to find them? Cheers!* Of course I wasn't going to bloody tell you.'

He squares up to me but I stand my ground.

'What the hell was Zac even doing with drugs in the first place?'

'Better if you don't know.'

'Is that why Connor has been keeping so many secrets these past few days?' I take a breath. 'Is Zac the one who's been spiking people?'

'I *told* you.' His hands curl into fists at his sides. 'It's better for you, for Connor, if you don't know. Just leave it.'

'I can't, Rob. Not while this is all hanging over Connor's head.'

He stares at me with bloodshot eyes, a scatter of red capillaries jagged against the white. He looks like he's aged ten years in the last few days. Finally, his shoulders slump, fists unclenching at his sides.

'So, what are you going to do?' he says, his voice raw. 'Tell the police?'

'I don't know,' I say. 'Maybe.'

He considers me for a long moment. Turns his head and spits out a gob of blood onto the ground.

'Well, I guess you'll have to do whatever you think you have to do.' He turns to walk away then looks back, his eyes coming to rest on mine one last time. 'And so will I.'

66

Even alone in the woods, my brother's words are still ringing in my ears. *Imagine you're a teenager, and you've lost your mum. Imagine how angry you'd be. Of course Zac hates her.* An outpouring of anger and guilt he'd been carrying with him since Vanessa was diagnosed, bottled up in the months since he'd lost her. Anger at the disease, at Cathy Ruskin, at the media, at himself, at the hideous unfairness of it all.

I will give Rob another chance before I make that phone call.

It's the least I can do.

I stand at the edge of the little clearing between thick gorse bushes and banks of nettles, next to the fallen tree with its thick twisted roots exposed to the air. Late afternoon is shifting towards early evening but the light is still good here, still enough sunshine penetrating through the trees to give me a proper look at this place. More than the fleeting glimpse I got last night before my encounter with Karl Crosby. Because there are hundreds of acres of woodland at Beacon Hill and how thoroughly has it actually been searched? The police had teams at the south end of the woods earlier in the week – near to where Emily's bike was locked up, near to Lower Farm Lane – but how well had they searched up here? Here on the north side, closer to the streets and houses, to the place where the five of them had been drinking around a fire as Saturday night turned into Sunday morning. And more to the point, how well had they searched *this* exact place, this little clearing next to the fallen tree, where I had followed Georgia last night after the vigil. Why *had* she come back here? Did she have her own suspicions about Karl Crosby?

I walk around the clearing in concentric circles moving nearer and nearer to the centre. Slow steps, eyes on the ground the whole time, scanning for any more of the little fish-shaped plastic vials we had found in Connor's room, an indication that they'd been used up here. Scanning for anything else man-made, out of place; for loosened earth or any areas that have been dug into and trodden flat again. Then standing in the centre and just observing, allowing my eyes the time to see, to *really* see the ground and its patterns. Using a long stick, I brush aside the leaves and undergrowth, shifting the beds of nettles, seeking out the places hidden to a casual passer-by. I look up into the trees in case there are any clues there; climbing a dozen feet into a hefty oak to look down on the site in case a different perspective reveals something I can't see from ground level.

I'm back on the ground, on my hands and knees at the base of a tree trunk, when my phone pings for maybe the sixth or seventh time. I sit back on my haunches, onto the hard-baked earth, to catch my breath. When I dig out my phone I see my hands are black with dirt, earth packed under the fingernails and lining my palms with dark contours.

The unanswered messages are stacked one on top of the other. The first couple are from Harriet:

Where r u?
Need to spk to u

The rest from my wife:

What did Rob say?
Have you talked to the police about Zac?
What did the police say?
Where are you? Call me

Her most recent message a statement rather than another question:

Tell me you're calling DS Shah or I'm doing it

I'm out of time.

It's possible that Georgia and Karl have already found incriminating evidence, taken it, disposed of it. Maybe there are microscopic traces that will only be found by a forensic team. Or maybe I'm clutching at straws again. Wanting on one level to carry on searching; knowing too that I'm putting off the inevitable, delaying the moment when I make the call to DS Shah to pass on my suspicions about Zac.

And about my brother, too.

Because if Emily came to harm in these woods, where is her body? If the police haven't found her here, then where is she? Unless someone carried her out of here – a deadweight – they had to have a vehicle. And none of the kids are old enough to drive or even have a provisional licence. In theory, I guess it's possible that one of them could have taken a family car without their parents knowing. But in practice, what were the chances in the middle of the night, all of them half-drunk or stoned, to take a parent's car, drive it up to Lower Farm Lane, load up a body and dispose of it somewhere else, then return the car without anyone noticing? Without driving into anything, without getting pulled over by the police? It seemed like a stretch to me.

Which meant an adult driver. An accomplice.

And Rob had dodged the question I had asked him, rather than denying it.

I wipe my hands off as best I can, take one last look at the clearing, and begin the walk back out of the woods.

At the entrance I go out through the gate, past a strip of police tape snapped and hanging limply from a tree, past posters of Emily Ruskin that are already starting to fade and curl in the summer heat. I stand there for a moment at the field's edge, looking down on the streets and houses stretching north across the river towards the scattering of high-rise blocks in the city centre. All those people, thousands of people, thousands of teenagers, and yet somehow perhaps in the end it all came back to my own family. To my own brother's son. No matter how hard I had tried to find a different culprit, a different answer.

I take my phone out and type a quick reply to my wife.

Calling them now

Even as I press 'send' on the message I have a powerful sense that I'm about to break something sacred and unique, to shatter it so completely that it will never be whole again. I wonder if my brother will ever speak to me again after today.

But this has to be done, for Connor. I have to do everything I can to protect him. *Everything.*

I know these things and yet still I feel like a coward, like the worst kind of traitor as I tap the green 'call' button on the screen of my phone and put it to my ear. It rings four, five, six times and just as I think it's about to go to voicemail – a welcome reprieve – it connects and DS Shah's voice comes on the line.

Instead of hello, she says: 'Can I call you back, Dr Boyd?'

'There's something important I need to tell you . . . about my nephew.' I ignore the roll of nausea in my stomach. 'Some information you need to know about his relationship with the Ruskin family, I think it could be significant for your investigation.'

At her end I can make out the sounds of a door opening, then clicking shut, a change in the background noise. The echo of a corridor.

'OK,' she says. 'I'm just in the middle of something at the moment but I was going to give you a call soon anyway.'

'It's very important,' I say. I need to get it out, to say it quickly, before I lose my nerve. But telling her about the drugs is too risky right now, it'll prompt too many extra questions that I can't answer. 'It's urgent, it can't wait. We've found out that Zac has been trolling Cathy Ruskin online, for months, in relation to his mother's own battle with cancer. He believes Cathy lied about having the disease and he's made a series of quite specific and graphic threats against the Ruskin family, including Emily and her sisters.'

'Anonymous threats?'

'Yes, but we know it's him. It seemed like something you'd want to know as well, to investigate properly. I'm going to send you screenshots in a minute of a particular account he's been using on Instagram, where some of the worst abuse has been coming from.'

The phone beeps in my ear with the call waiting tone and I check the display. Harriet is calling me.

'Hang on a second,' I say to Shah. 'I'll be right back.'

I switch lines to answer the call from my daughter.

'Harry, are you all right?'

'Dad?' Her voice sounds small and far away. 'Where are you? I need to talk to you about something.'

'Not right now, Harry, I'm in the middle of another call about your brother and it's really important.'

'I just need to tell—'

'Listen, I'll call you straight back, OK?'

I press 'end' and the phone switches back to DS Shah. There is a pause, nothing on the line apart from a very faint crackle of static, and for a moment I think the connection has failed.

'DS Shah?' I say. 'Are you still there?'

'Yes, I'm here.'

'So what do you think? About Zac threatening Cathy's family?'

'I was about to call you, actually.' The words are heavy, as if she is considering each one very carefully. 'Your son is here at the station.'

My stomach drops; a pit opening beneath my feet.

'What are you talking about? He's at home.'

'No,' she says. 'He's here.'

'Why?' I press the phone closer to my ear, the plastic hot against my skin. 'Have you arrested him again?'

'It would be better if you just came in,' she says. 'Are you able to come down right away?'

'Just tell me why he's there!'

'Because,' Shah says slowly, 'he just confessed to killing Emily Ruskin.'

67

The world sways beneath me as if tectonic plates are shifting, crashing against each other, shock waves rising up through the soles of my feet.

He just confessed to killing Emily Ruskin.

A wave of sadness, of grief for a young life lost. Final confirmation that this girl will never come home, never grow up, a family that will never be the same again. A mother, forever broken.

And the selfish thought tied to it, inseparable from it: *not my son.*

Not him. Not the sweet child who used to climb into bed with us when he had a nightmare, the boy who used to give his little sister endless piggybacks, the teenager who wanted to be a lawyer one day so he could help people. Not Connor.

I swallow. 'That can't be right.' I have a hundred questions but somehow I can't voice them. 'He's . . . I don't know, he's confused, doesn't know what he's saying. It must be a mistake.'

'No mistake, Dr Boyd. He was quite clear and specific.'

My legs are suddenly weak, muscles turning to water. I grab the fence rail behind me and lean on it, gripping the wood so hard I can feel the contours of the grain beneath my fingertips. My hands are shaking. *This is not happening.*

'But it *can't* be right,' I say again. 'Not Connor. He couldn't do that. He wouldn't . . . he's not capable of it.'

'I've just been in with him,' DS Shah says. 'He's given a full statement, voluntarily and without any preliminaries from our side.'

'Why is he even there, did you arrest him again?'

'No,' she says evenly. 'He walked in an hour ago of his own free will, asked for me by name at the front desk. Waived his right to his own legal representation although we made sure he talked to the duty solicitor anyway so he knew exactly what his rights were. Told us he didn't want a parent or guardian with him either, so we had a social worker in there as his responsible adult.'

'You should have informed us anyway!' I run a shaking hand through my hair. 'You should have told us!'

'I'm telling you now.'

My anger is doused instantly by the smooth wash of her words, leaving only fear behind. I need to *think*. And I need to see my son, to look in his eyes and ask him myself, to understand why he has done this. I start moving at a half-run along the path and through the field of wheat, stumbling over uneven ground as I head back down towards the streets below.

'Why now, why today?' The field is only a few hundred metres from top to bottom but it feels like an agonisingly long way to my car. 'Why not on Sunday when you first spoke to him?'

'He didn't say.'

'Tell me exactly what he said,' I say. *'Exactly.'*

She pauses, considering her words carefully. 'He said it was an accident. That he didn't mean to do it.'

I stop, feeling the air leave my lungs as if I've been kicked in the chest.

An accident.

'What else?'

She gives me a summary. According to Connor's account, he had told the truth about Saturday night – right up to the point where he had encountered Emily in the dark. He had doubled back into the woods and followed her so he could speak to her alone, try to talk her out of the plan she'd set in motion. He just wanted to see her. But when he caught up to her she surprised him in the dark, he said, and he had lashed out without thinking. Emily had fallen into a gully and hit her head on an old tree stump. There was blood, lots of it, and she never regained consciousness.

'He said he just panicked,' Shah adds. 'When he realised she wasn't breathing.'

I feel a roll of nausea as I recall Connor's own words from Sunday, the first time the police had pulled him in.

I panicked.

Talking to them on Sunday, a different version of this story. The *original* version, the one in which he was a normal teenager rather than a freshly minted killer. A common thread running between both versions: his own words.

I panicked.

A single thread, leading from the lie to the truth.

Shah is still speaking, saying something about a possible shallow grave site. A team was being assembled, she says, to search a specific area on the edge of the woods at first light tomorrow. Connor would spend the night in a cell and appear at the magistrates court at 9 a.m., a first appearance to enter a charge and a plea before the case is pushed up to crown court to be dealt with at a later date.

Nine o'clock in the morning, not much more than twelve hours until he was fed further into the legal meat grinder. They weren't wasting any time.

'He didn't . . . do this.' It must be the third or fourth time I've said it. A default back to denial. Simple parental denial.

Shah's voice is steady, unruffled. 'He just told us that he did. On the tape, under caution, having been advised of his legal rights and with a responsible adult present.'

'I don't believe him.'

She doesn't answer. But her silence is clear enough: *it doesn't matter at this stage if you believe him or not.*

I pass a dog-walker, one of the school dads I vaguely know who raises a hand in puzzled greeting as I half jog, half stumble past him with the phone clamped to my ear. I ignore him and keep going. There must be something I can do, something I can *say*, to alter the trajectory of this conversation.

'Listen,' I scramble for a medical answer, an off-the-cuff diagnosis that will make some kind of sense. 'Connor's been under a lot of stress this week, a lot of pressure with everyone pointing fingers and accusing him, it must have finally got to him and now he's had some kind of breakdown. Maybe a psychotic episode, a dislocation between what's real and what's not real.' I'm out of breath, my voice rising and falling with exertion. 'Everyone seems to have forgotten that he suffered a head injury at the beginning of all this. He should be in a hospital, not a police station.'

'He'll have a psych assessment in due course,' she says. 'And that will all feed into the legal process.'

I can tell she doesn't believe me. I'm not even sure I believe it myself anymore.

'So you've not actually found a body yet—'

'I've got to go,' she says, 'I'm finishing up a briefing. Goodbye, Dr Boyd.'

She rings off and I'm left with nothing but the sound of my own laboured breathing and an echo of far-off birdsong from the woods, the eerily quiet aftermath of the bomb that has just been dropped on my life. *My son.* These last five days we have been protecting him, shielding him, looking elsewhere to apportion blame. But according to what I've just been told, the culprit has been under our own roof the whole time.

I dial my wife's number and break into a run.

68

'He doesn't want to see you,' DC Harmer is saying to my wife. 'He said he doesn't want to see anyone.'

Laura is already at the front desk, hands on her hips, in a furious stand-off with the tall detective. She's come straight from home and has arrived at the police station before me, full of the same shock and disbelief, the same desperate anger, as the moment I'd phoned her with the news of Connor's confession. Harmer stands a foot taller than her but she's not intimidated in the slightest. She rarely loses her temper, but when she does, she's like a force of nature.

'I'm his mother!' she says, pointing a finger. 'I have a right to see my own bloody child!'

A scattered audience in the double row of plastic seats have fallen silent to watch the confrontation with interest. Harmer holds his hands up in what he probably thinks is a calming gesture, but is guaranteed to aggravate Laura even further.

'Why don't you just calm down for a minute and—'

'Don't tell me to *bloody* calm down!' She jabs her index finger into his chest. 'This is outrageous what you've done to my son! What you're *still* doing!'

'He was quite clear about it, Mrs Boyd,' the detective says, taking a half-step back. 'Your son's not under the influence of drugs or alcohol, he's been given a health and welfare check and he's stated he doesn't want to see anyone tonight, even his parents.'

'Because he knows we'll make him see sense,' she says forcefully. 'We'll talk him out of this madness.'

'All the same, madam, we can't force him to—'

'He's your prisoner, isn't he? So he'll do what he's told?' She crosses her arms. 'I'm not leaving here until I've seen my son, talked to him.'

I touch her lightly on the arm, her whole body rigid with tension. 'Hey.'

She flinches, noticing my arrival for the first time, and I see my own thoughts reflected back at me.

Not him. Not this.

I left a message for Kay Barber-Lomax on the drive here, asking her to call me back urgently. Connor will have known she'd advise strongly against a confession; that's why he didn't want her involved. But it won't feel real, it won't *be* real, until we hear it directly from Connor himself.

Laura's eyes are blazing. 'They're saying Connor doesn't want to see us, Andy,' she says, biting off each word. Her voice is a few notches louder, as if she wants everyone in the station to hear. 'So I thought we could give your journalist friend a call, explain to him how the police are keeping a child in solitary confinement and refusing to let his mother speak to him.'

Harmer looks from her to me, and back again. 'That really wouldn't be very helpful at this stage,' he says.

'Listen,' I say to him quietly. 'We're both going to stay right here, on this spot, until we see Connor for ourselves.' I meet his gaze. 'Ten minutes. That's all we want.'

The detective sighs and drops his hands to his sides.

'Let me speak to the boss again,' he says finally, reaching for the security door. 'Why don't you take a seat and I'll see what I can do.'

* * *

Fifteen minutes later we're sitting in a small interview room as Connor is led in. He's wearing a baggy grey tracksuit that's a bit too big for him, socks and no shoes. His own clothes have been taken, I assume, for examination. Laura pushes her chair back immediately and goes to hug him, wrapping her arms around him as if she'll never let him go. He hugs her back awkwardly, a head taller than his mother, and I'm not sure who's comforting who.

DC Harmer goes to wait outside but doesn't close the door all the way, and I can tell that he's still there in the corridor, his looming presence partially blocking the light.

Finally, Laura releases our son and comes to sit down next to me again, as Connor takes the seat opposite us. He looks smaller, thinner, diminished. A child lost in an adults' world. I try to discern any difference in him, any change that has come over him since he made his confession to the very worst thing one human being can do to another. Any outward signs of a mental breakdown, a temporary psychosis that might have pushed him into a false confession. Or perhaps an alteration in the way he looks, the way he holds himself, maybe a relaxation of his body language in the knowledge that he doesn't have to lie anymore.

But he doesn't look relieved, or resigned.

If anything, he looks more agitated than ever. His movements quick, eyes vigilant. He seems alert, checking over his shoulder that Harmer is just a few feet away in the corridor. Maybe he is already acclimatising to this new world, realising he has started down a road from which there is no way back.

The three of us sit for a moment, each waiting for another to break the silence.

Finally, Laura says: 'We're going to get you out of here.'

Connor nods, eyes down, as if he doesn't believe her.

I gesture to the detective in the corridor outside. 'Are they treating you OK?'

He nods again. 'Fine.'

Silence descends again. It seems as though he wants to say as little as possible, to get this over with.

'Connor?' I say quietly. 'Do you remember what I said to you the other day? Nothing you could ever do, or say, will make us love you any less. Nothing. I want to make sure you remember that.'

'I'm sorry Mum, Dad,' he says simply. 'For what I did.'

I cover his hand with mine. 'It was an accident, you said.'

'Tell us what you told them,' Laura says abruptly. 'Look at us, and tell us what you did. Tell us what happened.'

Connor's eyes flick to me, then back to his mother. 'I killed her,' he says. 'I killed Emily, in the woods. I didn't mean to.'

His voice is clear, unhurried. To hear him say it, to hear the words come out of his own mouth, is infinitely worse than having the confession relayed to me by DS Shah. A keen blade piercing my heart.

But Laura is shaking her head.

'No,' she says simply.

I half turn towards her. 'What do you mean?'

'No,' she says again. 'I don't believe you, Connor. I just don't.'

'I was there,' Connor says, without missing a beat. 'You weren't.'

'You don't have to—'

'I know what I did, Mum.' He stands up. 'I have to admit it.'

I stand up too and give him a hug. 'We're going to get you out of here, Connor. Until then, just look after yourself, OK? We'll see you tomorrow. We'll be there, tomorrow.'

I don't add the last words. *In court.*

He turns and walks out of the room without another word. We follow him out in time to see him disappearing through a blue steel door on the other side of the corridor. Harmer locks the door behind him, the mechanism sliding home with a solid metallic *thunk*.

'It doesn't make sense,' Laura says, her eyes shining with tears. 'I don't understand.'

I put an arm around her shoulders as we follow DC Harmer back towards the reception area. As we round a corner, DS Shah meets us coming the other way. She has a stack of files under her arm, her eyes shadowed dark with fatigue.

Laura moves towards her, jabbing a finger. 'This is *bullshit* and you know it.'

'Excuse me?' the detective stops walking, a deep frown lining her forehead.

'*You* did this,' Laura says. '*You* wound the pressure up until Connor couldn't take it any more. Sending people to follow him. Turning people against him. The leaks to the media saying you were about to make an arrest. It got to him in the end, didn't it?'

I register the look on Shah's face. 'Were those stories even true?'

'They were true enough,' Shah says.

'So you were about to arrest him anyway, he just saved you the trouble?'

Something passes across her face that I can't quite identify.

'We were close to rearresting him, yes.' She checks her watch. 'Now if you'll excuse me, I need to update the Ruskin family before the media gets wind of this.'

She walks away down the corridor.

Laura's anger has finally burned itself out; her shoulders start to shake under my arm as she dissolves into tears. I gather her into a hug and we cling to each other.

'It's going to be OK,' I whisper, rubbing her back. 'We'll figure this out, all right? The solicitor will know what to do.'

The clock at the end of the corridor says 6.52 p.m., its spindly metal hands seemingly frozen in place. Eight minutes before seven on a sunny Thursday evening in June. So this was our zero hour, our new midnight. The starting point for a new kind of life, the first step on a dark journey that none of us ever wanted to take.

Laura turns to see what I'm looking at. After a moment she glances absently down at her own watch with a sniff. Then at her phone. Then at me, with fresh alarm in her eyes.

'Have you heard from Harriet?'

69

Harriet is not answering her mobile.

She is not answering the home phone either.

Oh God. I had been so preoccupied with Zac, with my brother, with Connor's sudden confession, that I had barely given my daughter a second thought. Had put my phone on silent when we spoke to Connor and only realised when I switched it back that there were two missed calls from her. No message. Laura's face pales as she describes her panicked rush to the police station after my call, how she had left Harriet home alone, a belated text to Arthur next door – still unread – asking him to go over and stay with her. She also has a couple of missed calls from Harriet and a single, solitary message that makes my stomach drop into my shoes.

Going to Unc's house with Toffee

Unc was what she called her Uncle Rob. My brother.

Rob's words are ringing in my head, his parting shot after our brawl in the car park of the Three Tuns.

You'll have to do whatever you think you have to do. And so will I. And so will I.

What has he said to her? How has he lured her in?

Rob's number rings and rings before going to voicemail. I leave a frantic message as I'm running out to the police station car park. Laura is calling his landline but there's no reply on that either.

I drive fast, accelerating through amber lights and weaving through traffic, all the while scanning the pavement for a short red-haired girl. Praying with every turn, every new street, that I will catch sight of her and she will have a perfectly reasonable explanation. But knowing in my heart that I will not just come across her by chance. Too much has happened for it to be a coincidence. I remember my truncated call with her in the woods, while I'd been on the phone to Shah, just before the detective had dropped her bombshell about Connor's admission of guilt. Harriet had wanted to talk about something, but I had cut her short, forgotten to call her back in the rush to the police station, and that was more than an hour ago. I check her earlier texts again.

Where r u?
Need to spk to u

She hadn't sent anything since. Hadn't texted to say she was at home or to ask where everyone was. *Please let it be that her phone is just out of charge, or forgotten at the bottom of her bag.* Or maybe she'd just given up trying.

I'm almost at my brother's house when my phone rings on the hands-free, my wife's voice one notch below panic.

'She's not replying.' She suppresses a sob. 'God, Andy, what's happening? Why did she go to your brother's? Shall I meet you there?'

'No,' I say. 'You need to head home in case she turns up. I'm nearly at Rob's place now.'

I park half up the kerb across my brother's drive and run to the front door, ringing the bell and hammering on the brass door knocker at the same time. Peering through the frosted glass to make out any kind of movement. Nothing.

'Rob!' I pound on the door, the impact stinging the palm of my hand. 'Open the door! I know what you've done! I know you've got her!'

There is no movement from inside, no response, no sound beyond the echoing clang of the doorbell as I press it over and over again. The side gate is locked but the fixing has always been flimsy, the wood starting to give way to age and weather. I brace myself against the fence and kick it open on the first try, splinters of wood scattering onto the path behind. Moving around to the small back garden, I go to the back door. Locked. I bang on the glass, shouting my brother's name again, but I can't see anyone in the kitchen. I look around the back patio, find an old half-brick next to the barbecue and brace myself to heft it through the kitchen window.

I stop. *What am I doing?* There is a spare back door key in case they ever get locked out. I drop the half-brick, lift the yellow flowerpot by the back door and reveal a single brass key. I hurry back and let myself into the kitchen, listening for any sound.

'Rob!' I move into the hall. 'Harriet? Where are you?'

My own voice echoes back to me in unhelpful answer. I run into the dining room and the lounge – both empty – then take the stairs two at a time and check each of the three bedrooms, the bathroom and even the airing cupboard.

I hurry back downstairs, panting, confused, trying to ignore the drumbeat of fear thumping in my chest. My eyes fall on the small white door in the corner of the kitchen.

Cellar.

The musty smell of damp bricks and old paint greets me as I pull open the door onto a flight of rough stone steps descending into darkness. I flick the light switch. Nothing.

'Harriet?' I call into the dark, feeling my way down. 'It's Dad, can you hear me?'

A tiny rustle of movement. Leaning down to avoid the low ceiling, I switch on the torch on my phone and shine it into the first compartment of the cellar. Cobwebs and rusting paint cans, tools and boxes stacked haphazardly on a rotting wooden bookshelf. A broken stepladder on its side, a rusting bike with no front wheel, the bright eyes of a mouse scuttling away into the shadows.

The other compartment is more of the same, more half-abandoned stuff, more flaking bricks grimed with decades of dirt.

My daughter is not here.

I feel certainty slipping away, as if I can't rely on my own mind anymore.

I'm climbing back up to the kitchen when my phone rings with an unrecognised number. *Please let this be Harriet. She's at another friend's house, a parent calling to tell us she's safe or she's borrowed a stranger's phone.*

'Hello there,' a man's voice says. 'You don't know me but I got your number from—'

'Is Harriet with you?'

'I'm sorry?'

'My daughter, Harriet Boyd, she's not come home and she's not picking up her phone.'

The man sounds taken aback. 'Oh . . . no, sorry, I don't know anything about that.'

I don't recognise his voice. He sounds older, maybe fifties or sixties, traces of a southern accent.

'How did you get my number?' Before the words are even out of my mouth I realise there is no time for this. 'Doesn't matter. Listen, I need to keep this line clear in case she tries to get through, she might be calling any minute.'

I take the phone away from my ear and I'm about to hang up when his voice reaches me again, tinny and far away.

'It's about your dog,' he says hesitantly. 'I've got him.'

My thumb hovers over the 'end' button. I grope desperately for the meaning of his words, through a fog of unanswered questions.

I put the phone back to my ear. 'What?'

'You have a dog, Taffy, is it? Got your number from his tag.'

With a sickening flutter of panic, I remember the words of her text.

She had taken the dog with her. Of course she had. And wherever Toffee was, she would surely be nearby.

The caller is still talking in a monologue.

'. . . found him wandering around looking quite sorry for himself. The thing is, we had our spaniel, Missy, run off a couple of years ago and thank the Lord someone got a hold of her and checked her tag and was kind enough to ring me. She was filthy by the time we got her back but goodness only knows what might have happened to her if that kind person hadn't—'

'It's Toffee,' I say. 'Have you got him now?'

'Yes, I've got a hold of him for the moment but he keeps trying to run off again. Sparky little beggar, isn't he?'

I press the phone closer to my ear.

'Where are you? Exactly.'

'Well—' he sucks in a breath '—do you know a little road called Lower Farm Lane? There's a footpath there that's a back way into Beacon Hill Woods.'

I run back towards the street, fumbling for my keys.

'Stay right there,' I say. 'I'm coming to you.'

70

A stranger flags me down on Lower Farm Lane.

He's in his late sixties, with a white beard and a serious-looking walking stick that he waves in the air as I near the southern entrance to Beacon Hill Woods. I stamp on the brake and pull the car into a lay-by in a slew of gravel.

'Are you the guy who called me?' I run up to him. 'About my dog?'

He looks sheepish and I suddenly notice that he's on his own; Toffee isn't with him.

'I'm sorry,' he says, 'thought I had him by the collar but the little feller got spooked by something and took off running—'

'Did you see a girl?' I say breathlessly. 'Was there a girl? She's twelve years old, skinny, short red hair, about four feet nine.' I hold my palm out flat in an approximation of my daughter's height. 'Have you seen her around here? Or a man, around my height, my size, a little older, wearing a black T-shirt and jeans?'

'Sorry,' he says again. 'No, I don't think I saw either of them. Just the little dog wandering around on his own.'

'Call the police.' I'm already backing away. 'My daughter's been taken!'

His questions fade behind me as I run down the path into the woods. It's darker here, the air close and still as the dusk draws in, light giving way to shadows.

Me and my brother, back here in these woods.

Back where all of this started, four long days ago.

'Harriet!' I shout left and right as I'm running. 'Harriet!'

My voice echoes, unanswered, fading away into the trees. Has Rob brought her out here? Is she here somewhere, concealed, hidden, facing the same fate as Emily? The thought sends a jolt of terror through me as I pound up the trail, creepers and brambles whipping at my legs.

'Harriet! Harriet!'

I stop at the little river, breathing hard, and call her name again. Could she be in the water? She has never been a strong swimmer. *Oh God.* I run to the middle of the bridge and scan the water upstream and downstream for any sign of her, any clue to her presence amid the river burbling downstream over smooth grey rocks on either side.

Nothing.

On the far side of the river, the woods loom thicker, the trees closer together as the ground rises towards the ridge that gives Beacon Hill its name.

The day is fading fast now, the darkness of dusk gathering beneath the thick canopy. I remember the last time I was here, with Harriet on Monday, the police helicopter buzzing low over our heads and a search team going over the ground nearby.

It's getting harder to see. Finally, I have to stop for a moment, to get my laboured breathing under control.

Wait. Listen.

There.

A noise, so faint I wonder if I've imagined it. I move to my right, towards the sound as it comes again. A familiar, repetitive sound that I have heard a thousand times before. Small and indignant.

A dog barking.

My dog barking.

I run towards the sound, stumbling, skidding, tearing headlong through the trees, batting low branches out of my path.

'Harriet!' I shout. 'Toffee!'

Through the trees I can make out a shape, the moss-covered stone walls of the old woodman's hut, so overgrown with weeds and creepers that it has almost become part of the forest, a tree growing through a jagged hole in the slate roof. The place Harriet always used to say was haunted, as scary as the witch's hut in 'Hansel and Gretel', the last place she would choose to go. A strip of blue-and-white police tape hangs torn and limp next to where Emily's bike was found four days ago.

The barking comes again. Louder.

There is a painful thudding in my chest, my head, fear running so cold in my veins that I don't feel the scratches of low branches, the sweat at the back of my neck, the burning pain in my lungs.

Please let Harriet be OK. Please let her be OK.

Toffee is at the doorway of the old hut. He runs towards me as I approach, barking more urgently, jumping up excitedly and putting his paws on my legs the way he always does. My stomach lurches as I see he's still attached to his lead: my daughter didn't mean to let him go. After a moment he trots into the hut and I follow, whispering my silent prayer again.

Please let Harriet be OK.

There is no door, just a single dark gap in the wall bound around with weeds. I step inside, the fronds of a spider's web snagging across my face and something crawling in my hair, scuttling down the side of my neck. I drag strands of the web away, swiping at the spider and squinting into the foetid shadows as my eyes begin to adjust.

There is something in the far corner of the hut, curled among the dirt and creeping green weeds.

Some*one*.

A small figure, a child, laid on her back. Motionless.

But it's not Harriet.

And she's not OK.

71

A girl, skin mottled and grey in the shrouded twilight of the hut. Blonde hair knotted in thick strands, covering her face like a shroud. Arms splayed carelessly at her sides, a lifeless hand curled with grooves of dirt lining the palm, nails dirty and broken. Smells of bare earth, of dirt, of rot and decay. Of death.

Oh God. Oh no.

I kneel beside her and touch her arm, the skin cold beneath my fingertips. Dimly aware that this is a crime scene now and I mustn't contaminate it. Carefully, slowly, I move a tress of hair from her face, confirming the unthinkable, the unbearable. Confirming what I already know.

Emily Ruskin.

I fall back on my haunches, a hand going to my mouth. Toffee whines behind me and nudges at my shoulder but my mind is in free fall, spinning and tumbling, thinking about the police searching this area the day after Emily went missing. Because someone had been here since then, maybe today, maybe this evening, to dump her back in the woods, to rid themselves of evidence. But why here? How long would a body lie undiscovered in a place like this? The inside of the hut was hidden from casual passers-by, so maybe a day or two at most? Sooner or later she would have been found, without question. Perhaps her killer had been in a hurry, had been disturbed and couldn't take her any further into the woods.

Maybe that person was *still* here. And Harriet was here too. There was nothing I could do for Emily now, but my daughter . . .

A new sound reaches me, small and distant but wonderfully, terrifyingly familiar. I stumble to my feet and away from the body, almost tripping on a pile of rotten wood and out through the doorway, glad to pull in a lungful of fresh air. I stop and listen. I *had* heard something.

'Harriet!' I yell it into the silent trees, turning a full circle, searching the darkening woods for any sign of my daughter. 'Where are you?'

I wait, listening for a reply, the echo of my own voice mocking me.

'Dad!' Her voice is tiny, as if it's coming from a hundred miles away, but I know she must be close. Beyond the river, where the ground rises up. 'Dad!'

'Harriet! I'm coming!'

Toffee hares off in the direction of her voice and I follow, running to catch him up, sprinting through the trees and back onto the path to the river, my feet clattering across the little wooden footbridge and over the other side. Running, calling out, Toffee barking ahead of me.

Harriet has stopped shouting.

I keep going as the path winds into nothing and disappears and now I'm crashing through banks of nettles, brambles clawing at me, my lungs on fire as if they're going to burst, higher, higher, pounding further up the hill to the ridgeline, keep on going, keep calling to her. She's here and she's in danger, more danger than she's ever been in her life.

There.

A figure in the trees? Or a shadow?

'Harriet!'

A flash of blue beside the carcass of a huge gnarled oak laid flat on the ground, a glimpse of a pale blue T-shirt, of my daughter's red hair.

'Dad!'

My heart lurches, threatens to stop. The wave of relief is so intense, so overwhelming, that my legs almost buckle as I run towards her.

'I'm sorry, Dad.' She's crying, her eyes shiny with tears. 'He jumped out at us and Toffee ran away and—'

'Who jumped out on you?'

A *swish* of something hard swinging quickly through the air behind me.

I start to turn, but I'm too slow, too late—

There is a blinding explosion of pain at the back of my skull.

72

I drop and roll onto my back, raise my hands in a vain effort to defend myself against another blow. The pain in my head is unbelievable, a bursting red hot agony that consumes everything, every thought, every movement. I cry out, grit my teeth against the pain and gingerly feel the back of my head. My fingers come away sticky with blood. I blink, my vision blurring and shifting.

A figure stands over me.

Dark jeans, black sweatshirt, black balaclava. In a gloved hand, a hefty branch as thick as my wrist.

A wave of agonising nausea rolls over me and I shut my eyes. Everything is pain.

Harriet is whispering, her words seeming to reach me down a long, echoing tunnel.

'I'm sorry, Dad,' she says again through tears. 'It's all my fault. I shouldn't have come. I tried to find out what happened to Emily. I just wanted to help Connor, I didn't realise what might happen.'

'How did you . . .' Every word is an echoing agony. 'How'd you get here?'

She swallows down a sob. 'Uncle Rob.'

'Did he threaten your brother? Did he tell Connor to confess or else he'd hurt you?'

The hooded figure covers her mouth with a gloved hand.

Harriet's eyes bulge with fright.

I struggle to a sitting position. 'Take your hands off her.'

The gloved hand tightens over her mouth.

I haul myself to my feet. 'I said, take your damn hands off my daughter.'

For the first time since this nightmare week began, my fear is embodied, it's real and right in front of me, brought to life in this person who has tried to incriminate my son, to ruin him, to ruin my family. This person who has just dumped a girl's body in the woods as if it was nothing. I find I have rage on my side for the first time, a burning, blinding rage crowding out everything else. Crowding out pain, fear, reason.

Toffee must sense it too. He erupts from behind a bush in a furious brown blur, gums drawn back, teeth bared, a barking growl of warning at seeing Harriet manhandled by an aggressor. The figure releases her and swings out with the heavy branch. The little dog darts away, dodging the blow, snapping and snarling.

It's not much of an opening.

But it's enough.

I launch myself forward, barrelling into the figure before I can get hit again and then we're rolling and tumbling, crashing downhill through brambles and ferns, the world spinning end-over-end as we grapple and punch and kick. We finally come to a stop in a shallow gully and I'm on my back, pinned, straddled, dark eyes blazing back at me through the slit in the balaclava, hands on my throat, pressing down harder, harder, so hard I can't breathe. I'm trying to push away, fighting to release the pressure, but pain and nausea roll over me again.

Agonising pressure on my throat. No breath. No oxygen.

I feel my eyes closing. Everything fading.

No. A flare of adrenaline pushes my eyes open and I strain against the pressure once more, kicking out, trying to free myself, muscles burning with the effort.

It's no good. Not enough.

The hands on my neck grow tighter. I catch a glimpse of the canopy above our heads, of long branches swaying in the breeze. The evening sky above softening to a dark, inky blue. The first solitary star, a tiny silver pinprick. Spots dance at the edge of my vision, the edges greying, fading. Closing down.

I'm going to die here.

A sound reaches me as if from a long way away, a *smack*, like something heavy hitting the ground.

Suddenly the pressure on my throat is gone and I'm gasping for air, retching and coughing, pushing off a deadweight. The figure rolls off me into a bed of ferns, stunned, groaning. Harriet is beside me, wide-eyed with shock, her hand wrapped around a sharp rock the size of half a house brick.

I sit up, a hand on my throat, still gasping and retching, pulling in one strangled breath after another, air rasping into my lungs.

Harriet raises the sharp rock over her head, ready to strike my attacker again.

'Wait,' I croak. I stagger to my feet. Dizziness threatens to overwhelm me but I swallow hard, waiting for it to subside. 'Just wait a second, Harry.'

She lowers the rock but doesn't drop it.

The figure lies prone, helpless like a flipped crab, making whimpering, pitiful sounds, breaths shuddering with pain.

I lean down, grab the balaclava with a bloody hand and rip it off in one angry pull.

Alexander Saxton blinks back up at me.

73

'So it was you,' I say, my voice still rasping and raw. 'You did all this. You set my son up.'

He groans again, his eyes half closing.

'Everything I did was to protect *my* son. Just the same as you.'

'You knew Connor would make the perfect fall guy.'

He lets out a sob wracked with pain. 'I need a doctor.'

I put a foot on his shoulder, turn to my daughter. 'Harry, can you call the police? Tell them to come quickly. Ambulance too.'

She's crying now, her face ghost pale 'Lost my phone, Dad, when he first jumped out at us. Sorry.'

I'm patting my pockets for my own mobile when I catch a glimpse of movement lower down the hill. A figure emerging slowly, painfully, through the trees, staggering and stumbling up the hill towards us. His stride, his gait, so familiar.

My brother.

His face is streaked with blood, running down from his hairline.

'Rob,' I say. 'What happened, are you OK?'

Instead of replying to me, he walks up to Saxton's prone figure and swings a heavy kick into his ribs, prompting a strangled cry from the other man.

'Stop!' Saxton begs. 'Please!'

'You like dishing out the beatings, don't you, dickhead?' Rob wipes blood out of his eye. 'Not so good at taking one though, are you?'

He kicks him again and the air comes out of Saxton's lungs with a *whoomph*. I should probably stop my brother, restrain him, but it seems to me that Saxton deserves this and much, much more. Rob kicks him again for good measure then kneels beside him, pulling the man's expensive leather belt roughly from its loops before flipping the groaning man onto his stomach. He pulls his hands roughly behind his back and cinches the belt tightly around his wrists. Then he takes off his boots and hurls them away into the woods.

Saxton moans in complaint. 'It's too tight. You're cutting off the circulation.'

'You just dumped her in that hut like she was nothing,' Rob growls at him. 'I should be looping this belt around your fucking neck.'

'And what about your *son*?'

'You don't get to talk about my boy.'

'*Your son* is the reason we're all here!'

'Shut up.'

'He's the reason this all happened,' Saxton says.

'I said *shut your mouth*.' My brother's tone is heavy with menace.

'Oh, my son's not perfect, I know that. I know it better than anyone. But neither is yours. So why did Zac do it?'

Rob doesn't reply. He won't meet my eye either.

'What's he talking about?' I ask him. 'What does he mean? What did Zac do?'

'He's talking shite,' Rob says through gritted teeth. 'Just like he's been doing all week. Trying to get inside your head again. Don't listen to him.'

Saxton cranes his head around awkwardly to face my brother. 'You know it's true! Zac tried to spike Drew on Saturday night.'

'You'd best shut up,' Rob mutters, 'unless you want another kicking.'

But Saxton is near hysterical now. 'Because of some sort of feud between Drew and Connor! Payback for Drew, was it? Revenge for hitting Connor, fighting with him? Or was it just to get Drew out of the picture, clear the way for Connor so he could finally have a chance with Emily?'

I hold a hand up. 'Hang on, you're saying *Drew* was spiked on Saturday night?'

Saxton twists awkwardly on the ground until his eyes find mine.

'No.' His voice is shaking. 'I'm saying he was the *target*. But the drinks got mixed up – and Emily took the one intended for Drew. She drank it instead and set off into the woods on her little jaunt—'

Rob steps up and delivers another savage kick to Saxton's midriff.

'I told you to shut the fuck up!'

Saxton whimpers and his voice dissolves into great gasping sobs. He doesn't say anything else.

I step closer to my brother, putting a hand on his shoulder. His blood-streaked face is so full of anger and fear and despair that I almost don't recognise him. But all I can think of now is the body dumped in the hut, barely a quarter of a mile from where we're standing.

'Is it true?' I keep my voice low. 'What he's saying?'

'Of course not. Do you even have to ask?'

'Just want to hear it from you, that's all. From my brother.'

Rob stares at me for a moment longer, his eyes unreadable in the gathering gloom. 'I've called the police.' He turns away, stoops over Saxton's prone form to check the makeshift restraint around his wrists is cinched tight.

I give Saxton a quick check as well. He's bleeding from the head wound and clearly in a lot of pain; but he's conscious and lucid, breathing OK, his airway clear.

'Can you stay here with him a few minutes?' I say to my brother. 'I have to go back down there, to the hut, to where . . .' I point down the hill. 'Can you stay with him?'

'OK.'

'It's probably enough kicking,' I say to him. 'For now.'

Rob nods, wordlessly.

With Harriet's hand clutched tightly in mine I retrace my steps down the hill, back across the little footbridge and left, through the trees to the woodman's hut. Toffee trots along beside me, his ears low, tail down. Subdued.

I stop a few metres away from the hut's ruined doorway, put both hands on Harriet's shoulders.

'You need to stay outside until the police arrive, OK?' I hand her Toffee's lead. 'Just in the doorway where I can see you, but don't come inside.'

She throws a fearful look over her shoulder, back towards the place up the hill where Alexander Saxton lies pinned in the dirt.

'Don't worry about him,' I say to her gently. 'Rob's got him, he won't let him go. You're safe now.'

She gives a small, reluctant nod.

I go carefully back into the hut and kneel next to the body, wanting to help, to do something even though I know it's too late, far too late, knowing I shouldn't put my hands on her. In twenty years of practising medicine, of being a GP, I have never felt so useless.

So helpless. I shouldn't even cover her, give her a little dignity, in case it contaminates the crime scene. They will need to do forensics, gather evidence, all the things that need to be done. In the proper way. The right way.

I can at least wait and watch over her, make sure nothing is disturbed before the police arrive. Do her that small service if nothing else.

Emily looks tiny, skinny and frail, leaves stuck to the matted blonde hair that falls across her face. Little more than a child. Her skin is pallid and blotchy, dried blood around her mouth. She's dressed in a dirty white T-shirt and baggy shorts, her feet bare. Visible bruising around the grey skin of her lower arms and wrists.

My head pulsates with a hard, blunt pain. As the adrenaline drains out of me, I can feel a hard lump in my throat, a sob threatening to rise up. I've only ever been this close to a body once before in my life, more than twenty years ago in medical school. A sterile room, a cadaver donated for anatomy training. Nothing like this. I grit my teeth and swallow the emotion down. *Not now. Not in front of Harriet.* There will be a time for that later.

'Dad?' Harriet's voice comes from behind me. 'Is she . . .'

I shift my position to block her view of the body.

'Don't come in here,' I turn to her with a palm raised. 'Just stay where you are.'

In a small voice, she says: 'Is Emily dead?'

'Hey, you've got better eyes than me, Harry, can you go down to where the path opens up, just there?' I point to a spot perhaps twenty metres distant. 'See if you can see police coming. Stay where I can see you, but you'll have a better view.'

'I want to stay here with you.'

I nod. 'OK. All right. We'll wait for them here. Together.'

My daughter sees them first.

'Dad, look!' She points back towards the road. 'Over there.'

Through a ragged hole in the wall I can see a flash against the trees, like summer lightning. A faint flicker of blue lights, a reflection from some way off. Engines. Distant doors slamming. Running feet. Faint shouts, getting louder. Shouted commands, capital-letter voices. I take one last look at the girl in the corner of the hut, making a silent promise that I will do the right thing. A promise to her, to her family, to her mother.

And then the impossible, the inconceivable.

A movement so unexpected that I recoil in shock.

Emily's eyes flicker open.

74

**Transcript of interview with Alexander Saxton (AS)
conducted at Central Police Station,
Thursday 16th June 11.04 p.m.
Interviewing officer: DS Priya Shah
Also present: duty solicitor Matthew Francis**

DS Shah: We've gone through the charges with you, Mr Saxton. Is there anything you want to share with us at this stage?

AS: *[crying]*

DS Shah: Are you all right to continue?

AS: *[inaudible]*

DS Shah: Mr Saxton?

AS: Yes. *[inaudible]* Let's get it over with.

DS Shah: We want to establish what happened in Beacon Hill Woods. Saturday night, 11th June, into Sunday morning, the 12th. Primarily between 1 a.m. and 2.30 a.m.

AS: *[crying]* Drew called me.

DS Shah: And?

AS: He was in a panic. Total meltdown.

DS Shah: What time was this call?

AS: About 1 a.m. Maybe just after. He'd found her in the woods comatose, totally gone, barely—

DS Shah: Who?

AS: Emily. He says he followed her into the woods and he found her sitting by a tree, and then he was kissing her and . . . things, before he realised how far gone she was. She was barely breathing, her pulse was so weak and he couldn't wake her up. She'd clearly OD'd, maybe taken a double dose. Drew thought she was going to die.

DS Shah: So why didn't he call an ambulance?

AS: Because he thought he'd get the blame. Because of all the rumours at school about girls getting spiked, all the whispers that Drew was the one doing it.

DS Shah: And was he?

AS: Everyone would say there was no smoke without fire, right? And then you'd find his DNA on her, and that would be that. He was freaking out. Hysterical. Talking about going to jail, his life being over.

DS Shah: So you drove out there, to the woods, to help your son?

AS: Yes.

DS Shah: And what was Emily's condition at this point?

AS: Bad. Really bad. I knew I had to do something. She was hardly breathing.

DS Shah: And she was also bleeding at this point?

AS: [crying]

DS Shah: Mr Saxton?

AS: There was a bit of blood, not much. Drew thought she'd bitten her lip when she fell down.

DS Shah: What happened then?

AS: We were just about to move her to my car when someone else turned up. We waited for him to get close, then I hit him with a log. He went down.

DS Shah: And that was Connor Boyd?

AS: Christ knows why he'd followed her. But then I thought maybe I could use him, to cover our tracks.

DS Shah: You took Connor Boyd's fake ID and smeared it with Emily's blood, left it there at the scene for us to find?

AS: Yes.

DS Shah: Then you took Emily's phone and dumped it in a wheelie bin at the Boyd property later that day?

AS: [inaudible]

DS Shah: Can you speak up please?

AS: Yes. That was me.

DS Shah: So you've dealt with Connor Boyd. You've taken Emily to your car. What happened next?

AS: I was going to take her to A & E but then I realised there would be too many questions, too much risk. I didn't think she was going to make it. Drew would get blamed for this dead girl and the blowback for me, for my family would be . . . a disaster. I thought maybe I could drop her at the door and drive off but then CCTV at the hospital would pick up my number plate and trace it back to Drew. To me.

DS Shah: So you went home instead?

AS: Yes.

DS Shah: And what did you do with Emily?

AS: My house is . . . built to a European design, full-footprint cellar underneath, fully furnished, there's a gym, spare bedroom, larder, storeroom, study down there. The cinema room is soundproofed so we put her in there. It's barely ever used anyway. Kept her down there with the lights off. Put a blindfold on her and I wore a balaclava so she wouldn't see my face. I thought it was just a case of waiting for her to die and then we'd . . . figure out what to do next.

DS Shah: But instead, she came through it.

AS: Eventually. She was unconscious for almost a whole day, came round on Monday morning. Started ranting and raving and crying for her mum. I kept all the doors shut and music on throughout the house to mask any noise.

DS Shah: And you drugged her.

AS: *[crying]*

DS Shah: Initial results from the hospital suggest she's been repeatedly dosed with a central nervous system depressant, multiple times over the last few days. Is that how you kept her quiet?

AS: When she pulled through, after that first day, I realised I was screwed.

DS Shah: How do you mean?

AS: I couldn't safely hold on to her, but I couldn't safely let her go, either. I only really had three options. I could keep her in my cellar forever; I could take her out somewhere and drop her off, hope she was never connected back to me. Or I could . . .

DS Shah: You could kill her.

AS: I couldn't do that. *[inaudible]* I'm not a murderer. So I took her back to the woods this evening and left her there. But then the Boyd girl suddenly turned up with her uncle and . . . well, here we are.

DS Shah: Indeed. Here we are. But at least you didn't take that third option. Emily's alive, she's going to be OK.

AS: I just want to make two things clear, for the record.

DS Shah: I'm listening.

AS: It was all my idea, everything, keeping Emily in the cellar, the drugs, everything, it was all me. Nothing to do with Drew. It was me.

DS Shah: Noted. And the other thing?

AS: He swears he wasn't actually the one who spiked her.

DS Shah: I see.

AS: He admitted he took some drugs with him to the party, but only to take some half-doses with a bunch of his mates, see what the buzz was like. He says they were in his jacket upstairs and someone stole them earlier in the evening. He says Zac Boyd stole them. He used them on Emily. It was him.

DS Shah: Right.

AS: That's what happened.

DS Shah: Do you have any proof of that?

AS: Isn't that your job? Finding proof?

DS Shah: Well, since you mention it, I've just got some results back from a search of your home address, Mr Saxton. A search of Drew's bedroom. Is there anything else you want to tell us at this stage?

AS: [crying]

DS Shah: Do you want a break, Mr Saxton?

AS: [inaudible]

DS Shah: Interview suspended at 11.13 p.m.

– *Transcript ends* –

FRIDAY

75

DS Shah hands me a cup of strong, hot tea in a Styrofoam cup.

We're back at the police station but for once there's no recorder running, no caution read out, no solicitor joining us in the cramped little interview room. It's past midnight but the place is buzzing with activity, every interview room occupied, doors banging open and shut, footsteps and voices and phones ringing, a knot of camera crews and reporters thronging the car park outside.

I've just come from the hospital where a very young-looking registrar examined me and declared me mildly concussed, bruised, but otherwise OK. A dressing for my head and some hefty painkillers to keep me going for a few days until the swelling subsides. I'll take a few days off work. Right now, I just want to be home, in my bed. But DS Shah will be pulling an all-nighter and insisted on talking to me as soon as I'd had my injuries checked out.

She has an energised gleam in her eyes that speaks of a proper result, a job well done, a victim saved and a perpetrator in custody. A happy ending for the Ruskin family against all the odds, an outcome none of us really thought possible.

Emily is at the hospital. Dehydrated, malnourished, battered, bruised and disoriented. Long gaps in her memory of recent days.

Lucid dreams of being alone in the dark, of being restrained, blind-folded, of silent figures who brought occasional food and drinks that she desperately needed to slake her thirst even though she realised – after the first day – that they contained dose after dose of drugs that would make her sleep, make her passive and compliant and forgetful.

But according to Shah, the doctors say she will be OK.

Rob is there too, his head injury stitched. They want to keep him in overnight for observation, but I know he won't stay.

Alexander Saxton is in a cell down the corridor, his son in the cell next to him.

Laura and Connor are in the interview room opposite this one, with DC Harmer. They've already been told they can go home, but Laura refuses to leave without both her children.

Harriet sits beside me, a hot chocolate cupped in both hands.

'Explain it to me again, Harriet,' Shah says gently. 'I just want to make sure I've got it right.'

Harriet takes a sip of her hot chocolate.

'It was the door,' she says simply, as if that's all there is to be said.

'The door?'

'Yes.'

'OK,' Shah says. 'But how did you get to that point? I mean, what made you look for it?'

'Wasn't really looking for it. I was just looking at *everything* out there that I could find. I started with Drew, all the pictures he'd posted from the party on Saturday night and going back a few months. Then anyone else who'd been at the party, all the stuff they'd posted on Instagram, TikTok, on their stories and wherever. Like, as many people as I could find who were there. I thought there might be something in among all the pictures and videos and stuff.'

Shah is making notes. 'And what were you looking for, exactly?'

Harriet shrugs her small shoulders. 'Clues. To help Connor.'

'Sounds like you were very busy.'

'I went through, like, fifty people who'd been at the party, looked at *all* their pictures and posts, *all* the comments underneath to see what I could find, then I went through all the people who'd posted stuff on the *Find Emily* Facebook page. Checked all of them out. Then I started on the parents, first Emily's mum and Creepy Crosby, all their stuff, their whole digital footprint, Facebook posts, things they'd put on Twitter, Instagram, everywhere else. Even LinkedIn.'

'But not your cousin?' Shah says. 'You didn't check his posts, or your uncle?'

'Of course not.' Harriet frowns. 'I checked out Olivia and her mum next. Olivia had an absolute *ton* of posts and pictures about Emily, but her mum doesn't really do much online.' She's counting off on her fingers as she relates the stages of her search. 'And so then I started looking at Drew's dad.'

Now I've heard her describe it, I'm not surprised at all. Harriet has always been this way – always been the kid who gets fixated on one thing, who *has* to solve it, to understand everything about it, inside and out. All the hours she had spent in her bedroom these last few days, glued to her laptop, intent on finding the pattern, the key, the one thing that was out of place.

'I started watching his videos on YouTube. He's got loads. Most of them are a total yawnfest, about boring houses and buildings and stuff. The most recent ones are about Emily, and trying to get everyone to send in information and help find her, but there's like a hundred of them before that, all about building things. I watched them all. And then I watched the Emily ones again, quite a few times. And that's when I noticed it.'

Shah turns her laptop so we can both see it. A still of a YouTube video, Alexander Saxton in the centre, tanned and poised and perfectly groomed in a white linen shirt, his face a picture of concern. Behind him, in the background of the image, is the lounge-dining-eating area of his house, a huge, luxurious space with every imaginable facet and feature to enable a millionaire's lifestyle. An architect's dream.

Harriet points at the corner of the screen. 'Look. There.'

I sip my hot, sugary tea and squint a little closer at the laptop. My glasses are lost, somewhere in the woods, and there's been no chance to get my spare pair from home. But right in the corner of the shot, way back over Alexander's shoulder, is a door. To my eyes, it looks completely inconspicuous. There are four doors visible, actually, presumably leading to different wings of the house. Different parts of the Saxton mansion.

The one Harriet is pointing at is closed.

'There,' she says again. 'D'you see?'

I lean closer to the screen. 'It's just a door, Harry.'

'Yes, but on all three of the videos he made about Emily this week, it's closed. He used a still image with that same background on Instagram and Twitter. He likes that shot, with his back to the room. I think he likes showing off his big posh house and all his big posh things.'

I nod. 'I think he does, yes.'

'I watched all his other videos, going right back to when the house was first built and he first moved in. He sits in the same place, with the same background, on about half of them. Forty-eight of them, actually.'

Shah has a look of undisguised admiration on her face. 'And that door was never closed before?'

'No,' Harriet says. 'Not once. On all forty-eight of the previous videos, that door is open. *All* the doors are open. Something to do with airflow or thermal balance, or something. So then I zoomed into that little section of the picture, and enhanced it to focus on the door when it was shut, and the background when it was open, and I did a reverse image search on Yandex, and—'

'On what?'

'Yandex,' Harriet says, as if it's obvious. 'You upload a picture and it works backwards, helps you find similar images online. Helps you work out what your picture is.'

'Right,' Shah says.

'And the door, the handle, the grade of light behind it, the floor – the search said it was most likely a door to a basement or cellar. Then I'm like, OK, that might be interesting. I look for a floorplan of the house and it turns out Drew's dad had entered it for a competition when it was finished four years ago. He'd uploaded the floorplan as part of the entry and it was still there on the competition website, all the floors including the cellar. Staircases too. And you can see the whole layout of the cellar and there's *loads* of rooms under the house, and I'm thinking, why has he suddenly got that door closed when he never did before?'

Not for the first time this week, I shake my head in admiration of my second-born child. Of her dogged, determined work to help her brother. To help Emily. To expose Alexander Saxton and the lies he had told since the moment this nightmare started. I still can't believe he'd had the brass neck to hold a meeting of concerned parents in his own house just a few days ago, a meeting to mobilise community activity in the search for a missing girl, when she was *right there in his cellar* the whole time.

Because Saxton had used all of us, kept me close enough to find out what I was thinking, what Connor was doing. He had used my brother and Sophie de Luca too, brought them close to make himself look good. He had used us the way he had used the media and his influential friends, putting out an image of himself as the concerned friend, the determined organiser, galvanising the community in the search for a missing girl. An image pushed out to his extensive network too, to the thousands of people who followed him on social media.

And it had been his downfall.

76

'So I sent Drew's dad an email,' Harriet continues. 'Saying I had CCTV footage of Emily, and here's a link to see it, and of course he clicks on the link, and that uploads a remote access tool to his laptop and then I can look at *all* his stuff.'

I give her a tight smile. 'That's the bit that I'm not sure is completely legal, Harry.'

Shah shrugs. 'I think we can probably overlook the Trojan program she uploaded, Dr Boyd. Considering what your daughter found.'

The hours Harriet had spent poring over files on Saxton's devices had gleaned one crucial nugget of information – exercise data backed up to the cloud from his smart watch. The device had recorded movement, an elevated heart rate and bouts of strenuous activity on the night of Emily's disappearance, including several peaks around 1.30 a.m. that the software had designated as 'HIIT cardio' but detectives now believed related to the time Emily had been carried, unconscious, to and from his vehicle.

Using the remote access tool, she had uploaded a tracker to his phone to keep an eye on his movements. Seen him heading up to Beacon Hill Woods this evening, and followed him up there, getting a lift from my brother when she couldn't get hold of me or her mum.

Saxton, meanwhile, had sent Connor a series of messages to prompt his false confession – sent from the same Telegram account Emily had used on Saturday night. First a picture of Emily, blind-folded, bound hand and foot, a knife point pressed to her neck. Followed by a series of instructions.

Confess now or she dies
Mention this to anyone, she dies
Mess it up, she dies
You have one hour. Tell me when it's done
Remember, I can get to her anywhere, any time

'We think he timed it deliberately,' Shah says. 'He was going to dump her back in the woods at the same time as Connor would be making his confession. To make sure all our attention was focused on Connor rather than anyone – or anywhere – else. The messages themselves were all timed to disappear after ten seconds, using the self-destruct function on the app. But when we seized Saxton's phone tonight, he hadn't deleted the original photograph from his image gallery.'

Laura puts her head around the door.

'I've been told it's OK if I take the kids home,' she says. 'Need to get these two into bed.'

'Of course,' Shah says. 'I think we're done here.'

Harriet hops off her chair and gives me a hug.

'I'll see you in a bit,' I say to her quietly. 'Won't be long.'

Laura gives me a wan smile and shepherds our children into the corridor and away.

DS Shah gets up and quietly shuts the door, before sitting down opposite me again.

'Search teams executed a warrant at Saxton's house this evening and found a number of items of interest.' She holds up her phone, an image on the screen of a round silver tin with its lid off. Inside are perhaps ten of the small plastic fish-shaped vials, filled with clear liquid. 'Have you ever seen anything like this before?'

I pretend to study the image, my heartbeat rising from a steady canter to a gallop.

'No,' I say, as nonchalant as I can manage. 'Never.'

She fixes me with her intelligent gaze.

'You're sure? You're quite certain you've never seen anything like this?'

'Maybe . . . in a Japanese restaurant?' I shrug. 'For soy sauce, aren't they?'

She raises a quizzical eyebrow, then puts her phone back in her jacket.

'We believe they're doses of GHB, sometimes referred to as a "club" drug or "date-rape" drug. Found under a floorboard in Drew Saxton's bedroom, about an hour ago.'

'Right.' I swallow hard, my throat suddenly dry.

'The thing is,' Shah says, 'Alexander's been telling us for the last two hours that someone *else* spiked Emily's drink on Saturday night. Said it was your nephew, Zac Boyd. Drew says the same.'

Blood is thudding in my veins, every beat making my headache a little worse.

'Zac would never do anything like that.'

'You know, it's still not clear to me why your son went after Emily. Why he doubled back that night to find her.'

'He told you,' I say. 'He said he just got a bad feeling about it all.'

'You want to know what I think? I think Connor's been dodging questions all week, because that would drop his cousin in it. I think they walked back to your house, your son and your nephew, and Zac finally admitted what he'd done. He'd seen the drinks get mixed up, seen Emily downing a shot with a double dose of drugs in it, and he was terrified that she was going to overdose, alone in the dark. Thought he might have killed her. So he told Connor, and your son's instant reaction was to go back and help. To find this girl that he's in love with, rescue her. Zac said he would cover for him back at your house. Even sleep in his bed.'

I say nothing.

'So what do *you* think, Dr Boyd?' She leans forward across the desk. 'Do you think Zac was the one who set this whole thing in motion?'

'I think,' I say slowly, 'it sounds like it's his word against Drew's.'

'Perhaps.'

'And you already found more of these drugs in Drew's bedroom.'

'We did.'

'Well.' I shrug. 'There you go then.'

She sits back in her chair. 'I had a feeling you were going to say that.'

'My nephew's a good kid. He's had a really rough year.'

'I know.'

She holds my gaze as if waiting for me to say more. When I don't, she finally gives a small nod and closes her notebook.

She stands up, offers me her small, strong hand to shake.

'Andy, I'm going to need you to come in again tomorrow. You and Connor, to take us through everything one more time, make sure we've got it all nailed down. And Harriet too.'

'Of course.'

I turn to leave, but sense she has something else to say.

'You know,' she says, 'what your daughter did ... it's pretty amazing. You should be proud of her.'

'I am.' I nod, my throat thickening. 'Every single day.'

'I bet no one ever sees her coming, do they?'

For the first time since I met her, she smiles. A warm, genuine, easy smile, and for a moment she's not a police officer, not a detective, she's just a regular person you might meet on the street.

I smile back.

'Goodnight, detective.'

I turn and walk out of the little interview room, out of the police station, into the cool night air.

THREE MONTHS LATER

The TV is on mute. I'm not really watching it.

I have a book too, laid open on the arm of the chair. And the newspaper. And my phone.

I'm not really looking at any of them. Just looking at the clock. And waiting.

I check my watch again: it's still only 11.10 p.m.

Connor's not due back until 11.30 p.m. and he's already texted to confirm where he is.

He and Zac seem to have settled in well to the sixth-form college, making new friends and getting stuck into their A levels. It was good for both of them to get away from the school, I think, to make a clean break with the events of the summer. To rebuild their friendship and look to the future instead of dwelling on those five terrible days in June when one of their classmates set off alone into the dark. I'm watching Cathy Ruskin's new Netflix show on catch-up. It's not bad. The avalanche of publicity around Emily's rescue, her recovery, the moment she was reunited with her mother, have propelled the show to the top of the viewing figures. The internet conspiracy theories around her cancer haven't gone away but they haven't gained serious traction in the media either, especially not after the trauma of her daughter's kidnapping. No journalist would dare to go near the story; for the time being at least, Cathy is untouchable.

Emily was fully recovered from her ordeal, according to the media. She'd enrolled at a small private college where she was retaking some of her GCSEs, alongside her A levels. Karl Crosby didn't fare so well from the glare of attention focused on the Ruskin family in the aftermath of Emily's abduction. Various stories highlighted his chequered work history and allegations around his behaviour with female pupils. He and Cathy separated shortly afterwards; he's not returned to the school this September. From what I heard, he was strongly encouraged to move on by a head teacher keen to avoid any whiff of scandal.

The local reporter, Christian Dineen, was right about Alexander Saxton. Just for the wrong reasons.

Saxton is on remand, facing a slew of charges including kidnapping, false imprisonment, and administering a controlled substance without consent. Not to mention two counts of grievous bodily harm after his attacks on my brother and I in the woods. Despite Saxton's best efforts to take all the blame, his son faces a similar set of charges.

Emily's welcome home party was attended by more than two hundred people, with Olivia de Luca helping to organise the celebration and giving a heartfelt speech about her best friend.

Olivia and Emily remain very close, from what I hear. I had actually seen them in town a few days ago having coffee together, no doubt planning the next stage of their new campaign to raise awareness of the dangers of spiking. Olivia, in particular, seems to have got a taste for campaigning, with a new-found confidence in herself as the public face of the cause. She seems more comfortable in her own skin too – her hair shorter and back to its natural colour rather than a bleached-blonde copy of her best friend's style. DS Shah managed to conceal Harriet's role in hacking Saxton's laptop, after police investigators 'found' exactly the same incriminating data themselves during searches in the subsequent days.

And my brother . . . my brother is talking to me again, at last. It's going to be a slow process, but I'm trying to stay positive that we can get back to where we were before it all happened. Before we all turned on each other. I hope we'll get there, I really do.

We don't talk about that night.

Laura and I flushed the drugs we found in Connor's bedroom, and burned the vials to ash.

I check my watch again. There's still time before Connor is supposed to be home. He has a little while yet before his curfew.

Laura has told me not to stay up, not to watch the clock. Connor has never been late again since that fateful night in June, and he's promised he won't be this evening either. I know I can trust him.

But I've decided I'm going to stay up and wait anyway. Just until I hear his key in the lock.

Just a little bit longer.

Just to be sure.

Acknowledgements

Some books come together seamlessly, the story revealing itself smoothly during the writing until the first draft is finished. You stand back and look at it, nodding and smiling as if it's come out just as you expected, and the words are in mostly the right order. Raw lumber cut and carved and smoothed into a new shape, like it was always there underneath the surface just waiting to be revealed.

This was not one of those books.

Which is to say, there was a *lot* of extra cutting and carving, a *lot* of chiselling and re-shaping to get *The Curfew* where it needed to be. For that, and much else besides, I'm very grateful for the guidance and expertise of my editor, Sophie Orme, who showed me the way and helped make this novel better in more ways than I can list here. Likewise my amazing agent, Camilla Bolton, whose input at every stage was crucial to the book you're holding in your hands.

As ever, the team at Bonnier Books have done amazing work on my behalf and I'm particularly grateful to Felice McKeown, Ciara Corrigan, Eleanor Stammeijer, Francesca Russell and Kate Parkin; also to the very talented Emma Rogers for another stunning cover design. At Darley Anderson, I'm lucky to be supported by Georgia Fuller, Jade Kavanagh, Kristina Egan, Mary Darby, Rosanna Bellingham and Sheila David, who continue to do a fantastic job of bringing my stories to more people every year.

I'm indebted to Dr Helen Eeckelaers, who answered my questions about being a GP; and to Chris Wall of Cartwright King Solicitors, for his assistance on legal matters. Thanks to Tracy and Andy Cruickshank for their guidance on teaching; and to Alice and Cathy, the real owners of Toffee and Chester, for answering my strange dog-related questions.

I found a couple of books very helpful. *A Comprehensive Guide to Arrest and Detention* by Stephen Wade and Stuart Gibbon helped me to navigate the maze of police procedure in this area. And *The Secret Doctor* by Dr Max Skittle provided insights into the day-to-day life of a general practitioner. I also learned more about open source intelligence (OSINT) from Natalia Antonova, whose highly informative website and blog *Natalia Explains the Apocalypse* gives an eye-opening perspective on the amount of information we reveal with every single picture posted online.

Anyone familiar with Nottingham might recognise a few of the places mentioned in *The Curfew*, although I've fictionalised some streets and layouts around the suburb of West Bridgford. Sharphill Woods was the inspiration for Beacon Hill, but for the purposes of the story I made this area considerably larger than the real thing. Thanks to my children, Sophie and Tom, who gave me some background on Sharphill including stories of blazer-burning on the last day of school.

This book is dedicated to my wife, Sally, who many years ago was the first person to read my fiction and encouraged me to keep going. She is still one of my first readers, provider of very insightful feedback and I know how lucky I am to be celebrating 25 years together this year. Despite knowing about the weird stuff that goes on inside my head, she still puts up with me and always picks me up when I need it (except for that one time at Dairy Queen). One way or another, she is on every page. Happy silver wedding anniversary! xx

Enter the world of
T.M. LOGAN
Master of the up-all-night thriller
Join the Readers' Club
and get access to:
Regular giveaways
Cover reveals
Exclusive writing
Plus, get access to a free deleted scene
as soon as you join
Join today at www.tmlogan.com

Hello!

Thank you for reading *The Curfew*, I hope you enjoyed it.

I really enjoyed writing it, as the subject of the book felt quite personal to me. It's not long since my wife and I navigated the tricky teenage years as our kids started to seek more independence, going out with friends in the evening and returning home in the small hours. Our children are 19 and 22 now but I can still remember those anxious nights waiting for one or other of them to return from a night out or a party, waiting for a message or the sound of a taxi pulling up in the street outside, waiting for the sound of their key in the front door or a footstep on the stairs.

That was the inspiration for this story – a parent lying there in the dark, unable to sleep, spinning all kinds of doom-laden scenarios about an errant teenager who may or may not have missed his curfew. And what if that teenager *didn't* come home at all, but ended up in a police cell instead? What if one of his friends was missing? What if he refused to tell you what he knew? That was the starting point for the story that became *The Curfew*.

My next thriller starts with a miscarriage of justice. Heather Vernon – working mum-of-two, member of the school PTA and stalwart of the local choir – finds herself in court, in the dock, accused of the very worst crime. She has little memory of that night, only a powerful conviction that she cannot have done what they said she did. Alongside a steadfast faith in the legal system, and a certainty that the nightmare is almost over, that justice will be served and that she can begin to grieve properly for her loss, to rebuild her life.

Then the jury foreman comes back with the verdict: Guilty.

Nine years later, Heather walks out through the prison gates as a pariah: scarred, estranged, barred from contact with her two sons. Only one thing has kept her going: she's innocent. And the only way she'll ever see her sons again is to prove it. To prove that she was framed. To find out what really happened that night . . .

It is a story of deceit and betrayal, of redemption and revenge – coming in 2023.

If you would like to hear more about my books before then, you can visit www.tmlogan.com where you can become part of the T.M. Logan Readers' Club. It only takes a few moments to sign up, there are no catches or costs.

Bonnier Zaffre will keep your data private and confidential, and it will never be passed on to a third party. We won't spam you with loads of emails, just get in touch now and again with news about my books, and you can unsubscribe any time you want.

And if you would like to get involved in a wider conversation about my books, please do review *The Curfew* on Amazon, on GoodReads, on any other e-store, on your own blog and social media accounts, or talk about it with friends, family or reader groups! Sharing your thoughts helps other readers, and I always enjoy hearing about what people make of my stories.

Best wishes,

Tim